Maggie Dana

Beachcombing

Macmillan New Writing

First published 2009 by Macmillan New Writing
an imprint of Pan Macmillan Ltd
Pan Macmillan, 20 New Wharf Road, London N1 9RR
Basingstoke and Oxford
Associated companies throughout the world
www.panmacmillan.com

ISBN 978-0-230-74268-0

1 3 5 7 9 8 6 4 2

A CIP catalogue record for this book is available
from the British Library.

Typeset by Intype Libra Ltd
Printed and bound in the UK by CPI Mackays, Chatham ME5 8TD

Visit **www.panmacmillan.com** to read more about all our books
and to buy them. You will also find features, author interviews and
news of any author events, and you can sign up for e-newsletters
so that you're always first to hear about our new releases.

Advance praise for *Beachcombing*

'Maggie Dana has a light but perfect touch. *Beachcombing* is a rich tapestry depicting the comedy, tragedy and triumph of love in middle life'
Eliza Graham, author of *Playing with the Moon*

'With clear-eyed affection, sumptuous prose, and indomitable wit, *Beachcombing* examines loss, sorrow and redemption. Maggie Dana's first novel is proof that middle age offers no protection against vulnerability when it comes to love and lust. Fifty-something Jill Hunter is as vital, lively and optimistic about the future as any twenty-year-old'
Carrie Kabak, author of *Cover the Butter*

'Maggie Dana has crafted for us a heroine who is compelling, witty and refreshingly real. *Beachcombing* shines with sharp dialogue and richly rendered characters wrapped in vivid, charming settings. All this, and it's sexy, too!'
Kristina Riggle, author of *Real Life & Liars*

'*Beachcombing* is delightful and thoroughly inspiring. Jill Hunter slogs through heartbreak, financial disaster, and more car trouble than seems fair . . . and all with guts and good humor. Hurrah to Maggie Dana who's written a story that will resonate with many who've left the dewy-eyed category behind'
Becky Motew, author of *Coupon Girl*

'*Beachcombing* seduces easily and satisfies completely. Rich, funny and loving . . . reading this book is akin to sharing a perfect meal with old friends. I never wanted the story to end'
Jeanne Ray, author of *Julie and Romeo*

*For Judy, whose love and
friendship I value beyond measure*

Acknowledgements

No author writes a book without support, and my cheering team includes family and friends on both sides of the Atlantic.

In the U.S. where I live, my love and thanks to Carrie Kabak who encouraged me to write this story, and to Louann Werksma who gave it a final polish.

To my dear friends Judy Burns and Charlotte Lazor who graciously understood when I was too busy writing to come out and play.

To my wonderful family – Melanie, Paul, Peter, Kathy, Tim, Sarah, Noah, Sophie, Marya, and Alicia – you're the very best in the world.

To my online writing group (you know who you are), my most sincere and humble thanks for keeping me on track.

In England . . . my love and gratitude to Pat Waye, Julie Hoffman, and Wendy Newman for providing a home away from home, and to Eliza Graham who introduced me to Will Atkins, my truly brilliant editor at Macmillan.

Prologue

There's a party going on downstairs, and it's for me. A lunch party shrieking with voices of people I haven't seen in thirty-five years. I'm the guest of honor but I'm still in Sophie's spare bedroom stuffing myself into pantyhose and trying on shoes that hurt.

Someone raps on the door.

'Just a minute,' I yell.

My thumbs drill twin holes through a pair of tights.

'Damn!' I toss them in the waste basket and rummage in my case for replacements. Can't remember the last time I wore tights. Or real shoes, for that matter.

Sophie rattles the handle. 'Jill! What's keeping you?'

'Fashion adjustment,' I call out. 'Be with you in a sec.'

'Good,' Sophie says. 'But bloody hurry up. The natives are getting restless.'

She pads down the stairs, footsteps muffled by myriad layers of carpet, and I hear the doorbell ring, followed by Sophie exclaiming over the latest arrival.

'Hi, it's marvelous to see you again . . . How long has it been? . . . Yes, Jill's here, just tarting herself up a bit . . .'

Her voice is lost in the babble of others.

I finish tucking myself into tummy-control pantyhose, lurch off the bed, and jump up and down to make sure I'm properly squashed in. A final check in the mirror. Buttercream knit dress, a silk scarf of burnt umber and cobalt that matches my hair and eyes respectively, and brown leather pumps that want to rearrange my toes.

I look at my sneakers, longingly. Sophie will slay me if I wear them.

The stairs are narrow and steep and the handrail has gone missing. The treads are too shallow, even for my tiny feet, and with all that damn carpet it's like stepping in marshmallows.

He's standing at the bottom looking up. Tall and brown-haired, with a crooked smile and kind green eyes behind a pair of rimless glasses.

My foot slips. I miss two steps and tumble down the rest.

'Hello, Jilly,' he says, then chuckles as he bends to help me up.

His voice, his once oh-so-familiar voice, is the last thing I hear before passing out.

One

Sophie Neville and I are painting her bedroom. We're naked, or close to it, because Sophie insists it's easier to wash paint off skin than off clothes. Her bikini is two scraps of silk held together by lace. The back's no bigger than a child's hanky and the front barely covers all the rude bits. I try not to look.

She takes off her bra. 'I'm hot.'

'Sophie! What if someone comes in?' I'm wearing far more than her, but still feel exposed despite navy gym knickers and a size 34-B Cross-Your-Heart bra that I'm already spilling out of. Nobody runs around half dressed in my house. Certainly not my parents. I doubt Mum's ever seen my dad without clothes and I'm sure *she's* never bared herself to *him*.

'Don't worry, no one's home,' Sophie says, sloshing blue paint on the wall. 'Besides, we used to swim in the buff with Hugh and Keith. Remember?'

'We were five and the boys were six,' I remind her. 'It's a bit different now.'

'I'll say.' She grins. 'They're camping out this weekend.'

'In the fort?'

'Where else?'

3

I shrug because I don't want to seem interested, but I am. Desperately. Colin Carpenter hangs out with Hugh, Sophie's brother, and I lust for information about him. He's sixteen and they've built a tree fort in the woods behind Keith Lombard's house. Keith lives next door. He and Hugh have been best friends forever.

Hugh, Keith, and Colin.

They fancy themselves as the Three Musketeers. Sophie calls them the Three Stooges. I call them two twits and a miracle.

'Shall we go spy on them?' Sophie climbs down the ladder and strikes a pose. Hips thrust forward, head tilted. Her breasts don't droop like mine.

'Now?'

'No, this weekend, stupid.'

'What if they catch us?'

'They'll probably torture us.' Sophie pulls a tank top from her dresser and drags it over her head. 'But if you don't want to come, I'll ask Heather instead.'

That's all I need. The sexiest girl in school hiding behind a bush and making eyes at Colin. *My* Colin. I grit my teeth and scowl.

Sophie steps into her shorts. 'Only teasing.'

The floorboards outside Sophie's room are an early warning system. Step on the wrong one and it creaks. Me and Sophie know how to avoid it. So do Keith and Hugh. But Colin doesn't. He hasn't hung around here long enough to learn the ins and outs of the Neville family's house.

So, of course, it creaks.

I turn toward the noise and see the tail end of someone's shirt fly by Sophie's open bedroom door.

'The boys are back,' she says.

I glare at her. It's me that's half naked. I yank my shirt off the bed, thrust my arms through its sleeves, and do the buttons up all wrong. I'm redoing them when Sophie says, 'So, are you coming or not?'

I nod. Rabid cows wouldn't keep me away.

Snorts and muffled laughter drift across the hall from Hugh's bedroom and I wonder how long the boys have been spying on *us*.

Friday morning, I get my period. Bad cramps. Mum says it'll be less painful once I have a baby. I don't want one. I don't want to be like Mum, pinched face, always cross, always complaining. It's my fault. She was happier before I came along. I can see it in the photos of her and Dad on holiday. She was pretty then, with dark brown curls and a generous smile. Not like she is now, hair scragged back in a bun so tight it stretches her eyebrows.

I look at her hunched over the sewing machine, hemming another set of curtains for the living room. She never stops doing things over. Once, my dad came home late and didn't want to turn on the lights in case he woke us up. But he did because Mum had rearranged furniture in the living room, yet again, and Dad crashed into the gateleg table and broke his toe. I'd never heard him swear till that night.

Sophie rings up. Our phone's in the front hall. There's no chair so I have to stand and lean against Mum's antique bombé chest. I've begged for a phone in my room, but no luck. My tummy is killing me. Something in there is dragging a rake through my gut.

'Don't spend all day on the phone,' Mum yells above the whirr of her Singer.

'Is she in one of her moods?' Sophie asks.

'When is she *not*?' I wince as a wave of pain hammers me to the wall. I gasp. If this is what having a baby's like, I definitely don't want one.

'You still coming over?' Sophie says.

She knows I've got my period. 'I'm not sure.'

'Come on, Jill. It's only cramps. You'll forget all about them when you see Colin.' She blows a raspberry. 'You should see the junk Hugh's packing right now. You'd think he was going to China instead of next door.'

Shit, shit, shit. I don't want to miss out. 'I'll ring you tomorrow. Okay? Maybe I'll feel better in the morning.'

'Go to bed with a hot-water bottle,' Sophie says. 'And take an Aspro. Take two.'

How would she know? She's never had a cramp in her life.

Then she plays her trump card. 'If you don't show up, I'll tell Colin Heather fancies him.'

I saw Colin Carpenter for the first time last summer. Hugh and Keith had just started building their tree fort when Colin's family moved to Wickham Forge. Colin's father works in the City – investment banking, I think – and they bought a house on the posh side of town. Colin was good with his hands. He had all sorts of power tools that the other two lacked – saws, drills, and sanders – and he knew how to use them. The fort looked a whole lot better once he got through with it.

Except for one thing: it didn't have a ladder. The only way you could get to it was by climbing the adjacent tree – easy because it had plenty of low branches – then walking across a plank of wood the boys slung between it and the fort. The boys scampered across it like squirrels, then dared Sophie and me to follow. I didn't want to, but Sophie danced after them like a gymnast on a balance beam.

I held back, scared witless, while Hugh and Keith hurled insults at me. Colin told them to shut up, so I sat down and straddled the plank and bumped my way toward him. He reached for my hands, pulled me into the fort, and we fell backward amid a chorus of jeers. Then he rolled over and suddenly he was lying on top of me.

6

His hair flopped forward and tickled my cheek. His eyes were so close I could see yellow flecks among the green. He smiled. So did I. And when he helped me sit up, I could swear his lips brushed the top of my head.

I take a hot bath, using the last of Mum's pink bath salts. They're gritty and they don't dissolve very well because the water's not hot enough, so it's like sitting in sand but without the fun of being at the beach. If I could be bothered, I'd go and get a kettle of hot water, but then Mum would want to know why. So I ignore the grit and lie back with my feet propped on the taps and wonder what it's like to fall in love.

Is it like Sophie, who's ecstatic about one boy this week and head over heels about another the week after? Or is it like my parents, who're so different I can't begin to imagine why they got married in the first place? Mum bosses Dad around something awful, yet he puts up with it. Sophie reckons it's because he's got a girlfriend on the side. I think she's mad. My father would never do that.

I pull the plug and haul myself out of the tub. It's summer but the bathroom is cold. I wrap myself in a towel and peer in the mirror. Maybe I'll cut my hair. Or get a perm. Anything would be better than plaits. Yes, plaits. I'm fifteen and my mother insists on plaits. The only girls my age with hair like this are called Heidi and they're blond and they live in Switzerland and they know how to yodel.

I pick up Mum's nail scissors and trim off some split ends. I snip a bit more, then chicken out and drop the scissors in the sink. If I *really* wanted to piss her off, this'd be the way to do it. Cut it all off. Instead, I scoop my hair into a ponytail and secure it with an elastic band.

The door opens.

'Jillian Hunter, how many times have I told you not to

wear your hair like that?' Mum snatches the elastic. It snaps and my ponytail falls apart.

'Ouch!' I rub my head.

'Put something on,' she says. 'You're half naked.'

'Mum, I just had a bath.'

'Don't argue.'

I gather up my clothes and slope off to my bedroom.

Oh, God, my bedroom. My mother's memorial to the Flopsy Bunnies and apple-cheeked girls in long dresses, pantaloons, and poke bonnets. In one corner, Peter Rabbit wages war on Mr McGregor; in another, Mrs Tittlemouse tells Mr Jackson to get lost. Good for her. I wish I was brave enough to say that to my mother. I want Mick Jagger and Paul McCartney on my walls – not bloody Mabel Lucie Attwell and Beatrix Potter. And I want plain, ordinary paint – lavender, blue, yellow – I don't care, as long as it's not baby pink.

Dad comes in to wish me goodnight. 'Do you need anything?'

'A hug.'

'You feeling all right, love?' His brow is furrowed like a washboard. I run the tips of my fingers down it – bump, bump, bump – like I used to when I was little. He smiles, takes my hand, and kisses it. His mustache tickles. 'Will you be seeing Sophie tomorrow?'

'Yes.' I snuggle into bed. Right now I'm not fifteen. I'm back to being five, and my father's about to tell me the story of Katherine, his magic princess, who rides a giant cat with wings and a unicorn's horn.

'Well, then,' he says, getting up. 'You girls have a lovely time. Okay?'

Two

Wickham Forge
July 1970

The next day, Sophie and I go spying. We crouch behind bushes and wriggle through long grass in the Lombards' back garden. The boys are in the tree fort, unaware of our presence. I think. At one point, Keith runs across the plank and slides down the tree and I could swear he's looking straight at us.

'Shh!' Sophie warns. She's wearing shorter-than short shorts, a gauzy blouse, and no bra. How can I compete? Colin will take one look at her and melt.

We hold our breath and keep still. Keith walks past us, less than five feet from our hiding place, to go check on the line he's cast in the stream. It's not really a stream – more like a swampy ditch – but he's convinced it contains edible fish. He wades into the water and adjusts his pole. He's not wearing a shirt and his gray flannels are rolled to his knees. Must be a pair of his old uniform trousers. Hot and scratchy. Almost as bad as the rubbish Sophie and I have to wear – pleated maroon skirts that make you look fat no matter how skinny you are, and those miserable velour hats we stuff in our satchels the minute a boy walks by. Keith comes out covered with slime.

'Our very own swamp monster,' Sophie whispers.

'Shh! He'll hear us.'

But he doesn't. He obviously hasn't a clue we're watching because he reaches down the front of his pants and scratches. Or maybe he does know and he's just showing off.

'Stupid git,' Sophie says.

But she's smiling and I wonder if she fancies him. If she does, it'd be almost like incest, wouldn't it? I mean, she's known him for years. He's like a second brother. Or does she fancy Colin? I couldn't bear it if she does. So far, she's not shown any interest. He's one of the guys. Her brother's friend. Right? I'll die if she flirts with him.

We wait.

This isn't as much fun as I thought it would be. Crouching behind a hawthorn bush and talking in whispers is dead boring. I know Colin's up there because his bike's leaning against the tree. Otherwise, I'd go home.

Sophie says, 'I'm fed up.'

'Me too.' I stretch my legs. God, are they stiff.

'So, how about we go on over and see what they're doing?' Sophie stands up, tugs at her shorts. They're baby blue and really, really short, with gingham pockets on the back. My mother would never let me wear anything like that. 'We'll pretend we're out for a walk,' Sophie says. 'Don't you dare tell them we've been spying.'

As if I would!

They don't seem a bit surprised to see us.

Colin leans out the fort's window. His bottle-green shirt is unbuttoned and I can see a faint patch of light brown hair on his chest. I think he looks a bit like Burt Lancaster. Sophie and I watched *From Here to Eternity* on the telly last weekend. She was hot for Frank Sinatra but all I could do was gawp at Burt. I mean, he's old. Same age as my dad, but he was dead sexy. Just like Colin. They've both got crooked grins and their hair falls exactly the same way over their foreheads. Sophie says I'm barmy.

Colin grins down at us. 'Come on up.'

If I could fly, I'd be there in a millisecond.

'I'll go,' Sophie says. 'You stay here. I'll make them come down.'

'Thanks.'

Sophie scrambles up the tree, skips across the plank, and disappears. A minute later, she returns to earth with three boys following her like baby chicks after a mother hen.

We sit around the boys' campfire. They tell jokes, and although I try not to, I blush at the worst ones. They flex their muscles, beat their chests, and make Tarzan noises. They fart. They have burping and spitting contests.

Hugh and Keith lie down nose to nose and arm wrestle. Their faces turn red, their muscles bulge like tennis balls. They grunt and groan. It's hard to tell who's winning.

Sophie pokes her brother in the back. 'Your shoulder blades stick out like chicken wings.'

'Do not!'

'Gotcha!' Keith slams Hugh's arm on the ground.

Pissed at her for making him lose, Hugh forces Sophie's arms up behind her. 'So, let's see your shoulder blades then.' Her bones stick out. More than his. Then, suddenly, everyone's vying for biggest chicken wings. Even me. I arch my back and reach behind and of course this makes my boobs stick out too.

Keith leers at them. 'Jill wins. She's got the biggest ones right here.'

I look down. My blouse buttons have popped open.

'You dirty-minded little sod.' Sophie rams his thigh with her foot. Keith reaches for her, but Colin intercepts.

'Cut it out.'

I turn away and fasten my blouse. Maybe I'll go home.

Sophie says. 'Let's make tea.'

'I'd rather have a fag.' Keith holds out a packet of Players. Hugh takes one. Colin shakes his head. So do I. God only knows what would happen if Mum smelled cigarette smoke on my clothes.

Hugh and Keith light up. Colin tells them they're stupid to smoke, then goes off to gather more firewood. Sophie unearths a packet of Typhoo tea and a tin of sweetened condensed milk in the boys' stash of food. They've only got three mugs. Blue and white enamel. Chipped. Dented. One's missing a handle.

'I'll share with Hugh,' Sophie says, scowling at her brother. 'We're family. We've got the same germs.'

Colin comes back with an armload of wood. He dumps it by the fire. 'Oh, good. You found the tea.'

'We don't have enough mugs,' Sophie says. 'I'm sharing with Hugh.'

'Then I'll share with Jilly.' Colin flashes his Burt Lancaster grin. Good thing I'm sitting down or my legs would've given out.

Keith stubs out his cigarette and claims the third mug.

The tea is strong and sweet enough to make my teeth tingle. Grass clippings and specks of dirt float on top, but I don't care. I hand the mug to Colin. *Our* mug. The one without a handle. The most beautiful mug I've ever seen. He takes a sip from the same side I just took one from and hands it back.

His lips and mine have touched the same bit of mug. Does it count as a kiss?

I catch Sophie's eye and she grins. Colin's shoulder brushes against mine and I'm wondering how hard I dare lean into him when a spider the size of a Brillo pad runs up my arm.

I'm not scared of spiders, but I scream anyway.

Colin, who is, grabs it and hurls it into the fire.

12

'Aren't you the brave bugger,' Keith says. He pushes his friend in the chest. Colin pushes back. I hold my precious mug tight to keep it from spilling and the next thing I know, they're rolling on the ground laughing and yelling and it's a tangle of arms and legs, elbows and knees.

Someone's foot kicks a bit of burning wood. Sparks fly. They land in the grass and Hugh dumps his tea on them. He chucks his empty mug at his sister and joins in the fight. Sophie laughs. Is she egging the boys on? I can't tell if they're serious or just mucking about.

Keith crashes into me and I roll away from him. That's when the cramp hits. Groaning, I curl into a ball, wishing I was anywhere but here.

Sophie whispers, 'Did that idiot hurt you?'

'No.' I groan again. 'Cramps.'

The boys stop fighting, or wrestling, or whatever the hell they were doing. Keith shuffles off to check his fishing lines and Hugh disappears into the woods. To pee, probably.

Colin squats down beside me. 'What's wrong?'

I begin to shiver. Colin takes off his shirt and wraps it around my shoulders, then helps me up. 'I need to go home,' I whisper to Sophie. Home, of course, means Sophie's house. Not mine. My mother has no sympathy. She'd tell me to stop whining, that I was being a baby.

'I'll come with you,' Sophie says.

'Let me.' Colin cups a hand beneath my elbow.

Sophie clamps her mouth to my ear. 'This is your big chance. Don't fuck it up.'

I stumble beside him and wonder how much boys know about periods and cramps and having babies. Hell, I don't know much, and I'm a girl. Sex ed at school is a joke, and Mum certainly won't discuss it.

Sophie's mum is in the kitchen. The place reeks of paint.

Not the cheap, one-coat-covers-everything junk that Sophie and I used in her bedroom, but real paint. Oil paint. The stuff used by artists who paint pictures. Like Claudia Neville. Her blond hair is pulled back in a twist and secured by a couple of thin, long-handled brushes. Her face is dotted with paint – red, purple, and yellow – and a half-finished landscape leans against a wooden easel beside the fridge.

Claudia was twenty-one when Sophie was born. My mother was thirty-five when she had me, which means that Mum is now fifty and Claudia's only thirty-six.

Big difference.

Maybe that's the problem. My mum doesn't understand teenagers and Claudia does, because she can still remember what it's like to be one.

She takes one look at Colin, then turns her soft gray eyes toward me. 'Why don't you go and lie down on Sophie's bed? I'll be up in a minute with a hot-water bottle.'

Three

Sands Point, Connecticut
June 2007

Funny, isn't it, how you've not thought of someone in years and then, without warning, something as dumb as a bucket of nails triggers a memory and you're knocked almost breathless by it. This morning I was on the roof, nailing down loose shingles, and suddenly, there he was, up in that tree, fixing the fort Hugh and Keith had been trying to build all summer. Good thing I wasn't near the edge or I'd have fallen off. I blinked, and Colin Carpenter vanished.

Jeez. Where the hell did *that* come from?

I've not seen Colin in what? Thirty-four years? Longer?

I used to think about him. A lot. Mostly because I loved him to bits, but also because I never knew what happened to him. None of us did. Not even Sophie's brother.

Wiping the sweat off my face, I climbed down the ladder to begin my next project, which is where I am now – wedged inside the cabinet beneath my kitchen sink, trying to undo the trap and trying, mightily, not to think about Colin.

I tug at the wrench. Metal scrapes against metal. Nothing moves except rust. Grit adds more freckles to my face. I rub it off and try again. No dice. This sucker isn't planning to move any time soon. At least, not for me. The sink will have to stay stopped up till Monday when I'll call in a plumber.

If my bank account can handle it.

The fax phone in my office rings and startles me. I jerk my head.

Ouch!

Bad move. I grab my tools and wriggle out from under the sink. Who'd be faxing my office on a Saturday? Elaine Burke? Please, not her. It's bad enough putting up with her during the week. I don't want her invading my weekends as well. I'll ignore the fax. For now. Elaine can wait till I've mowed the lawn, had a shower, and washed my hair.

It's almost seven by the time I remember to check my office. The fax is lying on the floor. Mangled as usual. One of these days I'll treat myself to a machine that doesn't mutilate paper. I bend to pick it up and wince. My back's on fire. And no wonder. I forgot to wear sunscreen this morning.

The fax isn't from Elaine, thank God, and I'm about to toss it in the trash when I recognize the writing.

My dogs are multiplying, the dishwasher's on life-
support, and Keith turned fifty-three last month. We
had a party. A bunch of old faces showed up, including
Colin Carpenter. Nobody's seen him in years. He asked
where you were. I told him you live in America, and . . .

I stare at the end of the page where Sophie's last sentence breaks off. I turn it over. There's nothing on the back. Duh – this is a fax. Maybe there's a second page. Sinking to my knees, I check my fax machine's preferred drop zones – behind the file cabinet, between my desk and the bookcase, in the waste bin – but find nothing except dustballs the size of small sheep and enough rusty paperclips to build a pocket battle-ship.

I read Colin's name again and get a lump in my throat.

Three decades dissolve like ice in hot water. Memories bubble up. That picnic at Roddy Slade's in the pouring rain when we danced on the lawn with bare feet. The time we met in London for a Led Zeppelin concert and I missed the last train home. Keith's nineteenth birthday party when Colin and I went to the tree fort by ourselves.

Now I don't believe in clairvoyance or precognition or whatever they call it, but right now I'd believe in almost anything. I mean, what are the chances of my conjuring up Colin on the roof and then having him roll out of my fax machine a couple of hours later?

Zachary sidles into my office and leaps on the laser printer – his favorite spot in the house – and washes his paws.

'Out of bounds!' I shove him off. I've just spent a fortune having my printer repaired and all because one of his hairs got stuck inside the drum and fouled up the optical system. He lands with a thud and stalks off with his tail in the air.

I check the time. Almost midnight – in London. Will Sophie be at work or in bed? Hard to know. Her catering jobs take place at all hours, especially on weekends. I punch in her number and wait. Nobody answers, not even Sophie's machine which she has, no doubt, forgotten to turn on.

I sit down – my legs have gone wobbly – and read the fax again.

Colin Carpenter.

Where the hell have you been for the past thirty-five years?

My best friend, Lizzie McKenna, shows up at noon the next day with an armload of hydrangeas that match her eyes. Not the oversized purple and pink jobs from the supermarket's flower shop but those amazingly sky-blue blossoms that grow like weeds along the shoreline.

She pokes her head around my kitchen door. 'May I come in or are you still grumpy?'

'Of course not.' I grit my teeth and pull hard on my wrench. I'm back under the sink, having another go at the pipes.

'Does that mean "Of course I'm not pissed off" or "Of course you can't come in"?'

This sounds way too complicated for me to sort out. 'Lizzie, I'll be done in a minute.'

'Why don't you call Mike, or is he on your hit list as well?'

I grimace and twist the wrench again. Twice. Extra hard. Once for Mike the plumber and once for me. We'd dated a few times, a long time ago, then he met a girl half my age and married her.

Lizzie bends to my level and a wedge of gray-blond hair falls in front of her face. She pushes it to one side and grins at me. 'Well?'

I grin back because we both know what she's talking about.

Two nights ago, Friday, we'd had wine and pizza on the beach. It's a weekly ritual in the summer. Just the two of us. No kids, no men. Just Lizzie and me. She provides the pizza, we take turns buying cheap wine, and I provide the beach.

For once, it was blissfully quiet. We had the place to ourselves – even the sand flies were busy elsewhere – until a couple strolled by and wrecked my peace of mind. Complete strangers. Tourists, probably. They definitely weren't locals.

'That really frosts me,' I said.

'What does?'

I pointed. 'Those two. Valley Girl and Viagra.'

Lizzie squinted at the couple. 'It's just a guy out with his daughter.'

'Yeah, right.'

The man was at least sixty, bald, wearing bicycle shorts, gold chains, and a Rolex. The girl – long legs, cutoffs, and a crop top – clung to his arm like a cheap dress. Not the sort of clinging done by a daughter. He kissed the back of her neck. Definitely not the sort of kissing done by a father. She giggled and I looked closer. They both wore diamond-encrusted wedding bands.

'Okay,' Lizzie said, helping herself to more wine. 'So what? He's just another middle-aged stud with a trophy wife.'

'The minute she turns thirty, he'll replace her.'

'Like Richard did?'

'And keeps on doing,' I said. My ex-husband was on wife number three. 'They get younger and younger. His next will be in diapers. It's demeaning.'

'The diapers?'

'No. Men who choose girls instead of women their own age.'

'Here,' Lizzie said, handing me a slice of pizza. 'Have the last piece. You need it to keep up your strength.'

'What for?'

'Staying mad at a whole generation of middle-aged men.'

Turning over, I back out of the cupboard, taking care not to scrape my sore shoulders on the frame.

Lizzie dumps her flowers in the sink. It's full of dishes and dirty water. 'I take it the pipes are blocked up again?' she says.

'Third time this month.' I nod toward the flowers. 'They're lovely' – I hug her – 'and so are you.'

'I figured you could use a treat. You were spitting nails on Friday.'

'I spat a few more yesterday. I finally fixed the roof.'

'In your bathing suit?' Lizzie eyes the burn on my shoulders. 'Jill, for God's sake get help. You've no business romping around the roof at your age.'

'The guy who fixed your roof last year is older than me.' I

hand her two apples and a bag of corn chips. 'I'm thinking of asking him for a job.'

Lizzie sighs. 'One of these days you'll fall off that ladder and break your damn neck.'

We've had this discussion before. Lizzie, who calls an electrician to change a light bulb, doesn't understand my do-it-yourself approach or the acute lack of funds that makes it necessary. She also has no idea what it's like to run your own business. She works in a community college where students turn up on an annual basis, paychecks are deposited directly into her bank account, and a whole department of financial wizards takes care of paying the bills. Computers are fixed, the water cooler is filled, and her printer is never ruined by stray cat hairs.

'Here,' I say, handing her a jug of lemonade. 'Take this lot to the beach and I'll be out in five minutes. I've got a phone call to make.'

'Hot date with a new plumber?'

I flash my best Mona Lisa smile, knowing it'll drive her nuts.

'You gonna cough up or make me guess?' she says.

'I'll tell you later – on the beach.' I push my friend toward the door. 'Hurry, or you'll miss the best of the sun.' This'll get her moving. Lizzie's a born-again sunbather. But, unlike me, she never forgets to use sunscreen.

Wearing a loose dress that flatters her fullness, Lizzie sails out of my kitchen, through the living room, and onto the back porch where she fights for control of a floppy straw hat Zachary frequently uses as a cat bed. I think the hat suits him far better than it suits Lizzie.

We met sixteen years ago at McDonald's amid French fries and ketchup and small, exuberant children. After swapping phone numbers and marital details – I was newly divorced and she was still married to Fergus – we invited ourselves to each other's houses. Our kids grew up in the best of both worlds: rocks and trees at Lizzie's old house in the woods; shells and crabs at my place on the beach. The last time he was home, my elder son, Jordan, asked what Lizzie and I found to talk about after all this time. I said, 'Oh, we grumble about menopause and lower back pain and how we can't remember much of anything, and the next day she'll say, "Did I tell you about my hot flashes?" and I'll say, "No, I don't think so," and we'll discuss them all over again.'

I find a vase for Lizzie's flowers, dump Drano in the sink, and try Sophie's number again. This time, her machine picks up. I leave a message, change into a swimsuit, and set off to join Lizzie. On my way through the porch I see Zachary has won the battle of the bonnet. He's curled up inside it like a dollop of butterscotch pudding.

The flagstones I laid last summer scorch my bare feet. Why the hell didn't I think to wear sandals? I race across my patio and head for the path between the dunes that separate my back yard from the beach. The tide's coming in. I jump a line of seaweed and shells and plunge into the waves. The cold takes my breath away. Ducking under, I swim a few strokes, then tread water and watch windsurfers bounce like butterflies across the metallic blue chop. In the distance, a freighter ploughs its way toward New York, and just beyond the lighthouse a small fishing boat chugs into the harbor.

I've lived on the beach for sixteen years and this view still gives me goosebumps. It validates my life. It keeps me from knuckling under when cranky clients, clogged sinks, and leaky roofs gang up on me at the same time.

Lizzie's beach bag, the chips, and an apple core are strewn across her tartan blanket like the remains of a Scottish picnic. She's sitting in a sand chair, arms folded across her ample stomach. I flop down beside her.

'Come on,' she says. 'Spill the beans.'

I tell her about the fax, and she asks, 'Who's Colin Carpenter?'

'He was my first love.'

'Aah.' Lizzie's face softens. 'Did he fall in love with you, too?'

Did he? Did Colin love me the way I loved him? I have no idea. He never said. Boys didn't put their feelings into words back then. Mostly we hung about with the others. Sometimes, we'd go to the cinema by ourselves and cuddle in the back row, then fumble about afterward in his dad's car. Except for that last night in the tree fort, we never went much beyond snogging. Me, because I was scared of what my mum would say if she knew a boy had his hand inside my knickers; Colin, because, well, he was that kind of boy. He didn't push. He always asked if what he was doing was okay.

It always was, and I always wanted more, but never said so.

The week Sophie and I celebrated the end of our school days by stuffing our uniforms in the Aga, the Carpenters moved. Overnight. Nobody saw them leave. Two days later, newspaper headlines told us why. Colin's father had been arrested for embezzling. Colin idolized his dad and it must've destroyed him. He was an only child and his mother, from what little I knew, was considered neurotic. Rumor had it she took Colin with her to live in Scotland, or maybe it was Ireland. Keith and Hugh figured Colin was too ashamed to get in touch with his old friends and that's why none of us heard from him again. We were hurt and confused. Me most of all.

'Jill?' Lizzie nudges me with her foot. 'Did he love you?'

'Probably not. It was a teenage girl thing. You know how choked up we get over the first boy who makes us go weak at the knees.' I grimace. 'I bet he's bald and fat and nods off in front of the television.'

'With a child bride on his lap?'

I toss a corn chip at her. 'Probably.'

'So, what did he look like?'

'Burt Lancaster.'

'Jeez,' she says. 'No wonder you had the hots for him.'

'Remember that scene in *From Here to Eternity*?'

Lizzie thinks for a minute. 'The one on the beach in Hawaii with Deborah Kerr?'

'Yeah, that one.'

Sighing, Lizzie says, 'And now, after all these years, Colin shows up and Sophie leaves you dangling.'

'That's about it.'

'Would you like to see him again?'

'Of course I would, but I can't afford to go back. Besides, he's probably married.' I glance at Lizzie. 'All the good ones are, except Trevor, of course.'

'Hmmm.'

'Why won't you marry him?' I say. Trevor's fifty-two, eight years younger than Lizzie – a toyboy, almost – and he's been begging her to marry him ever since they met six years ago at a conference in Chicago.

'Trevor lives in Detroit,' Lizzie says. 'My life is here. Neither of us is willing to move, so we'll just go on having a nice little long-distance fling until he grows up and finds someone more suitable than me.'

'But—'

'Trevor's blissful in bed,' Lizzie says, stroking her thighs, 'and if I'd met him years ago instead of Fergus, then—'

'Your ex-husband,' I say, before she can stop me, 'is still in love with you.'

A flush spreads across Lizzie's suntanned face. 'Nonsense.'

'So why is he camped out in your driveway?'

Lizzie opens her mouth, then shuts it again and I laugh because Fergus's motor home hasn't moved an inch in six months and I predict it won't be long before he moves back into the house with Lizzie.

She pins me with a look. 'Aren't we supposed to be discussing *your* love life rather than mine?'

'I don't have a love life.'

'Then it's high time you did,' she says.

'I've forgotten how.'

'Rubbish. It's like riding a bicycle.'

'Well then, there's your answer,' I say. 'I never did learn to ride a bike.'

'You need to get out. Ever since you started your own business, you've hardly left the house.' Lizzie lifts a hand to shade her eyes. 'Come on, Jill. Be honest. When's the last time you had a date?'

'Harriet took me to lunch last month, and I had a root canal two weeks ago.'

Lizzie snorts. 'A *real* date, Jill. Soft music, great food, and—' She claps her hands. 'I've thought of the perfect man.'

'Who?'

'Dutch Van Horne.'

Ah. Lizzie's friend who comes up once a year for a college reunion.

'He's due for a visit,' she says.

'Don't be daft,' I say. 'Dutch lives in Savannah.'

'So?'

'It's not exactly local.'

'Perfect,' Lizzie says. 'There's nothing like a bit of distance between two lovers. It's kept Trevor and me going for years.'

No way can I argue with that.

Four

After Lizzie leaves, I wander around the house, unable to get my mind off Colin and the day we all went to the beach. I begged Mum for a new swimsuit. Sophie had a bikini, but I was stuck with my old elastic one-piece that rode up my butt. At least I didn't wear the smelly rubber bathing hat with flowers Mum shoved in my bag. Colin and I filled it with water to wash off our feet before getting back on the bus. We shared a bag of crisps and when the bus stopped to let me off, he kissed me goodbye. My first real kiss. Salty.

I could use a glass of wine, but there isn't any, so I settle for tea and discover there's no milk either.

Damn!

This means a trip to the village, and it's Sunday, and the place will be crowded and I'll never find a parking spot. I pull on a pair of shorts, shove my feet into espadrilles, and pick up my purse.

My Volvo crouches in the driveway like a crumpled toad. Poor thing. It suffered, without complaint, through two years of teaching teenage boys to drive. I slip behind the wheel and wince when my thighs are welded to scorching hot leather.

Turning the ignition, I offer a quick prayer to the god of internal combustion engines. When it fires, I roll down my window. The air conditioner is on the blink again.

It's a five-minute drive to the village. Knots of people – mostly tourists – clog the sidewalks and spill from shops and cafes along Bay Street. I edge my car into an alley, park behind someone's boat trailer, and nip in the side door of Tuttle's Market, a small, family-owned grocery store with narrow aisles, wooden floors, and clerks who know every local customer's name. I grab a carton of milk, six cans of Fancy Feast, and a loaf of French bread, still warm from the oven.

'Hey, Jill, I see you're out for blood,' Jim Tuttle says as he rings up my total.

'I am?'

'Your shirt.'

I look down. Printed across my chest are the words: IF IT'S CALLED TOURIST SEASON, WHY CAN'T WE SHOOT THEM? The shirt isn't mine; it belongs to one of my sons. Alistair, probably.

Jim hands me a brown paper bag.

I run to my car – no ticket, this time – and drive back to the beach in a fog of nostalgia. Does Colin still have that stomach-churning chuckle? Does that lock of hair still flop across his forehead? Do his cheeks still dimple when he smiles?

Does he ever think about me?

I miss my turn and have to back up.

Blacktop gives way to sand and dirt. My road, if you could call it that, has more holes than a colander. Gripping the Volvo's wheel, I slalom around them and pray nobody's coming the other way. A blue and white FOR SALE sign flashes by. My neighbor's house is on the market for three million dollars and I wonder how long it'll take Elaine Burke to sell it this time. I'm in the midst of designing the sales brochure for her. She's going to make a boatload of money on this one, provided she can find a buyer who's willing to pay a king's ransom for nine bedrooms, six baths, and a solarium with a panoramic view of Long Island Sound.

The Volvo's brakes squeal as I pull up in front of my house. I pat the dashboard, grateful it survived another trip to the village. My front garden is now in full shade and the flowers have perked up. Shy nasturtiums hide beneath a canopy of leaves; an early morning glory winds itself through a thicket of cheerful zinnias. Clutching my groceries with one hand, I deadhead cosmos and daisies with the other. My legs brush against clumps of lavender and catmint. Their scents mingle. I breathe them in.

The front porch sags beneath the weight of a wisteria I planted ten years ago. I make a mental note to find my pruning shears and trim it back. The steps are peeling. They could use another coat of paint. My window boxes need weeding.

The phone rings. I shove the front door open with my shoulder and race for the kitchen.

'Am I calling too late?' Sophie says.

'Heavens no. It's only six o'clock.' I dump my bag on the counter. It splits open and one of Zachary's gourmet dinners rolls into the sink, still full of dirty water. I'm dying to ask about Colin, but can't get a word in edgeways because Sophie's telling me about one of her puppies that got stuck behind the refrigerator. Finally, she takes a break and I jump right in.

'So tell me,' I say. 'What's he like?'

There's a pause as if Sophie's gathering her thoughts. 'Colin hasn't changed a bit, and he's still got that incredibly sexy laugh.'

My breath comes out in a rush.

'What did you say?' Sophie asks.

'Nothing.' I clear my throat.

She laughs. 'You always did unravel over Colin.'

'Did you tell him about me?'

'I said you'd been married and divorced, had two sons, your own business, and lived on the beach in an American state I can't pronounce.'

My life, summed up in one sentence. 'Where does he live? What does he do for a living?'

'They run some sort of guest house, or a bed and breakfast, in one of those terminally cute Cotswold villages.'

'*They?*'

'Colin and . . .' Sophie pauses. 'Oh, Jill. You know how bad I am with names.'

I swallow hard. 'His wife?'

'I've no idea,' Sophie says. 'Probably. He just called her Shirley, or maybe it was Sheila.'

'What's she like?'

Another pause. 'He was alone. Apparently one of them has to stay at the B and B, especially at weekends.'

I want to ask more, but what's the point? Colin's in England – another lifetime away. 'How's Hugh?' I say. A far safer question. 'And where is he?' Sophie's brother is rarely in one place very long.

'Hugh's in Saudi, selling software to sheiks.'

'What about Keith?' Unlike Colin, he's kept in touch with Sophie and Hugh.

'I forgot to tell you. He and Penny just had another baby.'

'Christ!'

Sophie laughs. 'He's making up for lost time.'

'No kidding.' Ten years ago, when he was forty-three, Keith married a woman half his age, and they're now on their fourth child. 'Sophie, come and see me before the summer ends.'

'Can't,' she says. 'The puppies are too young to shove in a

kennel, and besides, I'm booked solid with work till the end of August.'

'September, then?'

'Jill, it's your turn to come here.'

'I know, but—'

Thwoooop!

My sink lets loose with a gigantic fart.

'Holy shit!' Sophie says. 'What was that?'

Reaching for the sink, I plunge my hand through the scum and pull out a can of Fancy Feast. 'Let me call you back, okay?'

The pond water gurgles and drains away and I wonder how much money Zachary's gourmet dinner just saved me.

Enough to fix the leak in my bedroom ceiling?

A down payment on my next car?

A ticket to London?

Five

My business line wakes me at eight fifteen Friday morning. I bury my head in a pillow and groan because I stayed up half the night designing logos for the Contented Figleaf, a trendy new bistro on Bay Street. I was beyond tired, yet unable to sleep. Multiple deadlines for Elaine Burke had kept me working flat out all week. Finally, my restlessness turned to rebellion and I took it out on that innocent little restaurant by sketching a row of naked garden gnomes in pointy red hats leering over their shoulders and holding up fig leaves. *Snow White* meets *The Full Monty*. I doubt they'll go for it. Greedily, I snatch another thirty minutes in the sack.

Half an hour later I stagger into my office. The message light's blinking. I hit PLAY.

'Jillian?' There's a pause. 'Surely you're in the office by now.'

Elaine. Not a good start to anyone's day, especially mine. I pad into the kitchen to make tea, and while waiting for the kettle to boil I grab the wall phone and punch in her number. May as well get it over with.

She answers on the first ring. 'Where were you?'

I stifle a yawn. 'Good morning, Elaine.'

'I'm in a hurry,' says my most important client, before launching into a list of changes for a sales brochure I just finished. 'Are you getting all this?'

'Yes.' I head for my office but the phone cord pulls me up short. Can't find paper or pencil, so I scribble on a grocery bag with a laundry marker.

'You didn't do as I asked,' Elaine says, contradicting the instructions she gave me on Tuesday. 'That shot of the dining room needs to be much bigger. I can't imagine what you were thinking here. Nobody can see it.'

You told me to make it small, remember? 'It's an ugly room, Jillian. We don't want to draw attention to it.'

Elaine rattles on. 'The detail on the fireplace in the den is unclear.'

That's because the photos you gave me were low-res.

I turn the bag over.

'And there are ten bedrooms, not nine.'

Nine. Definitely nine. I clamp my elbow on the bag to stop it sliding off the counter.

'Jillian, are you listening?'

'Of course.'

There's a pause. 'Now, about the layout.'

Oh, God. Now what?

'I want eight pages, not twelve,' Elaine says.

'Then you'll have to cut copy.'

'Impossible,' she says. 'Everything stays.'

'But—'

'Make it fit.'

Well, there goes my weekend.

'Have it here by five on Tuesday. And bring me a CD. I don't trust e-mail,' Elaine says and hangs up.

I grind my teeth so hard, I'm in danger of loosening the

crown I just paid a fortune for. One of these days, that woman's going to push me over the edge.

Her priority-of-the-moment is the sales brochure for that overpriced house next door. She approved the final layout yesterday, said it was ready for her printer – a big, fancy outfit in Ohio – and now she's ripping it apart and blaming me.

Time to find another client. I'll start looking next week.

Zachary curls himself around my legs. I feed him, swallow a mug of tea, and get dressed. Then I sit at my desk and juggle appointments. If I cancel tomorrow's haircut, beg an extension on my article for *Paws and Claws Quarterly*, and persuade the chamber of commerce to wait till Thursday for my Fall Festival designs, I can pull it all off. Just to be sure, I check my calendar. Oh, hell. I forgot about the holiday and Jordan's flying in late Tuesday afternoon.

Maybe Lizzie will go and fetch him from the airport.

Turns out, Lizzie was dead right about Dutch. On Tuesday afternoon I get back from delivering Elaine's job to find him in my driveway leaning against his lopsided Cadillac wearing cut-offs, an Australian bush hat, and a Hawaiian shirt. He's barefoot and feeding peppermint sticks to a humpback brown dog that looks like a cross between an Irish wolfhound and a Chippendale sofa.

I hear a miaow and look up to see my cat on the roof.

'Hey there, Jill Hunter.' Dutch tips his hat. 'I'm mighty glad to see y'all.'

The good ole boy drawl slides through his walrus-style mustache like it belongs. But I know better. Dutch grew up in California and graduated from Yale with honors before earning a Purple Heart in Vietnam.

'This here's Murdock,' Dutch says, patting the dog's head with a bottle of Jack Daniel's.

I take a good look at the guy I met five years ago at one of

Lizzie's parties. Broad shoulders, narrow hips, long legs. A lived-in, weatherbeaten face with a generous mouth and eyes the color of slate. Lizzie's advice flashes before me. Is she right? Do I need to get back on that bike I never learned to ride in the first place? And, more to the point, should I get on it with Dutch Van Horne?

He grins and pulls me into a hug. 'Sorry to barge in without callin' you first, but I need a bed for the night.' He drops a kiss on my forehead. 'Can I share yours?'

'No,' I tell him, 'but you can have the couch.'

'Fair enough.' Dutch takes a shabby overnight bag from his car, hands me a bottle of Merlot, and follows me to the kitchen. He opens the wine and I pull cold cuts from the fridge to make sandwiches. I haven't eaten all day and the glass of wine I drink with Dutch goes straight to my head. He pours me another. I slice tomatoes and spread mayonnaise on French bread. I drink a bit more wine and open a jar of peanuts and we snack on those. I dump salsa into a dish, add grated cheese and corn chips, and shove it in the oven. We open another bottle of wine and by the time Lizzie shows up with my son, I'm totally wasted.

My unexpected guest and his dog take it upon themselves to step onto my front porch and act like greeters at a carnival sideshow. 'Howdy folks,' Dutch says, doffing his hat. 'Step inside and join the fun.'

I grasp a chair to steady myself. Is the room spinning, or is it me?

Dutch kisses Lizzie hello, then guides my bewildered son into the kitchen.

'Hi, honey. This is Dutch Van Horne,' I say, trying to keep Jordan in focus. 'He just popped in for a quick visit.' I make it sound like he's only staying five minutes. Then my legs give out and I sink to the floor and wrap my arms around Murdock.

Scowling at Dutch like a billigerent teen, Jordan tosses his bag in the corner and leans against the counter.

'I was on my way to a reunion in New Haven,' Dutch says, smiling at my son, 'when I remembered how close your mother lives. I made a detour to come and say hello. I'll be leavin' tomorrow.'

Lizzie whips up a sandwich for Jordan and tries to rescue us, but her efforts fall flat. The conversation stutters, then dies completely. Lizzie puts down her glass, stands up and says, 'Well, it's been a long day, so if you guys will excuse me, I'll be off.' Then adds, on her way out the door, 'Don't forget about tomorrow, okay?'

The way I feel right now, I seriously doubt I'll be up for a picnic.

Six

Sands Point
July 2007

I wake up with a mouth like the bottom of a bird cage. My head's on a turntable and my tongue is glued to my teeth. What the hell was I thinking? Falling into bed with Dutch isn't the answer. He has the sexual attention span of a rabbit.

There's a knock at the door. 'Are you decent?'

My bathrobe's nowhere in sight. I wriggle under the covers. 'Come in.'

Dutch, freshly showered and looking disgustingly cheerful, enters my room bearing a tray. Murdock, looking even more cheerful, trots beside him. Dutch places the tray on my bedside table.

Sitting up, I make a clumsy attempt to wrap the sheet around my shoulders. I squint at the tray. Is that coffee and hot buttered toast? A pot of marmalade, a rose in a bud vase? Jeez, it's kind of hard to stay pissed at a guy who delivers breakfast in bed. I give him a weak smile. It's the best I can manage. 'Thanks.'

Dutch hands me a glass of orange juice. 'Bad night, huh?'

'Um, did we, I mean . . .' I feel a blush staining my cheeks. 'You don't remember?'

'No.'

'Then I'm devastated. But you were fabulous.'

I groan and sink back into my pillows. The sheet slithers south, but at this point, it hardly matters. My first one-night stand, and I can't remember it.

Dutch grins. 'Your couch is real comfortable.'

I grab the sheets and cover myself again. 'So we didn't—'

'As tempted as I was, I didn't take advantage.'

My clothes are neatly folded on a chair. I don't recall getting undressed. Hell, I don't even remember climbing the stairs. Did Dutch have to carry me up? And where was Jordan while all this was going on? I blush even deeper.

'How about some toast?' Dutch says.

He really is rather sweet. Leaning forward, I kiss him on the cheek. 'You're a lifesaver.'

'Aw, shucks.'

I try to thank him for saving me from myself, but can't seem to find the right words. So I pat Murdock's whiskery nose instead.

Dutch stays until Jordan, who's been out walking the beach, comes back. I'm embarrassed by my son's surly behavior, but Dutch chooses to ignore it. He drives away just before noon in his elderly car with Murdock's hairy face hanging out the passenger window. A sticker on the back bumper says CLINTON AND GORE FOR '92.

I confront Jordan the minute I return to my kitchen. 'Why were you so infernally rude to him?'

'Because he's a jerk.'

'For your information, Dutch Van Horne's a decorated war hero, a Yale graduate, and—' I snatch up the kettle and pour cold water in the sugar bowl. 'Oh, sod.'

Jordan takes over making the tea.

Gingerly, I lower myself in a chair. 'Dutch is a good friend, that's all.'

Why do I feel the need to justify myself? Jordan's not a kid. He's twenty-six, for God's sake. Alistair would've said: 'Go for it, Ma!' and I'm reminded of the night, shortly after my divorce, when I tried to tell the boys, then aged eight and ten, that it was okay for me to date other men. Jordan looked at me wide-eyed; Alistair grinned and said: 'Does this mean you're gonna fool around?'

My anger, such as it is, fizzles out like day-old soda. Jordan's just doing what he always does – worrying about me. Seeing me drunk last night must've been a shock, especially when I was carried upstairs by a man he didn't know from Adam.

Jordan lets out a sigh. 'I'm sorry, Mom. I was out of line.' He touches my forehead.

I wince.

'Are you okay?'

'Not really. My hair hurts.' I take a sip of tea. 'Right now I could swallow a bottle of Tylenol.'

Jordan pulls an envelope from his pocket. 'This isn't a painkiller, but it might help.'

I put down my cup. 'What's all this about?'

'Go on,' Jordan says, handing it to me. 'Open it.'

I tear the envelope with clumsy fingers. It's a slip of paper with numbers on it, I think. My eyes keep crossing.

'It's an airline voucher,' Jordan explains. 'For a ticket to London.'

I stare at him, mouth open, gaping like a goldfish.

'It's from Alistair and me.'

'Are you serious?' My younger son's in graduate school. He's drowning in debt. He can barely afford to take the train home from Boston, let alone buy half an airline ticket to England.

'Al's promised to pay me back when he's a world-famous paleontologist,' Jordan says. He pulls out a chair, turns it around, and sits down with his chin leaning on the back rail just like he used to when he was a teenager and in need of a good chat. 'The voucher's open-ended. You can use it any time.'

'No, it's too much.' I push it toward him. 'You're sweet and wonderful, and I love you both for even thinking of it, but I can't possibly accept it.'

Jordan anchors the ticket to my table with a bottle of ketchup. 'You've been wanting to visit Sophie for years and besides, the airline had a special offer, so . . .' He tries to look convincing. 'No arguments, okay?'

I study my son's anxious, wide-open face and see the little boy who didn't buy my first fumbling explanation about dating other men. I don't think he bought the second one, either. I reach out and pat his thatch of streaky blond hair. 'This is fabulous. You have no idea.'

With Jordan's help I make the potato salad I promised Lizzie for her Fourth of July party. It's in full swing by the time we pull into the McKennas' driveway. Rock music pulses from an upstairs window and someone who can't wait for it to get dark – probably Fergus – is already letting off fireworks. Smoke from a barbecue grill spirals lazily upward and I hear the shriek of small children, the low thrum of adult conversation. Discarded toys and a shocking-pink tricycle litter the driveway. Jordan maneuvers past them to park beside Fergus's motor home. He turns off the engine and pockets the keys. I guess he doesn't trust me not to bugger off back home.

'Go and join the others,' I tell him. 'I'll take the salad inside.'

'Mom?'

'Yes.'

'I love you.'

I brush his cheek with my hand. 'I love you, too, and I'm sorry about last night.'

'You're entitled,' says my son. 'It's about time you had some fun.'

'Getting drunk isn't fun.'

Jordan winks at me. Maybe there's hope for this boy yet.

I find Lizzie in her kitchen about to dismember a trio of chickens. The sight of all that naked poultry makes me feel sick.

'You don't look so hot,' Lizzie says. 'You'd better sit down and tell me what happened after I left.' She waves toward a bottle of wine. 'Want some?'

'God, no.' I collapse into a chair and lay my head on Lizzie's butcher block table. Execution. That's what I need. Chop, chop. Head falls in basket. End of problem. 'I got seriously drunk last night.'

'You were pretty far gone by the time Jordan and I showed up.'

'I had more after you went home.'

Lizzie whacks the legs and wings off a chicken and tosses them into the blue and white striped bowl I gave her last Christmas. 'That's not like you,' she says, reaching for another carcass.

'I was only following your advice.'

'Since when did you start doing that?' She gives me a lopsided grin. 'And exactly which piece of advice were you following?'

'About having an affair with Dutch.'

'What does that have to do with getting drunk?' Lizzie takes a sip of her wine. Her fingers leave smeary prints on the glass.

I attempt a weak smile. 'Dutch courage.'

Lizzie spits Chardonnay all over the table. Wiping it up, she says, 'Well, did you or didn't you?'

'What?'

'Sleep with him.'

I shake my head. The room swims. I close my eyes and wonder if hangovers are terminal.

'Why the hell not?' Lizzie says.

'He didn't want to take advantage of me.'

'Well, *that's* gotta be a first,' she says. 'So, tell me, Jill. When *was* the last time you got laid?'

I shrug. 'I honestly don't remember.'

Early the next morning, I pull out my passport to make sure it hasn't expired, then phone Sophie to invite myself over.

'Come in September,' she says, 'and for God's sake bring decent weather.'

After promising to do my best, I take a cup of coffee and my sketch pad outside. I'm negotiating with Zachary for my share of the chaise when I hear a familiar screech. Two iridescent green parrots fly overhead, trailing twigs and grass from their claws.

The first time I saw them, digging for seeds in my lawn, I could barely believe my eyes, so I phoned our local pet shop and was told these birds are considered pests because they're not indigenous, that they're encroaching on the local bird population. Rumor has it they're descended from a shipment of parrots that escaped at Kennedy Airport twenty-odd years ago, or perhaps it was from an overturned tractor-trailer on Interstate 95. Nobody really seems to know.

Pests or not, I adore these crazy birds. I love it that they're ballsy enough to live here, and I make angry phone calls to power company officials when they remove parrot nests from the tops of utility poles. I pick up my sketch pad and flip through page after page of parrots – in trees, building nests, and flying in formation. Strains of *Turandot* waft through the back window. Jordan must be up.

Turning to a fresh page, I sketch a parrot with a puffed-up chest, outstretched wings, and a wide-open beak. I draw notes floating out. He's singing. He's taking a bow. The audience is clapping.

Jill, get a grip. Parrots don't love opera, they love sea shanties and pirates. They sit on their shoulders and say things like 'Ahoy there, matey!'

Skull and crossbones. Buried treasure.

Walking the plank.

The boys outgrew the fort the year I turned eighteen – the same year Colin's family disappeared and my father got sick.

Bone cancer.

He died the following February, two weeks before my nineteenth birthday. My mother presided over the post-funeral gathering like a dowager queen. Stiff and dry-eyed, she handed out cups of weak tea, plates of crustless cucumber sandwiches, and slices of fruitcake as if she were hosting a lunch for the Women's Institute. Sophie stayed glued to my side as friends hugged me and neighbors murmured words of sympathy, but I was numb. I kept looking for Colin. Some-how, I expected him to show up and put his arms around me and tell me everything was going to be all right.

But he didn't.

And it wasn't all right.

My dad was gone and I was alone with my mother. A year later, she married again and I became a stranger in my own home. So I moved to London with Sophie, threw myself into art school, and met a handsome, fair-haired American exchange student from Boston.

Seven

A light rain is falling when my Virgin Atlantic flight touches down at Heathrow the Friday after Labor Day. I'd forgotten how furiously green England is. After a summer of drought and bleached grass in Connecticut, my old home looks lush and verdant and I feel a bit strange, seeing it through the eyes of a visitor. This is the first time I've been back in almost ten years.

Sophie's waiting at the barrier, impossibly elegant in a simple linen dress with a scarf knotted around her neck that would've taken me half an hour to tie. Her blue eyes sparkle and her hair, still thick and still golden and as unmanageable as ever, is piled on top of her head and held in place with two tortoiseshell combs. Tendrils curl at the nape of her neck. People glance at her and smile. She doesn't seem to notice.

'I can't believe you're finally here!' Sophie's hug takes my breath away. 'You look absolutely fabulous. You're thinner and' – she holds me at arm's length – 'you've still got a complexion to die for.'

I hug her back. 'Liar.'

'Come on,' she says. 'Let's get you home. You must be

knackered. If I can keep those bloody dogs quiet, you can have a nap.'

Sophie's house is an unexpected treasure, a small brick oasis with a walled garden barely a stone's throw from the King's Road. The rumble of traffic, several streets away, isn't loud enough to keep me awake. I fall into Sophie's spare bed and doze off.

The light is fading when I wake up. Sophie comes in with a mug of tea. 'You still take sugar, I hope.'

'What time is it?' I sit up and rub my eyes.

'Seven.'

'Oh, hell. I won't be able to sleep tonight.'

'That's probably a blessing,' Sophie says. 'Ian's making another of those spy movies. He's invited us to stop by later and watch them filming. Do you feel up to it?'

'Sure, why not?' I'm curious about Sophie's latest boyfriend. A movie producer, this time. Probably bald, short, and aggressive, but that's just a guess.

Sophie sets my tea on the night table. 'Come downstairs when you're ready. Leftovers for dinner. Nothing fancy.'

But it is, and we dine by candlelight on chicken curry with strawberries and cream to follow. And when I'm feeling too full to stand up, Sophie hands me a towel. 'I'll wash and you dry,' she says, glaring at the dishwasher. 'Bloody thing's terminal.' She puts on a long, white apron that makes her look like a tall Mrs Tiggy-Winkle or perhaps a slender Jemima Puddle-Duck.

'How's your mother?' I say.

'Independent, impossible, and driving.'

I almost drop a plate. 'Driving?'

'Mum finally got her license.'

'You're kidding.' Last I knew, Claudia had failed her

43

driver's test so many times, they told her not to bother again. No point, the authorities said. You'll never pass.

'I wish I was,' Sophie mutters. 'She must've bribed some-one.'

Images of Claudia careening along narrow country lanes, scattering cows and tractors like confetti, flash through my mind. 'Does she like living in Cornwall?'

'Loves it. Why don't you go down and see her?'

'We could both go.'

'Maybe next week,' Sophie says. 'Now, it'll be cold by the river. Wear something warm.'

It's a ten-minute walk to the embankment. The Thames, thick and silent beneath a duvet of mist, reminds me of all the spy movies I've ever seen – suspicious figures in trench coats and trilbies leaning against lamp posts smoking cigarettes.

The movie set – cameras, lights, and clapperboards – fulfills most of my expectations. Ian Remmington does not. He's tall and slender with long hair and soulful brown eyes – a nineteenth-century poet masquerading as a twenty-first-century film mogul.

He asks Sophie to join him on location in Sardinia the following week.

'Not this time, Ian. Jill and I have other plans.'

He bends to kiss Sophie's cheek. 'Okay, how about Fiji, in November? We'll call it a honeymoon.' He winks at me and goes back to work.

'Are you guys serious?' I ask.

Sophie laughs. 'Ian's the ideal boyfriend, but he'd make a perfectly dreadful husband.'

'How would you know? You've never had one.'

'I think of Ian as dessert,' Sophie says, 'rather than the main meal. He asks me to marry him at least once a month and I always refuse. It works both ways. I feel desirable and he gets to indulge his romantic fantasy as the spurned lover.'

'Didn't you ever want kids? A family?'

'Once, maybe. But I got over it. Now I have dogs' – she grins – 'dogs and lovers.'

'What are you going to do about Colin?' Sophie asks the next morning. We're having coffee at her kitchen table. On the tiles beneath our feet, the puppies scarf down what's left of our scrambled eggs. Sophie's kitchen is comfortingly shabby, with mismatched chairs and faded chintz curtains. Along one wall lies an enormous Welsh dresser filled with Portuguese pottery, baskets of tarnished silverware, and a collection of Toby jugs I remember from Claudia's old dining room.

'Nothing. Everything. I don't know.'

'Can you be a bit more specific?' Sophie says.

'What the point? He's married.'

'We don't know that for sure.'

'He's involved. Same difference.'

'I wonder why he never got in touch.' Sophie feeds her last bit of bacon to the smallest puppy, then scoops up her hair and fastens it with a red plastic clip. 'You know, after his dad got in all that trouble.'

'Why didn't you ask him at Keith's party?'

'I didn't want to rake up old hurts.'

I get up to pour coffee. 'I can't imagine doing that.'

'Raking up old hurts?'

'No. Cutting myself off from old friends.'

Sophie looks at me. 'So, what do you call running away to the States, then writing two months later to say you got married?'

'A monumental blunder?' What began as an extended holiday – touring New England with Richard – turned into something neither of us bargained for: a baby we ended up losing. I feel a familiar stab of guilt. I should've told Sophie what was going on, but at the time I was so embarrassed over my dreadful mistakes, I hid from the world, including my best friend. In a brief, blistering phone call, Sophie told me I was a fucking coward. We didn't speak again for two, very long years.

It was Claudia who saved our friendship. She told me not to give up, to keep in touch with Sophie even if I didn't hear back. 'My daughter's a wee bit stubborn,' she said. 'Just give her time. She'll come round.' So I wrote cheerful letters and sent baby photos of Jordan, until one day Sophie telephoned to apologize for being, in her words, 'a bloody rotten excuse for a friend'.

She drops three lumps of sugar into her coffee. 'But there's one thing I can never forgive you for.'

My heart sinks. 'What?'

'You cheated me out of wearing peach chiffon and puff sleeves at your wedding.'

I relax. 'Silk ribbons? Stephanotis? Sweetheart roses?'

'Matching high heels, long pointed toes?'

'Winkle-pickers.'

Sophie grins. 'Fuck-me shoes.'

We had it all planned. She'd get married in ecru lace and I'd walk down the aisle in white peau-de-soie. We'd each have six bridesmaids and a flower girl to toss petals in our path. Our mothers would wear outrageous hats. Hugh and Keith would be in morning dress and Sophie and I would stand – veiled, virginal, and vulnerable – at the altar with the men of our dreams. In my case, it was always Colin. In hers? Who knew? Back then, Sophie dated one boy after another in a whirl of parties, point-to-points, and weekends at country houses. I figured it was only a matter of time before one of them put a ring on her finger. But here she is, thirty-five years later, still single and loving it, while I'm divorced with two grown sons, a crumbling beach cottage, and way too much debt.

Sophie asks again. 'What about Colin?'

I shake my head. What's the point? It'll only lead to more hurt. More loss. I take a deep breath. I'm in London. I'm with my oldest friend. It's time I got reacquainted with my heritage.

'Let's play tourist,' I say.

Sophie raises one eyebrow. 'Tacky.'

'Of course.'

Sophie drives me to Hampton Court, St Paul's Cathedral, and the Tower. We browse the markets in Camden Town, ride an open double-decker bus through a maze of city streets, and go shopping in Harrods where I buy a tin of Scottish shortbread for Lizzie to thank her for taking care of my cat. We stroll through Green Park and wander up the Mall toward Buckingham Palace to watch the changing of the guard. We view the Elgin Marbles at the British Museum and laugh at the mummers and clowns in Covent Garden. Tired and thirsty, we return to Sophie's house via a pub where we drink beer and play darts.

I sink into a squashy old wingchair by Sophie's fireplace and kick off my shoes. I haven't done this much walking in years, not on pavement, anyway. Sophie digs into a pile of paperwork that's accumulated on her desk.

'I've got to get this lot sorted before we can swan off to Cornwall,' she tells me.

The telephone rings and I answer it.

'Hi, it's me,' Lizzie says. 'Have you heard about Cassie?'

'Who?'

'The hurricane that's in the Bahamas right now.'

Is my flood insurance paid up? 'Will it hit Connecticut?'

'Too soon to tell,' Lizzie says. 'With luck, it'll blow itself out. They usually do.'

'How's Zachary?'

'He's fine,' Lizzie says, 'but he's not eating much. I've only had to refill his bowl twice.'

'No problem,' I say. 'He's probably out in the marsh, snacking on rabbits and mice.'

There's a pause. 'So, have you seen him yet?'

'Seen who?'

'Colin.'

'No, and I really don't expect to.' I glance at Sophie. She's frowning. 'We're going down to Cornwall,' I tell Lizzie. 'To see Claudia.'

Sophie looks up. '*You're* going. I'm staying here.'

I cover the mouthpiece. 'Why?'

'Because I've buggered up my calendar,' Sophie says, slamming her desk drawer and scattering papers all over the floor.

'Lizzie, I'm sorry, but may I call you back tomorrow? Sophie seems to be going into meltdown.'

Lizzie laughs. 'Sure. I'll be around all day.'

I hang up and Sophie waves a piece of paper in the air. 'That big catering job I booked for a week on Friday is really *this* week. Thank God I checked their purchase order.'

'Then I'll stay here and help you.'

'Better not. Mum'll kill both of us if you don't show up,' she says. 'You can either hire a car or take the train.'

I don't want to drive. 'Have you got a timetable?'

Sophie nods. 'It's around here somewhere,' she says, rummaging in her desk. 'Ah, here it is. Paddington to Cornwall. Mum can pick you up at the station in Truro. She often goes there to buy art supplies.'

'I think of Claudia every time I smell paint,' I say. 'Remember how she taught us to draw?'

'She taught you, not me. I was hopeless.'

'I wonder if she'd enjoy drawing on a computer.'

'You've got to be kidding.'

'No. Seriously. I bet I could teach her to—'

'My mother,' Sophie says, 'can't handle anything more complicated than a bamboo carpet beater.'

'She drives a car.'

'And you,' Sophie says wickedly, 'get to be her passenger.'

'Oh, shit!'

Sophie's grin widens. 'So, just how brave are you?'

'I'll rent a car.'

'Good idea.'

Eight

Cornwall
September 2007

Driving southwest, I think about Claudia. When her husband died last year, she was left with debts she didn't expect and a house she could no longer afford. Instead of feeling sorry for herself, she sold everything and trundled off to Cornwall to begin a new life – a gutsy move for someone just turned seventy-three.

The sun's getting low by the time I reach Claudia's village. It's so small, Sophie says, that if you blink while driving through it, you'll miss it completely. I stop and check my directions. I'm to go past the church and take the next right turn.

It's little more than a cart track.

Claudia's cottage lies against the landscape like a small brown animal that's burrowed into the ground but is slightly too large to fit into its hole. Its thatched roof, interrupted by the curving eyebrow of a blue-framed window, stretches up and out to embrace a center chimney that even now, in the warmth of a September evening, emits a small curl of smoke that hints of welcome.

For a moment or two, I feel as if I've stumbled into the

past . . . a place where things move at their own pace, where clocks and computers and airline schedules don't matter, and the only sound worth listening to is the muffled roar of waves pounding on rocks. It's familiar, yet elusive. An impression just out of reach, and—

I slam on my brakes.

Heart thumping like sneakers in a dryer, I roll down my window. 'Jeez, Claudia, I'm sorry. I almost hit you.'

'Come along and don't waste time with your suitcase,' she says. 'I need help with these squirrels.' Without waiting for a response, Claudia picks up two wire cages and disappears behind the cottage.

I abandon my car and follow her.

The vintage Morris Minor is almost hidden from view, obscured by a vine-covered trellis and a rusty wheelbarrow that's propped against the wall. Claudia heaves her cages into the back seat, takes off her gardening gloves, and tosses them on the floor.

'Let's go,' she says, climbing into her car. She turns the ignition and mashes the pedals with her Wellington boots. The car belches smoke. The engine snorts with surprise.

I jump in and slam the door.

Claudia grinds the gear into reverse. Her car shoots backward and hurls me against the dashboard.

'Oh, bother.' Claudia wrenches the gear lever in the opposite direction. 'Sorry about all this. I'll explain in a minute. Let me get out of here first.' She executes a clumsy three-point turn and we're off like the clappers, pitching through potholes the size of small bomb craters. I hang on to the armrest and hope Claudia's mechanic has plenty of spare parts because I think I just heard something fall off. We jerk to a shuddering halt at the end of Claudia's driveway. 'That miserable old bugger drove off half an hour ago,' she says.

51

My heart's still trying to catch up with the rest of me. 'Who?'

'With a bit of luck, he'll stay down the pub till dark.' Claudia cranes her neck, glances left and right, then swerves onto the main road. Her chin barely reaches the top of the steering wheel.

'Is it really ten years since the last time you were here?' she says. 'Sophie rang me this morning – said you haven't changed a bit. She's right, of course. And you look lovely. I like your hair. It's a bit shorter than I remember, and I hope you're not too hungry, but I've got to get these animals away from here first. I'll fix dinner when we get back.'

Have I blundered into the pages of a Beatrix Potter book gone horribly wrong? I turn to look at the tiny Squirrel Nutkins in Claudia's wire cages. 'What exactly are you doing with all these animals?'

'Relocating them.'

'Why?'

'That bloody farmer across the street is setting traps,' Claudia says, swerving around a corner. 'Then he drowns them in the pond behind his pigsties.'

'What have they done to deserve that?'

'They're eating his grain.' Claudia's grip on the steering wheel tightens. 'But his cows and pigs won't starve because a few hungry rodents help themselves to some corn now and then.'

'Gray squirrels are considered vermin where I live.'

'There are right ways and wrong ways to control pests. Keeping them in cages till they're half starved and then drowning them is unconscionably cruel.'

'Where are we taking them?'

'Right about here.' Claudia yanks up the handbrake and the Morris Minor judders to a halt. 'Hurry up. We've got to get back before he does.'

Legs shaking, I clamber out. 'Why?'

'I have to return his cages before he misses them.' Beneath the brim of her soft brown hat, Claudia's gray eyes twinkle with triumph. 'This is a nature preserve with plenty of old oak trees and lots of nice juicy acorns.'

That night I share my bed with a handsome silver-gray tabby named Max and wake up to the smell of bacon and eggs. I pull on a pair of old jeans and an Irish sweater, and follow my nose to the kitchen.

Its uneven plaster walls are colorwashed in lavender. Pine shelves, heavy and knotted, hold cookbooks and casserole dishes and blue earthenware plates I remember from childhood. Bunches of dried sage and rosemary hang from oak beams that criss-cross the ceiling; copper pans gleam from their hooks on the wall. The middle of the room is dominated by Claudia's bleached wooden table. The one she used to paint on. The window, unfettered by curtains, looks out across a carpet of heather. Beyond lies the sea.

'I hope you're hungry,' Claudia says, piling my plate with an old-fashioned English fry-up – grilled kidneys and tomatoes, bacon and eggs, and lashings of fried bread. Between her and Sophie, I've eaten more cholesterol and carbs in the past ten days than I have in ten years at home.

We gossip while eating and then Claudia shoves off to check on her traps. I head the other way, toward the water. The ground ends and I look down sheer granite cliffs to a small, crescent-shaped beach about two hundred feet below. How do people get to it? I don't see a path. Maybe it's one of those stubborn bits of coastline that refuses to give way to picnic hampers and daytrippers.

'Come along, Jill,' Claudia calls out.

Her back garden is an Impressionist painting – a tumble of textures and hues with bright points of light that focus the eye. Snapdragons and nasturtiums, all the colors in a box of crayons, spill across the path, alongside clumps of Michaelmas daisies that dissolve into clouds of white gypsophila and bright blue plumbago. I smell lavender and thyme. A hint of rosemary. Beside the back door, two stone rabbits crouch beneath a garden bench. A wooden squirrel perches atop a pile of clay pots. My shoes are muddy, so I scrape them on a hedgehog boot brush with beady eyes and an upturned snout. I pat its little head before going inside.

Claudia's picking up her car keys when I reach the front hall. 'Hurry up. We're wasting the best part of the day.'

'Why don't you relax and let me drive?'

She hesitates. 'Are you sure?'

'Absolutely,' I say.

It's a day filled with windswept beaches and tranquil bays; of solitary stone farmhouses and stunted trees that grow sideways out of the soil. We drive through sunwashed villages with streets barely wide enough for a car, and past tiny beaches where old wooden boats lie in the sand waiting for the next tide to release them.

At four o'clock, we stop for tea in a cafe near Land's End. Clotted cream and homemade strawberry jam. Milk bottles filled with sweet peas and freesia. Lace doilies, bone china cups. Starched napkins, white linen tablecloths.

'When's the last time you saw your mother?' Claudia says.

I almost choke on a scone. 'The day I left England with Richard. Why?'

'Just wondering.'

My mother, if she's still alive, would be eighty-seven by now. Does Claudia know where she is? If so, I hope she doesn't tell me because I really don't want to know. I never talk about my mother, not even with my own sons. Like all small boys, they used to be fascinated by monsters and gargoyles. They played scary games, and their unknown grandmother was always cast as a witch or a vampire. They weren't far off the mark. I gulp at my tea.

'Careful, it's hot.' Claudia looks at me, eyebrows raised, waiting.

Dammit, if anyone deserves an explanation, she does. 'I tried to see her, once, about twenty years ago. Richard had a business meeting in London. I phoned my mother and asked if I could bring the boys out for a visit. I thought, stupidly, it might be easier for us to patch things up if the kids were there.'

'Surely Edith wanted to see her grandchildren.'

'You'd have thought so,' I say. 'They're the only ones she's got.'

'What happened?'

'She called me a slut, said my sons were a couple of poor little bastards, and hung up.' Dear God, I can't believe I'm carrying on like this, telling Claudia stuff I've kept hidden for so long, I've almost convinced myself it never happened.

'I'm sorry,' she says. 'I shouldn't have asked.'

'Things got worse between us after Daddy died.'

'I know, but don't beat yourself up over Edith's lack of mothering skills. None of it was your fault. It was—' Claudia rearranges spoons and puts the lid back on the sugar bowl.

I lean forward. 'What?'

'Nothing.' Claudia stands up. 'I'll take care of this.' She places a ten-pound note on the table and something in the set of her jaw tells me to back off.

It's dark by the time we get back to Claudia's cottage. The phone rings, Claudia answers, and hands the receiver to me. 'It's Sophie,' she says.

'Jill, Lizzie rang up. I've been trying to get you for ages.'

All my alarm sensors go off at once. 'What's wrong?'

'Cathy's going to hit Connecticut.'

'Who?'

'The hurricane.'

'Cassie!' I glance at my watch. 'What time did she call? Did she sound worried?'

'I've been gone all day. Working. Lizzie left a message.'

When I finally reach Lizzie, the connection's so bad we both have to shout.

'Fergus and I are going to your place now to batten down the hatches,' she yells.

'Should I come back?'

'Don't be absurd,' she says. 'What would you do? Stand on the beach and pretend to be Moses?' There's a burst of static, then Lizzie again. 'Fergus has a truckload of plywood. We'll put some on your windows and—'

The line goes dead.

Claudia hands me a glass of wine. 'What's wrong?'

I fill her in and she suggests we turn on the TV. 'Maybe the news will have something.'

But it doesn't.

'In less than twenty-four hours,' I tell Claudia, 'my living-room furniture could be floating in three feet of water. Not,' I add, 'that it would be any great loss.'

Claudia pats her lap and the tabby jumps up. 'Tell me about your cottage.'

'A few small rooms with a fabulous view.' I shrug. 'It was my reward for enduring fourteen years with Richard. He got a new wife and the mansion in Mount Kisko; I got the kids and a beach cottage with rotten floorboards and bad plumbing.'

'Would you like to get married again?'

'Sure,' I tell her. 'I'd love to find the right guy, but most men my age want women twenty years younger.'

'Not all of them,' Claudia says. 'Look at Prince Charles.'

'I'd rather not.'

'Why did you really leave England?' Claudia offers more wine.

I hold out my glass. 'Because I needed to get away.'

'But why America? You could've moved to Ireland instead, or Wales.'

'I thought I was in love with Richard.'

'You were in love with someone else, though. Weren't you?'

The night of Keith's nineteenth birthday, Colin and I went to the fort. By ourselves.

While the adults chatted over cocktails in the Lombards' living room, us kids hung about in the kitchen. Sophie and Roddy Slade were wrapped around each other, slow-dancing, oblivious of everyone but themselves. Hugh and Keith were arguing politics with two boys from school. Colin took my hand and we slipped out the back door. I don't think anyone saw us leave.

For once, I had no trouble with the plank. Colin went across first. He turned and held out his arms. I let go of the branch I was holding and floated toward him, not caring about the ten feet of blackness beneath me.

We sat on the splintery floor amid dried leaves and bits of twigs and who knows how many dead insects, not daring to move, until Colin lay down. He tucked his hands beneath his head. I didn't know what to do. I continued to sit, looking anywhere but at him. This wasn't like being at the pictures. It wasn't like being in his dad's car. Music filtered across the Lombards' back garden. Everyone, except us, was at Keith's party.

Colin and I were in the fort. *Alone.* The possibilities scared me to death.

He reached for my hand and pulled me toward him. We

57

kissed. His tongue found mine and his hands fumbled beneath my blouse. It had a Peter Pan collar and puff sleeves and I absolutely loathed it. Colin's fingers undid the clasp of my bra – something else I loathed because it wasn't lacy or sexy like the ones Sophie wore. It snapped open and my breasts fell loose. He took off his shirt; then my blouse. My nipples grazed his chest and I gasped, all worries about my ugly clothes forgotten. We weren't Jill and Colin any more. We were Deborah Kerr and Burt Lancaster, and this wasn't the fort, it was a deserted beach in Hawaii.

'Oh, Jilly,' he moaned, wrapping his arms around me. One of his legs slipped between mine. He tensed, then shuddered, and I could feel warmth and wetness.

I had no idea what had happened. I honestly didn't.

Not then.

Colin kept hugging me. 'I'm sorry, I'm sorry. I didn't mean it to be like this.'

I hugged him back, bewildered, and willing to forgive him anything.

'I'll take you home,' he said, helping me on with my blouse. My fingers were shaking. I couldn't do up the buttons.

He dropped me at the end of my driveway. He kissed me goodnight.

I never saw him again.

Nine

Claudia's voice, yelling up the stairs, wakes me at eight the next morning. 'Jillian, come here. That storm's on the news.'

I leap out of bed and race down to the living room without bothering to put on my robe. Claudia's minuscule TV is on.

'The east coast of North America has been experiencing some very severe weather,' says the BBC announcer. 'Hurricane Cassie is approaching the south shore of Long Island. Power lines are down, some of the highways are flooded, and . . .'

The screen switches to a clip of generic storm coverage with waves crashing over a seawall and trees bent sideways by hurricane-force winds. The camera pans a deserted street, awash with water, where a solitary figure struggles to remain upright. Bits of lumber and cardboard fly past. The news item ends. It's followed by a report from the London stock exchange.

Claudia turns it off. 'How close is all this to you?'

'Too close.'

She nods. 'Tea?'

I follow her into the kitchen where sunlight streams through the window and the kettle welcomes us with a cheerful whistle. Hurricanes and floods seem half a lifetime away. Poor Zachary. He's terrified of storms. Last one we had, he scuttled under my bed and didn't emerge till I opened a can of tuna.

Claudia places two mugs on the table.

'I feel so helpless,' I tell her. 'I ought to be doing something.'

'Like what?'

'Coralling my cat and worrying about the roof blowing off, I guess.' I look around Claudia's lovely kitchen and notice a calendar on the wall. It's a delicate woodland scene with squirrels and badgers, rabbits, mice, and a fox. Butterflies dance like marionettes on hidden strings against a shaft of sunlight. Sprays of flowers – white daisies, blue forget-me-nots, yellow buttercups – grow amid ferns at the base of a large weeping willow.

'Did you do this?' I say.

Claudia nods. 'I do the odd painting for a wildlife society. They use them for greetings cards, wrapping paper, and calendars.' She takes it off the wall. 'Here. I've got plenty more.'

'Thanks. It's fabulous.'

The phone rings.

'It's my daughter again,' Claudia says. 'She wants to speak to you.'

Sophie sounds anxious. 'Heard anything from home?'

'The lines are down. I can't get through.'

'Jill, I know you were planning to come back tomorrow, but could you come up today, instead?'

'Why?'

'Because I prepared way too much food for last night's banquet. Keith and Penny Lombard are in town for the weekend, without the kids, so I invited them for lunch tomorrow.

Roddy Slade's coming, too.' She pauses. 'Oh, and bring Mum with you. Tell her the doctor can fit her in on Monday.'

'Roddy Slade?' Claudia says, when I tell her about the change in plans. 'That's a name from the past.'

'It sure is.'

'I wonder what he looks like now.'

'You'll get to see for yourself,' I say, then tell her about the doctor's appointment.

'Oh, bother,' Claudia says. 'Who'll take care of my squirrels?'

Max jumps on the table. 'What about your cat?'

'I'll ask Nora to feed him.' Claudia waves toward the front of her house. 'She lives right across the street.'

'You mean she's—'

'The farmer's wife.' Claudia grins. 'Her heart's in the right place. She doesn't like what her husband's doing to those squirrels any more than I do.'

'Will she tend to the traps?'

'No, but now and then she tells me where he hides them. I hate to think what would happen if he ever found out.' Claudia shudders. 'He'd probably drown her as well.'

We get back to London and find Sophie in her kitchen surrounded by stacks of disposable casserole dishes and large flat trays covered with tinfoil. Her hair's a mess and her hands are covered with pastry dough. While she and Claudia exchange floury hugs, I pick up the phone and try to reach Lizzie. No luck. The lines are still dead.

'Did you get through?' Sophie says, sliding a pie in the oven.

'Nope. Have you heard anything more?'

'Just what I saw on TV this morning. But it must be over by now, surely.'

'I hope so.'

Claudia takes my arm and pulls me into the living room. 'About this little party tomorrow,' she whispers. 'Sophie didn't cook too much food. This is really for you.'

'It is?'

'Don't let on I told you,' Claudia warns. 'It's supposed to be a surprise.'

I stare at her. 'Is there something you're not telling me?'

'Oh dear,' Claudia says. 'I said too much already.'

Lizzie rings up at noon the next day. 'It wasn't as bad as we expected,' she says. 'Hardly any damage. Just a few broken branches and a ton of leaves. Some areas are still without power, but your place is all right.'

'How about Zachary? Is he okay?'

There's a burst of interference and all I hear is '—'s fine.'

I relax. 'Thanks for taking care of things, Lizzie.'

'No problem. So, tell me. What's up for today?'

'Sophie's having a few friends for lunch.'

'Is Colin on the menu?'

'No.'

'Pity,' Lizzie says. 'When's your flight coming in?'

'Thursday, at seven thirty.' I pause. 'I've bought you a huge tin of shortbread.'

'In that case,' Lizzie says, 'I won't send Fergus. I'll come pick you up myself.'

I hang up and offer to help Sophie, but she shooshes me from the kitchen. So I go upstairs, have a bath, and get changed. Somehow, I've got to force feed myself into pantyhose, tie a scarf the way Sophie does, and make friends with a pair of malevolent shoes.

An hour later, I'm tumbling out of control down Sophie's narrow stairs.

Ten

I'm coming round, I think. I can hear people talking.

Claudia, her voice faint, says, 'Keith, clear that stuff off the settee and gather pillows. This leg needs to be elevated.'

'I'll get some ice.' Sophie sounds distant.

Oh, shit. My ankle.

It's killing me.

'Jilly, I'm so sorry.' Colin's voice. Deeper, older.

'Help me get her on the couch.' Claudia, loud and clear this time.

Strong arms lift me up and I'm swaying, weightless. The plank is stretched between us. I'm scared of falling.

Come on, Jilly, you can do it.

Why didn't Sophie tell me he was coming to lunch? Needles of pain shoot up my leg. I tighten my arms around Colin's neck. He's lowering me to the couch but I don't want to let go.

Something cold, ice cold, flops onto my foot.

'Ouch!' I open my eyes. A bag of frozen peas lies across my ankle. '*Peas?*'

'I didn't have enough ice in the freezer,' Sophie says. 'Poor Jill. You look wrecked.'

I close my eyes. This is a dream. I'll wake up in a minute, in bed, and this will be something to laugh about. I didn't really fall downstairs, did I? This is happening to someone else, isn't it? But the pain in my ankle is real, and so's Colin Carpenter, sitting at the end of Sophie's couch in a dusky pink shirt. A cotton shirt, heavy and well pressed, with bronze buttons shaped like miniature cartwheels. A corner of one cuff is frayed.

God! What if my ankle's broken? The peas shift. I feel fingers touching, probing. 'Damn! That hurts!'

'Can you wiggle your toes?'

I open my eyes. Colin's glasses are shoved on top of his head and he's examining my foot, moving it gently from side to side. 'A stretched ligament, but no broken bones.'

'I didn't think so,' Claudia says.

Colin replaces the peas. 'It's a sprain, Jilly.'

Jilly. No one else has ever called me that. Not even my dad.

Sophie's oven timer pings. 'Lunch is ready,' she says. 'Okay, everyone. Into the dining room. Not you, Jill. I'll set up a tray.'

'I'll stay with her,' Colin says. His hair is thick and streaked with silver. Lines add character to his face, and the dimples, thank God, are still there when he smiles. 'Does it hurt badly?' he asks.

I nod. 'How do you know it's not broken?'

'I was a medic in the army.'

Thirty-five years.

There's so much I don't know about him.

Sophie hands me a glass of champagne and asks Colin what he wants to drink.

'Ginger ale – or water.' He smiles again. 'I have a long drive home.'

Where does he live? Bubbles tickle my nose as I gulp my champagne, hoping Sophie will float by with more.

'Here you are, you two.' She refills my glass and sets a tray of food on the side table.

'I'm starving,' Colin says, leaning toward it.

He's as slender now as he was back then. I'll start my diet tomorrow. 'Sophie said you and your wife run a bed and breakfast.'

'Yes, we do, but Shelby's not my wife.'

So that's her name.

'I was married once,' Colin goes on. 'It lasted fourteen years and I never want to do it again.' He maneuvers the tray onto his knees. 'Would you like some of this?'

'No, thanks. Not yet. I'm still trying to cope with falling downstairs.'

And seeing you again.

He spears a piece of chicken. 'Tell me about your life in America.'

I watch his mouth and want to kiss it. 'I was married and then divorced,' I say. 'I have two sons and a cat, and I live on a beach.' Maybe we could sneak upstairs. No. I can't walk. He could hardly carry me up. Or could he? Does he want to kiss me? There's a speck of mayonnaise on his lower lip. What would he do if I licked it off?

'Do you have kids?' I ask.

'A daughter. She lives with her mother.'

'Did Sophie tell you I was here?'

'Yes.' Colin puts down his fork, turns to face me. 'She wanted to surprise you,' he says, glancing at my ankle. 'I'm sorry you fell.' His eyes, soft and warm behind his glasses, are the color of moss.

'Colin, are you happy?' I blurt out.

He looks at me, surprised. 'Yes, I suppose I am. Shelby and

65

I have been through a lot of ups and downs. I was a wreck when we met, and she helped me pull through.' He pokes at a wedge of cheese. 'I owe her for that.'

'Your marriage was as bad as mine, then.'

'Did you try a second time?' Colin asks.

'No.' How do I tell him I'm not brave enough to risk another loss?

'But what about you, Jilly?' he says. 'Are *you* happy?'

The clock on Sophie's mantel ticks off the seconds.

'I have good friends, a house I love,' I say, swallowing hard. 'The beach. My sons. I'm . . .' I grope for the right word. 'I'm content.'

'Don't you want more than that?'

Of course I do. But am I willing to admit it? To Colin? To myself? In a mad moment, I opt for honesty. 'I'm fifty-two and there are days I ask myself, "What else is there? Is this it? Is this all there is to my life?"' It's hard to believe I'm unloading like this but with Colin it seems so easy. So right, somehow.

There's a crash from the kitchen and the mood is broken. Colin sighs, and we move to safer ground – my life in Connecticut and his in Gloucestershire; his dog and my cat. He tells me about North Lodge, his seventeenth-century house in the Cotswold hills that's now a popular inn and hotel. A bit more than a bed and breakfast, he says.

I try to explain what I do for a living and discover Colin is only slightly less traumatized by computers than he is by spiders. 'I'm a graphic artist,' I say. 'I design brochures, logos, and promotion pieces for local businesses.'

The others drift in from the dining room. Roddy Slade, flushed and overweight, Hugh Neville, almost bald but with that same cheeky smile, and Keith Lombard whose once carroty-red hair is now totally gray. He introduces his wife. Penny Lombard has the sleep-deprived look of a mother whose infant keeps her up all night.

Roddy produces a digital camera and takes several group shots. He snaps one of Colin and me on the couch. 'Give me your e-mail address and I'll send it to you,' he says, before being waylaid by Sophie to take pictures of the dogs.

The boys – I still think of them that way – and I laugh over old memories and exchange bits of gossip, but nobody asks Colin why he disappeared without word.

Hugh and Keith slope off and Penny follows Claudia upstairs. Colin and I are alone. Again.

'Have you ever been to the States?' I ask.

'No, but I've always wanted to go.'

'Come over for a holiday.' Christ! Am I really saying this? What the hell. I'll keep going. 'You could stay with me.'

'That sounds great,' Colin says. 'I'll ask Shelby.'

Oh yes, Shelby. My face warms, reddens. What was I thinking?

His eyes lose their sparkle. His voice is distant and I turn away. For him, this has been nothing more than a pleasant interlude – a Sunday afternoon reminiscing about the past with an old friend.

After the last guest leaves, I round on Sophie. 'Why didn't you warn me he was coming?'

'And have you go into hiding upstairs with the dogs?' Sophie throws herself into the wing chair and hooks her legs over one of its arms.

I snatch up a pillow. 'I'm not a child.'

Sophie looks at my ankle, now the size of a small cantaloupe. 'Oh, Jill, come on. What would you have done if I'd told you?'

'For openers, I wouldn't have fallen down your bloody stairs.'

'I doubt that,' Sophie says. 'You always did have weak knees where Colin's concerned.'

I hurl my pillow at her.

Sophie catches it and says, 'So, what did you guys talk about?'

'The usual. Kids. Jobs. You know.'

'What about his wife? Shirley?'

'Shelby,' I tell her. 'They're not married – they live together.'

Sophie kicks off her shoes. 'Does Colin want to see you again?'

If only he did. I shake my head.

'He is *enormously* attractive.' Sophie's voice is a breathless gush.

I cover my eyes and she pounces. 'I knew it!' she exclaims, clapping her hands.

Eleven

On Monday morning, Claudia insists she doesn't want help getting to her doctor appointment. I don't need a chaperone, she says.

Sophie folds her arms and looks at me. 'Three weeks ago, the doctor's receptionist phoned and bawled me out because Mum didn't show up.'

'The sun was shining,' Claudia says. 'I went to the park instead.'

They leave ten minutes later, still arguing. A couple of Sophie's customers call, and one of them complains her photocopied price lists and menus are barely legible.

An idea takes shape. I look around for some paper and find Claudia's sketch pad lying on the coffee table, and good, there's a pencil tucked into its spiral binding.

I begin to draw.

Sophie's face is furrowed with worry lines when they return.

'What's wrong?' I bundle my sketches beneath a pillow.

'A touch of heartburn,' Claudia says, patting her chest. 'I ate too much yesterday, that's all.'

'Mum, doctors don't order expensive tests for indigestion.' Sophie frowns at her. 'I'm going to do the washing up.'

'What kind of tests?' I ask.

Claudia sinks into an armchair. 'Something electrical.'

'An electrocardiogram?'

'That was one. There were others. Quite unnecessary, so I refused them and now my daughter is' – there's a ferocious crash from the kitchen – 'a bit cross with me.' Claudia looks at her sketch pad, now back on my lap. 'What's all this?'

'A gift.' I show her the layouts. 'To thank Sophie for having me. Stationery, business cards, price lists and menus. I'll finish them off at home, on the computer.'

'Perfect,' Claudia says. 'Just what she needs, but wait till she gets through playing cricket with the crockery before you show them to her.'

The telephone rings and Sophie answers it in the kitchen. 'It's Colin,' she calls out. 'He wants to know how your ankle's doing.'

Claudia glances at my foot. 'Tell him it's Prussian blue with a nice touch of ocher.'

Sophie steps into the living room and hands me the phone. 'Here. You tell him.' She turns to her mother. 'Come on, Mum. Let's take the dogs for a walk.' She grabs a handful of leashes from a hook on the wall. 'We can continue our squabble outside.'

The front door slams shut.

'Jilly? Are you there?' His voice is so faint, I can barely hear it.

I grip the phone with both hands. 'Yes.'

'Look, I can't talk long, but I've been worried. Are you okay?'

My ankle throbs. 'I'm fine.'

'Jilly—'

There's a long pause. 'Colin?'

'I'm here,' he says. 'Look, there's no easy way to say this, so I'll just come right out with it.'

I hold my breath. He's going to tell me he's changed his mind about coming over. That it would be best to leave things as they are. I can handle this. No, I can't.

'I'd like to see you again,' he says.

I'd like to see you again.

My breath comes out in a rush.

'When are you leaving?' he asks.

'Thursday afternoon.'

'I'll come to the airport. Heathrow, right?'

I'm a teenager being asked out for a first date. 'Yes. Terminal Three.'

'What time is your flight?'

'Three thirty.'

'British Airways?'

'Virgin.'

'I'll meet you at their information booth. How does one o'clock sound?'

'Great.'

Wonderful. Perfect.

Colin says, 'I've got to go,' and hangs up.

I'm still clutching the receiver when Sophie and Claudia get back. 'Long conversation?' Sophie asks, removing the phone and putting it back on its base.

'No, rather short, actually.'

She lifts an eyebrow.

'He's coming to the airport,' I whisper, 'to say goodbye.'

'See,' Sophie says. 'I told you!'

Twelve

London
September 2007

Three days later, Sophie drives me to Heathrow. 'What you need is a bloody good love affair.' She swings out to overtake another car. 'Meet Colin a few times a year in places like Tahiti or St Tropez.'

'I couldn't,' I say, checking my seat-belt. Sophie's driving alarms me. She must take after her mother, or maybe Claudia takes after her.

'Don't be a prude.' Sophie steps on the gas. 'I bet he's looking for a bit of excitement. I mean, he's not exactly married.'

'He has a common-law wife.'

Sophie laughs. 'Don't be so bloody archaic.'

Airport signs flash overhead. A car swerves in front of us.

'Stupid git!' Sophie gives him two fingers. 'Besides,' she continues, 'in my book you're either married legally or not at all.'

'You, of course, are the expert,' I say, and Sophie gives me two fingers as well.

The line of people waiting to check in for my flight is long and slow-moving and we don't reach the information booth until almost one thirty. There's no sign of Colin.

'I'm going to leave you here,' Sophie says, hugging me, 'because I'm going back home to strong-arm my mother into taking those tests.' She grins. 'And because I don't want to get in Colin's way.'

'If he makes it.'

'He will.'

Sophie blows me a kiss and melts into the crowd.

'Hello, Jilly.'

I look up, startled, into Colin's smiling face. 'How long have you been here?' An inspired opening line.

'Not long. I waited till Sophie left.' He holds out his arm. 'Why don't we find somewhere less public than this,' he says, nodding toward a combination coffee shop and bar. 'Let's go over there.' He guides me inside and helps me into a chair. 'What would you like to drink?'

'I'll have a gin and tonic,' I say, not really wanting one, but if he's going to imbibe, I'll be polite and keep him company.

He looks at me for a moment. 'Right,' he says, and glances at the bar. 'I won't be long.' He comes back a few minutes later with a cocktail in one hand and a cup of coffee in the other. Oh, shit. Now he'll have me pegged as a borderline alcoholic.

When he sits, I don't dare look at him, and we're so awkward, it's like being back in the fort. We both speak at once. Then not at all. Finally, grasping for something neutral, I ask, 'How long did it take you to drive here?'

'A couple of hours,' Colin says, not meeting my eyes. 'I told them I had to see my accountant. In London.'

'Them?'

'Shelby's sister Diana lives with us.' Colin clears his throat and fumbles in his pocket, and I can almost feel his embarrassment at having to make excuses for his absence. He pulls out a photo. Jeez, no! Don't tell me he's going to show me a picture of Shelby and her sister. But it's a dog. A brown and white mutt with a feathery tail.

'Meggie's a border collie.' Colin hands me the photo. 'Comes from a line of prizewinning sheepdogs. She does a fine job of keeping our chickens in order.'

'No sheep?' I'm clueless about dogs.

Colin shakes his head. 'Best dog I ever had. I don't know what I'll do when she goes.'

I turn the photograph over. There's another, stuck to the back. A young woman with blond hair leans against a tree. She's wearing a halter top and shorts and her legs go on forever. 'Is this your daughter?' I hand it back to Colin.

He coughs. 'No.'

I don't want to hear what's coming next. I pick up my glass.

'It's Shelby.'

My gin and tonic – the drink I didn't want and am now profoundly grateful for – burns a trail down my throat.

'It's an old picture,' Colin goes on. 'This must've been taken twelve years ago. Meggie was a year old then.'

Avoiding his eyes, I do the math. Shelby has to be a good fifteen years younger than Colin. Maybe more – a mere infant when he and I were teenagers, eyeing one another in the fort and not knowing what to do about it.

'Look,' Colin says, 'I hate to think of you getting on that plane and disappearing for another thirty-five years.'

I want to tell him it wasn't me who disappeared. It was him, and now he has a life with someone else. A much younger someone else.

We sip our drinks.

Colin breaks the silence. 'Can I write to you?'

'Letters?'

'I could send you a fax now and then. Would you mind?'

No, but Shelby would. On the other hand, he and I are old friends – what's the harm in keeping in touch? 'I'll write back.'

'No, better not,' he says. 'My fax machine's in the office and whoever's passing picks them up.' He brightens. 'You could always e-mail me.'

'You said you hated computers.'

'I do,' Colin says, 'but I have learned how to handle e-mail – in one direction. I can receive them but not send any out.'

'Why not?'

He grins. 'Because I can't type.'

The loudspeaker interrupts with news about my flight. 'I guess it's time for me to leave.'

Neither of us moves.

'I really should go.' I reach for my purse and stand up. 'It's probably a five-mile walk to the gate.'

Colin looks down at my ankle, pink and fat in its elastic bandage. 'I could get you a wheelchair.'

Shelby wears a halter top and shorts and her legs go on forever.

'No, I'm fine.'

'How about I carry you?'

My legs tremble. 'I'd break your back.'

'You didn't before.' He holds out his arms.

Now what? Do we hug? Shake hands? Kiss one another on the cheek or wave goodbye? I'm still pondering the possibilities when Colin puts his arms around my waist and pulls me close.

'I can't tell you how wonderful it's been,' he says, 'seeing you again after all this time.' He's so tall that the top of my head barely reaches his shoulder. His lips brush my hair. 'There's so much we haven't talked about. Shared memories, that stupid fort—'

'It wasn't stupid,' I say.

'That spider.'

75

So, he remembers.

'I still hate them.' His arms tighten. 'You will write to me, won't you?'

'Yes,' I say into the rough tweed of his jacket.

Oh, God, what is this man doing to me?

A second flight announcement breaks the spell. Colin lets me go and I limp toward the barrier. I dump my stuff on the conveyor and turn around for another look. Colin's standing where I left him, watching me with green eyes and a crooked grin. He nods and mouths, 'I'll write to you.'

I walk through the security gate. A bunch of passengers push past me and the next time I look at the restaurant doorway, he's no longer there.

Thirteen

Sands Point
September 2007

We land in Boston on time, but my connection to Hartford is delayed and it's close to ten thirty by the time I meet up with Lizzie. She wears a floppy straw hat that's suspiciously like the one Zachary sleeps in. I take a closer look. Hell, it *is* the same one.

A narrow black ribbon encircles its crown.

'Very chic,' I tell her.

'Can't say the same about you.' Lizzie glances at my ankle. 'Those Brits didn't have another war, did they?'

'A minor skirmish at the foot of Sophie's stairs.'

Driving south, Lizzie asks about my trip. I give her the highlights, minus Colin, because I need to think about him a bit more before sharing, and we're a few miles past Middletown when Lizzie says, 'Trevor flew out while you were gone.'

'I'm sorry I missed him.'

'He came to say goodbye.'

'Why?'

'Because he's found someone else and wanted to break the news in person.'

'Oh, Lizzie. Why didn't you say something?'

'You were on vacation.'

'Lizzie!' I rummage in my bag for the shortbread. 'Here, you could probably use this.' I hand her a square and take one for myself.

Scattering crumbs across her lap, Lizzie says, 'We've had a good run, but it's time for Trevor to move on. He needs a family and I'm too old to give him one, but he's found a nice young woman who can.'

'How young?'

'Early thirties, I think.'

'Which means,' I say, keeping my voice even, 'she's about twenty years younger than—'

Lizzie sighs. 'Jill, don't even go there.'

Signs for Haddam, Chester, and Essex fly by. We take the next exit and cruise through downtown Sands Point, where out-of-season sidewalks are rolled up at dusk. Then Lizzie heads for the beach and we jolt down my dirt road. The lights are on in the house next door which means the new owners have moved in. My porch light's on as well, and as we pull into my driveway I can see ominous piles of leaves on the lawn. Looks as if I'll have some serious raking to do.

Lizzie slams on her brakes and misses my Volvo by inches.

'Christ!' I peel myself off the dashboard. 'You're worse than Claudia.'

'Holy shit!' Lizzie's jaw drops and she stares at the porch where my cat is washing his whiskers.

I try to open the door, but we're too close to my car. 'Move up. I can't get out.' We jerk forward. I glance at Lizzie. 'Are you all right? You look a bit pale.'

'Your cat. He got out this morning. I was late for work and didn't have time to go chasing him,' Lizzie says, reaching into the back seat. She pulls the ribbon off Zachary's hat, stuffs it in her purse, and hands the hat to me. 'Don't forget this.'

78

Holding the hat and my carry-on bag, I limp toward the house. Lizzie trails behind, pulling my suitcase. She drags it up the steps, gives me a quick hug, and scurries back to her car. She guns the engine and roars off.

Did I say something to offend her?

Zachary rubs against my legs. I unlock the door, leave my bags in the hall, and follow him into my office. He leaps on the laser printer where, no doubt, he's spent the better part of the last two weeks and I'm about to shoo him off when I see a piece of paper sticking out of my fax machine.

It's a single page, written in an unfamiliar hand, and it begins with *Dear Jilly*.

The front door bell rings. I check my watch. Five thirty. Is that English time or have I been sitting here all night? I read Colin's last sentence again: *When I saw you coming down those stairs, all the memories that had been buried for three decades came alive, and now—*

The sound of ferocious banging breaks my mood.

'Bloody hell.'

Ankle throbbing, I lurch into the hall and yank open the door.

Lizzie waves a carton of cream in my face. 'You don't have any.'

'I don't?'

'Jill, you've been gone more than two weeks. Anything left in your fridge will be yogurt by now.' She pushes past me and into the kitchen. 'Let's have a cup of tea, if only to make me feel better about going to the market at midnight.'

'But you don't like tea,' I say, as she empties half the carton into Zachary's bowl, 'and I hate cream.'

'Stop arguing and get out of my way.' Lizzie plugs in the kettle and pulls two mugs from the dishwasher.

I finger my letter.

'You look a bit shell shocked,' Lizzie says. 'What's wrong?'

'Just tired.'

'It's more than that.'

I take a deep breath. 'I saw him.'

'Who?'

'Colin.'

'And you didn't tell me?'

I hand her the fax. 'Read this,' I say, then finish making our tea while she skims the memories Colin has pulled from the past: *that party at Roddy's when we waltzed in the rain . . . that football match when Keith and Hugh got mad because you and I cheered for the wrong side . . . the log I tried to split with a blunt axe and broke the handle instead . . . you and Sophie painting her bedroom in your—*

Grinning, Lizzie looks up. 'You never told me about *that* one.'

'That's because gym knickers are top secret in England.'

She reads the last two lines out loud: '. . . *and now I'm a mish-mash of emotions; of regret for what didn't happen because I was too young and too stupid to know what I had.*'

'Oh, Jill. Tell me he's not kidding about this.'

'I can't.'

'Why not?'

'Because he's married,' I say, biting my lip, 'and he isn't.'

'He's one or the other,' Lizzie says gently. 'Which is it?'

I fish the tea bags from both mugs and Lizzie pretends to drink hers while I explain about Shelby, the photograph, and everything I can remember which, at this point, doesn't seem like much at all. My brain has shut down.

'When?' Lizzie says. 'When did you see him?'

'Sunday. At lunch.'

'You said he wasn't on the menu.'

'He was, but I didn't know that when you called.'

'Looks like you were as well.' Lizzie nods toward my foot, now propped on a chair. 'Did he take a very big bite?'

'Enormous.'

Lizzie raises her eyebrows.

'I fell down the stairs and landed on top of him.'

'You'll do anything for attention.'

Lizzie shows up on Sunday while I'm trying to reinvent Sophie's business image. One of Claudia's watercolors – a hedgehog wearing an apron and holding a saucepan – is providing just the right touch of whimsy.

The front door slams shut. 'I've brought goodies.'

I find her in my kitchen, making coffee. A bag of dough-nuts sits on the table. 'You're determined to make me fat, aren't you?' I say.

Zachary leaps up to investigate. Lizzie shoves him off. 'I guess foraging on your own for a week hasn't improved your manners.'

'What are you talking about?'

A blush creeps up Lizzie's face. 'I wasn't going to tell you.'

'Tell me what?'

She hesitates. 'Your cat ran off while Fergus and I were storm-proofing your house. I looked all over, but I couldn't find him.'

'How long was he gone?'

'Six days.'

'Which means,' I say, counting quickly, 'he didn't come back until I did.'

'I was planning to confess the night I dropped you off,' Lizzie says, 'but when I saw him sitting on the porch, it seemed kind of pointless. So I chickened out and—'

The penny drops. 'Went to get cream instead?'

Her blush deepens.

'That wasn't for the tea, was it?'

81

'Not exactly.'

'And the black ribbon on your communal straw hat?'

'I was in mourning.' Lizzie turns a deeper shade of red. I lean over and hug her. 'I didn't know you cared.'

'Neither did I,' Lizzie says, 'till I thought he was gone forever.'

'So, where was he?'

My cat, looking surprisingly well fed, slinks out of the kitchen. 'Somehow,' Lizzie says, fanning herself with a napkin, 'I don't think he's going to tell us.'

'Poor Zachary. He doesn't know it yet, but if I ever go away again, I'm going to leave him in a kennel.' I smile at Lizzie. 'I'm sorry he was such a problem.'

'Speaking of problems,' Lizzie says, 'what did you do about Colin's fax?'

'I wrote back.'

'Has he replied?'

'Yes, and Roddy Slade sent me a photo.'

'Can I see it?'

'Follow me.' I grab a doughnut and limp into my office. The enlargement I made of Colin and me on Sophie's couch is pinned to my cork board.

'He's quite the dish,' Lizzie says. 'But I feel sorry for him.'

'Why?'

'Having you land in his lap must've been a dreadful shock.'

Fourteen

Colin's next letter is another jolt from the past. Do I remember the school dance he'd been too shy to invite me to attend?

How could I forget? Sophie went with Keith, complaining it was worse than dating her own brother, while I stayed home obsessing over possible reasons for Colin's failure to speak up. It had to be because of my legs. They were too fat. Hugh and Keith used to call me Porky-stalks.

I tell Lizzie about this two days later when we're out walking the beach – slowly, because I'm still limping – and get gales of laughter instead of sympathy. 'It's not funny. I hated my legs.'

'Well, except for that bum ankle, there's nothing wrong with them now,' Lizzie says, bending to pick up an oyster shell. 'How's Claudia? Heard anything new?'

'Mild angina. The doctor's put her on a low-salt diet and told her to avoid stress.'

'Then she'll have to give up on those squirrels,' Lizzie says. 'Poor Sophie. I bet she's worried to death.'

'About the squirrels?'

Lizzie lobs the shell at me. 'Idiot.'

'Claudia's painting them.'

'How does she get them to stand still?'

'Come back to my office and I'll show you.'

I pull Claudia's watercolors from the battered brown envelope that arrived yesterday. Squirrels, wearing sunglasses and shorts, build a sandcastle under the watchful eye of a lifeguard; others in blue uniforms line up outside a school behind a teacher wearing a mortarboard and carrying a book.

'She ought to do this professionally,' Lizzie says.

I show Lizzie the calendar. 'She does.'

'Did you tell her about your parrots?'

'No.'

'Why not?'

'I'm not in the same league as Claudia.'

'Rubbish,' Lizzie says, pointing at the sketch of my opera-singing bird tacked to the cork board. 'You should do something with this.'

'Like what?'

'A picture book for kids.'

'Lizzie, get a grip. It's a specialized market. Very competitive.'

'That's what you said about writing for magazines.'

'So?'

'You broke into it, didn't you?' Lizzie says. 'Even when you insisted you couldn't.'

'Lizzie, there's a huge difference between writing an article for *Paws and Claws Quarterly* and' – I grope for a name – 'a book for Random House.'

After she leaves, I take another look at my tuxedo-clad parrot, beak open, wings extended, belting out arias from *Turandot*, *Carmen* or perhaps *Rigoletto*, and think, why not? His name could be Caruso. No, that's trite. Pavarotti? Even worse. How about Barnaby? No, because that's too close to that purple dinosaur Lizzie's grandchildren love.

Aria. Aria. What goes with aria?
Aristotle? Archimedes? Archibald?
Archibald's Aria.
Perfect.

My lawyer calls at noon on Friday. 'Jill, I need a huge favor.'

That's a switch. It's usually me calling on her for help, like the time a former neighbor falsely accused my boys of breaking into her house, and when Richard got into financial trouble and tried to prove my cottage really belonged to him. Harriet soon sorted those problems out, and we became close friends. 'What's up?' I say.

'Family funeral,' says Harriet Shapiro. 'Can you take care of Anna for a couple of days?'

'No problem.'

'You're a goddess. My nanny's back in Holland visiting her folks. Couldn't be worse timing.'

'Who died?'

'Uncle Willard.'

'Oh, I'm sorry. When are you leaving?'

'First thing in the morning. I'll drop Anna on my way to the airport.' Harriet hangs up and I'm left feeling warm and fuzzy at the prospect of having her daughter all to myself for two days.

I was there when she was born. Pink and squirmy and covered in green scum and the most amazing sight I'd ever seen. When my boys arrived I was so upset, no, make that angry, over Richard's absence that I shut my eyes and missed the actual moment of birth. A neighbor drove me to the hospital for Jordan. With Alistair, I arrived via ambulance. Richard didn't see either of his sons until they were several hours old.

Harriet and I giggled through eight weeks of Lamaze class and I'm sure the other couples thought we were partners. She lay on pillows and puffed while I counted and tried to keep a straight face. Our last night there I saw one of the other moth-ers-to-be glance at Harriet and mutter something to her husband about turkey-baster babies.

Twelve years ago, Harriet and her mother were in Bermuda on vacation when Harriet came out of the closet. Her mother promptly went to the hotel desk and demanded a separate bedroom. 'What did she think I was going to do?' Harriet grumbled when she got back. 'Jump her bones in the middle of the night?'

Harriet's a single-mother-by-choice. She chose Anna's father, carefully, from a sperm bank. Perfect health, genius-level IQ, and, according to the nurse at the clinic, an abun-dance of self-confidence. 'Maybe he jerked off in a Mensa mug,' Harriet said, the day I accompanied her to the insemi-nation.

'Thanks for pitching in,' Harriet says, when she delivers Anna at seven the next morning. 'I'd take her with me but I don't trust my family to behave themselves.' She sighs. 'Poor Uncle Willard. He's the only one who ever stuck up for me. If it were anyone else, I wouldn't be flying to Des Moines this weekend.'

Still in my bathrobe and barely awake, I yawn and give her a hug. Anna pushes by us, arms full of toys, and heads for the couch where Zachary's curled up on a pillow. Harriet hands me Anna's knapsack, bulging with books and clothes. A Cin-derella toothbrush peeks from a side pocket. Yellow socks, edged with lace, erupt from an open flap.

'When are you coming back?' I pick up the socks and stuff them in my pocket.

'Sunday night. Late.'

'Will you be in court the next day?' Harriet's specialty is employment law and for some reason, her busiest day is always Monday.

She nods.

'Let me keep her till then. I'll take her to school, fetch her afterward, and bring her back here. You can come get her when you're through.' I pause. 'My name's on the list of approved picker-uppers, isn't it?'

Harriet runs a hand through her unruly red hair. 'Yes, and are you sure? I mean, don't you have to work?'

'Go,' I say, pushing her out the door. 'Or you'll miss your flight. Anna and I will see you for supper on Monday.'

Harriet leaves and I turn to look at her daughter, cross-legged on the couch, introducing Zachary to her family of stuffed cats. Not quite seven, Anna's a perfect miniature of her mother – elfin face, velvety brown eyes, and freckles scattered across her cheeks like sprinkles on a peaches-and-cream dough-nut.

We dress Zachary in doll clothes and put him to bed in Lizzie's straw hat topped by a canopy we make from chop-sticks and cheesecloth. My cat worships Anna. He'd never let me do that to him. We stir gelatin into dishwashing liquid and blow bubbles on the front porch, cut snowflakes from paper towels, and mix up a batch of play dough. I print black-and-white outlines of Archibald for Anna to color in while I work. She gives him purple and green feathers, an orange beak, and red eyes with yellow polka dots.

That night, over fish sticks and baked beans with Oreos on the side, Anna begs for a story. So I invent tales about Clau-dia's squirrels and draw cartoons with bubble dialogue the way I used to with Jordan and Alistair to comfort them after Richard would bawl us out for no reason at all.

I bathe her sweet little body and shampoo her corkscrew curls until I'm intoxicated with the very essence of her. I dry her with soft towels and we frost my bathroom with baby powder. I help her into Little Mermaid pajamas and rock her and tell her more stories until she falls asleep. Tomorrow, we'll fly kites. We'll explore the beach and collect shells and bits of sea glass, and I'll teach her the Latin names for horse-shoe crabs, moon snails, and barnacles. Just like I did for my boys and would have done for the little girl I lost.

She'd have been twenty-eight now.

The doctor said it was a fluke. That an eight-month fetus is normally too well-protected to be compromised by a blow to the mother. It was my fault. I shouldn't have climbed on that ladderback chair. I shouldn't have bothered to wipe dust from the top of the bookshelf. But Richard had complained about my sloppy housekeeping and I knew better than to argue.

My foot slipped. The chair tilted toward me. Its back slammed against my huge belly and I folded over it like a piece of limp pasta. I went into shock and delivered a still-born, six-pound baby girl fourteen hours later. I was, mercifully, un-conscious at the time.

The Sunday before Thanksgiving, I drive Lizzie to the airport. She's flying to San Francisco for a meeting, then spending the holiday with her son, Adam, at his airbase in the California desert. I show her Colin's latest fax. Another list of old mem-ories that ends with: *I'm full of eagerness to come and see you, but I have to face up to the fact that I will be accompa-nied.*

'He's giving you mixed messages,' Lizzie says.

'I invited them both.'

'That was in September. His letters have moved the goal-posts since then. It doesn't sound as if he wants to bring Shelby.'

I pull up behind an airport shuttle bus. 'I wonder what she's like.'

'Let's hope you never get to find out,' Lizzie says, and I drive home with my feelings in a muddle to find a message from Colin.

88

'Jilly, it's me. I need to hear your voice, but –'

I want to climb into the answering machine.

'– my timing's off, as usual. One day we'll get together and you can show me that beach of yours.'

Cursing myself for not being here, I shove a can of cat food in the opener, but Zachary doesn't come skidding into the kitchen. Maybe he's still outside. I read Colin's fax again. Is he looking for diversion or meandering down memory lane? What about the phone call? What the hell is he trying to tell me? I stare at the phone and the noise of it not ringing gets on my nerves, so I go outside and look for my cat.

By ten o'clock he's still not home. The rain I drove through coming back from the airport has turned into a deluge. No way would Zachary stay outside in this. Unless he's in trouble. I grab a flashlight and open the door. It's worse than slamming head-on into a waterfall. I struggle to the end of my driveway and I call my cat.

Nothing.

The flashlight's battery conks out.

I'm drenched. I'm shivering. I'll try again tomorrow.

At noon on Monday, I give up trying to work. Zachary still isn't back and I'm way beyond worry. I go looking for him again and run into the mailman slotting letters into my box out by the main road.

'You haven't seen my cat, have you?' I ask.

'Not since Friday.' Bill stuffs a newspaper into the box next to mine. 'Why?'

'He ran off yesterday,' I say, 'and I know it's stupid to worry, but he's a purebred. Somebody might have pinched him.'

'Around here? Come on, Jill. Tourist season's over. Besides, everyone knows Zachary.'

I walk up and down East Bay Road, looking under hedges

and in front gardens and asking everyone I meet if they've seen a tawny-colored cat with yellow eyes. An Abyssinian, I tell them. One woman thought she saw a cat in her back yard, taking a nap on a pile of leaves, but then it woke up and she saw its tail, and realized it was a fox.

Foxes?

Do they eat cats?

Ramping up my search, I plough through beach grass and bamboo but find only a pair of frightened rabbits, a startled partridge, and one of the scrawny feral cats that live wild in the salt marsh.

On my way back home, I glance at the house next door. Two black Labrador retrievers are parked on the front steps. Zachary's going to love that, I mutter, before it dawns on me that my cat isn't available to voice his opinion, one way or the other.

I bite my lip, but the tears come anyway.

Thanksgiving turns into a chore. I lean against the counter, peeling onions and crying while making stuffing for the turkey. I scrub potatoes and scrape carrots. I bake pies. Then I empty Zachary's litter box and wash his dishes and store everything in the shed. I shove the straw hat into the back of my closet.

I phone Harriet.

'He'll come back,' she says. 'He did before.'

'But if he doesn't, what do we tell Anna?'

'The truth.'

'She'll be devastated.' I wipe my eyes. 'Maybe you'd better not come for Thanksgiving. It'll be like a morgue without Zachary.'

'All the more reason for us to be with you,' Harriet says. 'And I'll bring extra wine.' She pauses. 'Can I also bring an extra guest?'

'Someone special?'

'Yes.'

'Wonderful,' I say, and I mean it. Harriet hasn't been part of a couple since before Anna was born.

Lizzie calls from California. 'Stop worrying. He'll return when he's ready.'

I want, badly, to believe her.

The boys come home late Wednesday night.

'Hi, Mom. We're back.' The front door bangs shut and Alistair, clutching an armload of dirty laundry and a six-pack of beer, bounds into the kitchen. His brother, carrying a box of pizza, is right behind him.

'I left the cat outside,' Jordan says, dumping our dinner on the table. 'He'll only get in the way while we're trying to eat this.'

'What cat?'

'Zachary.' Jordan leans toward me for a hug.

I peck his cheek, race into the hall, and yank open the door. There, on the porch, is my cat. He miaows, arches his back, and leans against my legs as if nothing is wrong. I scoop him into my arms and bury my face in his fur.

'Where the hell have you been?'

Fifteen

Ten days before Christmas, I receive a call from the post office. 'Could you come down?' my mailman asks.

'Is anything wrong?'

'We've got a package for you.'

Why isn't Bill out delivering mail? 'Is it too large for your van?'

'No,' he says, 'it's small, but – it's a mess.'

'Who's it from?'

'No return address.'

'Can you read the postmark?'

'England.'

'Then it's probably from Sophie,' I tell him. 'She never did learn the art of wrapping things up.'

A line of people holding boxes and envelopes is snaking through the lobby when I get to the post office just before closing. Someone touches my elbow. It's Bill and his arm's in a sling.

'Come with me.' He grins at my look of surprise. 'Tripped and broke it, getting out of my van.'

I follow him into the adjacent lobby. 'What's all this about?'

Bill nods toward a beat-up package the size and shape of a loaf, lying in a shallow plastic tray on top of the counter. Its wrapping has come loose and the corners are torn.

I pick it up. It's heavy. Dirt trickles out.

'What is it?' Bill asks, looking a tad suspicious.

The handwriting, while not Sophie's, is achingly familiar. I shake the package and more dirt and bits of bark fall out. I rip off the remaining brown paper.

Bill scratches his head. 'Firewood?'

It's a log – or, more precisely, half of one – with a note stapled to the top that says: *I'll bring the other half with me.*

I lean against the wall, blinking back tears and hugging my log.

'Are you all right?'

'I'm fine. Really fine.' I turn the note over and read: *I'd like to come and see you – on my own. How's the second weekend in March?*

My birthday.

'Bill, I'm sorry if this was a nuisance.'

'No problem,' he says. 'Enjoy your fire.'

I drive straight to Lizzie's. She pours me a glass of wine and says, 'I admire his approach, but wouldn't it have been cheaper to send you a fax?'

'That's hardly the point.'

'He's wooing you with wood.'

'Better than boring me with bullshit.'

'Touché,' Lizzie says. 'Are you going to burn it?'

'Not till he gets here.'

'Will I meet him or are you planning to keep him in bed?'

I panic. 'What will I do about, you know, sleeping arrangements?'

'I'd have thought that was obvious.'

93

'Lizzie!'

'At the risk of repeating myself,' she says, 'it's time you got laid.'

The first snow of the season is soft and powdery like confectioner's sugar. It frosts the salt marsh, fills the potholes in my road, and adds a touch of realism to the plastic fir trees in front of Wal-Mart.

I decide to throw a party on Christmas Eve. My family, plus Lizzie's, Harriet and Anna, and Harriet's friend, Beatrice, who entertained us at Thanksgiving with one wicked lawyer joke after another. Should I invite the people next door? I caught a glimpse of them today on Bay Street and only recognized them because of the dogs. The man, with a small child astride his shoulders, held hands with his wife and they wore matching red and green ski jackets. The Labradors had red bows tied to their collars.

'I'm going to invite my new neighbors,' I tell Lizzie when I call about the party. Their name, I learned from Bill Edwards, is Grainger. Tom and Carrie and their daughter Molly.

'Don't bother,' Lizzie says. 'I was behind them at the post office this morning and they were putting their mail on hold. They'll be gone till after the New Year.'

'What are they like?'

'He's about my age. Beard. Nice smile. She's slender and pretty. Their little girl is adorable.'

'How old is she?'

'About three.'

'Not the child, his wife.'

'Mid-thirties would be my guess.'

I cover the phone with my hand and sigh.

Claudia's card arrives on Christmas Eve. Squirrels, dressed as choirboys, are holding sheets of music upside-down and singing while the choirmaster, resplendent in white surplice and red cassock, conducts them with one hand while playing a piano with the other. I place it on the mantel next to the card I got from Colin.

My party's a festive success. My sons are home for the holiday, my house oozes good cheer, and my closest friends are nibbling canapés and drinking wine and enjoying one another's company. Everything goes without a hitch until Anna and Beth, Lizzie's granddaughter, get into a tussle over Claudia's card.

'I saw it first!' Beth stamps her foot.

'Mine,' Anna counters. 'Those are *my* squirrels!'

I solve the problem by making two photocopies and giving one to each child.

'That friend of yours has talent,' Beth's father says. 'Lizzie tells me you have more of her pictures. May I see them?'

'Sure. I'll bring them when we come for dinner tomorrow.' This might prove interesting. Joel Barlow, Lizzie's son-in-law, is a rep for a greeting card company.

The first Sunday in March, I take a critical look at my bedroom. Peeling paint, cracked walls, stains on the ceiling. Are those worm holes in the door? No, that's where I hung a dartboard years ago.

Four days till Colin gets here. I'll have to work fast.

I scrub baseboards, wash windows, and haul out my painting supplies. I'm sponging on the second layer of glaze when Lizzie shows up with a bag of bagels, looking irritable and bored. Fergus, back from six weeks in Florida, has badgered her into letting him stay at the house until the weather gets warmer. He is, she claims, driving her potty.

'Don't have time to talk,' I say. 'And take those bloody bagels away' – my ladder wobbles – 'I'm on a diet.'

'Well, hello to you, too.' Lizzie makes room for herself on

the bed. It's covered with old sheets and the Sunday paper. The cat is snoring, somewhere, underneath it all. 'What are you doing, besides making a mess?'

Cream paint and green glaze stream down my arm. 'This is the Sistine Chapel. Can't you tell?'

'Why are you tarting up your bedroom,' Lizzie says, patting a lump that is probably Zachary, 'if you're planning to avoid sex?'

The ladder wobbles again. 'Where did you get that dumb idea?'

'From you.'

'I never implied—'

'You've been running scared ever since that log showed up,' Lizzie says. 'Here. Have a bagel.'

'I'm too nervous to eat.'

'Then how about some coffee?' Lizzie stands. 'Come on, Jill. Take a break. I promise not to annoy you for longer than five minutes.'

We abandon my masterpiece and go downstairs. I plug in the kettle for tea and tell Lizzie to help herself to the coffee I made earlier and didn't drink.

'You're right,' I say. 'I'm terrified.'

'Why?'

'Suppose I fall in love with him, really fall in love, but all he's after is a good time. What then?'

Lizzie grins. 'Isn't flying three thousand miles for a piece of ass taking things a bit too far? If that's what he wants, why can't he find it closer to home?'

'Keep reminding me of that.' I squeeze my tea bag and add milk.

'No sugar?'

'I told you. I'm on a diet.'

'You're a perfect size ten.'

'Not if you keep feeding me junk.'

'Get any smaller,' Lizzie says, 'and I'll cancel our friendship.'

I pick onion bits off a bagel. 'I'm scared of being let down.'

'Getting involved with a married man carries a huge risk.'

Colin isn't married.

'You have to ask why he's coming over,' she goes on. 'Does he want to recapture his past? Make a new future? Tie up loose ends?'

'Add another feather to his cap?'

Lizzie shoots me a guarded look. 'Whatever his reasons, accept them or reject them. Remember, the choice is yours.'

'That's the trouble,' I say. 'I make terrible choices.'

Lizzie sighs. 'Richard.'

'Yeah.'

'Whatever did you see in him?'

The tea is bitter and I change my mind about the sugar. 'He offered an escape, freedom. But when I lost—' There's no need to continue. Lizzie knows all about the baby.

'So why didn't you divorce him and go back to England? I mean, what the hell was holding you here?'

'Fear,' I say. 'I was in a strange country with no friends, no money, and nowhere to go. I burned bridges when I left England.'

'All of them?'

'Sophie was furious I got married first and told her afterward. I didn't tell her about the baby, either. We lost touch for a while. She moved. So did I. It's Claudia who kept track of me.' I pause. 'We joke about it now, but Sophie still chides me for not asking her for help.'

'Why didn't you?'

'Guilt. Pride, maybe. A stubborn case of "I've made my own bed and now I'd bloody well better lie in it" sort of thing.'

'Stiff upper lip?'

'Something like that.'

I make up my bed with fresh sheets, hang my newly washed muslin curtains, and buff the floor till the old wooden boards glow. My closet doors won't close, so I toss out clothes that no longer fit, sort through my shoes, and discover a box of candles I'd forgotten about. Citrus and sandalwood. I arrange them on my dresser beside a jar of dried hydrangeas and tuck a book of matches behind them.

How long has it been since I feathered my nest for a man? When's the last time I slept with one? Suppose he doesn't want to sleep with me? Who am I kidding? Colin's not coming all this way for tea and crumpets. He's expecting sex.

Oh, God! What if he wants a blow job?

Do I remember how to give one?

By Thursday morning, I'm a train wreck and Lizzie adds to my stress by calling with news of bad weather in Boston. Shit. Why didn't I tell Colin to fly into Hartford instead?

'They're forecasting two feet, maybe more,' she says. 'And don't forget about bringing Colin to dinner on Saturday. I've invited Harriet, Beatrice, and Anna. He may as well meet everyone in one fell swoop.'

Heavy wet snow starts to fall at the Rhode Island border and by the time I reach the outskirts of Boston it's six inches deep. Ploughs are struggling to keep up with the mess and traffic is snarled on both sides of the Southeast Expressway. I pull in to the airport at three. Colin's flight hasn't arrived so I join the crowd waiting for news at the British Airways information desk. All incoming flights are delayed while airport crews clear the runways and I'm told Colin's plane has been diverted. Nobody knows when it's going to reach Boston.

So I wait.

Three hours go by. I ask questions. No one has any answers. The storm eases up and other flights land, but not Colin's. My anxiety boils over and by eight o'clock I'm convinced that his plane will be the one to make grisly headlines on the front page of tomorrow's *Boston Globe*.

Finally, it lands. But when everyone in the world emerges from Customs and Immigration except Colin, my relief turns into doubt. He's missed the plane – or worse – he's changed his mind about coming over. Around me, couples hug, kids shriek, and families converge. Cabin attendants and a flight crew walk by with tired eyes and tight-lipped smiles, dragging black overnight bags behind them like booty.

More flights arrive. More people come streaming through the door and suddenly, he's here, hugging me. Solid and warm and best of all, safe.

'How long have you been waiting?' he asks.

I can't stop smiling.

'I thought we'd never land,' Colin says, still holding me. 'We were circling for hours, and when we did get down we still had to wait for a gate.' He drops his bag on the ground and stretches. 'Those seats were designed for midgets.'

He's taller than I remember. 'Have you any more luggage?' It's an effort to make myself sound normal.

'No. This is it. I travel light.' He picks up his bag and slings it over one shoulder. 'Where to now?'

'Home,' I tell him. 'I'm taking you home.'

Sixteen

Colin makes a valiant effort at conversation but falls asleep in the middle of Rhode Island and doesn't wake up till I pull into my driveway. I take one look at his face and decide that my anxiety and his exhaustion will make terrible bedfellows, so I guide him into the boys' old room. 'Would you like some tea? Something to eat?'

Colin dumps his bag on the bed and sits down beside it. 'No, thanks. I just need some sleep.'

I tell him where to find the bathroom and wish him good night. His face, when I leave, is a combination of relief and disappointment and I take comfort from the fact that he looks about as mixed up as I feel.

For once, I'm up early, and I collide with Colin in the hall at seven the next morning. Barefoot and wearing jeans, he's naked from the waist up. His hair is tousled and I want to run my fingers through it. He doesn't look much different from the lanky teenager who used to help me across a plank.

'Did you sleep okay?' I ask.

'Not bad.'

'Are you ready for a walk on the beach?'

He smiles. 'Can we eat first?'

I run downstairs and fire up a pot of coffee, then boil water for tea. I've no idea what he prefers. I'm toasting English muffins and slicing cantaloupe when he comes into the kitchen.

'Coffee – black – no sugar,' he says. 'And one of those muffins. I'm starving.'

Zachary wanders in as we're finishing breakfast. He rubs against Colin's legs and jumps in his lap.

'Damn!' Colin lurches to his feet. His chair crashes over.

My cat skitters across the tile floor and fetches up with a thoroughly ungraceful thump against the fridge. A magnet lets loose. One of Anna's drawings flutters down and lands beside him.

'Jeez, Colin. I'm sorry. Did he scratch you?'

'I'm fine. He just startled me, that's all.' Colin rescues his chair. 'How about that walk?'

'Sure,' I say, bending to pat Zachary, but he's too quick for me. With his tail fluffed out like a bottle brush, my cat stalks into the hall and disappears. No doubt he'll spend the rest of the day exacting revenge on my printer.

My garden is bare and bleached, devoid of color except for the stark outline of a storm fence rising like splintered red toothpicks from the wind-scoured sand. Not even my purple and yellow crocus are in bloom. Colin walks across the patio, turns to look at my house, and I watch him take in the old bricks, weathered clapboards, and bare trellises that bend beneath the weight of roses in June.

Does he see what I see? Drooping gutters, peeling paint, and loose shingles.

'This is charming,' he says. 'I didn't expect this.'

We follow the path through the dunes and onto the beach where a leaden sky leaks into a gunmetal Sound. Colin removes his glasses, wipes them on the front of his jacket, and stares with scrunched-up eyes at the water. The wind tugs his hair and he looks like a kid who wants to swim but can't because the sea is too cold.

Am I going to sleep with him tonight?

He takes my hand, and we walk toward the breakwater and I distract myself from thinking about what's going to happen later by babbling on about Sands Point, its history, and how it was one of the first permanent settlements in Connecticut.

'Why don't you show me?' Colin says.

After poking through a couple of antique shops, we stroll across the green and stop to admire the gingerbread-style gazebo where the Lions Club sponsors free concerts in the summer. I tell him about the typo in last year's flyer that promised wholesome, family-style entertainment hosted by the Loins Club of Sands Point.

Colin laughs and squeezes my arm. I think he's enjoying himself.

We bypass the gift shops, boarded up for the season, and wander down one of the alleys that connect Bay Street with the harbor, where a network of wooden docks creaks against the tide. A lone seagull sits atop a piling.

'This place will be full of cruisers and sailboats in a couple of months,' I say.

We have lunch at the Mexican restaurant.

'I haven't tried this before,' Colin says.

'You're kidding.'

'It hasn't really caught on yet – in England. At least, not where I live.' He scoops salsa onto a corn chip.

'Careful! It's hot.'

He gasps and reaches for his water.

On our way out of the restaurant we run into Tom

Grainger. He smiles at us, but doesn't stop because his little girl is running ahead.

'Friend of yours?' Colin asks.

'New neighbors. I don't know them. His wife is much younger—' I stop before putting my foot in any deeper.

Driving home, I point to a small red barn. It has one door, no windows, and its sagging roof supports a weathervane that tilts vaguely northeast as if waiting for gravity to finish off what winter storms began years ago. 'That's where the Rotary Club holds its annual shad bake.'

'Shad?'

'Fish,' I explain. 'They nail fillets to planks of wood, cover them with spices and bacon, and prop them around a bonfire. Everyone hangs about gossiping and drinking while the fish is cooking.'

'Sounds like fun.'

'It is,' I say. 'Especially when they throw away the fish and eat the wood.'

Colin gives me an odd look.

'Only kidding,' I say. 'It's a local joke.'

We cook dinner in a companionable sort of way and sit in front of the fire reminiscing over old pictures in my photograph albums. Colin produces the other half of the log and we burn both pieces. I see images in the flames. Sharing a mug of tea, a spider running up my arm, Colin giving me his shirt.

By ten, he's almost asleep. He lies back against the couch, puts his arm around my shoulder, and kisses my neck. His mouth finds mine. I melt into him, but he pulls away.

'Perhaps I'd better put myself to bed,' he says. 'I can hardly keep my eyes open.'

Is he waiting for a signal?

The choice is yours, Lizzie said.

'Would you like some company?' I ask.

His face crumples. 'I'm so glad you said that.'

'Go on up,' I say, rising above my panic. 'I need to . . .'

He turns and leaves me shaking with fear. Now I've gone and done it. There's no backing out now. I undress in the downstairs bathroom and wrap myself in Anna's Scooby Doo beach towel.

Great, Jill. Very sexy.

He's lying on my bed with the covers drawn up to his waist. The room glows from a dozen scented candles.

'We've both been waiting a long time for this,' Colin says, holding out his arms.

I drop my towel and climb in beside him.

Seventeen

My body tingles when I wake, and I reach for Colin, but the space beside me is empty. Damn! It *was* a dream, except how do I explain the damp spot beneath my thighs? I check out the dresser. The candles are burned down. Okay, so I wasn't dreaming, but where the hell is he?

'Jilly?'

I turn toward his voice. He's perched on a chair by the sliding glass door, elbows on his knees, hands wrapped around a mug, leaning forward as if poised for flight. Outside, on my balcony, everything is white.

'What time is it?' I ask.

'Almost six.' Colin hesitates. 'Coffee?'

'No, but thanks.' I shove a handful of hair from my face. 'I can't face that much caffeine this early in the morning.'

'Then I'll make you some tea.'

I stumble into the bathroom and attack my mouth with a toothbrush. Has last night's romance turned into morning-after guilt? Is he regretting whatever impulse made him come over? I have a shower but it does little to wash away the sight of Colin sitting on that chair with a mug of coffee and a smile that doesn't quite reach his eyes.

My tea's on the dresser when I emerge from the bathroom, swathed in towels and drying my hair.

'I'd like to ring England,' Colin says.

'Don't you have a mobile?'

'Yes, but it's dead and I forgot the charger.'

'Then be my guest,' I say, nodding toward my bedside table.

Colin clears his throat. 'I'd prefer a public phone.'

I stop toweling off. 'Why?'

'Because it's harder to trace.'

Oh boy, we're into serious guilt here. 'Then I'll drive you to the village.'

It takes an hour to shovel the driveway and it's almost eight when we pull into Sands Point. I park outside the drugstore between mounds of snow taller than my car. A sleepy-looking clerk is slumped behind the counter. He looks up from his magazine as we step inside on a blast of cold air. I point Colin toward the far corner where, amazingly, there's still an old-fashioned pay phone. In a booth, no less.

While Colin makes his call, I wander up and down the greeting card aisle. He's still talking, hunched like a penitent in the phone booth, when I circle around for the third time and I wonder, childishly, if he's now confessing his sins and seeking absolution from Shelby. I buy a bottle of shampoo and a gaudy St Patrick's Day card for Anna.

We have breakfast at the cafe next door. I order waffles. Colin asks for bacon and eggs and a large pot of coffee. He begins to talk, so softly I have to strain to hear him.

'I'm sorry for being distant, but . . . I've never been – you know – unfaithful before.' He pauses. 'I don't know how to handle it.'

'Furtively?'

He gasps.

My mouth needs a zipper. 'I'm sorry. That was flip.'

'No, Jilly. That's just you being you,' Colin says. He pulls a roll from the basket and spreads it with butter. 'Those three years in Wickham Forge with Hugh and Keith . . . and you and Sophie. They were the best. I'd never had friends like that before.' He pauses. 'Or since.'

I take a deep breath. 'So why did you disappear without a word?'

He flinches. 'You heard what my father did?'

'Yes, but that wasn't *your* fault.'

The waitress interrupts with food. I grab the syrup and smother my waffles. I need a sugar buzz to push this conversation forward. 'Colin, what happened after you left? Where did you go?'

'Scotland. My mother had relatives there.'

'Edinburgh?' I say, visions of him in a kilt. 'Dundee?'

'An island in the Hebrides.'

'Jeez! That's a bit remote.'

'Ferry twice a week to the mainland, electricity occasionally, and the only phone on the island was at the post office.' He shivers. 'I remember being cold, all the time. Even in summer.'

I swallow a chunk of warm, comforting waffle. 'Your mother?' I hesitate. 'Is she still . . .'

'She killed herself when I was twenty-four.'

My fork clatters to the table, bounces, then lands on the floor.

Colin hands me another. 'It was my fault. I wasn't watching her carefully enough.'

'You mean . . .'

'She'd tried several times before.' His mouth hardens. 'But

she finally got it right in the end. Sleeping pills. A whole bottle.'

He's detached. Dispassionate. Brutal, almost. I guess that's the only way to handle something as ghastly as this.

'And your father?' I ask. May as well spring all the family skeletons from the cupboard at the same time.

'Never saw him again. He got out of prison and buggered off to Australia.' Colin gives a bitter laugh. 'Appropriate, really.'

'Why?'

'Convicts. Penal colonies in Oz.'

'What about you? Where did you go?'

His voice turns soft. 'Back to Wickham Forge, looking for you.'

I choke and spit bits of waffle on the table.

Colin offers me a glass of water. 'Claudia told me you'd gone to America. That you were married.'

'She never said a word.'

'I begged her not to.'

'Oh, Colin.'

'So I put your memory on hold and tried to get on with my life. I did a stint in the army, got married, had a kid, got divorced.' He looks at me. 'But I never forgot about you, Jilly. Never.'

'Then why the hell didn't you write me from Scotland?'

'Because you deserved better than me. I had no money. No home. I had nothing to offer except trouble. My mother was suicidal, my father was in jail, and I was—'

His voice breaks and his shame is so palpable, so intense, I can't meet his eyes. My coffee's gone cold, but I drink it anyway.

'How did you find Keith and the others?' I say.

'I was at a computer show, trying to figure out what software to buy for the Lodge, and Hugh was one of the sales-men.'

'Did you recognize him?'

'The bald head threw me,' Colin says, 'but when he smiled, I knew it was Hugh. He sold me the right program and invited me to Keith's party. I almost didn't go, but thank God I did.' He wipes his mouth with a napkin. 'That day was a turning point for me.'

Our waitress bears down with the check and more coffee. I cover my cup and glance at Colin, but the light has gone from his eyes and he's retreated some place I can't follow.

He stands and lays a twenty on the table. 'Is this enough?'

'Plenty,' I tell him.

Across the street, two men are shoveling the sidewalk. A biting wind rips down Bay Street. Icy rain stings our faces. Colin shivers and pulls up his collar.

'It's a lot colder here. Colder than Scotland.'

'I'd like to explain about that phone call,' Colin says, coming in from the porch with an armload of wood.

I stuff newspaper and kindling in the grate, stand up, and wipe my hands across the seat of my jeans before collapsing on the couch. I've been wondering when he'd bring this up.

Colin lights the fire, then comes to sit beside me. 'I travel, quite a lot, for my business. The Lodge is Shelby's department. I buy and sell property. Small hotels, mostly. That's how I make a living.'

'I see.'

'So when I'm away, I always check in. Tell them where I am and when I'll be back.'

'Okay, so where are you supposed to be now?'

'Ireland.'

'Then I'll have to send you back with a shamrock,' I say.

'Or this.' I pick Anna's card off the coffee table and hand it to him.

'You don't let things get you down, do you?' he says. 'Or maybe you do, but don't show it.'

There's no answer for that. 'Tell me about your wife,' I say.

He sighs. 'I'd rather tell you about Shelby.'

Guilt taps a finger on my conscience. I push it away. It's not my job to worry about Colin's common-law wife.

Is it?

'Sure, go ahead.' I plump a pillow and settle back.

'I was a mess when we met. My marriage was over and my self-esteem was ten feet under. Shelby dug it up, nourished it. She helped me believe in myself again and I owe her for that. We traveled, we built up the business. Then we drifted apart. Probably my fault – most things are – but we don't do anything together any more. We're a couple of strangers who share the same house.'

Do they still share a bed?

Colin puts his hand on my thigh and I trace the veins with my finger. 'Looks like an old man's hand, doesn't it?' he says, smiling. 'Shelby's hands are smooth.'

'She's young.'

'That's the problem,' Colin says. 'The age difference between us is bigger now than it was when we first met.'

'*Yes!*'

Colin leans back, startled. 'What?'

'You. You're a man who finally gets it.'

'I am?'

Trying not to sound foolish, I explain my hangup over middle-aged men and younger women, and I'm barely finished when Colin grabs me. His mouth silences mine.

I guess he understands.

'Why didn't you ask Sophie for my address at Keith's party?' I say, coming up for air.

Colin kisses my nose. 'I didn't think you'd want to hear from me.'

'But when Sophie invited you for lunch –'

'– I took a chance. I had to see you. I wanted to see if that old magic's still there. It is, isn't it, Jilly?'

I nod, too choked up to speak.

'Then do you suppose,' Colin says, 'we could pull off a miracle and turn back the clock?'

'Why not?' I bleat. 'All it takes is a screwdriver.'

Colin puts a hand on my lips.

Oh shit, I've done it again.

'Jilly?'

'Yes?'

He unbuttons my shirt. 'Shut the fuck up.'

Colin asks to see my work. 'I still don't understand what you do, exactly,' he says. So I lead him into my office, pull out my portfolio and fire up the computer.

'These are great,' he says, thumbing through my Archibald sketches.

'We have wild parrots living here,' I say.

'You're having me on.'

'Am not.'

'Prove it.'

'It'll mean going outside.'

He shivers. 'If those birds can take it, so can I.'

I bundle Colin into one of Alistair's old ski jackets and a pair of warm gloves and take him outside.

'Look, up there.' I point to the top branches of a tall silver maple in my neighbor's side yard.

With no leaves to disguise them, the parrots stand out like green gauntlets. Obligingly, they squawk, as if to show they're not aberrant bluejays or mutant crows.

'How do they survive?' Colin asks. 'This isn't exactly the tropics.'

'They've acclimated. They're all over – San Francisco, Chicago, Atlanta.' I grin at him. 'Here, in balmy Connecticut.'

'What do they eat?'

'Birdseed, nuts, fruit. Last fall, I saw ten of them gorging on Lizzie's pear tree.' I pause. 'Which reminds me. We'd better get a move on. We're going there for dinner.'

'Will she serve pears?'

'Only if we show up wearing feathers.'

The McKennas' house is ablaze with lights, including those still in the evergreens, and there's a wreath, trailing pine cones and berries, clinging to the front door. By American standards, the house is old – built just after the Revolution – with narrow clapboards, a massive chimney, and haphazard additions whose proportions shouldn't work, but do because, as Fergus often points out, builders back then knew how to build houses.

'Currier and Ives,' Colin says. 'All it needs is a sleigh –'

'– and a couple of horses.' I climb out of the car and my feet crunch on corrugated snow.

'Hang on,' he says, taking my arm.

Lizzie's front porch is guarded by twinkling rhododendrons the size of woolly mammoths whose leaves – starched by the cold or perhaps embarrassment over wearing Christmas lights in March – have curled into pencils. Frost rimes the edges of the ivy in the wreath and reminds me of salt on the rim of a margarita glass. I hope Fergus is in full bartending mode because I could use a stiff drink. I'm a bit worried about Colin meeting my friends. Suppose he doesn't like them . . . or they don't like him.

*

'Why didn't you warn me he was this good-looking?' Lizzie says the minute she and I are alone in the kitchen. Fergus has taken Colin off to meet the gang – Lizzie's daughter, Paige, and her husband, Joel; Harriet and Beatrice. The kids are playing, noisily, upstairs.

'I take it you approve?'

She grins. 'Can I have a turn?'

'This one's all mine,' I say, relaxing. 'Besides, you've got Fergus.'

Lizzie pulls a face and hands me a plate of mini quiches, hot from the oven. 'Feed these to the masses and bring me a drink. Fergus is making margaritas.'

'Thank you, God.'

'No, thank Beatrice. She brought the tequila.'

A burst of laughter erupts from the living room and I hear Beatrice say, '. . . because changing lawyers in the middle of a case is worse than swapping deckchairs on the *Titanic*.'

'She's in good form,' Lizzie says.

I lean against the doorway and study Harriet's new partner. Wearing a shapeless tweed jacket, baggy linen pants, and topsiders with no socks, Beatrice French looks more like an upscale bag lady than the highly paid chemist she really is. Sturdily built, with cropped salt-and-pepper hair, Bea has unremarkable hazel eyes, a nose that's too long to be called elegant, and a radiant smile that transforms her face from plain to stunning. Her humor and kindness are legendary. I can see why Harriet loves her. Colin's at the buffet table, talking to Joel. I unload Lizzie's hors d'oeuvres and ask how he's doing.

'Fine,' Colin says. 'Joel's telling me about Claudia's squirrels.'

'Really?' I turn to Lizzie's son-in-law.

'Don't read too much into this,' he says, 'but the guys in marketing would like to see more. Do you have any?'

'A couple. I'll send them to you next week.'

Kids swarm through the room. Beth, her younger brother Tyler, and Anna are squealing and laughing and being pursued by the pink-faced nanny from Holland. A brass candlestick goes flying off the credenza. Lizzie walks by, picks it up, rubs it against her thigh, and puts it back.

Under his breath, Colin says, 'Are the children always this noisy?'

'No, they're usually much worse.'

He makes a noise in his throat.

'I'm kidding,' I say.

'They're not eating with us, are they?'

Fergus claps Colin on the back. 'Heaven forbid,' he says. 'They've had pizza and ice cream upstairs. Probably wrecked the joint by now.'

Lizzie calls out from the kitchen. We're to take our seats at the table. Paige asks Harriet how things are going at the courthouse and this launches another round of Bea's legal jokes.

Everyone laughs, but Colin barely smiles.

Beatrice leans across the table. 'Are you an attorney?'

'I run a hotel.'

'In that case,' she says, rubbing her hands with obvious glee, 'have you heard the one about the innkeeper's daughter?'

I try to catch Bea's eye but she's off and running and once started, there's no stopping her. Harriet, glowing in pearls and green silk, intervenes by asking Colin about the Lodge.

'It must be fabulous to live in a house as old as that,' she says.

After a couple of false starts, he loosens up. So, finally, do I, especially when he has everyone chuckling with a story about two elderly couples from California who muddled up their room numbers and climbed into bed with the wrong spouse.

'Don't the locks work?' Fergus asks.

'Not always. It's a really old house.'

Three scrubbed, shiny-faced, pajama-clad children are ushered in by the nanny to say goodnight. Anna hugs her mother and blows me a kiss. 'What did the snail say when he rode on the turtle's back?' she says.

Harriet groans and nudges Bea. 'See, I told you it would rub off.' She turns to her daughter. 'Okay, what did the snail say?'

'Wheeeee!'

I laugh so hard, soup threatens to come out my nose.

When we're through stuffing ourselves with boeuf bourguignon and debating the merits of restoring old houses, Paige and Harriet decamp to the kitchen.

They return with a cake.

Fergus sings Happy Birthday. The others chime in and I blush.

Colin says, 'Why didn't you tell me?'

'I forgot.'

'Jill's lying,' Lizzie says. 'She's in denial.'

Eighteen

Sands Point
March 2008

We light the candles and watch one another undress, and for once I'm not ashamed of my middle-aged body. Tonight my hips aren't wide, they're generous. My soft stomach is smooth and sensuous, and I'm proud of my full breasts that never passed the pencil test. Colin runs his fingers over them, around my nipples, teasing them to attention. He traces circles on my belly and probes between my legs, pushing them apart and licking me until I feel like a glove being turned inside out, one finger at a time.

I lose track of my orgasms.

Giddy and helpless and covered with sweat, we collapse in a tangle of arms, legs, and sheets. Colin looks at my alarm clock. 'Is this the right time?'

'I guess so. Why?' The numbers flash, then blink to one minute past midnight.

He leaps out of bed, wraps himself in Anna's Scooby Doo towel, and races through the door like Cinderella after the ball. Doors open and slam shut. Did I do something wrong? Is he venting his frustration on my kitchen cupboards?

The noises stop. Footsteps. Coming back upstairs. He slips

into my room, smiling and carrying the hunk of cake Lizzie insisted we bring home. A pink candle is stuck on top. He hands me a card.

'Lizzie told me your birthday's really today.'

My fingers tremble as I slit the envelope. It's the one I bought for Anna, and beneath a leprechaun perched on a pot of gold, he's written: *Happy birthday, my darling. P.S. Is it okay to tell you that I love you?*

'Oh, yes,' I say with a gulp. 'Oh, yes, please.'

'Then,' Colin says, taking my hands in his, 'I love you, Jilly Hunter, and I always have.'

I pull him back into bed and we find all sorts of ways to eat cake I never dreamed of before.

We spend most of Sunday in bed. Zachary, banished from the room, skulks in the hall but I'm too delirious with desire to feel sorry for him. Making love with Colin has blown me away. Literally. Lizzie's right. It *is* like riding a bike, except this time I seem to know what I'm doing.

I'm feasting on Colin the way my parrots feasted on those pears. I'm insatiable. The utter joy of being alive astonishes me. I'm vibrant – aware of myself in ways I never knew existed until now. I remember reading somewhere you're a different person every seven years. That's how long it takes the human body to slough off all its cells and replace them with new ones. Well, I've got news for the boffins who came up with that theory. It only took me three days. I'm not the same woman who met Colin off the plane last Thursday. She was flat. One-dimensional. The new me has more facets than a three-carat diamond.

Richard complained I was cold. Frigid. He's right. I was, but only with him. With Colin, I'm the sweet spot on a tennis racquet. A violin tuned to perfect pitch. Crystal that shatters at just the right note.

Colin's stomach grumbles and I plummet back to earth. He admits to hunger. So do I.

We make mushroom omelets, light the fire, and watch *The Bridges of Madison County*. I've seen it before, but Colin hasn't, and by the time we reach the scene where Meryl Streep is caring for her sick husband, Colin is crying.

'Shelby would never do that for me,' he says, taking off his glasses and rubbing them vigorously.

No, she probably wouldn't.

Colin sighs. 'Too self-centered. Too young, I suppose.'

But I'm not. I'd take care of this lovely man. I'd wash his socks and iron his shirts, providing I could find the iron, and I'd love him until we were too feeble to do more than blow kisses at one another from matching wheelchairs in the corridors of some grotty nursing home. I want to grow old with him. I want to fall asleep in his arms and wake up with him beside me. I want to remember things with him because I can. He's part of my past. We share memories nobody else has.

My cat is nowhere to be seen when I leave the next morning to take Colin to the airport. I'll worry about Zachary when I get back.

Colin wants to go shopping.

'What for?'

'I'm not going to tell you.'

The only place in Boston I know how to find, besides the airport, is Quincy Market. We have lunch there. I pick at a salad while Colin ploughs through a heap of pad Thai, then excuses himself to visit the men's room. He's gone a long time and I'm about to go looking for him when he comes up behind me and puts a small box on the table.

'What's this?'

'Happy birthday,' he says.

I open the box. In a nest of white tissue lies a heavy gold

chain. The kind of jewelry I've always admired on others, such as Elaine who can afford luxury like this.

'Do you like it?' Colin asks, sounding anxious.

'It's gorgeous – but . . .' I fight against tears. 'It's too much.'

Colin puts his fingers on my lips. 'I can afford this. It's the first of many things I want to give you,' he says, clasping the bracelet around my wrist, where it settles into a deeply satisfying curve.

At the airport we cling to one another and make plans for me to visit in May. Two months? Two whole months. How will I be able to wait that long?

How will he?

He walks backward through the security checks, clutching his bag and looking at me as if his heart is about to break.

Tense and aroused, I drive back to Sands Point. My thighs tremble. I squeeze them together, hard, to quell the ache down there.

That's what my mother called it. *Down there*, a bit of forbidden territory like the chocolate truffles she bought for Christmas one year and hid so Dad and I wouldn't find them. That wasn't her only euphemism. Having one's period was *being unwell*, submitting to sex with your husband was *doing one's duty for England*, and bearing children was *God's punishment for Eve's sin*. Poor Eve. She gets blamed for an awful lot of stuff.

One day, when I was seven or eight, I asked Mum if it hurt to have a baby. 'Of course not,' she replied. 'What's painful about finding a baby under a gooseberry bush?'

'Thorns?' Even then, I had a quick tongue.

Later, when I was thirteen and embarrassed by my rapid *development* (another bit of Mum's doublespeak), I asked if she'd fed me.

'What a silly question,' she said. 'You wouldn't be here if I hadn't.'

I looked down at my burgeoning bosom. 'I mean, did you—'

'Absolutely not!' my mother said. 'That's for gypsies and poor people. Not for those of us who can afford bottles and proper milk.'

Lizzie's in her kitchen, glasses perched on the tip of her nose, paying bills. The table is littered with bank statements, cancelled checks, and catalogs for clothes Lizzie will never, in a million years, fit into.

'I'm too wound up to go home,' I say, twisting my bracelet, loving the way it feels, sensuous and fluid against my skin.

'That must've cost him a dollar or two,' Lizzie says.

'Colin says he can afford it.'

'Good,' Lizzie replies. 'This means you can plan on being a very expensive mistress.'

'Oh, God. Is *that* what I am?'

'What else?' Lizzie says. 'Unless he's going to dump Shelby and marry you.' She adjusts her glasses and peers at me, pen poised for action as if she's going to take down my answer. 'Okay. Which is it? An illicit weekend now and then, or the start of something big?'

'I'm not sure.'

Lizzie sighs. She drops her pen on the table and pulls a bottle of Chardonnay from the fridge. 'Sounds as if you need to talk.'

I sink into a chair.

'So tell me everything,' Lizzie says, pouring wine.

It doesn't take long. A few broad brush strokes about Colin's years in Scotland and his life at North Lodge with Shelby and how they no longer have much in common.

'Do you feel guilty about her?' Lizzie asks.

'Horribly, and I wish I didn't.'

'It's Colin's problem, not yours. Let him deal with the guilt,' Lizzie says. 'Besides, it's not as if he's actually married to Shelby.'

'I know, but—'

'Jill, I know how your mind works, so stop feeling guilty, okay? You're not responsible for this. Sounds to me as if Colin and Shelby were on the rocks way before you came along.' Her eyes grow soft. 'Are you in love with him?'

'I think so.' I drain my glass. 'Yes, definitely. Love.'

He turned me inside out like a kid glove, one finger at a time.

Or is it lust? I think of the way I behaved over the weekend. Can Lizzie see it in my face? If she asks, I'll pretend it's the wine that's making me blush.

'Jill, is this what you want?' Lizzie asks. 'Are you okay with being the other woman in his life?'

Beneath the table, I cross my legs. The feeling's still there. Insistent, throbbing. Am I fooling myself? Am I willing to settle for dessert when what I really want is the whole meal? Peau-de-soie gown, six bridesmaids, and fuck-me shoes? The weddings Sophie and I planned but never had? Richard and I were married by a justice of the peace in a sorry little town in New Hampshire, with the JP's frumpy wife and her cleaning lady for witnesses and a hastily purchased bunch of carnations for the bride. I've always despised carnations.

Yes, it's exactly what I want. What I've always wanted. A guy to share my life with, but why do I have the feeling Lizzie won't approve?

'I'll take whatever I can get,' I say.

For now.

'In that case,' Lizzie says, 'I have only one question.'

'What?'

'Did you have fun?'

I let out a sigh. 'Oh, yes.'

She laughs and tops up our wine. 'A toast,' she says, raising her glass. 'Here's to your new sex life, and I know you find this hard to understand, but being pampered by an attentive man isn't a sin. It's manna for the middle-aged soul.'

I mumble something about not being used to this sort of thing.

'Rubbish. You've scrimped and saved. You've gone without so the boys could have it all. But now,' Lizzie says, 'it's *your* turn.'

Is it? Could I really sit back and let someone else swamp out the gutters, prune the wisteria, and point up the chimney before it falls down? Somehow, I don't think this is what Lizzie's talking about.

I try to stifle a very big yawn.

Lizzie pulls me to my feet. 'Jill, go home and get some sleep,' she says, shoveling me out the back door. 'You've just had a mind-blowing weekend. You probably have things to think about.'

Her words sit beside me all the way home. I try to leave them in the car but they follow me inside. Visions of champagne, filmy lingerie, and long, rocky beaches float through my mind. Is this where I'm heading? Three nights in Bora-Bora, all expenses paid? Am I about to become a kept woman? If so, I'll have to buy a whole new wardrobe. I don't think mistresses are supposed to wear sweatpants and old sneakers.

*

Dearest Jilly . . . Wow! I didn't think in my wildest dreams it would be like this. Thanks for the best four days of my life. I'm reliving each moment in the privacy of my mind. Everything was so special. The flight home was uneventful. The lady next to me fidgeted the whole

way. She prayed and crossed herself on take-off, and I
fell apart every ten minutes because I was thinking
about you.

My office overflows with unfinished work. Deadlines
approach. I need to find my cat. Pay bills. Write another letter
to Colin.

He falls apart thinking about me.

Must get motivated. Keep focused on what needs to be
done. Sod that. I'll cope later. Claudia's latest pictures, squirrels celebrating St Patrick's and Valentine's Day, lie on my
desk. I make scans and e-mail them to Joel. Then a pile of
unopened junk catches my eye and reminds me I'd better go
and check my mailbox. Grabbing my coat, I head for the main
road.

My box overflows with circulars and Wal-Mart flyers. I
riffle through them and find an alarming number of window
envelopes with PAST DUE stamped on the front. Walking home,
I worry about paying the bills while keeping an eye out for my
cat. He's been gone since Monday. It's now Friday. Where the
hell is he this time? Partying with the marsh cats? Lying dead
under a bush? Living with somebody else? My heart lurches
with the possibility of loss.

The phone is ringing.

Colin?

But it's Harriet. 'Are you busy?'

I close my eyes and pretend the heap of work on my desk
doesn't exist. 'No.'

'Good, then come for dinner tonight. We're making
samosas and chicken masala.'

'Fabulous.'

'See you at six,' Harriet says and rings off.

My business line trills and I race for my office.

'Is the Pinewoods layout finished?' Elaine says.

Pinewoods?

It has to be here, somewhere. I remember it arriving, shortly before Colin did. I rummage through all the piles.

Elaine says, 'When will I see the revisions?'

Shit. Where is the damned thing? Ah, there it is. In my filing tray. I open the folder and my heart sinks because I'm looking at hours of work, fixing mistakes Elaine has insisted I made. I didn't, but there's no point in arguing.

'How about Monday? Is late afternoon okay?' I check the file again, then the calendar, and heave a sigh of relief. This one's not due till next Wednesday. Counting the weekend, I have another four days.

'That won't do. I need it by ten.'

'Monday?'

'No, tomorrow.' Elaine hangs up.

Tomorrow?

The cow. The bloody-minded cow. I bet she did this on purpose. Jill, stop being an ass. Get over it already. This woman is your most important client. Her work pays the bills. Cancel your date with Harriet and get busy.

No.

I'll do both. I'll have dinner with my friends and *then* I'll deal with Elaine's latest crisis. Even if I have to stay up all night. A note from Colin rolls out of my fax machine.

Dearest Jilly . . . I can't sleep for thinking about you. I
lie in bed and relive all the details of our time together –
from the easy way we talk to the very easy way we
make love. God, you're gorgeous.

After too much wine and way too much of Harriet's delicious curry, I soak up a pot of coffee, pull an all-nighter, and deliver Elaine's job just before ten. But she wants more, and keeps me there till late afternoon, rearranging photographs and trying to come up with new things to say about the same old houses in the same old subdivisions that have been on the market for far too long.

This isn't part of the deal, but I do it anyway because I can't afford not to. The economy sucks and local business is tightening its belt. Elaine's the only one with money to throw around.

Must find more clients. But where?

Finally, Elaine is satisfied and I crawl home, fall into bed, and don't wake up till Lizzie bangs on the door at noon the next day, arms full of the Sunday *Courant*, with my cat leaning against her legs.

'Where did you find him?'

'On your front porch.' Lizzie dumps the newspaper on my table. Her eyes sweep over my bathrobe, my bare feet. 'I don't suppose you're up for a walk?'

'Give me ten minutes, and put the kettle on. I need a shot of caffeine.'

I check my office for a fax –

I printed your last e-mail and took it with me on a walk
with Meggie through the woods. It was misty. So was I.
Meeting you has woken me from a grey fog of no
emotion. I think about that odd time we had at
Heathrow when I drove down to say goodbye. Your
ankle was hurt and wrapped in a pink bandage. You
tried so hard to finish that G&T. Did either of us realize
what was happening? Even then?

– and neglect to shove Zachary off the laser printer.

For a while, we have the beach to ourselves. A brisk wind whips my hair into knots and I can feel ridges of hard-packed sand through the soles of my sneakers. Three months from now, this stretch of beach will be inundated with daytrippers, empty soda cans, and other people's problems. Last summer, two families from Brooklyn who'd apparently been feuding for years took up residence on each side of the breakwater and slugged it out every weekend from July to September.

Lizzie removes her sunglasses. 'Is that Tom Grainger?'

Coming toward us, I see my neighbor and his dogs. Labradors. Not my favorite breed. They're big and slobbery and like to shove their noses in personal places.

'Good morning,' Tom says.

The dogs, thank God, gallop off.

Lizzie says, 'Lovely day.'

While they chat about the weather, I scrape furrows in the sand with my heel and size up the guy next door. He's not much taller than Lizzie, a solid rectangle of a man with an unruly beard, silvery-beige hair that touches his collar, and eyes the color of a storm at sea.

He catches me looking at him and grins.

Perfect teeth, probably capped. False?

He's got a wife half his age.

Nineteen

I spend Easter Sunday with Lizzie's family. Fergus, dressed as a rabbit, organizes an egg hunt. Kids and eggs tumble around the garden like multicolored bubbles.

'Did you have this nonsense in England?' Lizzie removes a ham, smothered with apricots and raisins, from the oven.

I eat one of the raisins. 'Hams?'

'Egg hunts.'

'Eggs and bunnies weren't on my mother's list of approved Easter activities.' I swipe another raisin. 'We all went to church.'

'Probably a good thing,' Lizzie says. 'Do you have any idea how much money Fergus spent on candy and baskets, to say nothing of that outfit he's wearing?'

The back door crashes open and Tyler shoots into the kitchen pushing a dump truck full of foil-covered eggs. His father is right behind him.

'Jill, I've got another update on your squirrels,' Joel says.

A large, fluorescent-pink rabbit waddles in. Tyler shrieks and runs off, scattering eggs on the floor.

'Giant bunny turds,' Lizzie says.

Fergus pops one in his mouth and trundles after his grandson.

'The guys in marketing,' Joel says, 'still love the pictures –'

I cross my fingers. Claudia's latest, squirrels painting Easter eggs, arrived last week.

'– but illustrations, by themselves, aren't enough,' Joel says. 'They need more – a toy or a book. A puzzle.'

'Toys?' Lizzie says.

Joel nods. 'We make a few educational ones.' He hesitates. 'Sorry, Jill. It's a tough market. Let me know if you and Claudia come up with something unique. Something that'll grab parents by the pocketbook.'

The next day, I call Claudia to brainstorm about squirrels and she ends up solving the problem of where Colin and I will stay while I'm in England.

'You can have my cottage for a week,' she says, 'if you'll give Sophie and me a couple of beds at the beginning of July.'

'It's a deal,' I say. 'How long can you stay?'

'Just a few days,' Claudia replies. 'Then we're off to Hawaii. Ian will be on location and Sophie's agreed to join him on condition I go with her. Silly girl. She'd have a lot more fun if I wasn't breathing down her neck.'

'But your cottage?' I hesitate. 'Where will you be while . . .'

'Don't worry,' Claudia says. 'I won't be breathing down your neck, either. I'll be in London with Sophie.'

Does she need more tests? 'You're okay, I mean, you're not . . .'

She laughs. 'I'll be taking an art course. At Kew. Botanical illustration.'

I sneak off to the mall. Alone. Without telling Lizzie. She'll kill me if she finds out, but I don't think I can cope with her well-intentioned advice while trying on underwear. I haven't told her, or anyone else, about Colin and me . . . the way we are now. Lizzie just doesn't get it. She's never had to fend for herself. Not really. Not the way I have. Fergus has always been there for her, even after she kicked him out and had her fling with Trevor.

I love her to bits, but she's got a blind spot over my need for Colin. Not the physical need, which she thoroughly approves of, but my need for someone who shares a big part of my past. Lizzie still has friends she went to high school with, grade school even. She gets to attend reunions and reminisce with people who knew her as a tall skinny kid with knobby knees and flat feet. She has a history here. Mine, what's left of it, is back in England. My school doesn't even exist any more, so tracing former classmates is next to impossible, despite all those online reunion sites.

Lizzie's still teasing me about being Colin's mistress. The other day she got carried away and called me his concubine. I laughed louder than she did because it really is too funny.

I'm going to marry him.

> Sweet Jilly . . . I should never have let you go. I
> should've written from Scotland. I know now you'd
> have understood how desperate I was. This time, I'm
> strong enough and wise enough (I hope) to pull us both
> through the rough bits. It won't be easy. It'll take time
> for me to end my life here and begin a new one with
> you. I've never felt this close to anyone before. There
> has always been a gap not filled. With you, there is no
> gap. I am free to be me.

A spasm of guilt brings me up short. What will happen to Shelby? Colin owns the Lodge, but he and Shelby share the business. Maybe Diana has a share, too. I'm sure it'll be messy and as bad as getting a divorce. He's dreading it. I worry Shelby will figure it out before he gets up the courage to tell her. Or worse, somebody else will tell her, the way my gynecologist told me.

Seventeen years ago.

Two weeks after my annual physical, Mary Jane Mason called to schedule a follow-up visit. 'Nothing serious,' my doctor said in her sing-song voice. 'But it does need attention. Oh, and bring your husband as well.'

Richard refused to go. No way was he going to set foot in a doctor's office that dealt with female plumbing. His words, not mine.

So I lay on the examining table with my feet in the stirrups, trying not to panic while Mary Jane told me the lab had found suspicious cells in my pap smear.

'What sort of cells?' Cancer? Oh, shit! I've got cervical cancer. My father died of cancer.

'*Neisseria gonorrhoeae.*' Mary Jane told me to relax while she took another smear. 'Just to be on the safe side.'

Did she say gonorrhea?

'Sometimes the lab makes a mistake,' Mary Jane said, stripping off her gloves. 'More often than they like to admit, but since it's easy to solve this particular problem I'm going to give you a jab of penicillin. Hop off the table and bend over.'

After massaging my sore rump, I climbed into my clothes, and met Mary Jane in her tiny office next door. I loved this about her. She always talked to you afterward, when you were dressed and not lying half naked with your tender parts exposed.

'Why didn't Richard come with you?' she said. 'This won't work if he doesn't get a shot as well, unless, of course, you're planning to avoid sex with him from now on.' Mary Jane gave me a look that suggested I just might want to consider this a viable option.

I sat there, trembling, trying to digest it all, while she scribbled something on a prescription pad, slipped it into an envelope, and handed it to me. 'Give this to your husband. He can take it to his own doctor and get a jab.'

Jab?

I wanted to run him through with a sword. I wanted to slice his balls off and stuff them in his mouth. I wanted to . . .

Gonorrhea.

Oh, God!

I wobbled to my feet, gripped the chair till my head stopped spinning, and thanked my doctor. Then I paid her bill, in full, at the front desk. No way would I let this monstrosity go through our insurance.

Our insurance. Our life. Our kids.

I raced for the bathroom and threw up in the sink. How could he do this? To me? To the family? I needed revenge – right now – so I sat on the toilet and peed away the last bit of feeling I had for my husband, wiped myself clean, and flushed.

That bastard. That fucking bastard. Not only had he violated our marriage, he'd compromised my health.

Richard didn't see it that way.

'You slut,' he said, after opening the envelope.

I backed away. 'What?'

'I knew I should've stuck around the day your friend's brother came to visit. What's her name? The one you grew up with?'

'Sophie?'

'Yeah, her. And her fucking brother.'

'Hugh? What about Hugh?' Two months ago, he'd stopped by to visit on his way to Silicon Valley for some sort of computer seminar. I begged Richard to stay, but he refused and went off to play golf. Hugh and I fed the kids at McDonald's then took them to the park.

'He's the one,' Richard said, flecks of spit flying from his mouth. One landed on my cheek. I was too stunned to wipe it off.

'Hugh?'

'Yes, that filthy lout. Did you have fun with him? Did you do all the stuff you won't do with me?' Richard thrust his face at me. Red. Sweating. Pulsating. 'Didyoudidyoudidyoudid-you?'

'Hugh?' I said again, stupidly. 'He's like my own brother. I mean, that'd be in—'

Crack!

At first, I didn't feel a thing. Not even shock. Then it dawned on me that Richard must've hit me because my face hurt like hell and he wasn't there any more. Just an angry space. The garage door clanked open. Richard's car roared into life. Tires squealed and gravel crunched.

Then silence. Blessed silence.

I put ice on my jaw, checked on the boys to make sure they hadn't heard this latest horror, and gathered up fresh sheets for the bed in my guest room. I didn't want to sleep in my own bed.

Ever again.

We were divorced six months later and I didn't tell my lawyer about the gonorrhea because I didn't want it dragged into court where it would only hurt my sons.

Slipping into Victoria's Secret, I pull satin bras and lace panties from shelves while shop assistants with smooth hair and long legs exchange glances and hide their smiles behind well-manicured hands. I guess it's not often they see middle-aged women in here trying on silk teddies and camisoles.

I take my delicious loot into a dressing room and twirl in front of its three-way mirror. I run my hands up and down my body. I've lost weight. I'm firmer. Will Colin notice? I whisk one bra off and try another. Too much me. Not enough bra.

Need a bit more support. Underwire, maybe? Ouch, this one's too tight. How about a soft-cup bra that does up in the front? That ought to liven things up a bit. I lean forward and pour myself into it. Stand up, slouch a little. Hands on hips. Pout lips and look sexy. Try not to laugh. Does it have matching panties?

I shimmy into slips with spaghetti straps and pull on night-gowns that are mere whispers of silk. That emerald robe will do me just fine. I wrap it around me and imagine Colin taking it off, slipping one shoulder out, then the other, untying the belt, tying me up with it. I wonder if he'd go for that?

Holy shit! What am I thinking? What's happening to me?

My lovely Jilly . . . The magic, the physical longing is
getting harder to bear. I'm amazed this can happen at
our age! I want to hold you, touch you, kiss you, caress
your soft skin, talk to you, make you laugh and
tremble, and more besides. At night I curl up in the
cocoon of my mind and long for our next time together.
Why is May so far away?

What shall I buy him? A velvet smoking jacket? Too expensive. How about briefs? Those I can afford.

I leave Victoria with a bag full of her secrets and head for the men's department at Macy's, but the window display at Frederic's of Hollywood sidetracks me.

Do people really buy this stuff?

Crotchless panties, brassieres with tassels and cutouts for nipples? Leather girdles, spiked collars, velvet chains?

Fur handcuffs?

Oh, God, I'm not cut out for this. Neither is my relation-ships with Colin, so I scurry next door and plunge into the comforting world of men's underwear. Jockey shorts, pocket T-shirts. Terrycloth robes. I poke through packets of Y-fronts

133

and racks of boxers. I want something soft, sensuous. An assistant offers help. I blush and tell him I'm browsing.

I grab two pairs of Calvin Klein briefs.

These'll do. He won't be wearing them for long anyway.

Like a kid waiting for Christmas, I mark the days off my calendar. May first arrives, along with Claudia's squirrels twisting ribbons around a maypole. The rites of spring.

Sexual awakening?

Well, that shoots my concentration. Might as well go and help Lizzie sort donations for her college's fund-raising auction.

Her kitchen table is groaning with books. Moldy encyclopedias, how-to manuals, paperback romances, and hardcovers – thrillers and spy novels mostly. I pick one off a pile. Red and black dust jacket, man in trench coat, collar turned up. Trilby. No cigarette.

Lizzie whips it away. 'I was looking for that. It's a first edition, autographed.'

'Paul Lamont,' I say, impressed. This guy is Lizzie's absolute favorite author. 'Who donated it?'

'We don't know. The book just showed up last week.' She nods toward the scraggy-looking moose head propped against her fridge. One of its antlers is missing. 'Unfortunately, so did that.'

I shudder. 'Who on earth would buy it?'

'Fergus, probably.' Lizzie slides the Paul Lamont thriller into a plastic bag. 'This one needs to be kept safe.' She opens a drawer and slips her treasure inside. 'Any news on Claudia's squirrels?'

I pull the latest from my tote bag. 'Would you give this to Joel?'

'Maypoles?' Lizzie says. 'Isn't that a pagan festival?'

'Probably.'

'She'll be painting druid squirrels at Stonehenge next,' Lizzie says. 'When are you seeing her?'

'As soon as I get there. I'm spending the first weekend in London with her and Sophie.'

'Need a ride to the airport?' Lizzie consults her calendar, then yanks it off the fridge and drops it beside Claudia's drawing. 'I don't have any meetings that day.'

'I'm all set,' I say. 'But thanks.'

She turns back to her fridge, barely visible beneath shopping lists, empty seed packets, business cards, recipes, takeout menus, and kids' artwork, and I wonder why everyone, myself included, feels compelled to keep their lives stuck to the front of a kitchen appliance.

Lizzie begins to sort hers out.

I glance at her calendar, then at Claudia's artwork, back to Lizzie's calendar again, narrowing my gaze until one is superimposed on the other. Dates merge with squirrels and a maypole. What was it Lizzie just said? Something about druids and Stonehenge?

Calendars and clocks. Keeping track of time.

It all clicks into place.

'Jill, say something.' Lizzie is staring at me.

'You're a genius.' I stand up. 'I need to go home.'

'But you just arrived.' Lizzie shifts the moose to one side. 'This probably has fleas.'

'Then you'll have to charge more.' I grab my bag. 'Lizzie, I really have to leave. If I don't get my ideas into the computer, right now, they'll jump ship.'

Lizzie picks up her calendar. 'Is it something I said?'

'I'll explain later.' I slip out the back door.

The minute I get home, I ring Claudia and badger her into five more drawings. 'Thanksgiving, Halloween, something for June.'

'Weddings? Graduation?'

'Yes, and a snowman or sledding for January.' I grope for inspiration. 'Fireworks for July.'

There's a significant pause. 'A calendar?'

I glance at mine. Ten days and I'll be in London. Is that enough time for sketches, diagrams, a prototype of some sort?

'Yes,' I say.

'But I've already made calendars.' Claudia sounds disappointed.

'Not this kind.'

After I finish the mock-up, I clear my desk of the most important work, tell my clients I'll be gone for two weeks, and make decisions about packing. Jeans, sweaters, shorts. Maybe a bathing suit. I slip into my green silk robe, revel in its luxurious softness, and hold up my left hand. Yes, that's what I want. A socking great emerald surrounded by diamonds.

With this ring . . .

I fold the robe and wrap it in tissue with my lingerie and tuck it into my suitcase with a sachet of lavender. Then I coax Zachary into his cat carrier and take him to Happy Tails.

'We had one here just like him a few months back,' the kennel manager says. 'He's an Abyssinian, isn't he?'

'Yes, but he's never been in a kennel before, and—'

'Don't worry. He'll soon get used to it. They all do.'

I'm loath to leave him, alone in a cage with his straw hat and a bowl of food he'll probably despise. I feel weepy, so I go and see Lizzie to say goodbye to her, too.

'I feel like I've just abandoned a child.'

'You have,' she says.

I sniff. 'He'll hate me for this.'

'He'll probably move out permanently.'

'Gee, thanks.'

'You sure you don't need a ride to the airport?' she asks.

'I'm leaving the car in long-term parking. Don't want to drag you out at the crack of dawn.'

She laughs. 'When's the last time *you* saw a sunrise?'

'When I stayed up all night fixing that job for Elaine.'

Lizzie lets out a long sigh. 'What are you going to do about her?'

'I'd tell you, but it might incriminate me.'

'Don't do anything rash,' Lizzie says, folding her arms. 'You need her business, even though I keep telling you to dump her and find other clients.'

I give her a hug. 'I'll miss you.'

'Me too,' Lizzie says, hugging me back. 'Maybe I'll go to the kennel and hang out with your cat.'

Twenty

London
May 2008

'What, exactly, is it?' Sophie asks when I pull my creation from its nest of styrofoam peanuts. Luckily, the box had fitted into the airplane's overhead rack. I shudder to think what would've happened if it had been slung in the cargo hold.

'A calendar box?' Claudia says.

'An interactive, multifunctional calendar box,' I say, showing them how it works. I lift flaps and slide tabs in and out. They were a bugger to make. Gave me a whole new appreciation for kids' activity books. I spin it around. 'See, it's got twelve sides. One for each month.'

'Kind of like a pentagon,' Sophie says.

'Or a double hexagon,' I say.

Claudia nods. 'Ingenious, and I love it.'

Armed with staplers, glue guns, and sticky tape we spend all weekend revising my prototype and adding Claudia's new illustrations until late Sunday night when I'm satisfied we have something viable to show Joel's marketing boys. Claudia thanks me and goes to bed, Sophie folds herself into the wing chair, and I collapse on the couch.

Sophie scowls at her hands. 'I have terminal paper cuts.'

'And I overdosed on glue.'

'Will this make any money?' she asks.

'Joel says the card and toy business is incredibly tough.'

'But if it does,' Sophie goes on, 'how are you and Mum going to split the proceeds?'

'It's all hers. She's done most of the work.'

'But you're the one with brilliant ideas, Jill.'

'Come on, Sophie. All I did was—'

'But suppose it makes a fortune?'

When Sophie forms a set of opinions, she's slow to change them. 'I keep telling you. I don't want—'

'Jill, you've got to think of yourself as well as my mum.'

'This is for her,' I say, remembering the countless hours I spent in Claudia's kitchen. 'To thank her for being the mother I never had. I've always wanted to do something special for her. This is my chance. Don't bugger it up, okay?'

'But—'

'Sophie, drop it. We're probably wasting our time, anyway. The odds against success are enormous. Huge. Astronomical. Off the bloody chart, so let's call it a night and go to bed.'

Claudia produces a set of keys for the cottage and reminds me to let the farmer's wife know we're there. 'Don't forget to feed my cat, and if you've got time perhaps you'd be kind enough to check on my squirrels.'

Sophie looks up from stuffing my bag and the box with our precious cargo into the trunk of her car. 'Mum, Jill's got better things to do than worry about your blasted rodents.'

We drive west and London's suburbs give way to relentlessly green hills and chocolate-box villages that look as if they've grown up through the earth rather than having been built on top of it. In between bouts of admiring the scenery, I manage to convince myself that Colin and I won't click this time; that we've merely been fooling ourselves with marathon phone calls and gushy letters. Then Sophie adds to my stress by suggesting we take a detour and drive past North Lodge.

'No way,' I protest.

'We have plenty of time.' Sophie slows down. 'We can spy on the woman he lives with.'

Suppose Colin sees us? What then? He was quite clear about meeting me far away from his village. A roadside pub, ten miles down the road.

'Come on, Jill. It'll be just like old times.'

'That's what I'm afraid of.' I sigh. 'All right, but no cloak-and-dagger stuff. No hiding behind bushes and skulking in doorways.'

'I promise.' Sophie pulls off at the next exit.

Colin's house is breathtaking. So incredibly gorgeous, I struggle for words to describe its stately chimneys, its steeply pitched slate roof, and its golden Cotswold stone covered with honeysuckle and wisteria. Petunias and forget-me-nots tumble from boxes beneath tiny bow windows. Early roses bloom above the wooden front door.

Talk about picture-postcard.

'My God,' Sophie says, slowing the car to a crawl. 'I'd no idea the place was so grand.'

Neither had I.

The village recedes and I turn for one last look.

He's giving up all this, for me?

Colin sweeps me off the ground and swings me in a circle like a jitterbug dancer and my doubt evaporates. His bone-crunching hug tightens and something lets loose. Dear God, it's my bra. The flimsy one with spaghetti straps from Victoria's Secret. When my head stops spinning, I spot a sign with the letters WC and an arrow pointing toward a narrow pathway almost entirely hidden by overgrown shrubs.

'Put me down, crazy man. I've got to spend a penny.'

I give him a blistering kiss – sexy enough to earn piercing whistles from a man delivering crates of Guinness to the saloon bar – and head for the loo.

Once inside, I remove my sweater, then my bra. One of its hooks is broken. Fixable, but not without needle and thread, so I stuff it into my purse and pull my sweater on. The feel of it against my nipples is extraordinarily sensuous as I walk back to join Colin.

He's leaning against his car, waiting, smiling, passenger door open. It's lovely inside. A real wooden dashboard, leather seats. Moon roof. All mod cons. Luxurious. Seductive.

'Music?' Colin asks.

I fasten my seat-belt. 'Please.'

He slots in a CD – one of my favorites, an old Henry Mancini – and I lean back and lose myself in 'Charade' and 'Moon River'. We hit the road and I pretend we're Barbra Streisand and Robert Redford in *The Way We Were*, driving his tiny MG through the hills above Hollywood. I loved that film, but I'd have been happier if they'd gotten back together again. I hate sad endings.

Colin guns the engine and we zoom onto the motorway. The car purrs and eats up the miles. I look at his profile. Grecian nose, high cheekbones. Luscious lips. My nipples twitch. They're not used to rubbing against the rough wool of an Aran sweater.

Colin asks if I'd like to go and see a manor house in St Ives that just came on the market. It's only a few miles from Claudia's cottage and it would make a fine luxury hotel. An excellent investment. I nod, yes that would be lovely. How about tomorrow? I nod again. His hand is on my lap. Pretty soon it'll slide between my legs. How long does it take to get to Claudia's from here? Three hours? Four? Should we stop at a motel?

I pick up his hand and press my lips to his palm. 'You'd better keep your paws off me or you'll drive us off the road.'

Twenty-one

Cornwall
May 2008

We reach Claudia's cottage at dusk. I give Colin the keys. He opens the door and I'm overwhelmed with another attack of doubt. What if it's not the same? What if we disappoint one another? But when Colin presses himself against me in Claudia's tiny front hall I can tell he isn't disappointed.

'This place is gorgeous,' Colin says, 'and I'll admire it all later, but first . . .' Without taking his eyes off my face, he picks me up. The stairs, steep and narrow, squeak with protest under our combined weight. I look over his shoulder. Somber-faced Neville ancestors stare back from sepia-toned photographs that hang on the wall. Are we being censured, perhaps?

I steer him into Claudia's room. Bigger bed. Better view. We'll be able to see the ocean from here. He sets me down beneath a portrait of Alexandra Forbes, Claudia's maternal grandmother, ample-bosomed in bombazine and ostrich feathers, hands planted on the silver-topped handle of a walking cane. Should we turn her against the wall? Oops, no time for that now because Colin's kneeling, pulling off my slacks, and doing something unspeakably delicious with his fingers. His mouth brushes across my belly, slides down my legs. I shudder and lean back and forget all about Alexandra because Colin's nibbling the inside of my thighs.

I bite my lip to keep from crying out loud.

He hooks both thumbs into the crotch of my panties. 'Lovely,' he murmurs, kissing green satin. I tug at the elastic. 'Not yet,' he says. 'Leave them on for now.'

I catch my breath and slide my hands over his buttery leather jacket, slip it from his shoulders, and undo the cartwheel buttons of his shirt. The pink one. Did he wear it on purpose? Does he remember wearing it the day I fell back into his life? My fingers are thick, clumsy. I struggle with the last button.

He stands and shakes off his boots, unzips his jeans, and sheds his underpants. Jockeys. Gray cotton. Oh yes, I did the right thing, buying those Calvins.

He gathers me up, smothers my face with kisses, and lowers me onto Claudia's double bed. I raise my arms. He lifts my sweater and I wish I were wearing silk instead of scratchy Irish wool. Cables, twists, and bobbles rasp against my belly like a giant tongue. Up, up, and over my breasts. They tumble free like warm cottage loaves spilling from a basket.

'Oh, my God.' Colin's voice is thick. 'You're not wearing a—'

I'd forgotten about my busted bra.

Then he groans, and so do I because now he's cupping my breasts, stroking them and licking my nipples, and I want to French kiss the genius who invented those unreliable hooks.

'Oh, Jilly,' Colin moans. 'I don't know how I've survived without you, without—'

'Sshhh.' I pull him toward me. I want him to crush me. I want his weight to pin me to the bed. I also want him to remove my knickers, so I guide his hands down and raise my hips, sighing with relief when he rips off my double-digit lingerie and drops it on the floor.

I clamp my mouth onto his and devour him with all the pent-up desire and deprivation of the past two months. I want to swallow him. I vacuum up his tongue. Our teeth clink and I have a momentary panic about my crown. What if it falls off and I swallow it? What if it falls off and *he* swallows it? We rearrange our lips and laugh. A minor embarrassment. Time to catch our breaths.

Colin kisses me, then abandons my face to explore farther south. His tongue slides down my neck, between my breasts, beneath them, circling and licking, and I whimper while he sucks on one nipple and tugs at the other with his thumb and forefinger. I groan. Oh, God, don't ever let this stop.

I beg for more.

Whatever you want.

Leaning back, I wallow in the softness of down pillows and old linen. I reach behind and grab the brass spindles of Claudia's antique bed, hold tight and thrust myself toward him. Colin parts my legs, sinks between them, touching, probing. I spread my legs wider. His tongue flirts with me. It teases and tastes, and I gasp again when it plunges inside and brings me to the edge of a place I've rarely reached with anyone else and certainly not with Richard. I hated having sex with him. The more he tried – elaborate maneuvers gleaned from erotic movies and pornographic magazines – the less responsive I became. Sometimes, to make him feel better, I faked it, moaning and writhing and giving a performance worthy of an Oscar.

But I'm not faking now. I stiffen. I hold my breath. Waves peak, curl, and crash. I'm drowning. I shudder and cry out. I release the bars and reach for Colin, clutching his hair, his ears, anything to bring his face level with mine so I can kiss him and taste myself in his mouth.

'Your turn, your turn,' I whisper, biting his lips. His tongue. 'I want to do this again, with you. I want us to come together.'

He's ready. More than ready. Can I take all of him? He drives himself inside. Deeper, deeper. I'm throbbing, wide open.

More, more. I want more.

I dig my heels into the mattress and lift my buttocks off the bed. Ahh, that's good, but . . .

'More,' I say.

He lifts my legs onto his shoulders. I grab the bedposts and push myself higher. A wave, more explosive than before, gathers momentum. It crests and breaks. The room rocks and sways and while I seriously doubt I'm a reliable witness at this point, I could swear Claudia's grandmother winked at me.

Twenty-two

Cornwall
May 2008

What *was* I thinking? I'm too old for this. My nipples are on strike and my undercarriage is waving a white flag. Poor Colin. I took more than I gave last night – a whole lot more – and I'm going to make up for it by cooking breakfast. I lurch into the kitchen. Max miaows and curls around my legs, reminding me he's another mouth to feed. I pour food in his dish, plug in the coffee, and crack the farm-fresh eggs we bought yesterday into a bowl. I whisk them, leaning against the counter. Will I ever be able to stand upright again? Walk without a waddle?

'Are you up for St Ives?' Colin slides his arms around my waist. Nibbles my ear. 'Because if you're not, we could always go back to bed.'

'I'll pretend you didn't say that.'

'About last night,' he says.

Don't tell me he's eager for more.

'What about it?'

'Do you suppose others our age get fired up the way we do?'

'Judging by all those kids, I'd say Keith certainly does.' I drop six rashers of bacon in a frying pan. Tomorrow we'll eat nuts and grains. Today we sin. 'So does Sophie. She collects lovers and has them for dessert.'

Colin smiles and sets the table. I pour coffee and pile our plates with cholesterol and hot buttered toast. Wedges of orange, just to be healthy. A sprig of parsley I plucked from a flowerpot on the windowsill.

'Then how about people in their sixties and seventies?' Colin says. He folds blue cotton napkins into triangles, tucks them beneath our silverware. I forget he's a professional. 'Do you wonder what *their* sex lives are like?' he asks, pulling out my chair. 'Do you ask yourself if they even *have* sex lives?'

'All the time,' I reply. 'Geriatric sex fascinates me.' I sit down and sigh with relief that it only hurts a little. 'My latest hobby, in fact.'

Peering at me through the steam rising from his coffee, Colin doesn't look much older than he did the afternoon we shared a mug of tea. He and I had the one with no handle. Hugh and Keith arm wrestled. Sophie wasn't wearing a bra. I won biggest chicken wings. My God, how young we all were.

'Know what I used to think?' he says.

'What?'

'When I was a kid, a teenager, I thought old people didn't have nerve endings. That everyone over fifty was numb and there'd be no point in them doing anything that felt good, like drinking beer or having sex, because they wouldn't be able to feel it.'

My parents slept in separate rooms.

'But I was wrong, thank God,' Colin says, grinning. 'Sex gets better with age because we've had time to figure it out. We know how the bits and pieces fit together.'

I wince. 'You can say that again.'

'If it helps,' Colin says, 'I'm a bit fragile, too.' He sucks on a slice of orange. Offers one to me. 'I wasn't always this way.'

'Fragile?'

'No, sex mad.'

'Neither was I.'

Colin hesitates. 'Tell me about Richard.'

'Only if you tell me about your wife.'

For a second or two, his face looks as if somebody took it off and put it back on all wrong. Then it passes and he smiles again.

He nods. 'You go first.'

All I can remember is the bad stuff. Digging up the good is like looking for loose change between the couch cushions. You know it's there, but you can't, at this particular moment, put your hands on it. So I describe family vacations, the cocktail parties and the five-bedroom house in suburbia, and how Richard wanted nothing to do with the derelict beach cottage he inherited from a great-aunt. Then I go for broke and tell him about the final straw in my doctor's office.

'Okay, I've spilled the beans,' I say. 'Now it's your turn.'

Again, that look. Is he going to renege on his promise?

'Come on,' I say, hoping to lighten his mood. 'It can't be *that* bad.'

No worse than gonorrhea.

'My wife,' Colin finally says, 'left me for another woman.'

For once, I'm at a loss for words. If this were a scene from a movie, it'd fade away so the characters wouldn't have to cope. A novel would have those convenient little dots. But this, dammit, is real. It's not going to dissolve, or dot off, and now Colin's looking at me, waiting for me to say something.

'What about your daughter?'

He groans and I'm stunned by the rawness of his pain. 'I rarely see her,' he says.

'Why?'

'My ex-wife and her partner emigrated to New Zealand. They took Nancy with them.'

'Christ! That's the other side of the world.'

Colin wipes his eyes with a napkin. 'Tell me about it.'

'How old is she?'

'Sixteen.'

'Time for her to start thinking about college,' I say. 'Maybe she'll choose one in England. Or the States.'

'Nancy hasn't left New Zealand since they arrived.'

'Not even to come and see you?'

'I go down there, occasionally, but . . .' He shrugs. 'It's difficult. Uncomfortable.' His face clouds over again. I've seen that look before, in the cafe when he told me about his parents. So now I'm totally stumped. I didn't know what to say then, and I'm damned if I know what to say now. I can't imagine not seeing my kids. Yes, my two boys are grown and gone, doing their own thing, but they're only a phone call away. A short plane ride for Jordan down in Washington; a couple of hours by train or car for Alistair in Boston. And they're the foundation of my life.

'A lot can happen in two years,' I say, forcing myself to sound optimistic. 'By the time Nancy's eighteen, she'll be raring to go. When you and I were that age, going down to Brighton was a big deal. Not any more. Today's kids are global gypsies. Jordan hitch-hiked through Spain his junior year in college. Alistair went to China last summer. Told me they have the best bones.'

Colin looks up. 'Bones?'

'He's a paleontologist.'

Colin says it'll only take him an hour to deal with St Ives, so I send him off by himself. I need time to mull over what he told me about his ex-wife. Plus I'm too stiff and sore to walk around a big old house, listening to a hopeful estate agent gush about inlaid marble and fitted bathrooms.

Climbing upstairs is a challenge. I search out fresh linens

and change Claudia's bed – we made a proper mess of it – and scoop clothes off the floor. My green satin panties are torn. I toss them in the trash. A musky aroma – something old, something a little bit forbidden – lingers like the touch of a secret lover. I wipe the dust from Alexandra's portrait with my sleeve and examine her face, looking for the woman I saw last night, but her heavy-lidded eyes give nothing away.

Sunlight slants through the shutters and falls in diagonal stripes on the floor. I open the window and fill my lungs with the smell of salt air. If only it were this easy to fling open the windows in Colin's mind.

I wrestle pillows back into their shams. I fluff them and make a nest on the bed. I crawl into it, pull Claudia's old quilt over me, and wonder how I'd feel if Richard had left me for another man and taken my sons halfway around the world.

The manor house is a bust and Colin returns at noon armed with warm pasties from the pub, a bag of chips, and two bottles of brown ale. He doesn't say a word about Nancy, so I don't either. It's as if we never had that conversation. I guess this is how he copes, just like he does with his parents. Pretends it didn't happen. Sweeps it under the rug. Or perhaps it's a case of moving forward and putting the past behind you.

Whatever works for him is fine with me. It's not my past we're dealing with, but I can't help but wonder how I'd react if I were in his shoes.

We pack a picnic and follow a path I hadn't seen before, down the cliffs to that crescent-shaped beach. I kick off my sneakers and pad down the slope carved by years of violent tides. Waves fling themselves onto jagged rocks. Surf sizzles like soapy foam around my feet and the wind fingers my hair. I breathe in the familiar smell of damp seaweed; dig my bare toes in wet sand.

Colin pulls me down beside him and picks up a stone.

'This is me before we met,' he says, drawing a large, uneven circle. 'This one is you.' He makes another, overlapping the first. 'And both are you and me – joined forever.'

I catch my breath.

'Before we're born,' Colin says, pulling me close, 'our soul splits apart and half of it is given to someone else. So, all of our lives we're looking for the person with that other half.'

Me, I'm your other half.

'And if we're lucky enough,' Colin goes on, 'to ever find that person, our soul can say, "At last, I can rest. I have found my missing half." He takes off his glasses, wipes them on the cuff of his pink shirt. 'When I saw you last year, coming down those stairs, I knew the love of my life was the girl I met thirty-five years ago.'

Leaning forward, I trace the outline of Colin's circles. His hand closes over mine. I shut my eyes, but this crescent-shaped beach – this sliver of sand with its towering cliffs and vibrant ocean – is still there. It's branded itself onto my brain and I can't shake the feeling that in some strange, unfathomable way that has nothing to do with Colin, I've come home.

Our last afternoon, we tramp along the cliffs, ploughing through waist-high patches of purple heather. We scramble over tussocks of sea grass the color of driftwood and stop to kiss when bells from the village church strike up a simple carillon.

'Forever, Jilly,' Colin says. 'For the rest of our lives.'

Can't get much clearer than that.

Still, it'd be nice to have him on bended knee, asking me properly.

Colin challenges me to a game of tag and we chase one another around the huge thickets of vanilla-colored broom that Claudia says are called, appropriately, 'Cornish cream'.

Gasping for breath, I collapse among dense little mounds of thrift – clouds of pink blossoms like balls of crisp tissue – and decide to bring one of them home. A memory of Cornwall to plant in my garden.

'They'll never let you back in the country with that,' Colin says.

I ease a plant from the ground. 'They will if they don't know about it.'

'What is it, anyway?'

'*Armeria maritima*.'

'You're not planning to dig up one of those, are you?' Colin points toward a clump of broom the size of Claudia's Morris Minor. 'I suppose you know what that's called as well.'

I laugh. '*Cytisus scoparius*.'

'I love it when you talk dirty. Let's go to bed.'

My longing for him is suddenly so powerful I have to lean on him as we stumble the last hundred yards to the cottage. Colin takes the flowers from my hands and dumps them in the sink. I reach for his face and draw my finger down his cheek. It leaves a trail of sandy wet soil and makes him look incredibly young – a kid who's been out playing in the dirt. He picks me up and kicks open the kitchen door.

'A girl could get used to this,' I whisper into his ear, peeking at Claudia's ancestors. They don't seem nearly as censorious as they did the first time Colin carried me upstairs. Reckon they must be used to us by now.

Later, when we're sprawled on Claudia's brass bed, sweaty and spent from loving one another, I glance over Colin's shoulder at Alexandra.

This time, she smiles at me. I swear she does.

I'm glad it's gloomy and gray. I couldn't leave Cornwall, or Colin, if the sun were out. But unlike the journey down when neither of us stopped talking for more than a minute, we're quiet for most of the five hours it takes us to reach the airport. Colin, because I assume he's wrapped in thoughts about returning to his other life; me because I can't quell the fear that by loving Colin I'm somehow betraying Harriet. Does he realize she's gay? He was charming to her at Lizzie's dinner party. The only sour note was Bea's joke about the innkeeper's daughter, and now I know the truth about Nancy, I'm not surprised Colin didn't laugh.

So, how do I tell him about Harriet and Beatrice? Or should I say nothing? Just invite them for a picnic when he comes in July and let the chips fall where they may? I know I'm being idiotic. I know my imagination has run amok and I'm seeing problems where none exist. Colin hasn't said a word against gays – just against his ex-wife, and I can't say I blame him for that.

We arrive at Heathrow in a deluge, park the car, and race for the terminal. Steam rises from damp shoulders. People shake off umbrellas, fumble for passports and tickets, wait patiently in line. Loudspeakers blare, children cry. Armed guards keep watch.

Welcome back to the real world.

After checking my luggage, we ride the escalator up to the small, dimly lit restaurant where we said goodbye the last time. Colin nudges me and asks if I'd like another gin and tonic. I settle for coffee and a toasted ham sandwich. He elbows his way to the bar, orders our food, and carries it back to the booth I've just claimed.

We're almost finished with lunch when Colin hands me an envelope. 'Don't open this till you're on the plane,' he says.

'Why not?'

'Save it for later.' He stands and makes his way back to the bar. Returns with a huge gin and tonic. 'Tradition,' he says, and we take turns tasting one another like we did with that mug of tea.

The loudspeaker announces my flight.

We relinquish our table to another couple and edge sideways through the crowd. It closes around me and I lose sight of Colin. He reaches for my arm and pulls me from our intimate hideaway into the open concourse and I feel like a newborn being expelled from a dark, cozy womb into the bright lights and babble of a delivery room.

Trolleys loaded with luggage rumble by. Oceans of people surge back and forth in the midday rush to catch planes for Rome and Madrid, Amsterdam, Paris, and Boston. Colin and I stand in the midst of it all clinging to one another like two souls washed up in a storm.

His voice is a whisper. 'You can't leave.'

Then ask me to stay here and marry you.

'They're calling my flight,' I say.

We walk, holding hands so tight I don't think there's any blood left in mine, to the point of no return. I won't see him again until the end of July. A bored-looking official hurries me through security and now I'm on the other side and I can't touch him any more. I drop my bags and turn around. Colin takes a step toward me. A policeman bars the way.

He's carrying a gun.

The airplane is packed, every row full. I shove my box with Claudia's squirrel calendar in the overhead bin, squeeze past a couple of businessmen, and sink into my window seat. I pull Colin's envelope from my purse – what's he going to surprise me with this time? – and gasp loud enough to make the man sitting next to me lower his *Financial Times*.

'Oh. My. God.'

I count the zeros again to make sure.

But no, it really is a ten followed by a comma and three zeros.

Ten thousand dollars?

He's given me a banker's check for ten thousand dollars?

No way can I accept this. I'll have to send it back. Then I finger my bracelet and remember Colin's words the last time we said goodbye.

It's the first of many things I want to give you.

After two glasses of wine, the numbers begin to sink in. I look at the check again and imagine all I could do with this money. Fix the roof, buy another car. Pay off my credit card. Or open a savings account and put a serious dent in my home equity loan.

Tell Elaine to take her business and shove it.

Yes.

Well, maybe not quite like that, but I'll stop accepting her work. I'll finish off what I have, do a bang-up job on the Summerwind project I've already committed to, and walk away.

She can find someone else to kick around.

I have a third glass of wine and decide it's time to tell Lizzie the truth about Colin and me. No more pretending we're just casual lovers.

Better practice my speech.

Twenty-three

Sands Point
May 2008

By the time we touch down, I'm almost word perfect. I'm also losing my nerve. The wine has worn off and I'm worried about Lizzie's reaction. She's not going to like learning she's been left out of my loop.

I'll go straight home and call her tomorrow.

No. Get it over with. Now.

So when I reach the village I hang a right and drive out to Lizzie's.

Fergus is in the barn, cutting wood. 'Hey, Jill,' he calls out. 'Nice trip?'

'Fabulous.' I wave at him and climb the steps into Lizzie's back porch. I can see her through the window, bent over the kitchen table working on a crossword, glass of wine at her elbow. She looks up and grins.

Maybe this won't be as bad as I fear.

'You're glowing,' Lizzie says. 'I guess you had a good time, huh?'

'The best.'

'Then sit down and tell me all about it.' She points toward her glass. 'Want some?'

'God, no.' I sink into a chair. 'I'll pass out if I drink any more.'

I'll also forget my speech. Stalling for time, I pick up Lizzie's cow-shaped salt-shaker and fiddle with its cork. How will she react to my news? I feel like a shit for having lied to her. Well, not exactly lying. More like not giving her the full story. Lizzie's a dear and I love her madly, but she's got a bee in her bonnet about Colin. She doesn't think he's serious. Okay, time for me to set her straight. Maybe I'll describe Cornwall and Claudia's cottage first, then make her laugh over my delusions about Alexandra's portrait, and after that I'll—

Lizzie reclaims her cow. 'Come on, Jill. Stop messing about. I'm waiting.'

Something, jetlag probably, hijacks my script. 'I'm going to tell Elaine to take her work and shove it.'

I don't know who's more startled by this. Lizzie or me.

She recovers first. 'You're joking, of course.'

'Dead serious.' I flourish Colin's check. Wave it under Lizzie's nose. God, did I really do that? What the hell's gotten into me?

'Ten grand,' Lizzie says, nodding. 'Very nice, but it won't keep you for more than a few months. You need to work and right now you need Elaine's business.'

'Not any more.'

Lizzie sighs. 'Jill, you're having an affair. I bet your feet haven't touched the ground all week. But what happens when reality steps on your toes? What if Colin decides he's had enough? Or you do?'

'This isn't an affair.'

'Looks like one to me.' Lizzie glances at Colin's check, lying beside her crossword on the table. 'Jill, this is exciting and glamorous and right now I'm envious as spit because you're having all this fun while I'm stuck here with—'

Fergus's chainsaw fires up.

Lizzie closes the window, turns to face me. 'Jill, I'm—'

'We're getting married.'

She jerks as if I just slapped her. 'What?'

'Colin and I are going to get married.'

'On the basis of a weekend at the beach and ten days in Cornwall? Are you mad? This is a cruise-ship romance. You barely know this man.'

'I've known him all my life.'

Not exactly true, but I'm in no mood to split hairs.

'You knew him as a kid,' Lizzie says. 'A teenager. Thirty-five years of life have happened since then. His mother committed suicide, his father abandoned him, he had a shitty marriage, and now he's living with a woman he doesn't love.'

She doesn't know the half of it.

Better not tell her about his ex-wife and Nancy. That'd really send her up the spout. Lizzie looks at me. I glance away, try to stop the flush that's creeping up my face. Dammit, she's right, but she's wrong, too. Yes, all that shit happened, but—

Lizzie grabs me by the shoulders. 'He's changed. So have you. It's called getting older.' Her voice softens. 'Okay, so when did this turn serious?'

I hesitate. 'At the beach.'

'In Cornwall.'

'No. Here.'

Lizzie lets go of me. 'Back in March?'

'Yes.' My voice is so quiet I can barely hear it myself.

The atmosphere in the room shifts and I feel as if I'm in the eye of a hurricane. High winds have already blown through – trees are down, the power's out – but you know the worst is yet to come.

'Why, Jill? Why?' Lizzie says. 'Why did you plan a wedding behind my back?'

She points to the fridge where a Union Jack magnet holds

a postcard of Land's End I sent her last week. Colin and I stood on the rocks and waved at her.

'I suppose this means you're going to live in England?' she says.

'Colin's coming here.'

'I don't believe it. I don't fucking believe it.'

'It's true. He is.'

Her blue eyes glitter with tears. Her dear, sweet face twists with pain. I barely recognize her.

'No, Jill. Not that. What I don't believe is that you didn't trust me enough to tell me the truth.'

I went to the mall without telling her. Bought luscious underwear. I was right about those Calvins. They looked stunning on him.

'I suppose you told Harriet,' she says.

I shake my head.

'The boys?'

'They have no idea.'

'Great, Jill. The most important people in your life are the last ones to know.' Lizzie glares at me. 'So, when did Colin break the news to Shelby?'

Again, I hesitate. 'He hasn't. Not yet.'

She pins me with a look. 'But he *has* asked you to marry him?'

Forever, Jilly. For the rest of our lives.

'No.' The word slips out before I can stop it.

'Then what the fuck are you thinking about?'

The closest I've come to a ring are those circles Colin drew in the sand. I step toward Lizzie, hold out my arms. I want a hug and I bet she does too, but she backs away.

'We don't need words to tell us we belong together,' I say.

Lizzie groans. 'Just because you've had the greatest sex since Claudius's wife screwed half of Rome doesn't mean squat if he doesn't leave Shelby, and it means even less if he doesn't ask you to marry him.' She gives an obscene little laugh. 'Or are *you* planning to ask *him*?'

'You're out of touch. Lots of women ask men these days.'

'Jill, *you're* the one out of touch.' Lizzie grabs her wine, takes a slug. 'Remember your pet peeve? Middle-aged men and trophy wives? Well, this is *my* pet peeve, Jill. Strong women who turn to mush the minute a man scoops them up.'

'Colin hasn't—'

Lizzie narrows her eyes. 'He's transformed you from an independent, confident woman into a nineteen-fifties house-wife. I'm surprised you're not wearing heels and an apron.'

'You've no idea what it's like for me, do you?' I say. 'You have a secure job, a devoted ex-husband, and your mortgage is paid up.'

'That has nothing to do with it.'

'The hell it does.'

'Jill, be reasonable.'

My self-control snaps like frayed knicker elastic. I'm too tired, too bloody tired and too bloody mad to care any more. Why can't Lizzie see it *my* way for once? Why does she have to be always right, and me always wrong?

'Stop raining on my parade,' I yell. 'I've found a man I love who wants to take care of me and you're fucking jealous.' I grab the back of a chair for support. 'You've always been jealous. I'm thinner than you. Younger. You couldn't hold on to Trevor so you're taking it out on me.'

There's a dreadful silence, punctuated by a chainsaw.

'I think it would be best,' Lizzie says, in a voice I've never heard before, 'for you to leave before I say something I'll really regret.' She presses her hands on the table and leans forward, head down, not looking at me. 'I can't cope with you any more.'

My temper needs a time out. 'Lizzie, I'm sorry.'

'Now, Jill. Go away. Now.'

Choking back sobs, I stumble onto the porch. I lean against the wall, shivering and breathing hard. My heart's pounding so fast I'm afraid to open my mouth in case it leaps out.

Behind me, the door opens partway.

'You forgot this.' Lizzie thrusts Colin's check into my hand. 'Your fee for services rendered.'

The door closes and I hear the lock click into place.

Twenty-four

Sands Point
May 2008

Tears blur my vision and I run a stop sign at the end of Lizzie's road. Almost hit a guy walking his dog. What the hell have I done? Why did I make such a balls-up of telling Lizzie the truth about Colin and me? I knew this would happen. I should've gone straight home. Slept on it and told her in the morning.

Heart pounding, I grip the wheel and turn onto Bay Street. A crowd in evening dress lingers on the sidewalk outside the Contented Figleaf. Waiters circle with trays; ribbons and posies dangle from umbrellas. Silver balloons hang from the branches of a dogwood tree. Someone's anniversary? A graduation?

A wedding?

My car mounts the curb. Bounces off. *Clang.* Metal strikes the ground and I catch a glimpse of dull chrome as my last hub cap rolls into the gutter. I pull over and sling it in the trunk. Slam the lid. A boy on a bike rides by and gives me a funny look.

Somehow, I get myself home without further mishap. I fall into bed and thrash about like the guy in that TV commercial whose shitty mattress has him tossing and turning all night. Red-eyed and exhausted, I get up at eight and spring Zachary from the kennel.

He's gone before I even unpack.

Clients call with more work than I can handle and my days are filled, but sometimes sadness catches me off guard. It seeps in the window, slides beneath the door. I close my eyes and see Lizzie's face etched like an old china plate from myriad days in the sun. I remember the way her lipstick always leaks into the small lines above her mouth, no matter how often she blots it, and I feel her arms squashing me into her heavy bosom whenever I need a good cry.

I told her she was fat. Inexcusable.

Guilt hands me the phone.

'Lizzie, I'm sorry. Please—'

A gentle click and the line goes dead.

If she'd slugged me in the stomach, I'm sure I could've breathed more easily. I stagger from my office to the living room and collapse on the couch. I look around for my cat, but he's nowhere to be seen. Desperate for something to hug, I snatch up a pillow and bury my face in faded green velvet.

Harriet calls to ask if I had a great time in Cornwall and to regale me with details about the second-grade play I missed. Anna was an ear of corn. Spoke her lines like a pro, and do I have any idea how many egg cartons it took to make her damned costume? How much crepe paper? I admit I don't have a clue.

Should I tell her about my fight with Lizzie? No, I'm still too raw, too confused. What about Colin's check? Ditto, because if I tell Harriet it's now hidden at the back of my sock drawer, she'll rant and rave about putting it in the bank.

For services rendered.

Lizzie's wrong. I haven't given up my independence. I don't

need Colin's money to survive, nor do I need Elaine's business. I'll find other clients. So, for now, I'm leaving the check where it is. If I don't cash it, I can't spend it. And if I don't spend it, I've proved I don't need it.

End of discussion.

Colin rings up. His dog is failing and he's dreading that last trip to the vet. And no, he hasn't found the right time to tell Shelby. But he will, soon. He promises.

Dammit, what the hell is he waiting for? Is he scared of confronting her? I know all about that. I spent years watching my father tread on eggs around my mother. I asked him, once, why he let her push him around. His face turned kind of gray and I thought he was going to throw up. I never asked again.

Armed with clippers and gloves, I pull weeds, hack at the wisteria, and find a spot for my little clump of thrift that survived its journey from Cornwall inside a plastic bag at the bottom of my suitcase. I scrub mold off the patio furniture and stamp out the burrows that run like varicose veins through the lawn. Mole control is Zachary's job.

Where the devil is he this time?

My garden will have to wait. I throw down my tools and head for the beach to look for my cat. No sign of life at the Graingers'. No dogs either. They're an odd lot. Nobody in town seems to know much about them. Tom doesn't appear to have a job and if he does, it's something he does on the quiet. I study his multimillion-dollar house. Its soaring rooflines and cantilevered decks must've given some poor builder a migraine. The back is mostly glass and there's a green market umbrella propped up beside the double sliding doors.

A flicker of movement catches my eye. Curious, I step onto the boardwalk that runs between the dunes and up to his deck. Sunlight glints on the glass. Another movement. I walk closer.

Something's in there. Trying to get out. Not a kid or a dog—

Zachary?

How long has he been locked up? A few hours? Days?

A rag doll, sprawled like a hit-and-run victim, lies on a picnic bench. I pick it up and sit down in its place, holding the doll in my lap. I stare at my cat. He prowls back and forth, tail vibrating like a compass. Miaowing. What am I supposed to do now? Break a window? Call the fire department? They hold a dim view of rescuing cats.

Doors open and slam shut. Voices call out.

I drop the doll on the bench and retreat to the edge of the deck. A dog barks and Zachary stops pacing. The door slides open and my cat streaks out, shoots past me, and leaps off the deck into the bushes. I make a move to follow him.

Behind me, someone says, 'Can I help you?'

Whirling around, I come face to face with Tom Grainger's wife.

She's even younger up close, no more than thirty. Below her loose yellow shirt, apple green tights sheathe long, firm legs. Her toenails gleam with red polish.

'My cat,' I say, 'was locked in your house, and—'

'Cat?' She points toward the bushes. 'But – that's *our* cat.'

Zachary erupts from a juniper with a mole.

Traitor.

'No, he's mine.' I keep an eye on my cat as he treads with extreme care across the lawn to avoid the inexcusable blunder of tripping over his prey.

'But we've had him since—'

Her protest is cut short by the Graingers' little girl – a flurry of dimples and dark brown curls – who skids to a halt in front of me. She looks up, eyes wide with curiosity. They're heavily lashed, a deeper shade of blue than her mother's.

Carrie scoops her up. 'Molly, this is our neighbor – Jillian, isn't it?'

'Jill, actually.' I nod toward Zachary. 'And that really is my cat.'

'I want Elsa,' Molly says, squirming to get down.

I pick up the doll. 'This?'

'No, she's talking about the cat.' Carrie shifts Molly to her other hip. Runs a hand through her blunt-cut brown hair.

'Elsa?'

'After the lioness in *Born Free*.'

'My cat's a male.'

Carrie laughs. 'I know, but Molly—'

Tom Grainger and his dogs burst out of the house. The Labradors snuffle around my feet. One lifts its head to my knees. I cover my crotch. 'My cat's terrified of dogs.'

Tom looks at me, eyes faintly mocking beneath brows as ragged as a parrot nest. 'Really?' He turns to Carrie. 'I didn't know we had company.'

'I've come to fetch my cat.'

His beard twitches. '*Your* cat?'

'Elsa belongs to Jill,' Carrie says.

'His name is Zachary, not Elsa.'

'I see.' Tom transfers Molly into his arms. 'Come along, princess. Let's go and find – Elsa.' He glances at me, then hoists the little girl onto his shoulders and carries her off the deck.

'Look,' I say, with an effort at friendliness. 'My cat's been disappearing, regularly, since that hurricane last September.'

'That's when we first saw him. We'd just moved in and Tom said he was a marsh cat.'

'He's a registered Abyssinian,' I say. 'And where, exactly, did you find him?'

'Under our deck. Eating a mouse.'

'How did you get him to come out?'

166

'Tuna fish and brie. It's all we had in the house.'

'He'll suck up to anyone for cheese.'

I look toward the lawn where Molly sits beside Zachary. There'll be hell to pay when Anna finds out he's got another girlfriend.

Carrie says, 'We won't encourage him any more. We'll get Molly a kitten, maybe from the kennel where we left Elsa' – she shrugs – 'I mean Zachary, last March.'

They put my cat in a kennel?

'We have family in Vermont,' Carrie goes on. 'Took the dogs, but my brother-in-law's allergic to cats.'

It all falls into place. 'Did you leave him at Happy Tails?'

She nods. 'How did you know?'

I explain about the *other* Abyssinian who stayed there and we share a companionable laugh. I like her. Pity I don't care for her husband.

'We took him to the vet, as well,' Carrie says.

'Was he sick?'

'No.' She hesitates. 'Tom said it'd be better if he was fixed.'

I stare at her. 'But he already is.'

She grins. 'The vet thought we were mad.'

My phone rings when I'm halfway across the patio, arms full of indignant cat, so I run, holding on to him, because if I put him down he'll probably bugger off again.

Please God, let it be Lizzie.

I pour Zachary into his straw hat, race for my office, and snatch up the receiver.

'Where were you?' Elaine says. 'I've been trying to reach you.'

I won't apologize. Not this time.

'I'm sending Summerwind Cove,' she says.

The big one. The *last* one. 'I'm ready.'

'Make sure it's perfect,' Elaine says, and I bite my lip to keep from saying something I'll regret. Only another few weeks. You can hang in that long. 'Eight pages, four color,' she rattles on. 'Use plenty of photographs, and don't forget to include floor plans and the map.' I hear a rustle of papers, then she adds, 'I'm including the text copy. Use it as is.'

She can't spell for toffee. It'll need a thorough edit.

'No problem,' I say.

'Don't lose my slides. They're irreplaceable.'

I suck in my breath. 'I'm so glad you pointed that out.'

'Yes, well,' Elaine says, and hangs up.

Summerwind Cove. Expensive. Posh. Luxury condos and timeshares. Eighteen-hole golf course, members only. Two five-star restaurants, a marina, six tennis courts, and the best beach in town. Helipad, probably, judging by all the choppers that buzz the village, though that could be Channel 8's traffic news. Anyway, Elaine won exclusive rights to promote and manage the place and she's hired me to make sure everyone knows.

And they will. I plan to pull out all the stops.

Then I shall bow, quietly, gracefully, out of Elaine's life.

Her assistant – a pale young man with granny glasses and spots – shows up thirty minutes later. 'It's all here,' he says, dumping a box the size of a surfboard on my porch.

Christ, it's heavy. I haul it into my office and slit the tape with a razor blade, lift out layers of floor plans and site maps, architectural blueprints, photographs, and half a dozen huge travel guides. No wonder the box weighs a ton. Digging deeper, I find Elaine's instructions wrapped around a stack of transparencies held together with a rubber band.

Don't lose my slides.

The cheek. The bloody cheek.

Twelve slides. I check them, twice, against Elaine's list and drop them into a sturdy brown envelope.

The phone rings. Is it Lizzie this time?

'If you're not busy,' drawls a voice I haven't heard in almost a year, 'I'll be needing a place to hang my hat.'

'When?'

'The usual,' Dutch says. 'I'm coming up for the Fourth.'

Lizzie's annual bash. The one I haven't been invited to.

'Sorry, Dutch, I'd like to oblige but I've got company from England that weekend.'

'Can't I bunk in with you?'

''Fraid not.'

He chuckles. 'Then I'm glad it's *that* kind of company.'

'It isn't, but you still can't share my room.'

'Oh?'

Something inside me lets loose and I tell Dutch about Colin and our plans to get married. Funny, really, to be spilling my guts to a guy I rarely see, a stranger almost, kind of like sharing one's most intimate secrets with a shrink, I suppose. Never been to one, so what would I know?

'Then I'm real happy for you,' Dutch says. 'And remember. I'd make a mighty fine bridesmaid.'

Dutch Van Horne?

In peach chiffon?

I can't wait to tell Sophie she has serious competition.

Three days before Sophie and Claudia arrive, I go shopping at Sam's Club and bump into Fergus. He's choosing fireworks. Pawing through cartons of bangers and Roman candles with the gleeful expression of a kid.

'Lizzie's at the deli stocking up for the party.' Fergus grins. 'We'll see you there, won't we?'

I shake my head. 'I have other plans that weekend.'

'I'm sorry,' he says. 'We'll miss you.'

Clearly, Lizzie hasn't told him.

Five weeks and two days since I trashed our friendship.

I've called three times, been hung up on three times, written a long, apologetic e-mail, and sent two goofy cards.

Nothing. No response.

I've dropped off Lizzie's radar.

And I've no clue how to get back on it again.

Twenty-five

Sands Point
July 2008

Temperatures are in the mid-nineties when my guests fly into Hartford. Sophie, a veteran globetrotter, takes extreme weather in her stride. I'm not sure about Claudia. This is her first trip beyond England's gentle climate.

I reach the barrier as they emerge from the jetway. Sophie, cool as a flute of champagne in white silk and cream linen, doesn't look as if she's just spent eight hours on a plane. Claudia, wrapped in a raincoat and clutching an enormous umbrella, looks ready for a monsoon.

We haven't had rain since the end of May.

After rounds of hugs and kisses, I shepherd my guests downstairs to claim their luggage. I warn them about the weather. The automatic doors swish open.

Claudia gasps. 'Oh, my,' she says, fanning herself. 'I didn't think it could ever get this hot.'

But she revels in it. Wearing Zachary's straw hat, she prowls the dunes with her sketch pad. She examines the vines, the wildflowers. Asks questions about the local fauna.

'What's this?' She bends to look at a horseshoe crab half buried in the sand.

'One of the oldest creatures on earth,' I tell her. 'Older than the dinosaurs.' I flip it over and show Claudia the reason for its name – the outline of a horseshoe on the underside of its body. '*Limulus polyphemus*,' I say. 'It's a living fossil and it swims upside down.'

'Show-off,' Sophie says.

I blush. My one claim to fame at school had been the ability to memorize Latin. A useless talent except when it comes to identifying obscure plants at the nursery – and showing off, of course.

'Well, I think that's splendid,' Claudia says, patting my arm. 'Now tell me all you know about raccoons. Where would I find one?'

I point toward a trash can. 'Raccoons live on garbage. Tonight, they'll probably tip that over and make a horrible mess.'

Claudia is delighted. 'Then I'll sit out here and wait.'

And I'll worry about rabies.

'You'd best sit on the front porch. My dustbins are in the driveway. You'll see plenty of action.'

The next morning, lying on my kitchen table, I find a pencil sketch of two raccoons, bibs around their necks, holding up knives and forks. Fish heads, garnished with potato skins and tea bags, lie on a trash can lid. A cat, licking its lips, watches from behind a picket fence.

While everyone else gathers at Lizzie's for the holiday, I plan a picnic of my own. Three Brits on a beach amid a bunch of Yanks celebrating their freedom from England.

Sounds about right.

I pack a cooler with spinach quiche, pasta salad, and a variety of fruits and cheeses. I stuff paper goods and plastic glasses into a basket, and I'm filling two insulated jugs with

wine and iced tea when my fax machine churns out a note
from Colin.

> I miss you so much I'm turning to liquid. I'm afraid the
> barman will find a large puddle in the morning and it
> won't be spilled beer.

Sophie drifts into the kitchen wearing a black tank suit,
leather sandals, and aviator sunglasses.

'My mother has the fashion sense of a sponge.' She adjusts
her Ray-Bans. 'I can't bear to look.'

Swathed in yards of cotton covered with parrots and palm
trees, Claudia struts and spins like a runway model. 'It's a
muumuu,' she says. 'I found it in a holiday magazine.'

Sophie groans. 'If only you'd left it there.'

Claudia's dress is a Van Gogh canvas. Great daubs of
orange and purple, turquoise and bright yellow. I love it.
Especially the red and green parrots.

The tide's coming in by the time we settle into the curve of my
favorite dune. A few yards down the beach, a small American
flag flutters from the top of an elaborate sand castle. I spread
out my blanket, give Claudia the sturdiest chair, and dig a
hole for the handle of her umbrella. Someone's radio plays
music from the sixties. Claudia smiles and nods her head to
an old Beatles tune. At the high-water mark, kids with buckets search for treasures among piles of seaweed and shells.
Others paddle in the surf and a group of teens plays volleyball
in the hard-packed sand by the breakwater.

We tuck into our feast and demolish it.

'I ate too much,' Sophie says. 'Anyone up for a walk?'

'I'm too comfortable.'

'So am I,' Claudia says. 'Run along. Jill and I need to talk
about our squirrels.'

I stare at her. 'We do?'

'Lazy sods.' Sophie saunters off.

'No, we don't, but we do need to talk,' Claudia says, folding unused paper napkins in half and laying them in the basket. She collects our dirty plates, stacks them as if they were fine china, and places them beside the napkins, and I'm reminded of our tea in Land's End when she rearranged spoons instead of telling me what was on her mind.

'Talk about what, exactly?'

'Your mother.'

I groan. 'Let's not ruin a perfectly nice afternoon.'

'I'm sorry, Jill, but it's time you learned the truth.' Claudia's face is somber. Her eyes are wary.

'The truth?'

'The reason Edith was so tough on you.'

This is something I'd like to know. 'I'm all ears.'

'Edith Hunter isn't your mother.'

What?

'She's your aunt.'

Around me life slows to a crawl, but sounds are heightened – waves roaring up the beach, the drone of hidden cicadas, a breeze whispering through sea grass. The perfume of beach roses wafts over me. I breathe it in. Simple, pure. Innocent. Then I close my eyes and try not to think.

Twenty-six

Sands Point
July 2008

'Your mother,' Claudia says, 'was Edith's sister. She was also my dearest friend. Her name was Katherine, but everyone called her Katie.'

I hear the words, but they don't register right away. Katie. Katherine. A beautiful name. The one I remember from childhood. I gave it to my daughter as a second name because—

Oh, my God.

Princess Katherine, fearless heroine of my father's bedtime stories. Our secret, he said. Don't tell anyone about her or the magic will vanish.

Sophie was right. My father *did* have someone on the side.

My mother.

Claudia reaches into the folds of her dress, pulls a ring from her pocket. Two tiny pearls inside a twist of gold. A lover's knot. She lays the ring on my palm. 'Your father gave this to Katie the day you were born.'

My father.

Graham Alistair Hunter. He crept around the house in his bedroom slippers. Never raised his voice except the night he broke his toe on the gateleg table. Always helped with the washing up.

A man with two lives. Two women.

I tighten my fist around the ring, bring it to my lips.

With just a few words, Claudia rearranges my childhood. A middle-aged man falls in love with his wife's younger sister. She's charming, adventurous. A budding journalist who wants to travel the world with her camera.

'But instead,' Claudia says, 'she ends up pregnant with you.'

'Does Sophie know about this?'

Claudia shakes her head. 'Only me.'

My anger rises like bile. I scoop a handful of sand, and clutch it so tightly my knuckles turn white. 'Why didn't you tell me before?'

'Let me explain first,' Claudia says. 'Then you can be as furious as you want. Okay?'

Slowly, I let sand trickle through my fingers. 'Okay.'

'For the first time in her life, Katie was scared,' Claudia says, so softly I have to lean closer. 'She wanted an abortion, but Graham and I talked her out of it.'

Shock, like a big bully, shoves me back in my beach chair.

'Jill, I'm so sorry.'

'Give me a minute, okay?'

Claudia pours two cups of wine, gives one to me. I gulp it down without stopping. 'Now, remember, this was fifty-three years ago. Society frowned on unmarried mothers back then, so Katie quit her job at the paper and moved to Cornwall.' She looks at me, smiles. 'A small cottage on the coast.'

'*Your* cottage?'

'I inherited it from my grandmother. It was still empty, so I told Graham to take Katie down there.'

Holy shit.

'Was I born there?'

She nods. 'In the middle of a blizzard. They didn't get to the hospital till noon the next day.'

Home. Claudia's cottage on the cliffs. Her bedroom with a view of the sea. Alexandra Forbes, winking and smiling at me. Did my parents love and laugh in that bed? Well, maybe not *that* bed but one just like it with brass spindles and linen sheets, soft pillows and . . .

I can't handle this right now.

'What happened to her?' I say.

'Your mother loved the sea,' Claudia says, turning to look at the water, alive with sailboats and windsurfers, children paddling under the eyes of watchful adults. 'She swam all the time, even in bad weather. It drove Graham mad. One day, she was caught by a current. There were rocks. He couldn't reach her, and she . . .'

I swallow hard. 'Drowned?'

'You were four months old,' Claudia says. 'I was scared your father was going to kill himself. If it hadn't been for you, I think he would have. But, somehow, he pulled himself together and gave his wife an ultimatum: accept Katie's child, or he'd take the baby and leave.'

If only he had.

'And because Edith was a respectable married woman and wanted to stay that way, thank you very much, she agreed to Graham's terms. You became *their* child. Adopted, of course, if anyone was brave enough to ask.'

All those years, trying to please a woman I thought was my mother.

Katie's ring slips onto my finger as if it belongs. 'Why didn't you tell me this years ago?'

'I promised your father I'd keep his secret till you were mature enough to understand.'

'Jeez, Claudia. I'm fifty-three. How much more mature can I get?'

'Age has nothing to do with it.'

'Okay, so why didn't you tell me last September?'

'Because you weren't ready.'

'What the hell can change in nine months?'

'You,' Claudia says. 'You've changed.'

Lizzie called me a nineteen-fifties housewife.

'How?' I ask.

'Love,' she says. 'It's made you softer, kinder. Given you a dimension you didn't have before. You glow, like Katie did, from the inside. You know what it's like for a man and woman to love one another to the point where nothing else matters. You didn't feel that way about Richard, did you?'

'No,' I say. 'Not even close.'

'Or anyone else?'

I shake my head.

'So you see,' Claudia goes on, 'you'd never have understood the depth, the intensity of your parents' love till you experienced it for yourself. And now that you have, well . . .' She raises her face to the sun, smiles at a memory only she can see. 'Watching Katie and Graham was like seeing both ends of the same rainbow.'

Down by the water a young woman with blond hair bends to pick up a toddler. 'Do you have a picture of my mother?'

'I'll give it to you later.' Claudia hesitates. 'About Edith.'

Aunt Edith.

'Next time you're in England, go and see her.'

My God, she's still alive. 'You know where she is?'

'In a nursing home, as sharp as ever and still bitter about the past.'

'You've seen her?'

'I visit once in a while.' Claudia scoops a handful of sand, lets it trickle between her fingers. 'It's time for you to forgive her, let go of that anger.'

'Forgive?'

'Edith did her best. I don't condone the way she treated you, but it can't have been easy. You were a constant reminder of her husband's infidelity.'

'I'll have to think about it,' I say.

Later that evening, after Sophie goes to bed, I study the photograph Claudia has given me. It's a close-up, thank goodness. Not one of those awkward shots with more background than people. The colors have faded but I can still make out my mother's cobalt blue eyes and my father's golden hair, just like my two boys. And me, a solemn-faced infant wearing a long dress and a ridiculous lace bonnet.

'You may keep the picture,' Claudia says.

'I'll restore it and send you a copy.'

Claudia draws her hand across Zachary's fur. He's snuggled between us, snoring, oblivious. 'Tell me,' she says. 'Why haven't we met Lizzie?'

My stomach curls into knots. 'We had a fight.'

'Do you want to talk about it?'

Five minutes later, she's nodding, understanding how I feel. How Lizzie feels. 'Remember how devastated Sophie was when you left England and married Richard without telling her?'

I should've expected this. 'Yes.'

'And then the baby? You didn't tell her about that either.' Claudia fixes me with a look that reminds me of Lizzie. 'At least, not until it was all over.'

'Point taken.'

'Lizzie will come round, eventually,' Claudia says. 'Right now, she's hurt because you didn't trust her with the truth.'

'What should I do?'

'Keep calling, even if she cuts you off. Let her know you still care.' Claudia smiles at me. 'The way you did with my daughter. It took you, what? Two years to convince her?'

Two years?
Will it take me that long to win Lizzie back?

On Monday, I drive Sophie and Claudia to the airport, full of mixed emotions about saying goodbye. I don't want them to leave. On the other hand, I need time to think, to mull over what Claudia's told me; I also need to scare up enough courage to open the box she left on my back porch with instructions not to look inside until after she and Sophie had gone.

'Have fun in Hawaii,' I say, when we reach the security gate. 'I'll need a detailed report when you get back to London.'

'You can have that right now,' Sophie says. 'I'm going to lie on a beach and drink mai tais while my mother—'

'Paints wildlife?'

Claudia winks at me. 'Surfers and beach bums.'

'Just don't bring any of them home,' Sophie says.

I hear the phone as I pull into my driveway. Four rings, then Colin's voice, ragged and harsh, talking to my answering machine. 'Jilly, I took my—'

I sprint inside, grab the receiver. 'What's wrong?'

'I took Meggie to the vet this morning.'

'Oh, no. I'm so sorry.' I throw my purse on the table and flop into a chair. Zachary jumps onto my lap and I hug him so hard he leaps off again.

'I had to let her go,' Colin says, sounding bruised. 'I held her paw while we said goodbye.'

'You're a whole lot braver than me,' I say, and remember the look of anguish on a woman's face when she raced into the vet's waiting room last fall while I was there with Zachary for his annual shots. She was cradling a tiny terrier wrapped in a quilt. The dog had a grizzled nose and milky eyes and its owner was so blinded by tears she knocked over a rack of pamphlets about flea control in her rush to reach the vet's office. I shed a few tears of my own when she emerged a few minutes later, wiping her eyes with the quilt and clutching a small empty collar.

Colin keeps talking and so do I, treading on one another's words because our connection has that irritating long-distance delay, like one of those low-budget films where the sound track is two beats behind the script. We both speak at once, then stop, unsure whose turn it is next. I'm desperate to explain about my parents.

'Colin, I have something to tell you, but—'

'About us?'

'No, it's my—'

I hear someone's voice. A woman, calling out to Colin.

'Then I'll watch out for your estimate,' he says, and hangs up.

Dammit, I wonder who I'm supposed to be this time? The guy from the brewery or the builder Colin's hired to renovate the barn? I know he has to pretend he's talking to someone else, but . . .

Oh, what's the use. No sense agonizing over this. He'll tell Shelby when he's ready and not before.

'This was your mother's,' Claudia had said, placing a brown cardboard box on my coffee table. 'Graham gave it to me the day of her funeral. He didn't want Edith to find it.'

'What's in it?'

'Letters, mostly.'

'Did you read them?'

'Your father invited me to, but I couldn't. They're a part of Katie that belonged to him. And now, to you.' She drew me into her arms and I smelled lavender, felt the softness of her lips as she kissed my forehead.

She wiped her eyes. 'But I did look through her photos and sketches.'

'Sketches?'

'Katie was brilliant with pen and ink. Charcoal, as well,' Claudia said. 'Despite what you think, I didn't teach you to draw. You inherited that skill from your mother.'

My mother, the artist. A woman I don't know. All I have are Claudia's memories, a box of photos and letters. It's not enough. I feel cheated. My father should've taken me away from Edith and brought me up by himself. He should've told me the truth. So should Claudia. Anger at them both burns a hole in my throat. Scalds my tongue. I swallow hard. This must be how people feel when they find out they're adopted.

My stomach heaves and I race for the bathroom, but nothing spews up except bile. I spit, brush my teeth, spit again and look in the mirror, half expecting to see one of those black and white masks where one side smiles and the other cries.

Didn't anyone consider *my* feelings? *My* needs?

Bloody hell.

I've spent the last fifty years wishing for a different mother and now I've got my wish, I don't know what to do with it.

Yes, you do. Open the box.

Don't be such a wimp.

Gently, I lift the lid. Brown paper flakes off and lands like giant freckles on my knees. Two bundles of envelopes, tied with frayed satin ribbon, lie on top of photos and drawings. I'll cope with those first. Less painful than reading old letters.

Scattered among snapshots of wildflowers and beaches, I find sketches of harbors and fishing boats, seagulls, an abandoned tin mine. Lighthouses.

He couldn't reach her, and she drowned.

Waves of sadness sweep up my throat, fill my eyes, and I cry till my belly aches from crying. Zachary sidles up and leaps onto my lap. His solid, purring presence is a comfort. I touch the yellowed envelopes, dry and brittle like the paper-thin skin of a very old woman. The ribbons have etched shallow grooves in the bundles, and each is addressed in a different hand. One is my father's familiar scrawl; the other, more formal and slightly oblique, could be my own.

I untie the knots and begin to read.

Twenty-seven

Sands Point
July 2008

Dusk has fallen by the time I finish, and I almost miss the last letter, wedged beneath a layer of cardboard I'd assumed was the bottom of the box. I ease the fragile blue paper from its hiding place. Katie's writing. Another note to my father, dated 9 June 1955. Three months after I was born.

Except, it's not to my dad.

> *Your father came down again this morning. He can't believe how you've grown since the last time he was here. Has it been two weeks? It seems so much longer. We lay beside one another on our lovely brass bed and listened to the waves crashing on our beach. Your father cradled you on his bare chest. Big mistake! You curled your fingers round a couple of hairs and pulled. He almost exploded trying not to yell because he didn't want to scare you. I managed to uncurl your fingers but when I went to take you from him he smiled and brushed me off. He loves you with all his heart, my darling daughter, and so do I.*

Laughing through my tears, I gulp and try to catch my breath. I wipe my eyes and read my mother's letter, over and over, till I know every precious word by heart.

Could there be another? I tear into the box and rip out its false bottom, scrabble through the envelopes, unfolding and refolding my parents' love affair, but there is nothing else. Not for me.

But that's okay, because I have all I need.

Shifting my cat to one side, I stand up, stiff and sore from sitting too long. It's time, I think, to open another piece of my past.

Is Claudia right? Am I strong enough now?

Two weeks before Emma Katherine was born, I made her a treasure box and decorated it with red butterflies and sunny yellow daisies. I drilled holes for the tiny gold hinges, then attached the delicate gold clasp.

Richard had snorted. 'What's with all the girly stuff? Why not trucks and trains?'

We didn't have ultrasound in those days, and amniocentesis was used only if the doctor suspected a problem. Richard wanted a son. But I knew I was having a girl. A little girl with eyes like the ocean and hair the color of nutmeg.

Her box lies in my cedar chest beneath layers of lambswool blankets, monogrammed sheets, and damask tablecloths. Wedding gifts I've rarely used.

I open the lid, peel back the tissue.

Everything's exactly the way I remember.

Cream matinee jacket with satin ribbons and yarn soft as a newborn's hair. *K2, wrn, sl 1, K1, psso.* How I struggled with that pattern.

A bonnet no bigger than my fist.

Six undershirts with snaps.

Two pairs of booties the size of small mushrooms.

The cake decoration from my shower, a tiny stork made from tinfoil and toothpicks.

I return Emma's treasures to her box and place it, along with Katie's, inside my cedar chest.

When I least expect it, my mother's letter steals up behind me like a loved one who puts their hands over your eyes and dares you to guess who they are. Cherishing her words, I smile and write gushy e-mails to my sons, painting a cheerful picture of my newly washed past. I receive an automated response from Alistair – he's somewhere in North Dakota, digging up dinosaur bones – and a worried phone call from Jordan. I assure him I'm fine, yes, really fine, and I promise to fill in the blanks when he and his brother come home in September for Labor Day.

I'll also tell them about Colin, and about Emma Katherine.

It's a lot to swallow. I hope they can handle it.

Determined to make a good last impression, I finish my project for Elaine two days before deadline. I drop by her office, leave the box with Quentin, her assistant, and make an appointment to return at ten o'clock Monday morning. I'll wear a dress, or a suit, and real shoes and perhaps I'll even wear pantyhose, if I can find any without holes. I'll show up five minutes early. I'll smile and make small talk with the staff and be professional and dignified when I tell Elaine we're through. Maybe we'll manage to part on good terms, although I doubt it. Elaine's not the forgiving sort.

After picking up a loaf of French bread and a carton of milk from Tuttle's, I drive home with a delicious sense of accomplishment, kick off my shoes, and climb into cutoffs and a T-shirt.

Three more days and it'll be over.

I'll have paid my dues, with interest, which means I'll never have to deal with Elaine Burke again. To celebrate my freedom, I write a long e-mail to Colin and I'm about to push SEND when Quentin rings.

'One of the slides is missing.'

'That's impossible,' I say. 'Did you count them?'

'Of course.'

'Please check again.'

There's an awkward silence, then Quentin says, 'Elaine wants you to come right over. With the slide.'

'But it's not here.'

I hear a click and Elaine's voice interrupts. 'Jillian, where's that slide?'

'I don't have it.'

'Of course you do. Where else would it be?'

My self-control slips. 'I never lose photographs.'

'You have this time,' Elaine says. 'I trust you'll find it and bring it over without delay.'

Could I have lost that damn slide? Highly unlikely, but I give Elaine the benefit of the doubt and tear my office apart. I move furniture, upend boxes and waste bins, and reach into unknown territory between my desk and the file cabinet. I find several items I didn't know were missing, but Elaine's slide isn't one of them. I'm about to call her back when she beats me to the punch.

'Did you find it?'

'No, Elaine, and I didn't lose that slide. It has to be—'

'You do realize, don't you, all the trouble you've caused by—' There's a lengthy pause and I hear Quentin's voice in the background. A door slams, then Elaine's back on the line. 'Never mind. It's been found,' she says and rings off.

Just like that.

No apology. Not even a hint of remorse. All this trauma

over a fucking slide. Whoever said don't sweat the small stuff has obviously never worked for Elaine.

The bitch. The sodding awful bitch.

She's not going to get away with it. Not this time. I snatch my keys from the counter, race for my car, and roar out of the driveway, wheels spitting gravel like buckshot. I stamp on the gas and jackhammer down my dirt road as if the marsh cats had turned into tigers and were chasing me.

Halfway to the village, I cut my speed. No sense risking a ticket. Why the hell do I let Elaine goad me like this? Stumped for an answer, I swerve into the alley behind her building, slam the Volvo into a reserved parking space, and wrench open the door. Stop a minute and think. Maybe this isn't such a hot idea. Rampaging into Elaine's office, unannounced and barefoot, isn't the businesslike image I'd planned to present.

Jill, go home. Right now. Shower. Change.

No.

Revenge. I want full-blooded, face-to-face revenge.

Or, at the very least, an abject apology.

So, wearing grubby shorts and a T-shirt with the words CLEVERLY DISGUISED AS A RESPONSIBLE ADULT across the front, I charge into Elaine's front office and surprise everyone there by demanding to see the boss. Immediately.

'She's busy with a deadline.'

'Too bad.' I shoot Quentin an evil grin.

He shrugs and waves me into her office. 'It's your funeral.'

The door whispers shut behind me.

Elaine's inner sanctum is a cliché of chrome and glass, leather upholstery, and the overpowering smell of money. The whole back wall is a window that overlooks the harbor. Her forty-foot cabin cruiser is tied up below. Wearing a sleeveless black tunic over taupe linen pants, Elaine is holding a slide up to the light, head tilted in such a way that her glossy auburn hair looks as if it's been painted onto her skull and varnished with polyurethane.

Thick carpet muffles my approach. I halt in front of Elaine's desk, clear my throat. She turns, drops the slide, and gasps, her mouth a crimson O of surprise.

'What are *you* doing here?' Eyes like boiled marbles bore into me. She's wearing colored contacts. Emerald. Last week, they were turquoise.

'Well?' Elaine taps a blood-red talon on her desk.

Never mind. It's been found.

'You accused me of losing that slide,' I say. 'But when it turned up in your office, you didn't bother to apologize.'

'Don't be childish,' she snaps. 'I'm busy. I don't have time to—'

'Apologies,' I say, 'take no time at all.'

In the outer office, a telephone rings.

'Whatever,' Elaine says, baring teeth that are whiter than teeth need to be. 'Is there anything else on your mind?'

Every deadline she's blown, all the criticism she's lobbed at me, the all-nighters I've pulled, the freebies I've never been thanked for, rise to the surface like farts in a bathtub.

And boy, do they stink.

I clench and unclench my fists and step back to fling open the door. 'I want everyone to hear this.'

'Jillian. Stop the drama and close the door.'

Two of Elaine's staff move closer.

'Working for you has been the most disagreeable experience I've ever had,' I say, loving every minute of my revenge. 'And I've put up with your rude and demanding behavior because, quite frankly, I couldn't afford to do otherwise.' I allow my words to sink in. 'Until now.'

Gasps waft in from the other room.

'Close that door.'

'If you want it closed,' I say, folding my arms, 'do it yourself.'

Silence.

Behind me, someone snickers. Elaine strides across the floor, slams the door. Her Realtor of the Year Award falls off the wall, bounces twice, and lands upside down on three inches of beige broadloom.

'I don't know why—' she begins.

'All you need to know,' I say, loud enough to be heard through the door, 'is that I'm terminating our business relationship. We're finished.' I point toward the slide. 'This was our last project.'

'But—'

'Find someone else to kick around, because I'm through being a target for your vindictive temper.' I turn and stalk out of Elaine's office without looking back.

Someone applauds. Quentin, perhaps?

Twenty-eight

Sands Point
July 2008

A week before Colin arrives, three clients back out of projects I've been counting on to see me through the summer.

'We need to reconsider our options,' says the Mercedes dealer.

Pompous prat.

'We've exceeded our budget for this year.' This from the guy who sells million-dollar boats. Bowling alleys with rudders and lace curtains.

The third one makes me sad. 'We can't afford you any more,' admits the owner of the Contented Figleaf. I had such great plans for promoting that dear little restaurant and they didn't include naked garden gnomes, either.

Okay, so what's left? Flyers for Tuttle's weekly specials, an article for *Paws and Claws* about feral cats, and the village's fall festival. My presentation is due at the chamber of commerce tomorrow.

I'll deliver it today, instead.

Gary Kesselbaum, a portly, fretful man with a mottled face who favors three-piece suits and a pocket watch, even in summer, is reclining in his swivel chair and talking on the phone when I edge through the door, arms loaded with folders. I dump them on a table, help myself to a cup of the chamber's free but truly horrible coffee, and scan the jokes in last month's *Reader's Digest*.

When Gary hangs up, I smile and place my proposal on his desk. This is the best one yet. Banners wide enough to span Bay Street, pennants and posters to adorn lamp posts and shop windows. Maps of the village with discount coupons. An article for the *Hartford Courant*. Radio announcements and a promise from Channel 8 in New Haven to give us a plug on the six o'clock news.

With a flourish, I open the top folder, but Gary doesn't even look. His eyes, pale and anxious behind horn-rimmed glasses, slide over mine and come to rest somewhere beyond my left shoulder. I turn, expecting to see someone else but there're only the two of us here.

'I'm sorry, Jill,' he says, 'but we won't be needing you this year.'

I stare at him, too stunned to reply.

'It's out of my hands.' Gary eases the collar of his shirt with his thumb and reveals an angry-looking heat rash. 'I'm no longer in charge of the festival.'

Fumbling for a chair, I sit down with a thump. What the hell is he talking about? This is *my* festival. I'm the one who suggested it when the chamber was looking for ways to extend the village's tourist season beyond Labor Day. I'd just struck out on my own and was desperate for clients so I tossed out the concept of a festival like the ones they have farther north during leaf-peeping season.

Hayrides and pumpkins and hot apple cider.

Chrysanthemums and cornstalks. Arts and crafts. Antiques.

A carnival for the kids. Discount shopping for the adults. Jazz concerts in the gazebo, foliage cruises along the shore. The town fathers jumped on the plan, and my graphic arts business was off and running. That was ten years ago. Since then, the festival's expanded from a one-day sidewalk sale to a week-long extravaganza that attracts tourists from all over New England and I've handled all its promotion and publicity. Without a contract. The chamber and I have a handshake agreement.

The hairs on my arm stand to attention. Is it me, or has the air conditioning been cranked up? I shiver. What the fuck is going on?

'So, who *is* in charge?' I ask.

Gary Kesselbaum clears his throat. 'Elaine Burke.'

'That bloody woman has blackballed me,' I complain to Harriet. It's Friday and I've conned her into wine and pizza on the beach. Anna and Beatrice are down by the water, digging for clams.

'I'm not surprised,' Harriet says. 'You charged into her office like a menopausal cowboy.'

'Jilly the Kid with six-guns and a hot flash?'

Harriet laughs. 'So, how many clients do you have left?' *None.*

'Enough to get by,' I say.

'Are you okay for money?'

I have ten thousand dollars in my sock drawer.

'I'm fine, absolutely fine.' Colin's check is going in the bank. I'm through being stubborn. What the hell, I can't *afford* to be stubborn any more. My behavior in Elaine's office has back-fired all over the village. Even my bread-and-butter accounts have bailed out, including Tuttle's Market. I'm still smarting over Jim's apologetic e-mail which showed up this morning. Elaine owns half the commercial real estate in town, so I guess she put the screws on Jim and the others. Probably threatened to double their rent if they didn't cut me off at the knees.

Harriet nudges me with her foot. 'How's it going with your book?'

'Archibald?'

'Anna's hoping for a story.'

'So am I.'

'Then you'd better get busy.' Harriet hands me another slice of pizza. 'Who's that?' she says, looking over my shoulder.

I gather my scattered wits. 'Where?'

She points.

Beyond the breakwater, Tom and Molly are pushing a doll stroller. Its wheels keep getting stuck in the sand. Every few yards, Tom bends to free them and I can hear Molly's laughter from here. She's wearing a red sundress with white polka dots and a red baseball hat on back to front.

'My neighbors,' I say. 'Tom Grainger and Molly.'

'Adorable,' Harriet says.

I assume she's not talking about Tom.

While pretending not to, I watch him help Molly climb the breakwater, and when her foot slips, my heart skips a beat. But Tom grabs her and swings her around and around. Molly screams with delight. Her hat flies off and her curls tumble free, bouncing like corkscrews across her honey-colored shoulders. Tom sets her down, then lifts the stroller over the breakwater and onto our side. What on earth are they doing? Taking Molly's dolls for a walk?

Anna looks up, abandons her clams, and skips over to meet them. Beatrice trundles after her.

Tom waves at us. 'Come on down.'

'Let's go,' Harriet says. She stands and brushes sand from her legs.

I look up. 'Must I?'

'Yes.'

Sighing, I walk down to join them.

Tom reaches into the stroller and pulls out a handful of red and gold fur. It squirms and tries to leap onto his shoulder. 'This is Elsa,' he says, sounding proud. 'Molly's new kitten.'

Anna stares in amazement. 'It's a tiny Zachary.'

Tom catches my eye and grins.

And no wonder. Molly's cat is an Abyssinian.

At eight the next morning, I wake up with laryngitis. Good thing I don't need to talk to anyone about work. Colin calls, but can't understand a word I say. Neither can Harriet when she phones to deliver a pep talk.

She reminds me to get busy with Archibald.

'Do it for Anna,' she says. 'Write the story for her.'

For inspiration, I slip in one of Jordan's CDs. *The Phantom of the Opera*. The music soars, fills me with joy. I open my mouth to accompany Sarah Brightman, but nothing comes out.

Suppose my parrot has laryngitis? What if he can't sing, and . . .

Nope, that won't work.

How about this? I'll introduce Archibald to a diva with laryngitis and pit them against an evil mayor who's hired the opera singer for his fund-raising concert. But the diva can't sing, so she persuades the parrot to do it for her, hidden inside her huge, feathery hat, except he gets stage fright and . . .

It's a bold story. It needs bold illustrations, so I drag out my acrylics, my pens and ink. I fill my sketch pad with broad brushstrokes and crisp lines, and breathe life into Archibald's puffed-up chest and my diva's double chins, polishing my pictures and words until they glow. I cruise the Web and visit sites for writers, learn about submissions and the probabilities of success.

Slim to none.

On Monday, I stuff Colin's check into my purse and head for the bank. Plastic yellow tape surrounds the parking lot. Police cruisers and fire trucks stand guard. A guy in a hard hat and orange vest waves his arms, keeps the traffic moving. What the hell's going on? A bank robbery? In our sleepy little town?

Nothing as dramatic, I learn when I stop at the post office. A water main burst and the bank will be closed for several days. Customers who want cash are advised to use the ATM at the supermarket. All other transactions will be handled at the main branch.

Hell, that's thirty miles from here.

I'll wait.

Four days later, Colin flies over and slips back into my life as if he'd never left it. This time, there's no hint of awkwardness. No doubts. No hesitation. Our lovemaking is slow and sensuous. There's no need to rush. We have two whole weeks to enjoy ourselves. We walk the beach at sunset, romp in the surf, and spend hours in my room listening to the waves and talking about books we've read and the places we want to go. Colin drags my television upstairs and we rent a pile of old movies including *From Here to Eternity*, and I make love with my pretend Burt Lancaster while watching the real one on the screen.

Later, over dinner and a bottle of wine, Colin asks to see my mother's letter, her ring. He raises it to his lips, then slides it onto my finger.

Oh, my God.

Is this it? Is he going to ask? I close my eyes and wait for the magic words. *Come on, say them. Don't stop now.*

Dear God, I'm worse than a lovesick teen.

But the moment passes and now he's running his tongue down my neck, fondling my breasts. I grasp his hands to still them and ask about our future. He smiles and kisses my cheek, nibbles my earlobe. Be patient, he whispers. It'll come, I promise.

When, goddammit, when?

Colin wants to explore. His enthusiasm for New England is contagious, so I cross my fingers and pray the Volvo will go the distance. With gentle coaxing, it shudders up mountains in New Hampshire and slides toward the coastline of Maine where Colin and I stand on the beach in Kennebunkport, holding hands and talking about Cornwall. Someday, we promise one another, we'll return to Claudia's cottage.

We drive to Rhode Island and spend the day in Newport, tramping through mansions and admiring boats in the harbor. At sunset, we stop for dinner at a restaurant perched high on a cliff overlooking Narragansett Bay and Colin has his first taste of a New England boiled dinner.

I try not to laugh at his startled expression.

'Where do I begin?' he says, poking at the tangle of shells and legs on his plate.

I hand him the nutcrackers. 'Use these and put on a bib.' Then I reach for my camera. 'Smile.'

'Wait.' Colin cracks open a claw. 'See, I'm getting the hang of this,' he says, waving a piece of lobster as I click the shutter.

We return after dark and I coast into my driveway. I kill the engine and pat the dashboard. 'Thanks,' I whisper.

Colin grins at me. 'Relief?'

'I wasn't sure we'd make it.'

'Maybe it's time for a new one.'

I feel a rush of affection for the Volvo. 'I agree, but don't tell my car.'

Twenty-nine

Sands Point
August 2008

Zachary curls around my legs and complains the minute I step inside. I feed him and check for messages in my office. Nothing. No one begging for my services. No word from Lizzie, either. No reaction to my latest olive branch, a postcard of our beach with the words WISH YOU WERE HERE scrawled across it that I hoped was corny enough to make her smile. I walk back to the kitchen and find Colin spreading cream cheese and strawberry jam on a bagel.

'Dessert,' he says, licking his fingers.

'On top of all that lobster we ate?'

'Why not?' He leans forward and smears jam on my cheeks, my nose, my mouth. I lick my lips. He kisses me. 'You taste like that cream tea we had in Cornwall,' he says, kissing me again.

Dammit, now I want dessert as well. Pushing Colin to one side, I open the fridge and pull out a tub of vanilla pudding left over from Anna's last visit, a can of whipped cream, maple syrup, and more jam – apricot, I think. Or maybe it's marmalade. I dump it all on the counter and reach into a cupboard. What about this jar of honey, and who left that bottle of Grand Marnier in here? My hand curls around a packet of ladyfingers. Probably stale, but if I soak them in—

Colin pours syrup down the back of my neck.

'What the—'

He spins me around and pours more down the front. He's laughing, the sadistic sod. My blouse is soaked. I wrench it off and Colin squirts whipped cream across the swell of my breasts. Syrup dribbles between them. He shrugs off his shirt and unsnaps my bra. The one that fastens in front. I knew it'd come in handy one day. Grasping my shoulders, he bends to lick the syrup off my breasts. He sucks the cream off my nipples and I have to lean against the counter because my knees are about to give out.

'Let's continue our feast upstairs,' he says.

We load our loot on a tray and take it to my room.

We've perfected the art of shedding our clothes in a hurry and my panties hit the floor at the same times as his briefs. My green robe is draped across a chair. Colin reaches for it, removes the belt, and winds it around his hands.

'Lie back,' he says. 'Relax.'

I sink into the pillows and Colin ties my wrists to the bedposts and there's nothing I can, or want to, do about it. Fingertips dripping with honey, he draws cat's whiskers on my breasts and eyelashes above my nipples. He paints a smiley face on my belly with vanilla pudding. I twist and squirm, but the green silk holds firm and I'm about to explode when his tongue travels south to lap up the apricot jam he's smeared on the inside of my thighs, and I know I ought to be worrying about the mess we're making on the linen sheets he bought me last week and paid a fortune for, but multiple orgasms have a way of making one cavalier about the laundry.

He releases my hands, kisses my wrists, my fingers, but refuses to let me tie him up.

'Not fair.' I tickle his chest with emerald satin.

He slides both hands beneath his back. 'I promise not to interfere.'

I massage him with Grand Marnier, shampoo his hair with whipped cream until it stands up in stiff spikes. I dribble honey on his lips and savor the sweetness of him. But when I write *I love you* with maple syrup on his erection and lick the words off, Colin forgets his promise. He rears up and crushes me so hard I stick to him like Velcro. We pull apart to a chorus of slurpy, sucking noises and try to make love, but we're laughing too much. He can't keep it up and I can't stop giggling and we desperately need a shower. I climb off the bed and head for the bathroom.

Colin grabs my arm. 'I have a better idea.'

'What?'

'Let's go for a swim.'

'Like this?' I say, looking down at my naked, sticky body.

'Why not?'

'Someone might see us.'

'At this time of night? Don't be daft.'

We wrap ourselves in towels and race out of the house, across the back yard, and onto the beach. I jump over a piece of driftwood and my towel falls off. Colin knocks me down with a flying tackle and we roll toward the water, over and over, laughing and screaming, till we look like two Krispy Kreme doughnuts after they've been glazed and coated with sprinkles. Not exactly my movie fantasy, but close enough, I think.

I sit up and spit sand from my mouth.

'You're a mermaid,' Colin says, plucking a shell from my breasts.

I pull seaweed from his groin. 'So are you.'

'Hardly,' he says, looking down.

He pushes me over and climbs on top.

'Not here,' I whisper.

'Please.'

'I can't.'

He slumps on top of me and groans and I know how he feels, because I want it too, but not out here. Not on the beach. I'm about to shove him off when something large and hairy and definitely not human blunders into us, kicking sand in my face and digging its claws in my legs.

'What the fuck was that?' Colin says, struggling to sit up.

I look left and right. 'Watch out!'

Too late.

The second Lab crashes between us. Its tail slashes my face and another set of claws rakes furrows in my thighs. Colin puts his arms around me and I burrow into him. Our towels are way up the beach.

Behind me, someone whistles.

Shit!

Tom Grainger.

Oh, God. I can see the headlines now – LOCAL WOMAN FROLICS NAKED ON PUBLIC BEACH WITH LOVER. Village tongues will be wagging for weeks. Bad enough I've screwed myself with Elaine Burke, I've probably screwed myself with the neighborhood as well.

It feels like an hour but it's really no more than a minute before Tom and his dreadful dogs go back where they came from. I scramble to my feet and plunge into the water with an urgent need to wash myself off. Not just the sand and the syrup, but the sheer embarrassment of it all, the feeling of utter helplessness over being caught naked on the beach at 2 a.m. by a neighbor I dislike and knowing there's not a damn thing I can do about it.

Colin charges in behind me, laughing and splashing. He doesn't seem the least bit bothered by all this. And why should he be? He doesn't live here. He won't have to wonder, like I will the next time I walk to my mailbox, if that accusing look from the old biddy who lives two houses down is because she heard from her neighbor that *Jillian Hunter – you know, the woman with the odd-looking cat – was on the beach at midnight, naked, yes naked, as in no clothes, not a stitch, with a man and they were, well, doing it. I mean, it's obscene, that's what it is. Just think, it could've been me that found them, and let me tell you, if it had been, I'd have told that hussy a thing or two.*

Of course, I'm being totally ridiculous because I don't even know the woman who lives on the other side of Tom Grainger and I doubt she'd recognize me in full daylight, let alone in the dark, naked or otherwise. Feeling exposed and vulnerable, I try to wash. I scrub and scrape at my skin with my fingers, but discover that salt water doesn't cut it when it comes to removing apricot jam, maple syrup, and honey.

Or shame.

Colin grabs me from behind, runs his hands over my bare rump.

Ducking away, I try to explain I'm not in the mood for fun and games any more, that what just happened is really bothering me. I remind him he doesn't have to live here, and I do.

'Then let's go to New Zealand,' he says.

I stop scouring. 'Are you serious?'

He nods.

'When?'

'Late October, or maybe early November. It'll be spring down there. A perfect time to go,' he says, wiping sand from my cheek. 'We'll take a month. Five weeks, maybe. Can you get away for that long?'

I nod, because of course I can. Colin doesn't know about the mess I've made of my business. His check, dammit, is still in my purse. I never did get to the bank, but I will, the minute he leaves. I'll take care of my overdue bills and make arrangements for others to be paid while I'm gone. I can take four weeks, five if I want. No problem. Except for my cat. Maybe Harriet will have him. Anna would love it.

Shyly, I ask Colin if he's ever taken Shelby to New Zealand.

'She never wanted to go,' he says, hugging me. Water, black as ink, swirls around us. His arms tighten. 'Jilly, say you'll come with me.'

'Of course I will,' I mutter into his wet chest.

Harriet calls to reschedule our Friday-night barbecue. 'I'm sorry, but Bea's on a business trip. Could we come Saturday, instead?'

I hesitate because Colin leaves on Sunday and I don't want to share our last day with anyone. On the other hand, I'm anxious for him to meet my friends again, to get to know them properly this time. When I told him Harriet and Beatrice were coming over, he asked if Fergus and Lizzie were coming too, and I lied and hated myself for lying. I said they'd gone to Virginia and were sorry to have missed him. No way can I tell him the truth about my fight with Lizzie, not after what happened last night.

We were in bed, and although it wasn't exactly the best time to bring it up, I couldn't help myself. I asked when he was going to make the break with Shelby. Not that I was pushing him, mind you. I just wanted to know because, well, I had to figure out a few things for my business. Then, of course, I went whole hog and told him how I'd canned Elaine.

'That wasn't very smart,' he said.

At first, I thought he was kidding. I pretended to be indignant which wasn't easy given I was naked and straddling his belly. He pushed me off and turned away. I still didn't think he was serious, so I wrapped my arms around him and snuggled into the small of his back.

He stiffened, then told me I ought to mend my fences with Elaine.

I wasn't expecting that.

'It's for your own good, Jill,' he said.

Behind him, I buried my face in the pillow to muffle my sobs. I couldn't figure out what had upset me the most. The way he avoided the issue of telling Shelby about us, or what he said about my dumping Elaine. Or was it because he'd just stepped off his pedestal and I couldn't handle it? I closed my eyes and tried to will him back on it. I needed him up there where he belonged. Then he turned toward me and wiped my eyes and we tried to make love, but it kind of fizzled out.

Or rather, he did.

Harriet's voice hauls me back to the present. 'Jill? Are you still there?'

'Let's make it lunch instead of dinner, okay? Colin's flying home the next day, and . . .'

'I promise we'll leave promptly at four.'

I let out a sigh, grateful for friends who understand.

Harriet and family show up at noon armed with beach chairs and blankets and a positively sinful dessert with strawberries, meringue, and whipped cream. I shove it in the fridge and pull out the salads and chicken I prepared, and we take them outside where Colin is firing up the grill. He offers to cook.

'I see you've got him house-trained already,' Beatrice says.

'He mowed the lawn as well,' I say.

Anna tugs at my sleeve. 'Jill, can we go find that giant snail?'

'*Giant* snail?' Harriet raises her eyebrows. 'Should I be worried?'

'Absolutely. These guys grow to eight, nine inches or more,' I say, winking at Anna. 'They vacuum up clams and steal bait from lobster pots.'

'Impressive,' Beatrice says, 'for a measly old mollusk.'

Ever since I showed Anna a picture of a channeled whelk, she's been determined to find one. She wants to hum at it the way I've taught her to hum at smaller snails, like the periwinkle she's just found beneath a plant pot and is now handing to Colin. He puts down his spatula and examines the snail.

'Would you like me to cook this for you?' he says.

Anna squeals and snatches it back. 'No, you have to hum.'

Colin shoots me a puzzled glance, so I tell him that if you hum, in a boring sort of monotone, the snail will eventually poke its head out of its shell.

'Will it say hello?' Colin asks Anna.

'Don't be silly,' she says. 'Snails don't talk.'

'But if they did,' he persists, 'what would they say?'

She ponders this for a minute while the rest of us struggle to keep from laughing out loud. 'I think,' Anna says, with a perfectly straight face, 'they'd ask what the snail said when it rode on the turtle's back.'

'Wheeeeee?' Colin says.

After lunch I invite Beatrice for a walk because I want to ask her something and don't want Colin and Harriet to hear. We settle ourselves comfortably on a pile of smooth rocks and let our feet dangle in the shallow, sun-warmed water of a tide pool teeming with small, darting fish and dozens of hermit crabs.

'If this is out of line, tell me to shut up.'

'Okay,' Beatrice says. 'Shoot.'

'What's it like, moving into a house owned by someone else?'

Beatrice doesn't even hesitate. 'Difficult.'

'Suppose you bought half of it?' I ask, thinking about Harriet's painted lady on Bay Street. It's a pearl gray Victorian, with a rose pink front door, green and lavender trim, and a turret. Anna calls it their gingerbread house.

'We've discussed it,' Beatrice says, 'but it doesn't work because everyone, including me, always thinks of that house as Harriet's.' She bends to scoop a hermit crab from the water. Its shell is at least six inches. Maybe more. 'Is this one of those giants you were talking about?'

'Yes, and Anna will be thrilled,' I say. 'Even if the whelk is long gone.'

'D'you suppose the crab ate it before taking over?'

'More likely an angry lobsterman. They get pretty pissed at these things for pinching their bait.'

Beatrice tosses it back. 'We'll show it to Anna later. It's not going anywhere. At least, not till the next tide.' She wipes her hands on her shorts. 'So, where were we?'

'Sharing a house.'

'The only way it really works is for the couple to sell both their homes and buy something together. Fifty-fifty. Equal partners.'

'I was afraid you'd say that.'

There's a slight pause. 'Harriet and I just started looking.'

'You're not leaving the village, are you?'

'Of course not. We love it here. We want something with a bit more land, enough space for a garden . . . and a barn. Anna wants a pony,' Beatrice says, massaging her legs, 'and I want a house without stairs. I can't handle them any more.'

'Have you put Harriet's house on the market yet?'

Beatrice shakes her head. 'We're turning it into a professional center for attorneys, dentists, and doctors, with a sexy robot at command central for e-mail and faxing.'

We laugh, and then I describe Colin's lodge in the Cotswolds.

Beatrice sighs. 'Sounds utterly divine. How can he bear to leave it?'

'I asked myself the same question, but he is. He's coming here to share mine.'

'Big mistake.'

'Colin loves my house.'

'And I love Harriet's,' Beatrice says, 'but it just doesn't work. Trust me. I've been there and done that. Sell your cottage and buy something else with Colin.'

I'm about to argue when Anna runs up with a bucket, followed by her mother. Beatrice points to the giant hermit crab, tucked up against a rock.

Anna flops into the pool. 'Jill, what's it called?' she asks, poking it cautiously. The crab's claws are out and they're big enough to bite a small finger.

'A hermit crab,' Harriet says, peering over Anna's shoulder.

'No, the shell.'

'This,' I say, pulling it from the water, 'is a channeled whelk.'

'I know *that*,' Anna says, eyes widening at the sheer size of this precious monster. 'What's the shell's *other* name?'

I grin at her. '*Busycotypus canaliculatus*.'

'Bet you can't get your tongue around that one,' Harriet says, ruffling her daughter's unruly curls.

Anna sniffs. 'Mom, it's Latin, and Jill's been teaching me.'

'Really?' Harriet pretends to look surprised.

After promising Anna more lessons the next time she's over, I walk back up the beach to join Colin. He's sprawled on the blanket, eyes closed, one arm bent above his head, and his face is flushed. I rummage in my bag for the sunscreen and smooth it over his forehead, across the tops of his cheeks, and down his nose. He rolls toward me, deliciously rumpled and smelling, faintly, of the sex we had this morning. I instigated it. I don't normally, but after what happened the other night, I wasn't taking any chances. And the sex was fine. In fact, it was quite marvelous, despite Colin's rolling away afterward and turning on the TV. He wanted to watch the news. I wanted to cuddle, but made breakfast instead.

'Thanks,' he mumbles, sitting up.

I lean against him, feel the weight of his arm across my shoulders, the heat of his thigh pressed against mine. He takes my hand and circles my palm with his thumb. Pleasure zings through my body, turns into an ache between my legs.

Would anyone notice if we sneaked upstairs?

What will it be like when we're together all the time? Will the urgency fade? Will the humdrum of daily life turn us into a couple who has sex on Saturday nights and once every other Thursday? I can't imagine not wanting his body, his mouth . . .

Squeezing my legs together, I gaze at the water and count five sailboats, seven windsurfers. Two jet skis making more noise than enough. Beyond them, the tip of Long Island hovers like a mirage just above the horizon. Colin shades his eyes and looks toward my friends by the rocks, still heavily involved with the hermit crab. Anna's holding it up, quite confidently now, and Harriet's shaking her head, no doubt hoping to convince her daughter it's not okay to bring it home . . . that this creature needs to live here. On the beach, with its buddies.

Anna drops her crab in the pool.

'She's a sweet kid,' Colin says. 'What does her father do?'

I hesitate. 'She doesn't have one.'

'Come on, Jill. Everyone has a father,' Colin says. 'Even if they don't amount to much.' He shudders. 'Like mine.'

'Harriet chose Anna's father, carefully, and—'

'She did a damned fine job,' Colin says.

I hesitate. 'Anna doesn't see her father, because—'

But Colin interrupts. 'Then I feel sorry for him,' he says. 'Not knowing what a great little girl he has.'

'He doesn't want to know.' I pause. 'He isn't allowed to know.'

Colin looks at me. 'Why not?'

'Because he's anonymous. That's the deal.'

'I don't get it.'

'Harriet's a single-mother-by-choice. She selected Anna's father from a sperm bank.'

Colin turns away from me, back toward the group. Anna's crouching in the tide pool, peering into her bucket, and Beatrice and Harriet are sitting on the rocks, side by side, feet dangling in the water. And then Beatrice, not normally one for public displays of affection, even with Anna, takes Harriet's hand and Harriet lays her head on Bea's shoulder and these simple, loving gestures make it quite obvious how they feel about one another.

'You should have warned me,' Colin says, sounding brittle.

'I thought you knew.'

He shakes his head. 'Well, I do now.'

Thirty

Sands Point
August 2008

I spend the rest of the afternoon making sure the conversation is upbeat because I can feel Colin's tension and I'm worried he'll get up and wander off down the beach or go back inside and Harriet will guess something's wrong, or Beatrice will, and then I'll have to explain why he feels the way he does and I really don't want to.

Fuck.

I should've told him sooner, but I honestly thought he'd have figured it out by now.

'How about dessert?' I say.

'Yippee,' yells Anna.

Thank God for the innocence of small kids. We gather up our belongings and troop inside. I pull Harriet's confection from the fridge, serve generous portions, and set them on the kitchen table with spoons and napkins and glasses of ice tea. Colin inhales his without stopping. Would he like more? Harriet asks, clearly pleased. How about the recipe? Beatrice chimes in. He takes another helping.

Harriet glances at the clock. 'We'd better get going,' she says, scooping up wet towels, Anna's discarded bathing suit, and Beatrice's canvas bag. She lumps them together under one arm and holds out her free hand to Colin.

'I hope we'll see you again soon,' she says.

He nods, curtly. 'Yes. Of course. Same here.'

Beatrice takes over. She hugs me and punches Colin in the arm. I watch him tense up. He bites his lip, and when Anna wraps her arms around his legs he stiffens, visibly this time, before patting her head and disentangling himself, and I hear Harriet making a noise in her throat.

Oh, shit, this is all going wrong.

Zachary scoots past us and squeezes through the screen door. Anna runs after him. So does Harriet, and then Beatrice, and before following them, I tell Colin not to come with me. 'I'll handle this.'

He shrugs and turns away.

I force myself to go outside. Beatrice is strapping Anna into her car seat and Harriet's shoving their stuff in the trunk. She slams the lid, whips around to face me.

'Look, Jill, I know it's not your fault, and I know I'm making too much of this, but right now I'm incredibly hurt.'

'There's a reason,' I say. 'I can explain.'

Harriet leans against her car. 'Okay. Go ahead.'

'Colin's ex-wife took their daughter to New Zealand,' I say. 'He hardly gets to see her, and the ex-wife is, well, she's . . .' I find myself scrambling for the right words, but they won't come and no matter what I say, or how I say it, it's going to come out badly.

'I take it,' Harriet says, in a voice designed to shred opposing attorneys, 'you're trying to tell me Colin's former wife is gay?'

I nod and slump against the fender.

'And this is a big deal?'

'It is for him,' Beatrice says, coming to stand beside Harriet. 'But it isn't for Jill, and you and I know that, so let's not have this turn into something ugly.' She takes Harriet's hand and squeezes it. 'Everyone's entitled to an opinion.'

'Like my mother,' Harriet says, pushing Beatrice out of her way to climb into the car. She rolls down her window and looks up at me, eyes brimming with tears.

Beatrice takes my arm and pulls me aside. 'She'll be okay. Just give her a few days to cool off and then call us.' She pauses. 'Oh, no, wait. I forgot. We're leaving on Monday.'

This is news to me. 'Where are you going?'

'Didn't Harriet tell you?'

I shake my head.

'San Francisco,' Beatrice says. 'I'm taking Harriet home to meet my family.' She squeezes my hand. 'Better wait till we get back.'

'When?'

'Labor Day.'

Harriet drives off and I see Anna's small hand waving out the window like a tiny white flag. I wave back. How long before I see her again? Two weeks? Two months? Harriet's blue Subaru bounces twice, swerves to avoid the giant pothole at the foot of my neighbor's driveway, and disappears around the bend in a cloud of dust and I'm left standing in my front yard with no wish to go inside and face the other half of my problem.

Whatever you do, don't come unglued.

My legs tremble. I wobble up the porch steps and fold myself into the rope swing that Colin bought in Maine and hung up for me, and I spin around in it till I'm dizzy with indecision.

What should I do? Take the ostrich approach and pretend nothing's wrong, or be honest and make an issue of it? What would the old Jill have done? Tackled him head-on, that's what. But this new, softer Jill is a bit foreign to me. I haven't quite gotten used to living inside her skin. I don't know how to react, what to say. I'm scared to open my mouth because, like an adolescent boy on the verge of manhood, I don't know what'll come out. And if I don't like what comes out, then what?

Back to square one.

It's worse than pulling petals off a daisy. I'm screwed no matter which way I turn.

The screen door creaks open and Colin steps onto the porch. He's obviously had a shower because his hair is slicked back, but why is he wearing a shirt and a tie and a pair of well-pressed slacks? Did we have plans to go out tonight that I, in my current crisis mode, have forgotten about?

'What's with the fancy dress?' I say.

Colin tucks his cell phone into his pocket. 'I need to go home.'

I stop swinging. 'Home?'

'To England.'

'Like, right now? This very minute?'

'There's a train to Boston at five thirty. I'm booked on the eleven o'clock flight from Logan to Heathrow,' Colin says, looking at his watch. 'Will you drive me to the station?'

He turns away and I unfold my legs, trying to escape from the swing, but my big toe is stuck in the mesh. I yank it free and tear off a strip of nail. Christ! That smarts. I grab my foot and squeeze hard to keep the pain at bay. The screen door creaks again. Colin's maneuvering his suitcase onto the porch. He leans it against the wall and bends to adjust the strap that holds his carry-on bag to the handle.

My God, he's packed already. 'What the hell's going on?'

'Problem at the Lodge,' he says, straightening.

'What sort of problem?'

'Something's come up.'

'Can't it wait until Monday?'

Colin shakes his head.

I study his face, searching for clues, but he's like a book I've opened at random. I can read the words and understand the phrases but they don't make sense because I've just landed in the middle of a puzzle, much like poor Alice when she fell down the rabbit hole.

'Then let Shelby and her sister cope with it,' I say.

He hesitates. 'They can't.'

Letting go of my sore foot, I lurch out of my rope nest and feel like screaming. Not because my toe is on fire, but because I've bloody well coped. I've spent a lifetime coping because that's what you do when there's nobody else to pick up the pieces, and when I think about women like Shelby and Diana who fall apart because a guest complained or the bartender quit or, heaven forbid, the florist delivered the wrong flowers, I get seriously mad.

'Come on, Colin,' I say. 'What's gone so horribly wrong it can't wait a few more days?'

He grips the porch railing and stares at my front lawn which he mowed, just this morning, into rows of neat, diagonal stripes. Sweat beads up and glistens on his forehead. He's flushed, partly from the shower, but mostly from too much sun. I should've gotten to him sooner with the sunscreen. I limp toward him and reach up to stroke his cheek. He grasps my wrist.

'Hadn't you better get changed?'

My bathing suit's covered with sand. It chafes the tops of my legs. 'Are you leaving because of what happened just now? Because if so, then we need—'

'Of course I am.' Colin drops my hand. 'That's why I have to get back and get it sorted.'

It takes a moment for this to sink in, but when it finally does I realize he doesn't have a clue. He has no idea my friends are hurt and that the reason I've been sitting out here, stewing, is because I don't know how to handle the confusion

I feel. He obviously thinks I was referring to his problem back at the Lodge, not mine, which has just driven off in a fury.

I let out a small sigh. I've been handed a reprieve, a bit of breathing room, which is a relief because I don't feel up to dealing with this right now. Not with Colin shifting from one foot to the other, anxious to take off. Issues this complex, this fraught with emotional liability, require lengthy discussions and copious amounts of patience and we don't have time for either at the moment. It'll have to wait till we get to New Zealand. I'll see about a ticket on Monday. Probably way beyond my means, but I'm sure Colin will help pay for it.

'Then I'll drive you to the airport.'

He glances toward my car. 'I'd rather take the train.'

I catch my breath.

'That Volvo's ready to give out. It'll never make it to Boston and back,' Colin says. 'So why don't you put on some clothes and take me to the station. Once everything's sorted I'll give you a call.'

'When?'

He frowns. 'Tomorrow afternoon. Okay?'

I sigh. 'Okay.'

'I'm sorry,' he says.

'So am I.'

Thirty-one

Sands Point
August 2008

Amtrak's five thirty to Boston pulls into the station as Colin and I race onto the platform. Breathless, he bends and kisses my cheek. My lips search for his, but a kid carrying a duffel bag bumps into us and we never connect. Colin's mouth grazes my hair. He turns, reaches for the handle of his suitcase, pulls it away.

Wheels groan, hydraulics hiss, and the train grinds to a laborious halt. Doors slide open. People alight and hurry off to waiting cars, eager loved ones. Colin steps on board, hesitates, then looks over his shoulder and flashes me a crooked smile.

'Bye, Jill.'

I put a hand to my lips. Another kiss. But he's gone. Swallowed up by passengers and luggage, herded inside by a zealous conductor who keeps checking his watch.

A whistle blows.

The train jerks as if impatient to be off. Doors swish closed.

Scuttling along the platform, I peer in windows, hoping to catch sight of him as he edges down the aisle, lifts his bag into the overhead rack, or settles into a seat, but all I see are reflections of myself, wide-eyed and anxious, with a mop of salt-stiffened hair and Colin's pink shirt hanging to my knees.

The station master raises his hand, looks up and down the platform, and tells me to step back. He signals the engineer.

'All aboard.'

Expelling a huge sigh, the train shunts forward and gathers speed, and as I stand on the platform and watch it shrink to the size of a toy, I curse myself for not insisting that Colin tell me, precisely, what the problem is that's hauled him back to England in such a terrible hurry.

I look down at my toe. It's bleeding.

Unable to face my empty house, I grab a towel from the porch and head for the beach. Waves roll up the sun-drenched sand, whipped by a skittish wind that turns their tips into froth. I paddle beyond the surf and swim in long, lazy circles until my arms and legs refuse to work any more. Limp with exhaustion, I flip onto my back, close my eyes, and drift with the current.

In the distance, something rumbles.

Thunder?

Without warning, a roar blasts through me. Waves chop and churn, and I'm being sucked under, caught in the wake of a speedboat racing too close to the beach. I surface, spluttering and choking, and if I could get that guy's registration I'd nail his balls to the wall.

I punch a hole in the air with my fist.

Thoughtless git.

Head down, I trudge out of the water and bump into my neighbor, standing in the shallows with Molly thrashing around his legs, pretending she knows how to swim. No sign of the dogs.

'You almost lost it back there,' Tom says.

If he mentions the other night, I'll throttle him.

'Hold still a minute,' he says.

I freeze. 'Why?'

'This.'

Something slithers off my back. I shudder and turn around. Tom holds up a strip of bilious green kelp.

'Lasagna!' Molly cries.

'No, princess. It's seaweed,' Tom says, dropping it back in the water. Molly grabs it.

'Actually,' I say, 'its botanical name is *Laminaria longicarpa*.'

Tom Grainger looks at me.

'And,' I go blathering on, 'sea urchins thrive on it.'

'So it would appear,' Tom says. He retrieves the kelp before Molly sinks her teeth into it.

Where's that damn zipper when I need it?

I snatch Colin's shirt and my towel off the beach and march back to my cottage with the feeling that, somehow, Tom Grainger has one-upped me.

I drink half the bottle of wine I'd been saving for my last night with Colin and fall into bed, restless and unable to sleep. Finally, I doze off and wake four hours later, sheets knotted around my ankles, my quilt a puddle on the floor with Zachary, fast asleep, on top. It's still dark, for Christ's sake.

What the hell woke me up?

Colin.

Is he home yet? I squint at my clock till the numbers swim into focus. Five thirty. Twelve hours since I put him on the train. He ought to be landing right about now. Another two hours, three at the most, and he'll be back at the Lodge dealing with whatever it is that neither Shelby nor Diana can cope with.

He said he'd call in the afternoon. His time or mine?

I forgot to ask.

Zachary jumps up and treads about on my legs, looking for a place to settle. I rescue my quilt, rearrange the sheets, and sink into a dreamless sleep, arms wrapped around my cat, and it's almost ten when I open my eyes again. If things had gone according to plan, Colin and I would've just finished taking a shower together and I'd be wandering into the kitchen to fix breakfast, and then he'd drift down to join me and maybe we'd take our coffee onto the patio and afterward we'd stroll along the beach, holding hands, and I'd look with mild pity at those solitary women who have no one to walk with, except their dogs, and feel rather smug because I'm no longer one of them.

After skimming the Sunday paper, I kill time in my office sorting through bank statements and unopened bills, not daring to look at the numbers. I'll cope with my debt tomorrow.

Keep busy. Keep moving.

I finish my submission for Archibald. Everything's ready to go. I address manila envelopes to the first ten editors on my list and fill them with manuscript, sample illustrations, and a cover letter that took me almost as long to write as the story did. I'll drop this lot at the post office on my way to the bank.

At six o'clock, when Colin still hasn't called, or faxed, I ring his cell phone and leave a message on his voice mail. Suppose he doesn't check it? I shoot off an e-mail – *Thinking about you and hoping everything's all right* – and have an overwhelming urge to get out of my house. Away from the phone and the waiting.

But what if he calls?

He'll leave a message.

What if he doesn't?

Stuffing the cordless phone in my pocket, I follow my well-worn path to the beach. I kick at seaweed and scuff my bare feet through loose clumps of sand. The sky is overcast, filled with a threat of thunder and a peculiar, gray-gold light that sets fire to the dunes. Squadrons of insects attack my legs. Slapping them off, I walk as far as the rocks and peer in the tide pool. No sign of Anna's hermit crab.

Come on, phone, ring. Dammit, why don't you ring?

Could I be out of its range? This phone is brand new. State-of-the-art digital technology and guaranteed up to five hundred yards. I pull it from my pocket and check for incoming calls, but the message window is blank. I slouch back to my house.

The wind picks up and makes a weary pass through the willows alongside my patio. Narrow leaves, still quite green and probably surprised at finding themselves on the ground in the middle of August, drift into corners. I stack chairs, lower the umbrella, and haul cushions onto the back porch. No point leaving them outside with a storm on the way. Then I pull two buckets from the shed and take them upstairs. If it rains hard enough, the roof will undoubtedly leak.

My stomach grumbles and reminds me I haven't eaten since breakfast. Opening the fridge, I contemplate the leftovers, but this isn't the time for sensible eating, so I fish around in the cupboard and exhume that package of stale ladyfingers. I finish them off, scattering crumbs on the floor, and stare at the phone. How the hell does an instrument that's designed for human communication have the gall to remain so stubbornly, persistently silent?

Is something wrong with the lines? I check to make sure they're okay – they are. Maybe there's a problem with the ones in England – the international operator assures me there isn't.

So why hasn't he called?

Iris O'Reilly, the assistant manager, is chatting with a teller when I race through the rain and into the bank at nine thirty the next morning. Her bracelets glitter as she waves me into her office, her purple dress sweeps the ground. She closes the door and offers me a seat. The chairs are new, as are the carpet and drapes. Those burst pipes must've wrecked everything. Even the wallpaper's been replaced.

'Jill, I was about to call you,' Iris says.

'You were?'

Iris lowers herself into a well-padded chair, swivels toward her computer. She taps the keyboard and frowns, then rotates the monitor so I can look at the screen. Columns of numbers make me dizzy, especially when they're red and they're mine. *Thank God for Colin's check.*

'How about I pay three months on the mortgage and put fifteen hundred against my loan?' I say.

Iris's face breaks into a smile. 'Sounds good to me.'

'I'd like to open a savings account as well.'

'Statement or passbook?'

'Passbook.' I haven't had one of these in years, not since the boys were small. I'm kind of surprised they still offer them, and I have visions of watching my nest egg grow, compounded by interest and the money I'll add by whipping up the odd logo or selling a kids' book now and then. Maybe I'll help Alistair pay off his college loans, give Jordan a down payment for a house instead of his wasting money on rent, or—

Iris hands me a form to sign. 'How do you want to handle this?'

'With a banker's check.'

She waits, smiling, hands resting on her desk while I dig into my purse. Where the devil is that check? When's the last time I saw it? The day the water main broke, right before Colin arrived. Have I switched bags since then?

No.

Then it's here. Somewhere.

Wallet, address book, and credit cards spill onto my lap. I fan the pages of my checkbook, paw through receipts, old shopping lists, a reminder from the vet about Zachary's next checkup. I plunge deeper and rummage in the detritus at the bottom of my bag – pens with no tops, broken pencils, half an emery board, a comb sprouting brown and gray hairs.

Gray?

In desperation, I upend my bag and shake it. Two pennies and a dime roll across Iris's desk. Three paperclips tumble out.

But no check.

Shit.

'How about your car?' Iris says.

Brilliant.

Ducking my head, I bolt from the bank in a downpour and tear through the Volvo, groping under seats and reaching inside door pockets. I lift floor mats and search the trunk while rain pelts my shoulders, sluices down my legs.

My toe starts to throb. Shivering, I slide into the passenger seat and pull off my sneaker, ease the sock off my foot. Doesn't look good. Red, a little puffy. With wet, clumsy fingers, I tear the wrapping off a Band-Aid I find in the glove box, wrap it around my toe, and limp back to Iris's office.

'Any luck?' she asks.

'No.' Slumping into my chair, I scowl at my purse, flat and empty like a deflated balloon amid a scatter of loose change. It swung from my shoulder throughout half of New England. Colin's check could be anywhere – a motel in New Hampshire, a restaurant in Maine, the ladies' room at Rosecliff. Feeding the fish in Newport harbor.

Lining someone else's pocket?

'Can anyone besides me cash it?' I ask.

'Sure, with adequate identification,' Iris says. 'But for now, let's assume it's lost, but not stolen. Okay?' She pulls another form from her desk, asks who issued the check and when. And yes, we can stop payment on a banker's check but it has to be authorized by the person who actually purchased the check. You'll have to contact them to arrange for this to be done.

She hands me the phone.

'Now?'

'The sooner the better.'

Colin doesn't know I didn't deposit his check.

Do I want to call and admit my stupidity with Iris sitting across from me, listening even though she'll pretend not to?

'I'd rather handle this from home.' I scoop up my belongings and stuff them in my purse. 'Can we talk about this tomorrow?'

'No problem,' Iris says, 'and if all else fails, I'm sure we can refinance your loans. Just remember to bring your last two tax returns, and a P-and-L for this year.'

'P-and-L?'

'Profit-and-loss statement.'

Profit?

Iris signals to a couple waiting outside her office. 'Be with you in a minute.' To me, she says, 'Jill, don't waste any time. Arrange for that stop payment as soon as you can.'

My fingers tremble as I punch in Colin's number. Please, please pick up. Please, please. I hear a click. Then another. The tone changes. Damn, I'm getting his voice mail again.

The number you called is no longer in service.

What the hell?

I must've misdialed, or mispunched, or whatever. Come on, Jill, get a grip. Stop mucking about and do it right.

Click. *The number you called is—*

Now what?

E-mail? But when I fire up my computer and launch AOL, I discover the note I sent him last night bounced back.

Unable to deliver, yada, yada . . .

I've got one option left. Call the Lodge. But suppose Colin's not there and I end up with Shelby, or Diana? What then? Do I hang up? Pretend to be somebody else? No, because this isn't multiple choice. I take a deep breath and make the call.

But nobody answers.

Another storm hits at dawn, and I wake up, groggy and slow from the sleeping pill I took with reluctant desperation four hours ago. Rain pummels the roof, batters the balcony. My gutters overflow. Staggering out of bed, I close the sliding door and lean against it, hands and face pressed to the glass. The wind lifts a willow branch, shakes it and lifts another, and then another until the whole tree is shaking and leaning into the one beside it as the wind tears into that one as well, and the next, one by one, like a line of dominoes, shaking each one in turn before circling back and tearing through them all over again.

Over and over again.

Like me, yesterday, trying to reach Colin. Finally, I connected with an English operator who told me there'd been storms there as well. Many lines were down. Everything's messed up, she said. Try again later.

Water plops on my head, trickles down my cheek.

That damn ceiling's leaking again.

I gather towels and spread them on the floor, place buckets beneath the worst drips. Lightning strobes across the dunes, chased by cracks of thunder that rattle my windows. Zachary streaks between my legs and dives beneath the bed. More lightning, closer this time. Something pops, fizzles; the lights flicker and die, come back on again. Better unplug my computer, just to be safe. I stumble downstairs in the gloom and head for my office.

A crumpled fax lies on the floor.

Jill,

What we had was a wonderful adventure, one that allowed us to miraculously continue and complete all those feelings we had for each other all those many years ago. Perhaps our flame burned too brightly or too soon. Or maybe too late. Who knows? But now, for reasons that are hard to explain (even to myself), I find that I cannot go through with all that we planned.

So my decision now is to pick up the pieces of my old life and move forward. Please try to do the same. You've created a lovely life in Sands Point. Live it without me, as I know you can.

By the time you read this, I'll be on my way to New Zealand. I have much unfinished business down there.

Colin.

Thirty-two

Sands Point
August 2008

Do hearts stop beating with shock? With grief? Or do they thrash about like fish in a bucket the way mine is thrashing now? I sink to my knees and fold inward like the spines of a broken umbrella and everything hurts more than I thought it possibly could.

He's on his way to New Zealand?

The phone rings.

I lunge for the receiver. 'Colin?'

A recorded message asks if I'd like to buy life insurance. I drop the phone and begin to shake. I'm cold, very cold, so I haul myself upstairs, feet hitting the treads like sandbags, and pull on a sweater, a pair of wool socks.

Back straight, hands on my lap, I perch on the bed.

I am *not* going to fall apart. I am *not* weak. I am *not* one of those women who can't cope. I can handle this. This is *not* the end of the world.

I *can* cope.

No, I can't.

Snatching up a pillow, I wrap my arms around it and hug it so hard, feathers burst out. One settles on my nose, another on my lips. I blow them off. Damn, I ought to be crying, for God's sake. I certainly *feel* like crying. I'd prefer an honest sob session to this dry-eyed stoicism. I blink, and blink again, but the tears refuse to come. They will eventually, of course they will, and I'll quietly unravel and have a cleansing, therapeutic howl. I'll destroy a whole box of tissues, and then . . .

What?

What, precisely, *will* I do?

I'm still trying to wrap myself around the enormity of this question and all it implies when Zachary leaps on the bed. He rubs against me and purrs with comforting familiarity. Grateful for a warm, sympathetic body, I gather him up. My heart races, then skips a beat, and I fold my arms across my chest to keep it from escaping. Tears prick at my eyelids and I let them come, because they must, and I wonder if the pain I'm feeling now is the pain I ought to have felt, but never did, at the end of my marriage.

Justice, I suppose, has a way of catching up.

So, too, does loss.

It's a vague, formless dream in which I'm falling an immeasurable distance with ample time to contemplate all manner of horrible landings. I keep fighting to the surface, and sometimes I get close, but then I remember why I'm sleeping and why I don't want to wake up, even though it's the middle of the day and I shouldn't, really, be in bed.

I held his heart in my hand but he snatched it back.

The room's almost dark the next time I open my eyes.

Pain. I'm aware of pain. A physical, pulsing pain. But where? It takes me a second or two to locate the source.

My foot.

I turn on the light and pull off my socks, ease the Band-Aid off my toe. It's so swollen I can barely see what's left of the nail. I need help.

Medical help.

'You have a nasty infection,' says the doc at the clinic. 'Why did you let it get this far?'

I shrug.

'You'll need antibiotics,' she says.

What I really need is an anesthetic. I need to sleep and sleep and not wake up until some time next year. The doctor jabs me in the thigh, wraps my toe, and tells me not to get it wet. Come back and see her on Friday. And get someone else to drive you, okay?

Sure.

I limp into the waiting room and lean against the desk while my insurance card is scanned. This has expired, says the nurse. She hands me a bill. Check or credit card?

My insurance has expired?

Iris understands when I explain about my foot, and did I stop payment on that check? Well, no, I didn't. Then come and see me next Monday, Iris says, and don't forget your paperwork.

Paperwork.

The damn stuff is spread like an accountant's nightmare all over my desk. For three days, I've struggled with overdue bills, taxes, and a warning from a collection agency. Debts I have no way of paying off. One good thing, I suppose, to be said for my financial problem. It keeps me from obsessing over the other one.

What made him leave? Harriet and Beatrice? The fact I didn't tell him about them? Or is he pissed at me for something else? Maybe I pushed him too hard about breaking with Shelby. I know he wants to leave her. He said so. And I know he wants to marry me because he said—

No he fucking didn't. He never once said it. I'm the one who said it, over and over, to myself. But it was obvious, wasn't it? I mean why tell me he's going to leave England and come to live here if we're not getting married? Hell, we don't even have to actually get married, just as long as we live together.

Here. In my house.

Shit! Maybe he didn't like my house but knew how I felt about it, and was too sensitive to tell me we ought to sell it and buy something together. Stop, Jill. That's ridiculous. Beyond ridiculous. He wouldn't leave over something as dumb as that. He'd talk to me about it, wouldn't he? My stupid Burt Lancaster fantasy rears up to taunt me and my brain turns to mush as I search for other clues, but all I do is circle back to one thing.

Colin hates gays. One of my best friends is gay. He can't handle it. Or . . .

Maybe he's right. Maybe we burned our candles at both ends and ran out of wax. My world tilts on its axis. I feel dizzy and lay my head on the table. Biting back tears, I contemplate the mess I've made of my life. My foot is infected, the bank's about to call my loans, and the man I love has swanned off to New Zealand without me. Oh yes, I almost forgot. My two best friends despise me and my business has gone belly-up.

What comes next? Rats? Locusts?

Bankruptcy?

The bank won't refinance my loan unless I can prove a steady source of income. My business is dead, or having a long, embarrassed nap, and so now, obviously, I need a job. But where? Elaine's made sure nobody in the village will hire me, so I'll have to travel farther afield – Middletown or Hartford – and my car may not hold up, which means I'll have to buy another, and God knows where I'll find the money for that, and—

My head hurts, my toe throbs.

The front door bell rings. I really don't want to see anyone.

I wait.

It rings again. Longer this time.

Damn! I limp down the hall and wrench open the door.

'I couldn't find an olive branch,' Lizzie says, handing me a box of pizza, 'so I got this instead.'

I stare at her, open-mouthed.

She holds up a bottle of wine. 'And I got this because it's Friday.'

Thirty-three

Sands Point
August 2008

From the pocket of her long, shapeless dress, Lizzie pulls out a card – the WISH YOU WERE HERE postcard I sent her last month.

'I sure hope you meant this,' she says.

My stiff upper lip crumbles and I burst into tears. Shit, I hate this. I hate breaking down in front of somebody else, even Lizzie. No, make that *especially* Lizzie. She's intimidatingly strong. She'd never unravel over a man.

Lizzie hesitates. 'Should I leave?'

'Don't you dare.' I wave her inside. There's a moment's uncertainty as we jostle in the hallway, then she grins and so do I, although I'm sure it looks more like a grimace, and we hug one another awkwardly because Lizzie's holding a half-gallon jug of Chardonnay and I'm trying not to drop the pizza. Zachary leans against my legs, miaowing pitifully as if I haven't fed him in days.

'I'm sorry for being such an obstinate old fool,' Lizzie says.

I gulp. 'My fault. All mine.'

'Will you forgive me?'

'Nothing to forgive,' I say, sniffing and trying to wipe my nose on my own sleeve and not hers.

She pats my back. 'Best friends should know better, huh?'

I let out a sigh that feels as if it's been trapped inside me forever.

We disentangle ourselves and Lizzie's eyes sweep over me. 'Jill, I hate to be critical, especially right now, but, to be honest, you don't look too hot.' She brushes toast crumbs off the front of my bathrobe. 'Are you sick?'

A lump of self-pity surges up my throat. I choke it back. 'No, not sick. Just—' I rake a hand through my hair. Can't remember the last time I washed it.

Lizzie glances at my foot, still bandaged, and raises her eyebrows. I shrug and she squeezes past me, into the kitchen, and clears a space on my table for the wine. 'Got any clean glasses?' she asks, eyeing the pile of dishes in my sink, the mugs and plates stacked on my counter.

'Probably not.'

Lizzie runs the tap and rinses a couple of plastic tumblers. She turns toward me, worry lines creasing her face. 'Jill, it's really none of my business and I have no right to ask, but—' She catches her breath. 'What the hell has gone wrong?'

I point to a chair. 'Maybe you'd better sit down.'

It pours out, a torrent of words about my mother, the mess I've made of my business, Colin's check, his letter, his reaction to Harriet. Lizzie pulls me into her arms and rubs my back. She makes soothing noises and doesn't say 'I told you so', even though she has every right to. Greedily, I suck up her sympathy, her warmth and her uncritical love, and I don't feel quite so alone any more.

'Jill, he's no good.'

I speak the truth in a whisper. 'I know, but I still love him.'

Reaching for Colin's fax, Lizzie skims it again. 'Jill, listen to this: "You've created a lovely life in Sands Point. Live it without me, as I know you can."' She looks at me, shakes her head. 'That's plain cruel.'

Bloody hell, I'm going to cry again.

Lizzie hands me a tissue. 'Let it out, Jill. Cry, scream, throw things. Allow yourself to be angry with him.'

I have to get over loving him first.

I blow my nose. 'How?'

'Focus on his bad points,' she says. 'He's a coward, he's a cheat, and he's homophobic. That'll do for a start. And after you get good and mad, you can tear up his letters and flush them down the toilet.'

'Scribble on his picture with a laundry marker?'

'That's the general idea.' Lizzie pours us more wine. 'Jill, I hate like hell to repeat myself, but all you had with Colin was a cruise-ship romance. Nothing more.'

So why didn't I see it? The evidence was right there, all along. Colin's obsession with the past – our past – and his need to turn back the clock. The way he brushed off my questions about our future with a kiss and a promise.

Always a promise.

Never a plan.

He had no intention of settling down over here. I was confusing reality with a movie star I once had the hots for. I'm exactly what Lizzie said I was. A nineteen-fifties cliché with her head in the clouds.

Love gave me wings, then took away the sky.

I remember reading that somewhere, but never thought it'd apply to me. I mean, I never really expected to fall in love. Not the way I fell in love with Colin. The joy I felt with him is hard for me to imagine now that he's gone. All I feel is pain, as if someone has wrapped my chest in bands of steel, like a barrel. They tighten and I fight for breath.

Lizzie tells me to put my head down. Lower, Jill, between

233

your knees. That's it. Now relax and breathe deeply. Her strong hands comfort my shoulders.

In, one, two, three . . . out, one, two . . .

I remember the lessons I learned in Lamaze class with Harriet, and more tears well up. Another loss. Shit, how many more do I need?

'Thanks,' I say, once my breathing is steady. God, I hope this doesn't happen again. I fumble in my pocket for a tissue. My hand closes around a soft, familiar lump, and I wipe my eyes with Anna's yellow socks. 'You must think I'm dumber than a bag of hammers.'

'No, I don't,' Lizzie says, 'because this was Colin's fault. Not yours. He charged into your life, turned it upside down, and broke your heart.'

If I knew *why* he'd left, it might be easier to deal with. At least it'd give me something to mourn and put behind me so I could move forward. But the not knowing, the niggling doubt that somehow it could have been my fault he bailed out, is eating at my insides like rats gnawing on cheese.

Lizzie voice is soft, gentle. 'It's been what, not quite a year, since you met? Nearly three hundred and sixty-five days. How many of those did you spend with Colin? Thirty, forty? Most of them making love, walking the beach, and watching old movies in bed. Celluloid, Jill. But not real life.' She pauses. 'You had a fabulous affair, and now it's over. He isn't coming back and you have to move on.'

'I don't think I can.'

'Yes, you can, but it'll take time,' Lizzie says, 'and remember that the guy you fell in love with last year isn't the same one you remember from childhood. He doesn't exist any more.' She drains her glass. 'Have you told the boys about any of this?'

'No.'

'Good.'

'Why?'

'Because kids, even grown-up ones, don't want to know everything about their parents. So, for what it's worth, I suggest you tell your sons about Katie –'

'I already did.'

'– and Emma Katherine,' Lizzie says, 'but leave the rest in the past. Where it belongs.'

Lizzie leaves and I keep busy, loading the dishwasher, wiping the counters. I scrape egg off a plate and wonder what it'd feel like to chuck it across the room, watch it shatter on the tile floor. Would it help? No, because I'm not angry. I'm fucking miserable, and miserable people don't throw crockery. They curl up in a corner and cry.

Biting back more tears, I have a sudden, overwhelming urge to hear another friendly voice, so I pick up the phone and call Dutch. If he's surprised to hear from me, he doesn't say. He asks about Colin and I hesitate because I really don't want to whinge.

'Come on,' Dutch says. 'I can hear something's not right.'

So I tell him.

'Then I'll be expecting you here tomorrow,' he says, 'for vintage champagne, good conversation, and straightforward sex.'

I close my eyes. 'Thanks. I needed that.'

'One hundred days,' Dutch says.

'What?'

'A hundred days. That's how long it'll take you to recover.'

I count the weeks. 'I'll come down right after Thanksgiving.' I won't, of course, but it's nice to be asked.

'For you,' Dutch says, 'the porch light will always be on.'

After a much-needed shower, I pull on shorts and a T-shirt and head for the beach. A chill wind walks up my spine and I shiver. My arms are covered with gooseflesh and I'm about to run back to the house for long pants and a sweatshirt when somebody calls my name. I turn. Damn, it's Tom Grainger and he's alone. No sign of Molly or the dogs.

'Hey, how's it going?' he says.

I shrug, digging at the sand with my heel.

'I'm by myself for the next few days,' Tom says. 'Would you like to have lunch with me?'

Lunch? Is he mad?

More gooseflesh erupts on my arms.

'How about tomorrow?' Tom says. 'We could—'

'We could not,' I say, glaring at him, 'even stampede in the same direction. Much less go to lunch.'

His brow wrinkles and for a second or two he looks genuinely puzzled. Then he turns and walks off, hands in his pockets, shirt tails flapping loose in the wind.

I stare after him. The toad. The unspeakable toad.

On Monday, Iris tells me what I've already figured out for myself. The bank won't refinance my loans unless I have a steady source of reliable income.

'How long can you give me?'

'A week. Two at the most,' Iris says, with the look of someone who suddenly hates her job. 'I'm sorry, Jill. If it was up to me, I'd—'

'That's okay.' It isn't, but what else can I say?

Lizzie takes charge. 'You can't go looking for work with scratches on your knees and clothes fit for the trash,' she says, forcing me to wear pantyhose for the first time in almost a year. I turn around in front of the mirror. My body, accustomed to T-shirts, shorts, and no shoes, feels unwieldy in the blazer and black linen dress Lizzie has unearthed from the depths of my closet. I'd forgotten they were there.

She hands me a brush.

I drag it through my hair and adjust the tiny gold earrings

that Lizzie has also insisted upon. I glance down at my dresser. The bracelet, whose intolerable presence I have yet to deal with, lies in a mocking curve behind my candles.

Lizzie reaches for it. 'What are you going to do with this?'

'Leave it. I haven't made up my mind.'

'Why don't you put the damned thing out of sight?'

I stop brushing, place both hands on the dresser, and lean my head against the mirror. 'Just leave it, okay?'

There's a small, complicated silence.

'Lizzie, I'm sorry. Forget I said that.'

'Said what?'

There are times when I wonder why Lizzie puts up with me.

As I suspected, the local job market sucks. Nobody needs help, at least not from me, so I look farther afield and wind up with a three-month assignment doing data entry for an insurance company in West Hartford. Fifty-two miles away.

This is going to kill my car.

Alistair phones from North Dakota. His work-study program has been extended another month and he won't be flying back for Labor Day weekend. How about Columbus Day instead? Fine, I say, and then I call Jordan in Washington to make sure his plans haven't changed as well.

They have. He's bringing home a new friend.

Her name is Bridget. Like Jordan, she's a virtual reality programmer, and I spend most of the holiday weekend trying to understand what they're saying. Finally, they switch to a subject I know something about. Jordan's found a small house in Bethesda – a fixer-upper – and he wants to buy it, then rent out the extra bedrooms to help cover the mortgage, and I wonder if Bridget will be in one of those rooms or sharing my son's. I hope they're planning to share because I rather like this young woman with auburn hair, freckles, and emerald green eyes.

Of course, seeing them together, holding hands and finishing one another's sentences, reminds me of what I had and what I lost. I plaster a smile on my face and keep my sadness firmly under wraps. I *will* get through this, I know I will. Hearts aren't like eggs. They're like rubber balls. Unfortunately, mine seems to have lost its bounce.

Late Sunday night I snatch a moment alone with my son. I tell him about Emma Katherine and we kneel on the floor in front of my cedar chest, looking inside her treasure box and crying. I show him Katie's letters and we shed even more tears.

I say nothing about Colin. I mean, what's the point? It's over, well and truly over, and I'm not about to upset my son in exchange for a shoulder to cry on. Besides, Lizzie told me not to and right now I'll take her wisdom over my own.

Jordan hugs me. 'Poor Mom. You've had a horrible time.'

'I'm okay,' I say, feeling good just being held by someone who loves me.

One evening, after work, I bump into Beatrice at the library. She asks after Colin.

'Things didn't pan out,' I say. 'He went back home.'

'I'm sorry, so sorry,' Beatrice says, looking down at her feet, festive in orange socks and blue plastic sandals. 'Despite everything, you guys were good together.'

And we were. For a while we had it all.

'Give Anna and Harriet my love,' I say.

She nods and trundles off, arms full of books, her Day-Glo feet a startling contrast to the library's somber gray carpet. But Harriet doesn't call so I send her a card that says MISSING YOU. It worked once before. Maybe I'll get lucky again.

Joel calls to say his marketing guys have finally decided they're interested in Claudia's squirrels. They've pulled my mock-up to bits and rebuilt it with several improvements, and it'll tie in nicely with a line of educational toys and books they're developing for their English market. It all sounds rather exciting. Should they talk to me about this, Joel wants to know? Best to call Claudia, I say. She's in London with Sophie. I give Joel the number and hang up with a sigh of relief.

At least something's going right.

Lizzie talks me into attending a surprise party for her next-door neighbors. Ruth and George have been married for sixty years. Some of the guests look as if they've been married even longer and as I observe the silver-haired couples, frail and stooped and leaning on one another for support, I think, why them and not me? Why couldn't I have looked forward to sixty years of memories with the same man?

Fergus hands me a glass of wine and tells me the old geezer in the corner is making eyes at me. I glance toward him. He raises his cane and grins, exposing oversized false teeth.

'You have an admirer,' Lizzie whispers.

'Christ, Lizzie. He looks about ninety-two.'

'Perfect,' she says. 'You'd be the younger woman for a change.'

September slides into October and suddenly it's Columbus Day weekend and Alistair fills my life with dirty laundry and stories of his adventures among the fossilized rocks of North Dakota. After I show him Katie's letters and tell him about Emma Katherine, Alistair gets choked up and hugs me till I can barely breathe.

'Mom, what can I do to help?'

He bristles with energy, a need to let off steam with hard labor, so I point him toward my clogged gutters, the peeling paint on my bedroom ceiling, and the tool shed's broken window. He fixes them all while I bake cookies and apple pies for him to take back to college.

The parrots are busy, too, ferrying twigs to a large, untidy nest they're building on top of a utility pole at the foot of Tom Grainger's driveway. Like me, they're getting ready for winter, except they don't have to put up with a soul-destroying job that requires them to spend endless gray days in a cubicle half the size of my bathroom.

Renee Dodd, my supervisor, is ruthless. Behind her back, people call her Attila the Hen. Last week, she fired a temp for surfing the Web. Another was shown the door because she used the company's computer to update her résumé. I could be next, so I watch my back when I call home during lunch to retrieve messages.

Today, I have two. The first reminds me that my phone bill is overdue; the second chills my blood.

'Nothing serious,' says the nurse at Anna's school, when I return her call. 'Just a tummy ache, but she'd be better off at home. We can't reach her parents, and you're next on the list.'

Obviously, Harriet didn't take me off. 'I'll be there in an hour.'

Renee's not in her office, so I scribble a message – *Sick child, will make up time later* – and leave it taped to her computer.

Anna sits, hunched over, on a plastic chair in the nurse's office. She looks at me with frightened brown eyes and tries to smile.

'Has she been throwing up?' I ask.

'Not so far.'

Her brow feels cool and damp beneath my fingers. No fever. 'Did you try reaching her mother again?'

'Yes, but her cell phone doesn't answer.'

'Then she's probably in court.' I pause. 'What about Bea French?'

'Her office said she's at a conference in New Orleans.'

'The nanny?'

In a small voice, Anna says, 'We don't have one any more.'

The nurse hands me Anna's knapsack bulging with books, papers, and spare clothes. I bundle Anna into her jacket and carry her out to my car.

'My belly button hurts,' she says, curling up.

That's it. I'm not taking any chances. We're going straight to the clinic. I tear out of the school's parking lot, hit a speed bump, and my car bottoms out. Anna groans and clutches her stomach. Maybe I should go to the hospital instead. It's a twenty-minute drive. The clinic's less than a mile from here, but it's just a clinic, and if this is serious, they'll send her straight to the hospital.

I stomp on the gas and head for the highway.

Thirty-four

Sands Point
October 2008

'You saved her life,' Harriet tells me later, much later, after we've paced the floor and drunk too many cups of bad coffee from the hospital's vending machine. I tell her she's exaggerating, but have to eat my words when the doctor informs us that Anna's appendix was close to bursting and it's a good thing I bypassed the clinic and brought her in right away.

'But she'll be fine,' he says, smiling. 'Kids her age are tough.'

Harriet sits by Anna's bed trying not to look scared, Beatrice calls every half-hour from New Orleans, asking if she ought to fly home, and I feel faint when I think what might've happened if I hadn't phoned home for my messages. The only one not terribly fazed by all this is Anna, despite being hitched up to IVs and a tube that goes from her nose down to her stomach. 'To prevent vomiting and gas,' the nurse says.

Anna begs for stories about Archibald and as I embellish my tale with details about the diva and the evil mayor, I catch Harriet's eye, but there's no need for words because her face says it all.

Forgive me?

And I'm okay with this because while Harriet's a verbal wizard in the court room, she's hopelessly inept at coping with simple apologies. I see her struggling, trying to find the right words, and I wait because maybe she has a need to say them.

She does.

'I hate that it took all this,' Harriet says, waving her arm at Anna's hospital bed, 'to get us back together again.'

'Me too.'

'Jill, I'm sorry, but I have to ask. Did Colin leave because of—'

'He left for a lot of reasons.'

If only I could figure out what they are.

We spend the night in Anna's room, and I doze, fitfully, in an armchair while Harriet alternates between the cot they set up and lying beside her daughter, the two cuddled up like a pair of spoons. In the morning, Anna's in better shape than we are. I offer to stay because I know Harriet has another grueling day in court with needy clients and a demanding judge. She doesn't want to leave, but I shove her out the door, remind her the courthouse is less than five minutes from the hospital.

At nine, I call my office and leave a message for Renee that I won't be back till tomorrow, but when I show up for work the next day, I discover I no longer have a job, because, as my supervisor informs me, she takes a dim view of employees who go traipsing off to cope with somebody else's child.

'You can't fire me for this.'

Renee looks at me. 'I just did. Now please get your things and leave. Right now.'

Driving home, I wonder how the hell I'm supposed to find another job with a black mark like this on my résumé. Should I even admit to having had this job? It was only temporary; on the other hand, it's the only current reference I have, and I'm so busy worrying about my lack of options that I'm halfway down Bay Street before I notice the festival decorations.

Oh, my God, the colors.

Red and turquoise bunting droops between the lamp posts; matching posters leer from shop windows. A banner the color of cat vomit hangs from a telephone pole, and I'm wondering who's guilty of such appalling taste when a gunshot glues my hands to the steering wheel.

What the hell was that?

I glance back. Clouds of exhaust hang over the trunk of my car. Dammit, my wretched muffler has let loose.

The driver behind me honks his horn. I press, tentatively, on the gas. Another explosion rends the air, followed by a throaty roar that propels me down the street and into Dave Norton's garage.

'Are you practicing for the Indy Five Hundred?' he asks.

I have to yell. 'No. I need a muffler.'

'So does your car.' Dave grins, wipes his hands on a cloth, and bends down to investigate. 'That muffler's got a hole the size of a baseball and the pipes are rusted out.'

'Can you fix it while I wait?'

'Yes,' Dave says. 'But it'll mean a whole new exhaust system.'

Shit. This won't be cheap. 'Go ahead.'

Dave does the job in less than two hours. 'Your brakes need relining,' he says, writing up my bill. 'And you're due for another timing belt. Do you want to make an appointment?'

'Not yet.' I open my checkbook and glance at the register, but there's not nearly enough to cover this little repair. 'Dave, can I come back and pay you later?'

'No problem,' he says.

Colin's bracelet fetches three hundred dollars at the pawn shop behind Wal-Mart. I'm sure it's worth more, but it's enough to cover Dave's bill and that's all I care about right now.

Feeling a bit shattered and in need of a hug, I drive out to see Lizzie. After telling me she'd like to nail my ex-boss to the wall, she asks about Anna and I tell her she's doing just fine. 'She'll be home in time for Halloween.'

'Which reminds me,' Lizzie says, 'Fergus and I are going to the dance Friday night. Come with us.'

'I'm not in the mood.'

'Rubbish,' Lizzie says. 'It'll do you good to get out. I'm going as a pumpkin.'

'That's original. What about Fergus?'

'Do you really want to know?'

'Yes.'

'The Energizer Bunny. He's got a drum.' Lizzie grins.

So do I.

'It's good to see you smiling again,' she says. 'And I won't take no for an answer. You're coming with us, and if you're worrying about Elaine, you can stop right now. I doubt she'll dare show her face.'

'Don't be daft. The whole bloody festival committee will be there.'

'But not Elaine Burke.'

'Why?'

'Because she screwed up,' Lizzie says, grinning hugely. 'The festival hasn't exactly been a whopping success. The money they were supposed to raise for the new library hasn't materialized, and now' – her grin widens – 'some of the village elders are pissed at her.'

'I had no idea.'

'That's because you haven't been paying attention.'

Claudia calls to tell me she's in touch with the toy company representatives in London and that finally things are looking up for the squirrels. I swallow my own disappointment over not having heard anything positive about Archibald and tell Claudia I'm thrilled for her.

She wants to share it with me. 'Fifty-fifty.'

'No,' I say. 'Absolutely not.'

'Then I'll give you sixty percent, and—'

'Claudia, the squirrels are yours. I only gave things a bit of a leg-up, that's all.'

'Nonsense,' Claudia says. 'Without you, nothing would have—'

'Please, don't argue. I told Sophie six months ago I did this for you. To thank you for being the mother I never—'

'I insist you get something.'

'What I really want from you,' I say, suddenly over-whelmed with thoughts about mothers, 'is Edith's address.'

'You're going to write to her?'

'Yes.'

Claudia sighs. 'I'm glad,' she says. 'For your sake.'

After I jot down Edith's address – a nursing home in Sussex – I pull out my photograph album and turn to the second page. I remove a small photo. Edith's strong features – high cheekbones, prominent chin, and deep-set dark eyes – still have the power to control. I swallow hard and prop my aunt's picture on the shelf next to one of Jordan and Alistair fishing for crabs by the jetty. I'll find a suitable frame for it later. In the meantime, I have a letter to write.

The words come slowly. My fingers freeze on the keyboard more than once. Then I change my mind; I'll write this by hand. I rummage in the cupboard and pull out a plain white card, folded, with a raised scroll across the bottom. Matching envelope. Edith will appreciate this. So I pen my words of rec-onciliation in a careful script and hope her eyes aren't too old to see them. I'm sure someone, a nurse or a volunteer, will read them to her.

Before I can think again, I seal the envelope, slap on a stamp, and drive it to the post office where I stand, hesitantly, in front of the sturdy blue mailbox. Opening the flap, I sigh deeply and let go of another piece of my past.

Disguised as a cat – black sweater and tights, velvet ears, and bristly whiskers borrowed from a broom – I join Lizzie and Fergus at the village's annual Halloween dance. There's no sign of Elaine so I relax and enjoy myself by pretending to be someone else for an hour or two. I hadn't planned on staying longer than that, but when some guy dressed as a monk in long, black robes and a mask shows up and nobody knows who he is, I'm intrigued enough to stick around.

Using sign language, he asks me to dance.

I shoot a nervous glance at Lizzie. She grins and tells me to get on with it, so I follow him to the middle of the room and we jerk about in the awkward way middle-aged people do when they dance to young people's music. God only knows how old this guy is. I can't see his face. It's covered by a cowl and a hideous mask – blank eye sockets, dripping fangs, the works. He doesn't talk, just shrugs and points, and when the music speeds up he gets tangled in his cloak and trips over his feet. One of his sandals is missing a buckle.

At midnight, he wanders off toward the bar and disappears.

'Maybe he turned into a frog,' Fergus says.

Lizzie grins. 'Or a prince.'

Much to my disgust, the fun I had at the party is obliterated by problems with the plumbing. I crawl out of bed the next morning, bleary-eyed and a little hungover, to find the kitchen sink is stopped up and the downstairs toilet is leaking.

Nothing I do solves either problem. The door bell rings

and I answer it, clutching a pipe wrench and still in my bathrobe.

My next-door neighbor smiles at me. 'Need any help?'

'No.' I try to close the door, but his foot's in the way.

He points at my wrench. 'I'm a fabulous plumber.'

I'm tempted, oh so tempted, to smack him, but I hear the sound of running water and race for the downstairs bathroom. He follows and takes the wrench from my hands and in less than ten minutes he fixes both toilet and sink, and I wish, nastily, that he'd had at least half the trouble I had. It must be some sort of strange male conspiracy in which pipes and plumbing refuse to cooperate with any female over the age of fifty.

'Have I earned a cup of coffee?' Tom places my wrench on the kitchen table and sits down, and I glare at him while Zachary hops into his lap and starts to purr. Traitorous beast.

'I'd rather you went back to your wife and daughter.'

'But I'm not—' He stares at me. 'My daughter?'

'That little girl with brown hair and dimples.'

'Molly?'

'Who else?'

Tom laughs. 'She's my granddaughter.'

Zachary leaps on the table and licks the butter. I'm too stunned to stop him. 'But what about Carrie?'

'What about her?'

'She's your wife.'

'You've really got things screwed up, haven't you?' Tom says. 'Carrie's my daughter, and Molly is hers.'

Feeling like a prize ass, I duck my head and stumble into the hall, pulling my bathrobe together with one hand while gesturing toward the front door with the other. 'Thanks for the sink, but I'd like you to leave.'

'Why?'

'Because—'

'How about having dinner with me?'

'No. Please leave.' I take a deep breath. 'Right now.'

'But why?' Tom says. 'I'm available.'

'No, you're intolerable.'

He grins at me. 'Then I'll have to do something about that,' he says, picking up the broom I've left by the door. 'Nice bristles. I hear they make wonderful whiskers.'

The blush I've been dreading sweeps up my neck like a tidal wave and I slam the door with a force that rattles its frame. Breathing hard, I lean against it while anger and embarrassment battle for control.

Thud.

When I'm positive he's gone, I open the door.

One leather sandal, minus a buckle, lies on my door mat.

Thirty-five

Sands Point
November 2008

I'm about to kick Tom's sandal off the porch when the telephone rings. If that's him, I'll throw the damn phone at the wall. I'll—

But it's Lizzie.

'Hey, what's up?' she says.

'I don't believe it,' I say, heading for the downstairs bathroom. 'I don't bloody believe it.'

'Huh?'

Cradling the phone with one shoulder, I rummage in the cabinet for a Tylenol. My head is reminding me I have a hangover. 'He's not married. He fooled us.'

'Who did?'

'Tom Grainger.'

'Jill, what the hell are you talking about?'

I swallow the pill without water. 'Carrie's his daughter, not his wife. He just unclogged my sink.'

Silence from Lizzie's end, and I imagine her pursed lips, her wrinkled brow and cocked head, as she tries to solve this equation.

'And the connection here is?' she finally says.

I explain and she snorts with laughter. 'That's not all,' I say, glaring at the toilet my neighbor just mended. 'Remember that stupid monk?'

'The one you danced with till midnight?'

'Did not.'

'What about him?'

I spit out his name. 'It was Tom Grainger.'

'Jill, that's priceless. How did you find out?'

'He left a sandal on my porch.'

'Sandal?'

'The one missing a buckle.'

'Holy shit,' Lizzie says, laughing even louder now. 'Cinderella the Monk.' She catches her breath. 'Which, of course, makes you Princess Charming.'

'Bloody hell!'

'Your anger,' Lizzie says, with exasperating patience, 'is bombing the wrong target. Stop beating on the guy who's taken care of your cat and fixed your sink and get mad with the man who really hurt you.' She pauses. 'Think about it and call me tomorrow.'

The phone clicks softly and disconnects.

I stomp into my office and stare at the photo I ought to have tossed in the trash. Reaching forward, I drag my fingernail over Colin's face, his nose, his lips; along the curve of his shoulder and down his arm, across those lean fingers that touched and teased . . .

He brought me to a place I never reached before.

Just rip the damned thing off the wall.

I can't.

My hand trembles and I snatch it back. What the hell am I supposed to do? Stick pins in his eyes? Burn his letters? Cut the sleeves off that pink shirt?

Does he remember wearing it the day I fell back into his life?

Why the hell do I still love him so much?

If I could just hear his voice, ask why he left the way he did. Does he think of me at all, or am I a regrettable memory he's thrown in the trash? My hand reaches for the phone, my fingers punch in his number, and my heart lurches. Suppose he answers. What will I say?

'North Lodge. May I help you?'

Christ, it's him.

I hang up.

Two days later, I pluck up my courage and try again. This time I don't chicken out when he answers. 'Colin, it's Jilly. I need to—'

'Sorry, there's no one here by that name.'

I've never felt so betrayed by anyone in my life.

The Sunday paper has plenty of openings for systems analysts, home health aides, and database managers, but precious few for people with my skills and I'm about to give up when a small ad catches my eye. A media publisher – whatever that is – needs a typesetter. Call for appointment.

I can handle that.

'Come and see me tomorrow,' the man shouts above the noise of machinery in the background. 'Five o'clock. Bring a résumé.'

Even though he didn't ask, I'm going to take my portfolio. Maybe I can convince him they need a graphic artist as well.

After several wrong turns, I reach my destination – a dismal, one-story building with a cement floor and no windows. People hunch over keyboards; others sit at long tables reading proofs. A woman with a haircut that reminds me of a corn muffin hurries past carrying a clipboard and yelling instructions above the roar of presses that churn through miles of paper in a room the size of a supermarket.

Phones ring.

Nobody smiles.

My interview is with the production manager, a thin, hollow-cheeked man who reeks of cigarettes. He glances at my résumé, ignores my portfolio, and offers me a job.

Surprised, I say, 'When do you want me to start?'

'Thursday.'

'Then I'll see you the day after tomorrow.' I hold out my hand.

He grasps it with nicotine-stained fingers. 'Seven thirty sharp.'

The wall outside his office is stacked high with boxes of coupon books, begging letters, and credit card offers. Stuff that clogs mailboxes and drives everyone mad.

A plow with flashing red lights pulls into the parking lot. How can so much snow pile up in less than half an hour? Slipping and sliding, I make a mad dash for my car. It takes forever to start and I drive back to Sands Point ambivalent about working for an industry that destroys millions of trees in order to piss off an equal number of people. But, what the hell. It's a job and I need it so I'll keep my opinions to myself.

By the time I pull off the highway, heavy wet snow has given way to freezing rain and I can barely see where I'm going because my windshield wipers have turned into Popsicles. The heater groans with effort. Can't afford to have it fixed, so if I'm to survive this dreadful commute, I'll have to wear extra clothes. And socks. Plenty of socks. My feet are getting numb.

The village has no lights.

Neither does the beach road.

Damn. The power must be out and I don't have any dry firewood. No kindling, either. My cat is probably freezing. Was he inside or out when I left, and why is my steering wheel suddenly heavy?

My car slows and coasts to a stop.

Sod it.

I crank the ignition, hold the key too long, and flood the engine. Very good, Jill. You know better than that. It's bloody cold in here. I breathe on my hands, rub them, and count the seconds till I can safely try again. A minute, maybe two, crawls by. Is that enough time? I turn the key.

Click. Wheeze. Click.

Careful. Don't fuck it up. I give it one more go, but my car sighs as if it's too tired to move another inch.

I bang my fists on the dashboard.

Don't give up on me now.

But it already has.

My flashlight, thank God, is still in the glove compartment. I fumble with frozen fingers for the switch. On, off. On, off. Come on, damn it, work. I shake it, but the batteries are dead. *Wonderful.* I open the door and the wind wrenches it from my hand.

Shit, shit, and more shit.

Clutching my jacket to keep it closed, I stumble forward in the dark. Can't see a thing. Sleet stings my eyes and sandpapers my cheeks. A vicious wind slices through my clothes. Why didn't I wear a heavier coat, and what possessed me to wear such silly little shoes on a day like this? Black leather pumps with cutwork – holes, for God's sake – that spew like a lawn sprinkler as I walk.

I must've been mad.

Headlights approach. A sports utility vehicle roars by and sprays me with ice water. Mud dribbles down my legs. Into my shoes.

I'm too fucking cold to care.

It stops by my Volvo, the driver sticks his head out the window and yells back at me, but the wind hijacks his words.

He reverses, wheels tearing into the sand bank, and halts beside me.

'You're soaked.'

No shit!

My neighbor grins at me, leans over, and opens the door. I don't want to, but I climb inside. Even I'm not stubborn enough to refuse a ride home in these conditions.

He reaches behind his seat. 'Wrap up in this.'

A rough blanket smelling of wet dog lands in my lap. I shrug into it, shivering despite the hot air swirling around my feet. Can't feel my toes any more. Maybe I have frostbite.

Tom guns the engine, performs a gravel-crunching three-point turn, and speeds back to the beach. 'You'd better come home with me.'

'No.' I put a hand on the door.

He clicks the lock. 'Don't be stupid.'

We jerk down our dirt road, past one gloomy house after another, and Tom's is the only one with lights. Lucky sod. He must have a generator. My house, just beyond the willows, is dark as a tomb. Tom's garage doors open and he drives inside.

They bang shut behind us. I'm trapped.

I can't open my door.

Tom unlocks it, and I squeeze out of his car, edge sideways past a sack of sunflower seeds, and squelch up the steps into a mud room. Old newspapers, dog bones, and stray boots litter the floor. A ladybug umbrella leans against a stepladder and Tom's mask, propped on top of a recycling bin, has a pink mitten drooping from its mouth and looks as if it's just bitten off a child's hand. His black cloak hangs from a hook on the door.

Cinderella the Monk.

If he mentions Halloween, or, worse, the night he caught Colin and me on the beach, naked, I'll die blushing.

And then I'll leave town.

Permanently.

Tom ushers me into the kitchen, drops his keys on the counter, and picks up a bottle of wine and a mug. He turns to me, smiling. 'What'll it be? Cabernet or cocoa?'

I shiver. 'Cocoa – and thanks.'

Tom supplies me with dry clothes – socks, sweatpants, and a sweatshirt that hangs to my knees – and I change in a small bathroom off the kitchen. When I emerge, he's holding two mugs of cocoa.

'My office is warm,' Tom says, pushing open a door with his foot.

The room is alive with flickering light. A log fire burns in the grate and Molly's cat lies curled in a basket on the hearth. I'm tempted to join her.

'Where are the dogs?'

'In Vermont, with Carrie and Molly,' Tom says. 'My daughter and her husband are trying to patch things up.' He shrugs. 'I love having her here, but she needs to get on with her own life.'

That's what Sophie said yesterday when I called to talk about Colin. She called him a sodding awful bastard, then told me I was better off without him. That I've raised two kids, renovated a cottage, and run a business by myself. What the hell do I need him for?

Good question.

Tom hands me the cocoa and I take small sips, standing with my back to the massive stone fireplace, soaking up the heat. My toes tingle. My shoulders relax and I look around Tom's comfortable room, at his shelves full of books, the half-finished crossword on the coffee table, his desk and computer equipment – silent and dark because of the power failure – and realize you can never really know a man till you've seen the inside of his home, his personal space, the way he arranges his furniture.

'Make yourself comfortable,' he says, pointing at the couch.

I lower myself into down-filled leather cushions, soft as butter.

I slide my hands over his buttery leather jacket . . .

Tom sinks into a faded, chintz-covered wing chair, crosses his legs, and appears ready for polite conversation. Stalling for time, I pick a *National Geographic* off the table, flip a few pages, and come face to face with a green and red parrot.

'How about those birds, huh?' Tom says, leaning forward.

That sack in the garage. 'Are you feeding them?'

'Constantly,' he says, grinning. 'I'm a sucker for parrots.'

The headline I'm looking at says THE WILD PARROTS OF TELEGRAPH HILL. 'Have you done this before?'

He nods. 'I had a neighbor in San Francisco who had a huge nest hanging over her driveway. At first, she was thrilled, but when the parrots shat on her car and woke her family at dawn, she hired a guy with a cherrypicker to take it down. So I bought a bird feeder and tried to lure them to my yard.'

'Any luck?'

'Pigeons and squirrels.'

'But no parrots?'

'Not till I moved here.'

'Don't tell me you came east just for the parrots?'

Tom grins. 'They were an unexpected bonus.'

Outside, sleet lashes against the windows and a determined wind howls down the chimney. Logs shift and settle. Sparks fly out and land on the hearth. Tom sweeps them up, then bends to stroke Elsa's tiny gold head. She yawns and stretches, first one elegant paw, then another. Lovely, her body language says. Do that again.

The mirror above Tom's mantel is made from a weathered

old window. Beneath it, amid photos of Molly and the dogs, stands a small picture in a black metal frame. It shows a much younger Tom – beardless and wearing one of those multi-pocket vests favored by photographers – with his arm around a slender, dark-haired woman. A little girl, also dark-haired and unmistakably Carrie, stands between them with one foot in front of the other, squinting at the camera. Tom's free hand rests on her shoulder.

'That was taken twenty-five years ago in Hawaii,' Tom says, reaching for the picture. 'Six months before Peggy died.'

'Your wife?'

He nods. 'Ovarian cancer.'

'I'm so sorry.'

'Me too,' Tom says, wiping the glass with his cuff. 'I still miss her.' He hands me the picture and picks up our mugs. 'More cocoa, or would you prefer wine?'

'Wine would be great.'

'Red or white?'

'White.'

Twenty-five years. That's a helluva long time to miss someone. I turn the frame over and the photo slips out. I'm sliding it into place when I notice writing on the back.

Hawaii, 1983: Carrie, 5; Tom, 34; Peggy, 42.

Forty-two?

Oh, Jeez.

Shame surges up my neck and floods my cheeks like a hot flash. I return the photo to its frame, glance in the mirror, and see Tom's reflection. He's leaning against the door, a glass in each hand, looking at me.

'There's something I need to know,' he says.

I grip the mantel. 'What?'

'Why do you dislike me so much?'

His wife was eight years older than him.

'I think I'd better go home.'

He walks up behind me. 'Do you have a generator?'

'No, but—'

'Then why not stay here?'

'Because of my cat,' I say, groping for inspiration. 'He'll freeze.'

'If you go home, you'll freeze as well.' He's so close I can feel his breath on the back of my neck. 'I'll go and fetch him. He can share a bed with Elsa.'

'And me?'

'You can sleep on the couch,' Tom says. 'Where it's warm.'

'What about you?' I turn slowly to face him.

He hands me a glass. 'I'll be upstairs, with a paraffin heater.'

'How many bedrooms do you have?' My question shoots out of nowhere.

'Eight. No, wait a minute. Nine, I think. I've never had a house this large before.' Tom shoots me a puzzled look. 'Why do you ask?'

'Because I designed the sales brochure.'

'For Elaine Burke?'

'She insisted it had ten bedrooms.'

'That sounds just like her,' Tom says, placing his wine on the coffee table. 'Is your house locked?'

I shake my head.

'Then I'll be right back,' he says, and returns ten minutes later with my bad-tempered cat wrapped in a quilt.

Thirty-six

Sands Point
November 2008

Tom's voice wakes me at seven the next morning. 'You couldn't fax me because the lines were down. Where are you?' There's a pause and I struggle to sit up. Is he talking to me? No, he's on the phone, leaning against his desk. 'The Philippines?' Tom says. 'What the hell are you doing there?'

I toss my quilt to one side. Zachary, who despises other cats, is curled up with Elsa in the basket. They're washing one another's faces. Go figure. My teeth are scummy and my back is killing me. I'm too old to be camping out on other people's couches.

Tom covers the mouthpiece. 'Jill, I'm sorry, but this is going to take a while. Can you make it home by yourself?' Into the phone, he says, 'No, of course I'm listening.'

'I can probably stagger that far.' I glance out the window. No more freezing rain. Just a plaintive sun that looks about as washed out as I feel. 'I'll wash your clothes and return them later,' I tell Tom, but he's bending over his keyboard and doesn't hear me.

Should I go out the way I came in? Better not. I'll never find the switch to open the garage doors. I gather up my quilt and my cat, who doesn't seem anxious to leave, retrieve my clothes from the bathroom, and head in the general direction of Tom's front door. Beside it, hanging on the wall, is a scruffy old moose head. Two dog leashes and Molly's red baseball hat dangle from its solitary antler.

So that's what happened to Lizzie's white elephant.

According to Dave, my Volvo's a lost cause. Time to shoot it and buy another, he says, offering me a nice little used car with low mileage, new tires, and an air conditioner that works.

'How much?'

'Nine thousand, Jill. It's a bargain.'

Yeah right, and now all I need is a miracle. Somebody to wave a magic wand and take all my troubles away.

My fairy godmother awaits in my mailbox, but instead of a crown and pink tulle, she wears neon yellow paper festooned with black stripes and she promises to solve my financial dilemma with a low-interest loan.

No questions asked.

Am I brave enough – no, make that desperate enough – to take the plunge? What choice do I have? Short of selling my house and starting over, I've run out of options. I need wheels to get to work; I need a job to pay for the wheels.

Case closed.

So I call the toll-free number and yes, they'd be delighted to help. How much do I want? Ten thousand? No problem, just sign on the dotted line. I don't even have to give them my first-born child.

I'm scared to death about this, but it's only for three months. A short-term loan. After that, I'll refinance everything with the bank because Iris has told me I'll be qualified by then, as long as I have a job. Okay, today is Wednesday. With luck, I can pull it all together by next Monday. Buy another car, get it registered – damn, the DMV is closed Monday, Tuesday then – and start work on Wednesday.

One more week. That's all I need.

It's like asking for a stay of execution.

'Tomorrow,' the production manager says. 'We're expecting you tomorrow.'

I suggest a compromise. 'How about noon on Tuesday?'

'No good. We need someone right now,' he says, and hangs up without giving me a chance to explain.

This is great, just great. Now I have no job and way more debt than I had yesterday. Maybe I'll ask Dave to shoot me as well as my car.

Tom drives me uptown to rescue my portfolio from the Volvo before it's disemboweled and chopped up for spare parts, and he looks the other way while I shed a couple of tears in Dave's back lot to mark the end of an era.

Another loss.

My clunky old Volvo, the first car I bought with money I earned myself, is finally dead. I close the door, pat the hood, and after we stop to pick up bread and milk, Tom takes me home.

He glances at my portfolio. 'I'd love to see your work.'

'Now?'

'Sure, if you have time.'

I've got all the time in the world, so I lead him into my office and show him the layouts I've done for Elaine, the rejected designs for this year's festival, Archibald and my naked garden gnomes.

'This is great stuff,' Tom says, flipping through my sketch book. 'I love your parrots.' He looks at me. 'You must be swamped with work.'

He obviously has no idea I'm the local pariah.

'Business is a bit slow right now,' I say. 'I was on my way back from an interview when the car broke down.'

'Did you get the job?'

I tell him about the sweatshop.

'Sounds as if your work would be wasted in a place like that,' Tom says. 'Look, I don't want to interfere, but I know an outfit that pays well for talent like yours.'

'Around here?'

'Boston.'

'Rather a long commute.'

'Doesn't matter,' Tom says. 'They'll let you work at home.' He pulls out his wallet, thumbs through a stack of business cards, and hands one to me. 'Give them a call.'

'Wow, thanks,' I say.

'Feel free to mention my name. It might help.' Tom grins. 'Then again, it might not.' He nods toward the picture of Colin and me. 'You still seeing that guy?'

I hesitate. 'No, not any more.'

Tom looks at me, then at the photo. 'Good luck with the job hunt,' he says, turning to leave. 'Those people in Boston work hard for their clients.'

The Volvo's successor is a gray, nondescript little thing with the soul of a shoebox. Dave has pronounced it safe and reliable; I consider it a blemish on wheels, but I mustn't complain because it gets me to Boston for my interview with the agency Tom recommended. They give me a couple of freelance illustration jobs with a promise of more to follow. Nothing spectacular, but enough to keep the creditors off my back.

I call Tom to thank him.

My pleasure, he says. Any time.

Lizzie has a hard time believing Tom and I are now friends. Some days, so do I. It feels odd to walk by his house and have him wave at me and for me to wave back instead of turning the other way. I've learned my lesson, I tell Lizzie over coffee and bagels in her kitchen. I'm never going to jump to conclusions again. Hmmm, she says, not believing that one either, then suggests we invite Tom and his family for Thanksgiving which is something I've been doing my best to ignore.

My sons won't be here.

Jordan's going home with Bridget to meet her family and Alistair's been invited to go heli-skiing in British Columbia. All expenses paid. I told him I'd disown him if he refused, then patted myself on the back for having cut the apron strings so well that neither of my sons feels guilty over not spending the holiday with me.

'So, you'll ask them?' Lizzie says.

'Huh?'

'The Graingers,' Lizzie says. 'Invite them for Thanksgiving. I don't have their number. It's unlisted.'

I spot the dog about a mile from the beach and recognize it immediately – a black Lab – which means Carrie and Molly are back from Vermont. I stop the car and get out.

'Here, boy,' I call, and the Lab limps toward me, dragging a front paw. It doesn't even hesitate before lumbering into the back seat where it parks its heavy wet nose on my shoulder and refuses to budge till I pull into Tom's driveway.

'Thanks for Hemingway,' Tom says, opening the car door. Molly peers at me from behind his legs.

'Who?'

'The dog.' Tom bends to examine its paw.

'Oh, no problem.'

'When you get to know him better,' Tom says, straightening, 'you'll be allowed to call him Ernest.' The other Lab squeezes between him and Molly. 'And this one is Austen.'

'As in Texas?'

'No, as in Jane.' Tom grins at me. 'Would you like coffee? I just made a fresh pot.'

'No, thanks,' I say, having tanked up at Lizzie's, 'but if you guys aren't busy for Thanksgiving, you're invited to the McKennas'. Lizzie has a couple of grandchildren Molly's age.'

'Then we can't possibly say no,' Tom says. 'Tell her we'll be there. What time, and what can we bring?'

'I'll have to let you know,' I say, and go home with an odd feeling of pleasure.

I know before I'm fully awake this is going to be a tough day. For one thing, it's bloody pouring which means I'll be fussing with mops and buckets and wondering if my roof will last another winter; for another, it's Thanksgiving and I'm not sure I want to get up and face the crowd, mostly couples, at Lizzie's.

Couples.

I'm beginning to hate that word, and hate myself for hating it.

Richard and I were never a couple. We never connected with each other the way I figured a married couple ought to connect, like the people next door to Richard and me whose house overflowed with love and laughter. They had five kids, barely enough money, and two elderly cars, one of which was always in the shop. Compared to us, they were practically paupers, but a whole lot happier. Or so it seemed at the time. Maybe they were miserable, but hiding it, the way I did. Back then, I didn't know what real love was like, and if you don't know what something is like, then you can't miss it when it's not there.

Now I know, and I miss it like hell.

I miss knowing someone special is thinking about me the same way I'm thinking about him. I miss the touch of his hands on my breasts, my belly, the tantalizing ache between my legs. Will it ever come back?

I turn over and my bed gives a solitary sigh as if to

exaggerate the aloneness I feel, the uncoupling of a couple I thought would last forever. This time last year, Colin was living inside my heart, curled up like a luscious little secret that kept me warm while I laughed and celebrated the holiday with my sons and my friends. I remember smiling a lot, drinking a bit more, and e-mailing Colin when everyone else had gone to bed, telling him about an American Thanksgiving and the welcome return of my vagabond cat.

Lizzie asked me if I'd do it all over again, fall in love with Colin knowing what I know now, and I said yes, I would, because I'm trying to convince myself it's better to have loved and lost than never to have loved at all.

Or some such rot.

An hour later, I'm in the kitchen making pies and determined to play hooky from self-pity and the stress of bills I can't pay. If the agency in Boston doesn't come up with another project next week, I'll be scouring the help-wanted ads again and hoping I don't have to settle for cashier at Wal-Mart or selling trinkets at Target to holiday shoppers.

Another leak erupts through the ceiling so I add another bucket to the brigade in my bedroom and drop more towels on the floor. If this keeps up, I'll have no choice but to have the roof fixed before winter.

By the time I arrive at Lizzie's, my neighbors and the McKennas are getting acquainted over drinks and hors d'oeuvres in the living room. Molly and Tyler crawl across the floor, taking turns with the remote-controlled bulldozer I bought him last Christmas. The bestest ever, he told me.

Lizzie hands me something pink and frothy in a glass.

'Where's Harriet?' I dump my pies on the kitchen counter. 'Isn't she coming?'

'Anna's got the flu, but Bea's stopping by to pick up food. I insisted.'

After another round of cocktails, Fergus dons a chef's hat

and apron to carve the turkey. His new mustache, long and droopy, reminds me of Dutch and I wonder what he's doing for the holiday. Is he alone? Probably not. More than likely he's curled around a blonde and a bottle of expensive champagne. I help Lizzie ferry food from the kitchen while Tom and Joel round up the kids. They want to sit together, so Paige and Carrie form an alliance of young mothers at one end of the table while their offspring make a mess at the other, leaving Tom, Joel, and me to cope with the consequences of sitting near children armed with gravy and mashed potatoes.

I take a seat beside Tyler and cover my lap with a napkin.

Beth points toward Lizzie, then nudges Molly with her elbow and says, 'That's my grandma. Where's yours?'

'My grammy,' Molly says, 'is buried in the chemistry.'

Conversation stalls. Forks halt midway between plates and mouths, and I bite my lip, wondering how Tom's going to handle this.

'She's quite right,' he says, ruffling Molly's curls. 'And I'm sure her grandmother would appreciate her choice of words.'

Fergus clears his throat and nobody speaks until Carrie says, 'My mother was a pharmacist, and' – she glances down the table and smiles at her daughter – 'Molly's middle name is malaprop.'

We're still laughing when the front door opens and Beatrice limps in, leaning on her cane. Her arthritis must be kicking up again, but I doubt she'll whinge about it because she never does. We make a space for her at the table. I fill my glass with wine, pour one for her.

She leans toward me. 'There might be an opening at work.'

'For me?' I say.

'Our publications department needs an assistant art director.' Bea hands me a slip of paper. 'Call them on Monday. I already put in a good word.'

'You're a lifesaver,' I say, hugging her. The job sounds perfect.

Perfect.

Fergus starts in with a shaggy dog story but can't remember the punch line, so Beatrice conjures up a substitute and Fergus says it's better than the one he forgot. My sons call to wish me a happy holiday – Jordan from Bridget's home in Pennsylvania and Alistair from a helicopter, judging by the racket. I can barely hear him.

Laden with leftovers, Beatrice thanks us and leaves, and for some idiotic reason I feel abandoned, sitting on my own at the end of the table, ever so slightly drunk and watching the others laugh and talk and swap stories. Paige and Joel engage Carrie in lively conversation about nursery schools, while Tom and Fergus discuss, of all things, golf. I didn't even know Fergus played. Lizzie stands behind her ex-husband, hands resting lightly on his shoulders, and when I catch her eye, she smiles and nods as if to say, 'You were right and I was wrong.'

How long before they're a couple again?

Couple.

Maybe I'd better leave before my rampant self-pity lures me into another glass of wine, and another. Shit, I hate to bug off before the party's over, but Lizzie will understand.

'Call me later,' she says.

I'm at the door, reaching for my coat, when Tom asks for a ride home.

'I need to let the dogs out,' he says, 'but I don't think Molly's ready to leave.'

His granddaughter tumbles past me, shrieking with glee as Beth teaches her to turn somersaults.

Rain pummels my face as I run for the car. Tom reaches it first. Opens the passenger door for me. 'Let me drive,' he says, and I don't argue because my head is spinning.

He seems to sense I'm in no mood for conversation and

doesn't say a word till we turn into our dirt road. 'The dogs are okay,' he says. 'They've been left alone far longer than this.'

My car skids over ruts slippery with rain. 'Oh?'

'Do you feel like talking?' he asks.

'What about?'

He shrugs. 'I figured you're upset and might need a shoulder.'

How the hell does he know? Was I *that* transparent?

He glances at me. 'Well?' he says. 'Your place or mine?'

We slide past his driveway.

'Guess that answers my question,' he says.

Thirty-seven

Sands Point
November 2008

We sit at opposite ends of the couch, Zachary between us, and it's obvious I had too much wine at Lizzie's because my lips are flapping up and down faster than a pair of tart's knickers. Tom strokes my cat and listens with a quiet, focused concentration while I blather on about my parents' love affair and mine with Colin and how he loved a memory rather than loving me.

'I wonder if that's all I loved, as well,' I say, and this is alcohol talking, not me, because now I'm plunging into the purple prose of a romantic novel. 'He was a mirage, a man I invented from misty old memories.'

Dear God, I'll be speaking in tongues next.

'Real or not,' Tom says, 'it still hurts, doesn't it?'

'Yes,' I say, with a thick sort of shame. 'But I feel like a fraud.' He lost a wife. All I lost was a middle-aged boyfriend who wouldn't commit. Oh yes, I lost my self-esteem as well. And my business, but I won't complain to Tom about that.

'A loss is a loss,' he says. 'Your pain is no less than mine. It's just different.'

I begin to speak, then catch sight of him looking at my

reflection in the night-blackened mirror of the sliding glass doors, and can't say anything at all.

Tom reaches for my hand. 'We can try to understand one another's pain,' he says, 'but the truth is we can't, because pain is unique. You have yours and I have mine. And when somebody says, "I can feel your pain," they're kidding themselves. It's their own pain they feel, not yours.'

'Does it ever go away?' His hand is warm and dry. Friendly, but not suggestive. No thumb running around my palm or fingers squeezing mine, and I'm glad because I wouldn't know what to do with a come-on right now.

'Yes, eventually, it does,' Tom says. 'But I tried to hurry mine along by getting married again.'

Another wife? 'Did it work?'

'No,' he says, standing up and stretching. 'It was a disaster that lasted two years.'

Is he going to leave? Jeez, I hope not, though I wouldn't blame him if he did. He's probably tired of hearing my woes. I can't believe how much I've unloaded on Tom. Village gossip says he was some sort of journalist but doesn't like to talk about it. That could be right because he certainly knows how to listen and ask the right questions.

Outside, something clunks and the wind shifts direction. It bullies my house and taunts the gutters, tempting shingles to fly off the roof. I'll have a mess on my hands tomorrow. I hear a noise in the chimney, a rattle, and a clump of soot lands in the grate. Seconds later, a tiny black creature – a field mouse, probably – scurries out, leaving a trail of sooty footprints on the hearth.

Zachary leaps off the couch to investigate.

Laughing, Tom says, 'Adventurous wildlife around here. First the parrots, building a nest on top of my utility pole, and now this.'

'You ain't seen nothing yet.' I tell him about the raccoon

that fell down Lizzie's chimney last spring and left a smelly calling card in her coal stove before climbing back out again.

Tom wrinkles his nose and picks up a log. 'How about a fire?'

He's wooing you with wood, Lizzie said.

'Sure.' I roll and knot newspaper because I don't have any kindling and my hands are suddenly in need of a job.

Tom builds a fire, lights it, and asks, 'How many times have you been married?'

'Just once.' I hesitate. 'Tell me about your second wife.'

He sits down, opposite me this time, on the loveseat. 'Must I?'

Shit. Now I've stuck my foot in it. 'Is it painful?'

He grins. 'No, it's embarrassing.'

'Then I promise not to laugh.'

'All right,' Tom says. 'She was self-centered and glamorous, and very, very young.'

I look at him and wait.

'She ran off with a surfer. Guess I wasn't exciting enough for her.'

Biting back a smile, I say, 'What do you do, for a living, I mean?'

'Loaf about, mostly.'

Is he independently wealthy? I study his hands, the thickening of the middle finger on his right hand that tells me he's right-handed, the short, square nails. Blunt fingers. The pale scar that curves around the base of his thumb. Not the hands of an idle man. 'But you must've done something else besides that,' I say.

He hesitates. 'I was a war correspondent.'

So the gossips were right. 'Vietnam? The Middle East?'

'And other places,' he says. 'Wherever trouble broke out. But now I'm retired and, like I said, I just loaf.'

'My mother was a journalist,' I say. 'And an artist.'

'Guess it rubbed off on you, then,' Tom says. 'Did you ever finish that kids' book?'

How does he know about that? Did I tell him? Did Lizzie?

He grins. 'I saw those parrot sketches in your office, remember? Figured maybe they were heading for a picture book.'

'I sent it to a bunch of editors,' I say.

'Any luck?'

'Seven rejections, three to go.'

He winces. 'Must be tough.'

I shrug. 'I'll just send out more submissions, that's all.'

'Tell me about your father,' Tom says. 'Was he a journalist, too?'

'He owned a company that made fencing,' I say. 'Chain link and barbed wire. On Saturday mornings, I'd go in with my dad and watch the men work. A tall guy named Will was missing an arm and I remember being fascinated with his empty sleeve, pinned to his shoulder. One of the other men told me a machine had jammed and Will reached in to free up a length of wire, got his arm caught, and would have followed it to his death if my father hadn't reversed the machine and saved Will's life.'

'Quick thinking,' Tom says. 'He sounds like a great man.'

'He was, and I adored him. I was eighteen when he died. Thought I'd never get over it, but I did and I honestly don't remember grieving very long.' I sniff. 'I'm so ashamed of that.'

'Don't be.' Tom leans forward, elbows on his knees, and steeples his fingers. 'Loss is easier when you're young because you have most of your life ahead of you. Later on it's much tougher. We're pushed for time, desperate for another chance. Some of us panic,' he says, looking chagrined, 'and wind up making idiotic choices.'

A log shifts, and sparks fly out. I grab the brush and sweep them back into the fire, add more wood.

'Know what I miss the most about Peggy?' Tom says.

'What?'

'Not having someone to remember things with.'

I swallow hard.

Gently, Tom says, 'You feel the same about Colin, don't you?'

I nod, then tell him how I felt at the anniversary party Lizzie and Fergus dragged me to. How envious and yes, let's be honest here, how jealous I was of all those gray couples.

'They were probably jealous of you, too,' Tom says.

'Why?'

'Because you're younger than them.'

'Yeah, right.'

'Relatively speaking,' he says, grinning. 'Just remember, you won't always feel like this.'

'Is that a guarantee?'

'Trust me,' he says. 'There are days when you feel that you'll never recover. But you do, or at least you pretend to the rest of the world you've hauled yourself back. Then one day, you wake up, and find that you have.'

'I'm not sure I'll ever,' I say, 'be able to haul myself back.'

'Of course you will, but you can't put a time limit on grief, or a measure on how you feel, or how you think you ought to feel,' Tom says. 'The wound will heal, but the scar will remain. It won't fade completely, but you'll learn how to cope with it. Most of the time.'

'How do you cope?'

'By keeping busy.'

Doing what? I wonder, but don't ask.

Tom stands and stretches, checks his watch. 'I ought to be going. Those poor dogs will *really* be crossing their legs now.'

Beatrice's company, a rising star in the biotech world, grants me an interview so I tart myself up and drive to New London.

274

The main office lies on the outskirts of town among tasteful plantings and winding brick paths. An elevator whisks me from the underground parking garage to the third floor. Dense carpet, mellow lighting, tinted windows. No wonder Bea likes working here.

The woman who interviews me wears a dark gray suit and a pale pink blouse. Yes, they're impressed with my portfolio, and my qualifications fit their needs, but they'll have to check with my previous employers. Standard procedure, she tells me. Just to verify dates and time spent on the job, that's all.

'Assuming it's all satisfactory,' she says, 'we'd like you to start right after Christmas.'

'That would be fine,' I say, as she goes on to explain company benefits. Health insurance, profit sharing, retirement plan.

Security.

Another month. I can hang on till then.

Dutch's one hundred days have come and gone, but memories of Colin cling like burrs on a blanket. Drinking tea from an enamel mug with no handle, playing tag among thickets of broom, painting one another and sticking together like Velcro. I struggle to keep him at bay, but he pushes inside my head, demands I pay attention. Is he thinking about me? Does he regret that letter? Should I write to him? No, of course not, stupid. Remember his reaction when you phoned?

Sorry, there's no one here by that name.

I spend hours walking the beach, trying to make sense of it all, of my need to have someone special in my life. After all these years of living alone, you'd think I'd have gotten used to it by now.

But that's all it took. One taste of togetherness and I was worse than a kid with an incurable crush.

He dumped you. It's over. Get on with your life.

*

That little clump of thrift is still alive. Despite withered stems and brown leaves, it'll bloom again next year. To make sure, I scoop mulch around its base and tuck it in for the winter. Dammit, if this plant can survive, then so can I. I'll bloom. I'll get back to that place where I was before Colin showed up.

Independent, sure of myself. Content with my life.

Feeling a new spring in my step, I walk farther than usual, past the breakwater to the end of the beach. For a moment I stop to admire the black and white striped lighthouse that sits on a pile of rocks, guarding the entrance to the harbor. What else, I wonder, have I inherited from my mother besides the ability to draw and a fascination with lighthouses?

Falling in love with unavailable men?

It's a day with dim colors and soft edges and such perfect stillness not even the sea grass is moving. Suddenly, and without warning, Cornwall and Claudia's cottage on the cliffs come out of hiding. I take a deep breath and hold it till the memory subsides.

Funny, but it doesn't hurt quite as much as it once did.

I hear a shout and turn. Tom's picking up trash from the rotting pilings of an abandoned dock, shoving soda cans and a pizza box into a plastic bag. Hands in my pockets, I walk toward him.

'Think I should salvage this?' He points to the skeletal remains of a long-dead Christmas tree caught between two poles and decorated with driftwood and kelp.

'Beats the hell out of a plastic one.'

'How's that agency working out?' he says.

'Fine,' I say, 'and thanks for the lead.'

If the job in New London comes through, I'll do the agency work at night, on the weekends. I can't afford not to. I'm slipping behind again. The bank just sent me a letter, a polite reminder about money owed, and I dread to think of the one I'll get in February from the loan shark.

Tom dismisses my gratitude with a wave. 'I did them a favor, not you.' He stoops to pick up a newspaper, straightens, then invites me for lunch. 'I make a killer macaroni and cheese.'

I grin. 'In that case, you're on.'

Thirty-eight

Sands Point
December 2008

'You never answered my question,' Tom says.

'Which one?'

'The reason you don't like me.'

I choke on my last mouthful of food. Why the hell did he have to go and spoil a perfectly nice lunch?

'If I promise not to bite, will you tell me?' Tom says. 'More coffee?'

'No.' I stare at my plate. How the hell do I handle this?

'Come on,' Tom says. 'What have I done to piss you off?'

I swallow hard. 'I can't tell you.'

'Why not?'

'Because I feel stupid,' I say, looking through the open door toward the fireplace with its mantel of photos.

He pushes back his chair, stands up. 'Would you feel less stupid in my office?'

'No, it's better in here.'

'Okay, so tell me,' he says, sitting again.

Short of running away, I don't have much choice. I lay down my fork and stare out the window. Dunes, beach grass, Long Island Sound. 'Nice view.'

'It's the same as yours.'

Blushing furiously, I say, 'I've got a really dumb hangup.'

Tom leans forward. 'Is it kinky?'

'It'd be easier to explain if it was.'

'Try.'

It comes out in a rush. 'I have a problem with men who marry women half their age.'

His gray eyes bore into me. 'That's it?'

'Women young enough to be their daughters. Grand-daughters, even.' I pause. 'If a woman snags a guy half her age, people call her a cradle-robber. What do they call a man who does the same thing?'

'Gay?'

I glare at him. 'Men never marry women older than them.'

He sucks in his breath. 'I did.'

'Oh, God, I'm so sorry.' My hands fly to my mouth. 'Look, I'd better go. I've been thoughtless.' I stand and my chair falls backward and scrapes across the tile with a sound worse than nails on a blackboard. 'I can't believe I just said that.'

Tom says, 'I think I can see your point, but I still don't know why you're mad at me.'

'I'm not mad at you. At least' – I gulp – 'not any more.'

'Why not?' He doesn't wait for a reply, which is just as well because I haven't a clue what to say. 'Oh, I get it.' His face crumples into laughter. 'My God, now all that nonsense in your kitchen finally makes sense.'

The door from the mud room bangs open. Molly and the dogs arrive on a tidal wave of energy.

'Grampy,' she says, flinging herself into his lap. 'I'm going to misery school with Tyler.'

'You are?' Tom says. 'Can I come too?'

Molly tugs at his beard. 'You're too old.'

Carrie slides sideways through the door with an armload

of bags. Tom takes one from her, sets it on the counter. 'Molly's right,' he says, winking at me. 'I'm too old. Much too old.'

I blush even deeper.

'And,' he goes on, with an air of complacency, 'I shall go on growing older, disgracefully.'

'Dad,' Carrie says, 'you already have.'

I race home along the beach because I can see Ed Bigelow's truck bouncing down the dirt road for our two o'clock appointment. He sets up his ladder and climbs on my roof, pokes around lifting shingles and shaking his head, then delivers his verdict.

'You can patch it up and pray for mild weather, or play it safe with a new one,' he says.

Bloody hell. 'What happens if I do neither?'

Ed whacks a stray shingle into place with his hammer, then another. Some are curled like slices of stale bread; others went missing in the Thanksgiving storm.

'It might last the winter,' he says, climbing down. 'But if we get a couple of nor'easters like last year, you'll be shoveling snow from your bedroom.'

Ed leaves me with a written estimate for a new roof – slightly less than I paid for my car – and tells me not to wait because once the weather gets too bad for his guys to work outside, I'll be out of luck till next spring. Oh yes, he'll have to repoint the chimney as well because if he doesn't, it'll probably fall down, and my gutters are a disgrace. Do I want new ones?

Maybe I'll move to Mongolia and live in a yurt. Do they require chimneys? Gutters?

Sighing, I tramp inside and pick up the phone. No sense procrastinating. The folks at Loans-R-Us are delighted to help, and in less than five minutes I've almost doubled my short-term debt.

Within a week, men with crowbars are ripping shingles off my roof. Hammers crash and boots stomp above my head. To escape the noise, I grab a coat and walk to the main road. Tom's SUV idles at the curb while he empties his mailbox. He nods hello and leans against the fender, thumbing through a fistful of envelopes. I pull Christmas cards from my box, more bills with PAST DUE stamped on the front, and a letter from Beatrice's biotech company. Probably that insurance form I'm supposed to fill out and return right away.

Tom throws his mail in the car, climbs inside and lowers the window. 'Heard any more about your book?'

'The last three editors are taking a long time to say no.'

'Have you thought about entering a competition?'

I glance at the Publisher's Clearinghouse envelope in my hand. 'Like a sweepstake?'

'No,' Tom says. 'A writing contest.'

'I'm not ready for a Pulitzer.'

'Few people are,' Tom says, grinning. 'But there's an article in last Sunday's paper about an award for children's writers. If I can find it, I'll bring it over.'

'Thanks.'

'How's the agency been treating you? Any problems?'

'None,' I say. 'Things are a bit slow at the moment.' A serious understatement. The work's fizzled out and probably won't heat up again till the spring, but I'm not about to tell Tom. Don't want to sound ungrateful for his help.

'Then I'll catch you later,' he says, and drives off.

I walk back to my cottage to find the hammers have ceased. The roofers are taking a break, drinking coffee and smoking. Styrofoam cups litter the driveway and cigarette butts sprout like birthday candles from a bucket of sand.

Wood shingles and broken bricks lie in heaps on the lawn. My bushes sag beneath the weight of tarpaulins and bent gutters.

Ed's foreman assures me his men will clean up the mess.

After tossing the junk mail, I set my bills to one side and open the cards. Angels in braces from my dentist, a reindeer with its leg in a cast from Zachary's vet, and from Tom, a card with eight birds perched on telephone wires like the notes of a musical score. GOD NEST YE MERRY GENTLEMEN, say the words beneath. I smile and open the envelope from my future employer, read the letter, and—

What the fuck?

They're sorry, but the position I interviewed for is no longer available and they wish me every success finding employment elsewhere.

That's it?

Forget about us and good luck for the future?

My body slumps as if it's just been released from a corset. I drop the letter and it lands beside a card from the bank wishing me a joyous holiday season.

Does Beatrice know about this? I call her office but she's as baffled as me, and no, there isn't a hiring freeze, as far as she knows. She'll contact a friend in HR and try to figure out what's going on.

Doors slam, someone laughs, and I hear the rattle and clank of men climbing ladders. The hammers start up again, pounding nails till my head hurts. I can't deal with this. Hell, I can't even think. I have an urgent need to do something, but what? Where do I begin? Where do I find another job? Another life?

The pile of bills on my table seems to double in size.

Is Lizzie home from work yet? It's two o'clock, no three. She'll be in her office. I punch in her number, leave a message, then sit down in front of my computer to surf the Web, track down yet more places to send my résumé. It's too close to the holidays. I won't find anything this side of the New Year. Probably won't find anything the other side, either.

I lean back in my chair. Spin around twice, kick off my shoes. Now what the hell do I do?

Take in a boarder?

Sell my house?

Charming cottage on the beach. Fabulous view. New roof.

Should I mention bad plumbing?

Lizzie calls at four thirty. I'm still at my desk, turning over possibilities, trying to fight my way through this. I'm screwed. Totally screwed. I have no reserves, no place to go but down. Right now, if I could afford it, I'd drink myself stupid.

'You sound a bit ragged,' Lizzie says. 'What's wrong?'

'I lost the job.'

There's a pause. 'With the agency?'

'No, the one in New London.'

'Why?'

I read her the letter. She lets out a sigh. 'Jill, I'm sorry. This is shitty bad luck.'

No, it's bad planning. If I hadn't been blinded by my own fantasies, my own foolish, middle-aged illusions, I wouldn't be in this mess. I'd still have a business and I wouldn't be heading for bankruptcy.

'I really needed that job,' I say, in carefully measured tones, 'because I owe the bank rather a lot of money.'

'Don't we all?'

'There's more.'

'Credit cards?' Lizzie says, sounding worried.

'Worse.'

'Do you want to tell me about it?'

'No, but I will anyway.'

'Oh, shit,' Lizzie says, when I'm through explaining about the loan shark. 'There was a dean at the college who borrowed money like that. She missed a couple of payments and the bastards terminated her loan.'

I take a deep breath. 'What did she do?'

'Sold her house to pay them off,' Lizzie says. 'Jill, don't do anything rash. There's got to be another way.'

Except, right now, I'm not seeing it. Everything I have is tied up in this house, but if I sell it and pay off my debt, how much will I have left? Enough to buy a condo? Not around here. Rent an apartment? No, that's worse than chucking money down the drain.

My cottage.

The one my ex-husband inherited twenty years ago from an aunt he never knew and couldn't have cared less about.

For me, it was love at first sight, a dream come true, but Richard declared the cottage beyond redemption and insisted it be put on the market right away. 'Why do we need a hovel with no bathroom when we can fly to Palm Beach and stay in a hotel?' he said.

One of the floorboards gave way under his foot.

Through the cottage's broken window, I stared across a wilderness of weeds toward sand dunes shaped like portobello mushrooms. Beyond them, fringed by beach grass, lay the frosted blue water of Long Island Sound.

Buckets and spades, sandcastles, children playing in the surf.

My boys will love this.

'With the money we get for this dump,' Richard said, brushing the dust off his slacks, 'I could buy that Mercedes I saw last week.'

I didn't bother to point out his BMW was less than a year old. Instead, I watched a beetle crawl along what was left of the windowsill and calculated the driving time between our house and this quiet corner of Connecticut. Two hours, maybe less if the traffic wasn't bad and my station wagon didn't overheat and force me to stop along the way.

So, while my husband flew off on business trips, the boys and I drove east to a shack with an outside toilet and a leaky roof. We explored the beach at low tide and I taught them the Latin names for blue crabs, ospreys, and quahogs. We collected driftwood and shells, and reveled in sunsets shot with mauve, pink, and pewter no painter would ever dare copy. Then, after timeless days spent camping out, we'd roll up our sleeping bags and return to the pristine house in the neighborhood my husband had picked out where I'd bathe the boys in the first hot water they'd experienced in over a week, have a quick shower, and be ready with a tray of drinks when Richard came through the door. He rarely asked about our trips to the cottage; he also never got around to selling it, thank God.

And now, I contemplate the home I created from the shambles of my divorce, this shack I rescued from a wrecker's ball. For months, the boys and I suffered splinters from walking barefoot on plywood floors. We coped with a cantankerous toilet and took showers outside while I learned to use power tools, drive a straight nail, and mix cement. I tore down walls and rebuilt them. I caulked windows, installed light fixtures, and hung doors. My hands bear the scars of mistakes and success, and I savor the hours, the years I've lived and breathed in this space, raising my sons and watching them turn into men.

By myself.

I was ready, finally, to share it with someone special.

An elaborate cobweb stretches from my bookshelf to the curtain rod. A large spider crouches at its center, one of those hairy jobs with racing stripes and hobnailed boots. Colin would've had a fit if he'd seen this. 'Every smudge has eight legs,' he'd said, 'when I'm not wearing my glasses.'

My heart sinks, but my hands aren't quick enough to catch it.

Outside, I hear the guys pulling ladders off my roof, shouting to each other as they climb into trucks. Going home to wives and girlfriends, watching TV, putting kids to bed. My stomach grumbles, so I heat a can of baked beans, pop two slices of bread in the toaster, and plug in the kettle for tea.

Comfort food.

Thirty-nine

Sands Point
December 2008

I fall asleep on the couch and wake just before midnight. Something rustles outside. Is it the wind, fumbling around, chasing leaves and twigs across the front porch? I hear a thump. Must be the rope swing I've yet to take down. Feeling stiff and disoriented, I wobble into my kitchen and peer out the window, catch glimpses of light coming toward me, down my driveway. A flashlight? Would a burglar carry one of those? Yes, but he wouldn't wave it about like a kid with a jack-o'-lantern.

Where the hell is my cat? Outside or in? Can't remember, and I have a fleeting, improbable image of being defended by Zachary, fangs bared, claws extended, in full attack mode. I hesitate, then back away from the window and I'm about to reach for the phone when a face looms out of the dark. I scream. The face stiffens, captured in a cone of light from beneath. Hooded eyes, hairy cheeks. Heart pounding, I'm ready to scream again, when a voice calls my name. I race into the hall and yank open the front door.

'I could kill you for this.'

Tom steps inside on a blast of cold air. 'Hey, I'm sorry. Didn't mean to scare you, but—'

'It's midnight,' I say, still shaking.

'Ah, but your light's still on,' Tom says, pulling a scrap of paper from his pocket. 'Here's that article I promised.' He clears his throat, begins to read. '"The Bessie Walker Award for New Voices in Children's Literature is open to unpublished writers in Connecticut. Deadline, December thirty-first."'

'Hey, I appreciate this, but it sounds a bit too fancy for me,' I say. 'Archibald's not exactly Alice in Wonderland or *The Hobbit*.'

'Be fun to enter, though.' Tom hands me the clipping. 'Why not give it a try? The judges include agents and editors in New York.'

What the hell. I've got nothing else to do.

On Christmas Eve, the boys and I drive out to Harriet and Bea's new house on a rise overlooking a pond at the north end of town. The sprawling ranch, with its vaulted ceilings and plaster walls, has antique pine floors, a retro kitchen full of pink and chrome appliances, and a basement rec room with track lighting and wall-to-wall shag carpet.

'Eclectic,' Jordan says, nodding approval. He runs his hand over the burled maple dresser in Harriet's front hall. 'Beautiful wood.'

I turn away to hide my smile. Is this the same boy who grew up living out of laundry baskets because putting clothes in drawers was too much trouble? Harriet catches my eye and winks.

'We have a little work to do here,' she says.

After touring the house, we settle down to exchange presents by the fire. Anna unwraps my gift – a wooden stegosaurus – and begs Alistair to help her assemble it, and as

288

I watch his agile fingers fit the pieces together it's easy to imagine them chipping at layers of rock and brushing away dirt to reveal the prehistoric treasures underneath.

Bea whispers in my ear. 'I found out why you weren't hired.'

'You're gonna love this,' Harriet says. She refills my glass with champagne and settles on the couch beside me.

I look at Bea, then at Harriet. 'I am?'

'Your old boss, up in Hartford, gave you a bum rap,' Bea says.

'Renee Dodd?'

Bea nods. 'The bitch.'

I'm not sure which shocks me the most, Bea's uncharacteristic language or her revelation about Renee. What could she have said? That I blew off work for two days because I was at the hospital helping a friend cope with her sick child?

'I think we may have a case,' Harriet says.

'A case? What do you mean?' I turn to Bea. 'What, exactly, did Renee say about me?'

She hesitates. 'That you were unreliable. Dishonest.'

I inhale a mouthful of champagne and choke on the bubbles.

Harriet thumps me on the back. 'We can sue her company for this,' she says. 'And why the hell didn't you tell us you were fired?'

I shrug. 'Didn't seem important.'

'Well it was.' Harriet shoots me a wolfish grin. 'Finally, I get to pay you back for everything you've done for me.'

'Pay me back?'

'I owe you,' Harriet says. 'Big time.'

'Idiot,' I say. 'You don't owe me a thing.'

'Are you forgetting my skiing accident?' she says. 'If it hadn't been for you, God knows how I'd have managed.'

Three years ago, while test-driving a pair of parabolics at

Killington, Harriet hit a patch of ice and collided with a rather stout tree. She broke her nose, busted three ribs, and shattered her left ankle. I took care of Anna till she got out of the hospital. Then I took care of them both until Harriet could walk again. Three months, more or less.

'Anyone would've done the same,' I say.

'My family didn't.'

'Yeah, well.'

She leans over and hugs me. 'Will you let me handle this case?'

'You're mad,' I say. 'The judge will toss it out the window.'

'He won't have a chance,' Harriet says, 'because I plan to settle out of court.'

'How much?' Bea asks.

Harriet rubs her hands. 'I'll go for sixty and settle for forty. That okay with you, Jill?'

'Forty dollars?'

She laughs. 'Forty thousand, you numbskull.'

Well, after that, I drink far too much champagne and for a few hours I allow myself to think everything's going to be okay. Forty thousand dollars? Just because Renee Dodd lied about me? I mean, come on. Is this ridiculous, or what? But, as Harriet reminds me, people sue for much flimsier reasons and sometimes they win. She reckons we have a fighting chance.

After dinner, I sober up and tell Harriet I appreciate her concern, but I'd rather she didn't tilt at windmills on my behalf. What's the point? She isn't going to win. Not against a huge insurance company. She argues, so I tell her I'll be okay. Really.

Liar.

Harriet has no idea I'm all tapped out. Nobody does, except Lizzie and I swore her to secrecy. I haven't even told my boys. This is *my* problem. I created it, and it's up to me to find a way to fix it.

I'll call a realtor and put the house up for sale next week. Exclusive listing. By appointment only.

No way is Elaine Burke getting her hands on my cottage.

The day after Christmas, Boxing Day in England, Sophie rings up. She always does, or else I call her. 'The boys are about to leave,' I say. 'Hang on a minute. I'll be right back.'

Shoving the phone in my pocket, I step onto the front porch and watch my sons load Alistair's car with loot – two boxes of pies, a cooler full of leftover turkey, cranberry jelly, and stuffing, the remains of a sweet potato casserole, and the gifts I gave them. Nothing extravagant this year, just underwear and shirts, leather work gloves for Alistair and a set of sheets for Jordan.

He's wearing mismatched socks and faded blue sweatpants with pockets that stick out like puppies' ears. I resist the urge to tuck them back in, the same way I no longer move glasses of milk away from his elbow at mealtimes or remind him to brush his teeth.

I settle for hugs instead. Jordan gathers me up and it's like being embraced by a sheepdog and I'm reminded of the time he was sixteen and playing bass guitar. His group performed at a high school dance and he invited me to come and watch. I slipped in the side door, late, and stood in the shadows, but Jordan spotted me, beckoned me onto the stage and hugged me.

Right there. In front of his peers.

Alistair shoves his brother to one side and squeezes me so hard he puts my ribs at risk. I feel the solid muscles of his arms, the strength that comes from digging up rocks and swimming the butterfly for his college's swim team. No wonder his shoulders are twice the width of mine. Last year he qualified for the intercollegiate finals and won but Alistair couldn't care less about that. Swimming provides him with a scholarship, but that's all. He's more interested in fossils than gold medals.

Two parrots fly over. I'll miss those birds when I move.

My sons climb into Alistair's old Saab, and I wave till they're out of sight, bumping down my dirt road the way they did on their bicycles years ago, pretending to be Evel Knievel. Once, I caught them setting up ramps and I watched, horrified, as Alistair roared up the plywood on his bike and leaped over a trash can with Jordan lying inside it. Memories like this make me wish I'd had a brother or a sister.

Sophie.

I pull the phone from my pocket. 'Sophie, I'm sorry, but . . .'

Silence. Have we been cut off? Is Sophie pissed because I put her on hold? I hear a sniff, someone crying.

'Sophie?'

'Jill, it's Mum. Can you come over?'

Forty

Sands Point
December 2008

Between them, Lizzie and Tom haul me through the next twenty-four hours. Tom calls the airline and books my ticket with the one credit card I have left that isn't maxed out. Then he tells me to go and find my passport and not to worry about the mail. He'll phone me at Sophie's if anything looks urgent.

Threatening letters?

Men in black with buzz cuts and bicycle chains?

Lizzie rummages through my closet with the zeal of a bargain hunter in Filene's Basement. She tosses skirts, pants, and sweaters on the bed, resurrects my black linen dress with the scoop neck and short sleeves.

'That's for summer,' I say.

She folds it with tissue paper and lays it in my suitcase. 'It's the only black dress you own.'

Please God, I won't need it, will I?

Lizzie adds my black blazer to the mix. A black and tan paisley shawl, black shoes. 'Will you have to wear a hat?' she says.

'Christ, Lizzie! Claudia's in the ICU, not a fucking funeral home.'

She puts a hand on my arm. 'I'm trying to be practical.'

'I don't give a shit about clothes.' I glare at the phone. 'Why don't they call?'

'Because hospitals don't allow cell phones and because no news is good news,' Lizzie says. 'Now go downstairs and do something useful like polishing your doorknobs. I'll take care of things up here.'

'What about my other stuff?' I wave toward the bathroom. 'Toothbrush, shampoo. Makeup.' Dear God, I'm worried about lipstick and mascara at a time like this?

Lizzie holds up my cosmetics bag. 'All taken care of.'

The front door bangs open and I hear Harriet calling out. She's here with Anna to collect Zachary. I pull my reluctant cat from beneath the couch and try to coax him into his carrier. He arches his back, braces his paws against the frame, and acts like a terrified skydiver about to be pushed from an airplane. I wait for him to relax his grip, then shove him inside. Taking care not to pinch his tail in the lid, I snap it shut and follow Harriet outside. We fill the trunk of her car with Zachary's litter box and cat food, his dishes and Lizzie's straw hat, and I wonder what state of mind I'll be in the next time I see him.

Myocardial infarction.

That's what Sophie called it. Her tongue tripped on the words, but she finally got them out. Maybe it's easier than saying heart attack, less threatening because it sounds foreign. Rude, almost, as if the heart merely farted rather than stopped.

'Jill,' Harriet says. 'Give me Sophie's phone and fax numbers in London, and can you access your e-mail from there?'

I look at her, bewildered. 'I think so. Why?'

'Because I'll probably have questions.'

'About my cat?' I heft Zachary's carrier into the back seat. Already he's complaining loudly enough to be heard in the village.

Harriet bends to buckle Anna in her car seat. 'About our case.'

'Forget it,' I say. 'It's a lost cause.'

Straightening, she grasps my shoulders and fixes me with the same penetrating stare she uses to skewer opposing attorneys. 'Jill, I'm determined to make this work,' she says, nodding toward my house. 'No way am I going to let you lose all this.'

How does she know? I don't remember complaining, or—

'It doesn't take a genius to figure out you're in trouble,' Harriet says. 'No business, no job, and don't think I haven't noticed you tightening your belt.'

Which all seems so bloody insignificant compared to Claudia.

Heart attack.

Oh, my God.

How can everything turn into something as big and black and bottomless as this in the blink of an eye?

Tom drives me to Boston. 'No sense leaving your car in long-term parking,' he says, then listens while I reminisce about Claudia.

Like the time Sophie and I were five and Claudia filled an inflatable dinghy with water for us to play in. We didn't have bathing suits so we all stripped, even Hugh and Keith, and it was the first time I ever saw a boy's willy. Trying not to stare, I backed up and sat down hard on the dinghy's rubber edge and squashed a bee that left its stinger in my bum. It swelled so badly I had to eat supper standing up. Claudia told Edith that the bee had crawled inside my knickers, not that we were frolicking in the Nevilles' back garden without our clothes.

Claudia saved me again and again, including the year I turned seventeen and had just gotten my license. Edith gave me her car keys and a shopping list. 'No need to dawdle,' she said. 'I don't want you gallivanting around in my car. No stopping at Sophie's and don't you dare go anywhere near that boy.'

She disapproved of dating, especially going steady, so I had to meet Colin in secret. Sophie always covered for me. This time, I asked Edith if it was okay for me to stop at the library and she allowed that to be acceptable. After running her errands, I drove to Colin's and broke down at the end of his driveway. In a panic, I rang Sophie. She borrowed her father's car and showed up with Claudia who promptly called for a breakdown truck and made the mechanic promise to tell Mrs Hunter he towed her car from the greengrocer's shop, not the Carpenters' house. Then Sophie drove me home and Claudia informed Edith she really ought to pay more attention to her car's maintenance because poor Jill was stranded in the village with a pound of corned beef and two cabbages, and wasn't it lucky she and Sophie were available to come and rescue her?

'Did she buy it?' Tom asks.

'Hook, line, and sinker,' I say.

We emerge from the tunnel that runs beneath Boston harbor. Colin had clenched his fists every time I drove him through it. His face lost its color and his lips formed a thin line. The first time it happened, I thought he was angry. Turns out he was scared.

Couldn't handle being tied up with emerald satin, either.

'I like the sound of your Claudia,' Tom says. 'She's a brave woman.'

Signs for Logan Airport flash by. Airplanes drone low overhead. Tom navigates the ever-present maze of construction and says he'll be in Europe some time in the New Year. 'I'll call you at Sophie's if I get to London,' he says, pulling up at the international departures terminal. He opens the trunk and lifts out my suitcase. Sets it down on the curb.

'I appreciate this,' I say, 'but you don't have to come inside.'

'I'd like to keep you company.'

'No, but thanks all the same,' I say, shrinking from the memory of other farewells. Colin walking backward, face crumpled with emotion. Me at the barrier, waving and wanting another kiss. Him, stepping forward, and a man in uniform barring the way. Watching his train disappear because he said my car wouldn't make the journey to Boston.

A problem at the Lodge that couldn't wait.

Tom puts his hands on my shoulders the way Harriet did. 'Take care of yourself, and take care of Claudia,' he says. 'I'll miss you.'

After checking my luggage, I browse airport bookstores in search of something to read on the plane. A familiar name catches my eye. Paul Lamont, Lizzie's favorite author. Is this another thriller? I read the back cover. Sounds more like a love story, so I toss the book in my basket along with two bars of chocolate and a magazine.

To my surprise, Paul Lamont's bittersweet novel holds my attention from the very first page and I arrive at Heathrow on the trailing edge of a smudgy winter dawn, stiff and tired, eyeballs scratchy from reading all night.

If nothing else, it kept me from panicking.

I take a taxi from the airport and it drops me at Guy's Hospital. Sophie told me only immediate family are allowed to visit patients in the ICU, so I pretend I'm her sister and almost snatch my pass from the volunteer's startled hands. Dodging crowds, I race along corridors and try to keep clear of orderlies pushing gurneys. The lifts are taking too long, so I climb three flights of stairs to the ICU and find Hugh, unshaven and bleary-eyed, slumped in a chair outside Claudia's cubicle. He pulls me into a clumsy hug and I feel the dampness of tears on his cheeks.

Am I too late?

'Sophie's with her now,' Hugh says. Arm resting on my shoulders, he guides me toward a gap in the curtain. 'Go on, Mum's waiting for you.'

Lights blink, monitors beep, and a nurse bends to adjust the clamp on a tube that runs from Claudia's nose and mouth to a machine on a trolley. Another makes notes on a clipboard and hangs it at the foot of Claudia's bed.

Sophie looks up and I rush into her arms. We sway back and forth, murmuring platitudes and clutching one another. I whisper it's going to be okay. She rubs my back and sobs into my shoulder.

Loss is easier when you're young, Tom said.

'What happened?' I say.

'Not here,' she replies.

Claudia's eyes are closed, but her lips quiver. She can't speak because of the tube in her mouth. I take her hand in mine, stroke the brittle skin, run my fingers over the bones in her wrist. When had she gotten so old? So frail? Is this the same woman who prowled my beach last summer in a muumuu covered with parrots and palm trees, sat up half the night sketching raccoons, and told me to forgive Edith? I kiss her wrinkled brow and tell her I love her, then follow Sophie through the flowered curtains that hang from U-shaped tracks on the ceiling.

She nudges Hugh awake and he shuffles into Claudia's cubicle to take our place. We head for the waiting room and help ourselves to strong tea and stale pastries from a vending machine. Sophie collapses in a brown leather armchair. I throw myself onto a slip-covered couch whose soft pillows are a pleasant surprise, and wish I could fall asleep.

'Okay, give it to me straight,' I say. 'And don't hold anything back.'

'I was in the living room,' Sophie says, 'going over a job order when Mum came downstairs and stretched out on the sofa, saying she didn't feel well. We'd eaten a ton of Christmas pud the night before, so I didn't pay much attention because I figured she had indigestion. Then Mum told me her chest hurt, like something heavy was sitting on her breastbone.'

A man in a rumpled suit enters the room and pours a cup of tea from the urn. Distractedly, he nods at us, then leaves looking as worried as we do.

Sophie takes a deep breath. 'I told her to stay put while I fetched the car, but when I got back, she was upstairs brushing her teeth and about to take a bath. So I threatened to call an ambulance if she didn't cooperate; then I brought her to Guy's. After that, everything happened fast. Mum was whisked off to an examining room. The walls were a pukey pale green. She had a cardiologist and three nurses. One of them stuck electrodes on her chest and plugged her into some sort of machine, another hung an IV drip, and the doctor put tubes up her nose.'

I shudder. 'When did Hugh get here?' From Sophie's garbled explanation on the phone, I'd learned her brother had left on Christmas Eve for a skiing holiday in Austria and she'd had a tough time tracking him down.

'Yesterday,' Sophie says. 'The nurses said Mum was doing better. They'd moved her out of the ICU and into the cardiac ward by then, so I felt okay about leaving for an hour to fetch him from the airport. When we got back, Mum's bed was empty. I freaked. Good thing Hugh was here because I was a gibbering idiot at that point.'

'Where was she?'

'Back in the ICU, where they could keep an eye on her,'

Sophie says. 'Apparently, Mum decided she was fit enough to go home, so she ripped out her tubes and when all the monitors went off at once the nurses rushed in and found her on the floor. She went into atrial fibrillation and they spent two hours bringing her out of it.'

'Christ.'

'Remember when our mothers used to tell us to always wear clean knickers in case we were hit by a bus?' Sophie says.

I nod.

'Well, it doesn't matter,' she goes on, 'because they cut your clothes off with surgical scissors. Mum will be furious when she finds out they shredded her favorite track suit.'

For the first time since leaving home, I smile. 'Then let's go to Marks and Spencer and buy her another one.'

Forty-one

We take turns at Claudia's bedside, reading to her and rubbing her chapped lips and hands with aloe which is all we're allowed to use. Working in shifts, we rotate back to Sophie's house to shower and change our clothes, feed the dogs, and gather up more books and magazines to keep Claudia entertained. She's beginning to look better. More color in her face and her eyes seem a bit brighter than before.

'How long can you stay?' Sophie asks.

'As long as you need me.'

A look of relief sweeps across Sophie's tired face.

Finally, after three days, I reach the bottom of my suitcase and discover Colin's pink shirt wrapped around my funereal black shoes. Is this Lizzie's idea of a joke? Of course not, Jill. Get a grip. She never saw the damned shirt, except for that picture above my desk. I unroll the sleeves. Sand trickles out; a tiny shell tumbles from the cuff and bounces on Sophie's spare bed.

Is there no end to the memories?

Did anyone, Hugh or Keith, call Colin to tell him about Claudia?

Jeez, I hope not. Last thing we need is him showing up.

I run downstairs to make tea and glance at the calendar on Sophie's desk and realize it's New Year's Day. Her message light is blinking. I hit PLAY and listen to an angry woman complain that Sophie had blown off her New Year's Eve dinner party.

I erase the message.

Claudia's condition improves, and by the end of another week she's well enough to be moved back into the cardiac ward, but not without dire warnings from her doctor.

'Pull that stunt again,' she says, adjusting Claudia's drip, 'and we'll strap you to the bed.'

Dressed in a pale blue bed jacket with satin ribbons, Claudia looks more like Barbie's grandmother than the woman in Wellington boots who rescued squirrels and roared around Cornwall in her ancient Morris Minor. Soft curls frame her face and a hint of blush dusts her cheeks. Is that lipstick I see?

Sophie nudges me and grins.

I pull Paul Lamont's book from my bag and turn to page one.

'Let me see that.' Sophie leans over my shoulder. 'Hey, Ian's making a film with this guy.'

'I didn't know he was an actor as well.' I look for a picture of the author, but don't find one.

'No, silly. He's written the screenplay for one of his thrillers and Ian says it's going to be a blockbuster. The next James Bond, but with more violence and sex.'

'Just what we need.'

Claudia pipes up. 'That nice young doctor told me to wait at least six weeks before having intimate relations,' she says. 'Do I really have to?'

Sophie blushes. She grabs a pillow and threatens to suffocate her mother. I keep reading aloud, and as Claudia tells

Sophie to mind her own business, I feel as if something huge and horrible has just been lifted from my heart.

But when Claudia nags me into visiting Edith, I know she's really on the mend. 'Do you have her address?' she says, pulling her handbag from the night table. 'Because if you don't, then it's in here somewhere. Now promise me you'll go?'

'Of course I will.' At this point, I'd walk barefoot over glass for her.

I help Sophie get her business back on track. We take orders, cook massive amounts of food, and hire substitute caterers for the functions we can't handle. In between, we visit Claudia. She's getting better, slowly, but not yet well enough to come home.

Finally, early in February, Sophie takes a day off, so I borrow her car and drive south to Brighton. A steady rain stutters on the pavement as I park the car and stumble onto the beach. Mounds of pebbles threaten to twist my ankles, salt spray dampens my face. The wind whips my hair into knots and numbs my fingers. I pull up my collar, shove both hands in my pockets. Down by the water, a woman attached to a leash is being pulled along by a dog the size of a pony. Two pale-faced boys share a cigarette beneath an umbrella. Maybe if I hang out here long enough, visiting hours will be over by the time I get there.

As sharp as ever, and still bitter about the past.

Claudia will have my guts for garters if I chicken out now.

The nursing home's director is an angular, middle-aged woman who introduces herself so quickly I don't catch her name.

'Didn't you get our letter?' she asks, when I explain why I'm here.

'What letter?'

The woman opens a diary. 'It was sent just before Christmas.'

'Air mail?' I say.

She sighs. 'Surface. We're on a strict budget.'

No wonder it never showed up. Probably still hasn't arrived or Tom would've called to let me know.

'So, you obviously didn't receive it,' she says.

I shake my head.

With an air of being quite used to this sort of thing, the woman tells me Edith died on 21 December. 'This must come as a shock, but it was very peaceful, and believe me, she wasn't in pain.'

No heart attack then. Not like Claudia. I feel a sense of relief and ask, 'Did she ever say anything about me?'

'Not till your letter arrived.'

I stop fidgeting and lay both hands on my lap while the woman, whose name I'm still trying to remember, sorts through piles of paper on her desk.

'That letter meant a lot to your aunt. We were surprised because we didn't know she had any living relatives. Anyway, she left this for you.' Leaning forward, she gives me a padded envelope. 'I was waiting to hear from you before sending it.' Then she stands and walks to the door. 'You'd probably like to be alone for a bit,' she says, before slipping away.

The envelope is soft and thick, its surface worn and wrinkled as if it's been used several times before. I remove the tape and pull out a small, tissue-wrapped object with a plain white card attached to the top: *This belonged to your mother.*

I tear off the last piece of paper. A slender chain forms a puddle of gold in my hand; an oval gold locket nestles on top.

With clumsy fingers, I pry it open, blinking through my tears. Inside the locket are two tiny pictures, grainy black-and-white images of infants, and I only recognize myself because of the ridiculous lace bonnet. I lift the other picture from its shallow nest and turn it over. On the back, in faded brown ink, is a single word.

Katie.

Clutching my treasure with one hand, I hang on to my chair with the other. The room tilts and sways. I close my eyes and count slowly to ten, then open them again. The room has stopped spinning.

There's a soft knock on the door and the nursing home's director comes in with a tray of sandwiches and tea. 'I thought you might need this,' she says.

I remember her name. 'Thank you, Ms Holt.'

'Daphne,' she says, lifting the teapot. 'Please call me Daphne. Shall I pour?'

After buying a bunch of narcissus for Claudia, I drive back to London, straight to the hospital. She's alone, looking tired. The nurse on duty tells me she had too many visitors today.

'I'll only be a few minutes,' I say, holding up my flowers. 'Long enough to give her these.'

She nods approval.

I bend to kiss Claudia's soft cheek. It smells of Yardley's face powder, a scent I remember from childhood.

'Did you see her?' she says.

'No, but Edith left this for me.' I show her the locket. 'It belonged to my mother.'

Claudia lets out a sigh. 'Oh, my dear. How sad for you.'

'She died just before Christmas.' Tears prick at my eyelids. I blink, but one escapes and rolls down my cheek. Poor Edith. What a sad, unhappy woman. How different would my life have been if she and I had gotten along? For a start, I wouldn't have left England and married Richard. Or had my two boys.

My boys. I can't imagine life without them.

I guess, when all is said and done, Edith did me a huge favor by driving me away. I kiss the locket and slip it around my neck.

'At least she got your letter, and that's good,' Claudia says. Her eyes close and I see blue shadows around them, not Yardley or Revlon, but exhaustion and illness. Her lips move. 'He came to see me.'

I reach for her hand, squeeze it gently. She must've seen her beloved husband, Guy, in a dream. God forbid she's getting ready to join him.

I won't let her go.

'He came with Keith and Penny,' Claudia says, her voice barely audible.

I lean closer. 'Who did?'

Her breath whispers across my face. 'I wish he hadn't come. He hurt you. I can't forgive him for that.'

Colin was here, in this room?

The nurse takes my arm. 'She's had a rough day.'

My mouth goes dry. I look down at Claudia, at this woman who gave me the love I didn't get at home, and my feelings about Colin harden into a malignant lump. If he's caused a relapse, I'll drive up to the fucking Cotswolds and kill him.

Forty-two

After I drive the night nurse mad with questions, she tells me to go and find Claudia's doctor. It's almost midnight when I track her down in the cafeteria, hands wrapped around a cup of black coffee. She looks almost as exhausted as I feel.

'This isn't a relapse, just a minor setback,' Dr Schaaf assures me. 'Mrs Neville got a little over-stimulated today, so I prescribed something to help her sleep. She'll be fine tomorrow.'

But I'm not fine. I'm so mad at Colin I can barely see straight. I can't believe how angry I am.

Angry with Colin?

Rage surges up my throat. I swallow hard, choke it back down. My fists clench into claws. How could anyone be that insensitive, that clueless? Is Colin so self-centered, so oblivious of others' needs, he thought Claudia would be glad to see him? Doesn't he realize she'd be protective of me? That by showing up without warning he might cause a problem for her? I mean, come on. The woman's just had a heart attack, for God's sake. She doesn't need any more shocks.

Sophie's still up when I storm through her front door.

'Trouble parking?' she asks. That's usually the reason for frayed tempers around here. Some nights we have to circle her block three or four times before finding a space large enough for the Range Rover, which makes me really appreciate my driveway back home.

I slam Sophie's keys on the table, throw my coat on the couch.

'What's wrong?' she says.

'Colin Carpenter, that's what.'

She shoots me an exasperated look. 'Don't tell me you saw him.'

When I asked to borrow her car, I didn't tell Sophie I was going to see Edith because I wasn't convinced I'd be able to pull it off, so I tossed off an excuse that I needed to get away by myself for a bit. She probably assumed I was driving up to confront Colin.

'No,' I say, 'but Claudia did.'

'Holy shit,' Sophie says. 'When?'

'This afternoon,' I say, and assure her Claudia's okay, except she had too many visitors, including one who upset her.

'Stupid git,' Sophie says. 'What the hell made him think he'd be welcome?' She sighs. 'The only day I don't go to see Mum, and this happens. Good thing I wasn't there or I'd have killed him.'

'You wouldn't have had a chance,' I say through clenched teeth. 'Because I'd have killed him first.'

Sophie raises her eyebrows. 'Really?'

'I'm so fucking mad at him, I could—'

'Hallelujah!' she says. 'It's about bloody time.'

Oh, my God. Did I say that? Out loud? Has the old Jill finally come back? I guess she has, because Sophie laughs and says, 'I was wondering when the real you would get around to showing up.' Then she grabs my hand and hauls me into the dining room, or what *was* her dining room when I left at nine thirty this morning. Drop cloths cover the floor. A mountain of furniture lurks beneath a blue plastic tarp and Sophie's paint-spattered stepladder leans against the far wall. Her oriental rug lies rolled in a corner with a tangle of dogs snoozing on top.

'What's all this about, then?'

'Mum,' Sophie says. 'She can't live alone any more, so she's coming to live here. I'm turning this into a bedsit for her.' She points toward the tiny bathroom whose claw-foot tub and willow-patterned lavatory would fetch a fortune in an antique shop. 'She'll have everything on one floor. No more fussing with stairs.'

'And she's agreed to all this?'

'Not yet, but she will,' Sophie says. 'Providing you help me talk her into it.' She hands me a stack of paint chips. 'I need your opinion about color. Can't make up my mind.'

Closing my eyes, I conjure up Claudia's cottage in Cornwall, the scabiosa and purple-belled heather that grow wild on the cliffs. Through her kitchen window, I glimpse vanilla-colored thickets of broom and the myriad blues and greens of an ever-changing ocean.

'She'll be less bolshie about moving here if it reminds her of home,' I say. 'Go with lavender walls and cream trim, sage accents and splashes of Prussian blue.'

'Brilliant,' Sophie says. 'Tomorrow, we paint.'

I grin at her. 'Naked?'

'Is there any other way?'

After a quick trip to the local DIY store to buy decorating supplies, we visit Claudia. She's still tired, but her eyes sparkle, and when Sophie tells her we're turning the dining room into a bed-sitting room for her, she doesn't argue. Just nods and says, 'We'll see.'

'Better than an outright no,' Sophie says.

We drive home and get busy. I prime the woodwork while Sophie climbs the ladder and swipes lavender emulsion on the wall as if conducting a symphony. Blobs of paint fly from her roller, specks land in her hair. She leans to reach into corners.

'Watch out,' I yell.

Too late.

Sophie's ladder wobbles. The tray tilts and lavender paint slops all over her.

'Shit!' She pulls off her shirt, balls it up, and dumps it on the floor. 'Okay, smartass,' she says, glaring at me because I'm trying not to laugh. 'Now it's your bloody turn.'

'Sophie, get real,' I say. 'We're not kids any more.'

Hands on hips, she strikes a pose. 'Tit for tat.'

'Does that mean you're taking your bra off as well?'

'Why the hell not?' Sophie unhooks it.

Dammit, her breasts still don't droop.

'Come on,' she says. 'Don't be shy.'

I wriggle out of my jeans and yank off my sweatshirt.

Sophie grins. 'No more gym knickers?'

'Used the last pair for dust rags years ago,' I say, twitching the elastic on my gray spandex briefs. I've abandoned Victoria's Secret in favor of L. L. Bean.

'That's what we need,' Sophie says. 'Rags. There's a pile of old clothes in my room. See what you can find. A cotton shirt would do.'

Pink cotton? Heavy and well pressed?

Dropping my brush in a bucket, I run upstairs and rummage in my case, pull out Colin's shirt and race back to the kitchen. Sophie's scissors lie on the counter. The hospital reduced Claudia's favorite track suit to shreds. Can I do the same to Colin's favorite shirt? Like Sophie just said, why the hell not?

I grab her scissors and chop off the collar and cuffs, cut the sleeves into ribbons. Gripping hard, I slice up the back and both fronts. My heart lurches and my hands shake, but I keep hacking at the shirt till there's nothing left but a pile of pink rags.

There, I've done it. I've shredded Colin's memory the way he shredded my gut. And, you know what? It feels good, really good. In fact, it feels rather marvelous. With a feeling of triumph, I take my rags into the dining room and give one to Sophie.

'This isn't one of mine, is it?' she says, wiping her hands.

I open a can of paint with a screwdriver. 'Nope.'

'Didn't think so. I never wear pink.'

'It's Colin's. He was wearing it the day I fell down your stairs.'

Sophie waves her rag in surrender. 'Jeez, Jill. Remind me never to piss you off. My wardrobe couldn't take it.'

Footsteps clatter across the kitchen floor.

Another early warning system?

'Quick.' I toss more rags at Sophie.

She covers her boobs. Hugh pokes his head through the open door. 'Oh, sorry.' He coughs and turns away. 'I've come to pick up stuff for Mum. She wants her sketch pad and paints.'

Thank God I'm still wearing a bra.

'They're in the basket on top of my desk,' Sophie yells at her brother. 'Her pastels are there, too.'

The front door bangs shut.

Sophie shoots me an evil grin. 'Remember how we used to spy on the boys?'

'Of course I do.'

'Let's do it again.'

I groan. 'Must we?'

'Just a suggestion,' she says. 'We'll go antiquing instead. I need to find a comfy chair for Mum's new room. How about Saturday? There are some great shops up near Stroud.'

Which, of course, is less than twenty miles from where Colin lives.

After finding the perfect armchair for Claudia in a second-hand furniture store, we stuff it into the back of the Range Rover and head for home. Half an hour later, Sophie pulls off the main road and makes a detour through Colin's village.

'Just a quick drive-by,' she says. 'No stopping. Once up and down the high street and then we're out of here, okay?'

I ought to know better.

She spots a teashop across from North Lodge and declares she can't drive another mile without something to drink.

'Then let's find a pub,' I say.

Sophie checks her watch. 'It's four o'clock. I want tea, not alcohol.'

Yeah, right.

Five minutes later we're sitting in the Buttery's bay window at a round table with a blue gingham cloth and a vase of snowdrops in the center. Sophie wears dark glasses and a headscarf. Makes her look like a middle-aged Royal in disguise. I lurk behind the menu and try to decide between cucumber sandwiches and scones with clotted cream. Maybe I'll have both. We're the teashop's only customers and it's getting late. The waitress who takes our order yells it into the kitchen before putting on her coat. She waves goodbye and slips out the door.

Across the narrow street, North Lodge is bathed in the glow of a late afternoon sun. Barren vines embroider the honey-colored stone like dark threads on a golden tapestry and the wooden tubs out front are ablaze with winter pansies. A robin perches on the bare branches of an almond tree. Through a narrow archway, just wide enough for a coach and horses, I see the corner of a barn, a strip of lawn still shockingly green, and a splash of purple crocus beneath the silver trunk of a birch. Smoke curls from crooked chimneys, and I have an image of guests sipping cocktails in front of a large open fire.

'Gorgeous, isn't it?' Sophie says.

Someone comes up behind us. 'Ay, that it is.'

We turn and look up.

A tall, ruddy-cheeked woman with hair pulled back in a bun and a shelf-like bosom holds a large silver tray. She sets it on the table next to ours. A knitted cosy warms an earthenware teapot. Spoons jiggle on saucers and scones spill from a basket. 'Two cream teas,' she says. 'And who gets the sandwiches?'

'I do,' I say.

Sophie removes her Ray-Bans. 'Would you like to join us?'

Why do I get the feeling she's about to take espionage to a whole new level? I shoot her a warning look, but the damage is already done. The woman pulls up a chair.

'Don't mind if I do,' she says. Her voice has a soft country burr. She's probably lived in this village all her life, knows everything that goes on around here, which is exactly what Sophie wants. 'I'm Doris,' the woman says. 'Doris Tidworth.'

'Rebecca Bond,' Sophie replies, 'and this is my sister, Kristina.'

Bond? As in 007?

To keep from laughing, I bite into a sandwich while Doris sets out china plates, bone-handled butter knives, and silver spoons. She pours the tea, offers milk and sugar, then slathers cream and strawberry jam onto a scone.

Best to let Sophie handle this. She's better at spying than I am.

It doesn't take long. In no time at all, she's chatting up the teashop's owner about the weather and the lack of business in winter, and we learn how Doris wishes young people in the village weren't so eager to scarper off to London because she can't find any decent help any more and what with those charrybangs full of tourists coming in all summer long and her bunions acting up, she can't keep on her feet all day, can she? Especially when those city folk come traipsing in from the Lodge because they don't serve afternoon tea over there.

I'm exhausted listening to her.

'Such a nice man, that Mr Carpenter,' Doris says, waving her scone toward the window. Crumbs bounce off her plate and onto the table. 'And don't you believe a word of those rumors about that accident, neither.'

Forty-three

England
February 2009

Sophie leans forward. 'What accident?'

'There's some folks around here think he's to blame because the missus can't walk any more.'

Missus?

Dear God, don't tell me he lied about that as well.

Sophie kicks me under the table. 'His wife?' she says.

'They're not married, but they may as well be,' Doris says. 'They've been together for years.' She takes a noisy swig from her cup. Its delicate porcelain handle makes her gnarled fingers look even larger. 'Anyway, after the accident Shel gave up her fancy job in London and turned her house into a hotel. Must've cost a pretty penny. Very posh it is too.' Doris takes a huge breath, looks at us. 'You should see the goings-on over there. They've got one of them cajuzzi things. Big enough to hold six people.'

'A Jacuzzi?' Sophie says.

Doris nods vigorously. 'Don't hold with all that community bathing, myself,' she says. 'Stuff like that's got to be done private. I never let my old man see me without me knickers.'

Stifling my grin with a napkin, I'm torn between laughter

and disbelief. Colin's common-law wife is a former career woman who, according to Doris, switched gears when life tossed her a curve?

There's a problem at the Lodge and Shelby can't cope.
Like hell she can't.

'Tell us about the accident,' Sophie says.

God only knows how she's keeping a straight face.

Doris glances over her shoulder as if expecting to see the village constable, ready to arrest her for gossiping. She lowers her voice. 'Four, maybe five years ago, she and the mister had a big fight. The cleaning lady overheard them. Now, she wasn't snooping, mind you, but they was yelling loud enough to beat the band.'

'What about?' Sophie asks.

'Money, more'n likely.' Doris leans forward. 'Her money, not 'is. He don't have any, you see. Anyway, like I said, the cleaning lady, who's a regular customer of mine, swears blind he shoved her, and Miz Burnside went—'

'Burnside?' Sophie says.

'Our Shel,' Doris says. 'Well, she went arse over teakettle down the stairs. But Shel insisted it was her own doing. Says she tripped and fell. She's like that, you know. Generous to a fault, she is. Wouldn't hurt a fly. Well, the thing is, her career up in London was over, so she's back here where she belongs, at the Lodge.'

My head is spinning.

I expect Sophie to start pumping Doris for more, but she doesn't need to. Thoroughly warmed up, Doris prattles on.

'Burnsides have lived in that house for generations. One of them fought with the Bonnie Prince, and –'

Another lie. Colin said the Lodge belonged to him.

'– I remember Shel as a little girl, and then a teenager and mad as could be because her mum had a new baby. At *her* age, Shel told me, and I agreed. Well, really, she was almost forty and you'd have thought she'd be all done with that sort of stuff. Poor Shel. She used to come here a lot in those days. Get away from her little sister. That would be Diana, of course. She's fifteen years younger than our Shel. Got herself a fancy education over in Switzerland. One of them finishing schools. Came back a few years ago to help out after the accident, but I think she's got her mind on something else these days. 'Tisn't the mister's fault she's always throwing herself at him.'

Sophie says, 'Oh?'

'Speakin' of the devil,' Doris says, hauling herself upright. 'There they are now.'

We turn and look out the window.

Across the street, Colin pushes a wheelchair through the archway. Dusk looms above the rooftops and shadows lengthen on the ground, but I can see well enough to make out the woman's pale hair hanging loose around her shoulders. A blanket covers her legs, her hands grip the arm rests. She can't walk.

And to think I was jealous of her.

A younger, dark-haired woman stumbles beside Colin. She wears a calf-length red cape and matching miniskirt and she trips over the cobbles in her high-heeled black boots.

Diana?

She links her arm through Colin's. He smiles, then bends to kiss her and his hair flops over his forehead. I bite my lip to keep from losing all my hard-won resolve. Shelby looks straight ahead. Doesn't she have any idea at all what's going on behind her back?

I've never been unfaithful before, Colin said.

My mouth turns sour. Disgust mingles with anger and shame. 'I need another cup of tea,' I say, reaching for the pot.

So, Colin doesn't own the Lodge, and according to Doris, he doesn't have any money, either. How many more lies did I swallow? That check I lost must've come from Shelby's account. I wish there was some way I could apologize, tell her how sorry I am about all this.

After making sure we don't need any more scones, Doris loads our tray with empty plates and lumbers off to the kitchen.

The minute she's out of earshot, Sophie says, 'What the hell went wrong with Colin? What turned him into such a bloody shit?'

I tell her what happened in Scotland. 'And that's not all,' I say. 'His father swanned off to Australia, then Colin got married and his wife left him for another woman and took their only child to live in New Zealand.' I pause. 'Unless he was lying about all that as well.'

'Cripes,' Sophie says. 'If true, it's enough to curdle anyone's blood.' She reaches for my hand. 'Poor Jill. You must hate this, seeing him again. I'm sorry I dragged you here.'

'I'm glad you did.'

'Why?'

'Because it's helped me figure out the truth.'

'Like what?'

'That Colin took me for a fool. I was hoping for something else, some other reason he dumped me and ran. But Lizzie was right. He was a cruise-ship romance. Nothing more, and I was a prize idiot for believing him.'

'Oh, Jill.'

'Yeah, I know. There's no fool like an old fool, huh?'

Sophie sighs. 'He used to be such a nice guy.'

'And he could be again,' I say. 'People *can* change, you know.'

'But only if they want to.'

'Exactly,' I say. 'And Colin doesn't want to. I mean, why should he? He's got the best of both worlds. Freedom to travel and pick up with women whenever he feels like it, and Shelby and her sister at home, holding the fort because somebody has to.'

'Shelby's a bloody saint,' Sophie says. 'Or a bloody fool.'

'Or maybe she really does love him.'

'And what about you?' Sophie says. 'Do you love him?'

I think about the place where I am now and how hard I've worked to get here. Something inside me lightens and shifts, and I feel myself slide beyond the reach of soft green eyes and a crooked grin. My road forward is suddenly clear. I'll sell my cottage and buy something else to fix up and call home. Find another job or stick a Band-Aid on my business, get it up and running again. Whatever I do, I'll work damned hard to make it happen.

It won't be easy, but I've done it before and I can do it again.

'Jill?' Sophie says.

'No, I don't love him, but I've forgiven him.'

Sophie cocks an eyebrow. 'Are you sure?'

And I nod, because the past is a pair of jeans that don't fit any more.

Forty-four

Rain lashes the Range Rover's windshield as we drive back to London. Sophie turns on the radio. I hunker down and try to sleep, but images of the Colin I once knew keep colliding with the sight of him kissing Diana behind Shelby's back. Did he really push her down the stairs? Is he responsible for her landing in that wheelchair? Somehow, I can't get my arms around that one. It's nothing more than idle speculation, village gossip at its worst. Colin's a pathological liar, but he isn't violent.

With a shudder of distaste, I give his memory a final shove and it slithers out of my heart. Relief washes through me; then comes a trickle of pity for the man he's become. I suppose that's healthy, really. Better than hating him. Thank God I don't love him any more.

Sophie's mobile rings.

The hospital? Is it Claudia? Suddenly alert, I sit up and watch Sophie's face as she answers, then relax when I see her nod and smile. 'Sure, come on over,' she says into a phone no larger than a credit card. 'We'll be home by seven, so come over around eight.'

Company? 'Who's coming?'

'Ian,' she says. 'He's bringing Paul with him.'

'Paul?'

'Paul Lamont. The guy who kept you up all night on the plane.'

I groan.

'Come on, Jill. This is exactly what you need.'

'Another sleepless night?'

'No,' Sophie says. 'Meeting new people. Socializing.'

Right now, I'd rather fall into bed with a good book.

'Okay, but do I have to get dressed up?'

'Wear whatever you want.'

'Sweats and fuzzy slippers?'

'Of course,' she says.

Yeah, right.

We hit heavy traffic around Reading and arrive home later than expected. The closest parking space is three streets away. Running through sleet and freezing rain, I'm numb with cold by the time we reach Sophie's front door. She takes a shower upstairs and I opt for a decadent soak in the old claw-foot tub. Wallowing in hot water and a froth of vanilla-scented bubbles, I fold a towel into a pillow, lean back, and wait for my body to thaw out.

I wash one leg, then the other, and stick my big toe up the water spout like I used to when I was a kid. Instead of making small talk with Sophie's guests, maybe I should just loll about in Claudia's new bathroom and pretend my life's in perfect order.

Steam fogs up the mirror and my bubbles collapse. The rosy picture I painted earlier about selling my cottage and fixing up another one gets stuck in my throat like a ball of wadded-up duct tape. What the hell was I thinking? Power tools and ladders have no place in my life. Not right now, anyway. Without medical insurance, Murphy's Law would be sure to kick in and I'd fall through the roof, chop off a finger, or—

There's a rap on the door. 'Jill, get a move on. They'll be here in a minute.'

Wrapping myself in a towel, I scurry upstairs as the doorbell chimes. I push a snarl of coat hangers to one side and pull chinos and a lambswool sweater from the wardrobe, then scrabble in my suitcase for clean undies and socks. I shove my feet into loafers and run a brush through my tangled wet hair. No time for makeup, just a spritz of cologne.

Sophie yells, 'Jill, do hurry up.'

Carefully, I descend the stairs. Last thing I need is another sprained ankle.

'Here you are,' Sophie says, handing me a whisky. 'Jill, you remember Ian, don't you? And this is Paul Lamont.'

He steps out from behind Sophie's boyfriend. 'Hi, there.'

'Oh, my God.' I suck in my breath. 'What the hell are you doing here?'

'D'you two know each other?' Sophie says.

'Kind of,' he says, winking at me.

'Why didn't you tell me?'

'I take it you guys are acquainted,' Ian says.

The whisky burns my throat. 'We're neighbors.'

He wears tan corduroys and a blue Oxford shirt over a navy turtleneck. Docksiders, no socks. Aren't his feet cold? This is London in February, not July on the beach.

'Neighbors?' Sophie says. 'In Sands Point?'

'Yes,' I say, staring at the bearded man now leaning against her mantel. 'Except I know him as Tom.'

Sophie takes Ian's hand. 'Let's go and see about supper.'

I let Tom pour me another drink. If nothing else, just holding the glass gives me something to do while I reassemble what's left of my composure. My face feels tight and shiny, my hair feels like a haystack ravaged by rain and high wind. I forgot to brush my teeth. We both speak at once.

'My God, to think we—' I say.

'Quite the coincidence,' Tom says. 'I had no clue that your Sophie was Ian's Sophie as well.' He tugs at his beard. 'I must say, it was quite a surprise, seeing you come down those stairs.'

'You probably think I'm an idiot,' I say.

'Why?'

'For not knowing who you are.'

'And who is that?'

The guy who wrote that charming story I read on the plane.

'A best-selling author.' I haven't read any of his thrillers, but Lizzie has and she thinks he walks on water. She'll be gobsmacked when I tell her who he really is.

'You flatter me,' Tom says.

'Why did you keep it a secret?'

He abandons the fireplace and sits beside me on the green linen couch I once shared with Colin. Funny, but my heart doesn't lurch like a drunk when I think about him. No anger, no sense of loss either, just a calm, rhythmic pulse that feels different, as if readying itself for something quite new. I feel richer, somehow. Deeper and wiser for having invested myself in a relationship, even if it didn't work out the way I wanted.

'How would you have reacted if you'd known?' Tom says.

'Reacted?'

'To me.'

I shrug. 'I don't know. The same, I guess.'

'No, you wouldn't.' Tom puts a hand on my knee.

It feels warm, familiar, as if it belongs there.

He says, 'Jill, I've grown up with groupies. My father was once a successful politician. He had them, and then so did I.

Surrounded by people who fawned over us for what we did, what we had, but not for who we really were.' He pauses. 'I didn't want to risk that sort of friendship with you. My fame, or whatever you want to call it, would've gotten in the way. It always does.'

My heart pokes me in the ribs. 'So, who else knows your real identity?'

'My daughter, my agent. The publisher in New York.' Tom grins. 'I suppose Molly's guessed by now, but I'm not sure about the dogs.'

'But no one in Sands Point?'

'I like being anonymous.'

Lizzie's auction. The autographed first edition. 'Then it must've been you who donated that book.'

'And bought the moose,' Tom says. 'It makes a great hat rack.'

Who'd have thought he was Paul Lamont? I certainly didn't, but now I know he's a celebrity, I have to keep reminding myself he's also my neighbor – an ordinary guy with two stroppy dogs who picks trash off the beach, fixes my plumbing, and makes a killer macaroni and cheese.

He asks after Claudia and I tell him she's going to be fine, that she's coming here to live with Sophie. Then you'll be coming home soon, he says.

Home?

Do I still have one? Maybe the bank's already repossessed it. I ought to have called Iris but I'm operating in *what I don't know can't hurt me* mode. Before I left, I called to tell her about Claudia and how I had no idea when I'd be back and she promised to hold off the bank's SWAT team as long as she could. I haven't heard, so I assume she's succeeded . . . so far.

But Tom's right. It's time for me to go home. Claudia's on the mend, Sophie's pulled her shit together, and I need to go and gather up mine. I glance toward Tom. He's looking at me, smiling. He has such sweet creases at the corners of his eyes. His beard lies peacefully on his jaw and his hair no longer curls over his collar. Even his eyebrows are less shaggy. Carrie must've forced him to visit the barber before flying over.

'What brings you here?' I ask.

'Emergency script conference,' Tom says. He pulls an envelope from his pocket. 'I brought you this.'

A letter from the loan shark?

'But how did you know I'd be here?'

'Before leaving, I rang Lizzie. She said you were staying a while longer and suggested I deliver your mail in person.' He nudges my arm. 'Well, go on. Open it.'

The return address doesn't ring any bells. I don't know anyone named Bessie Walker, do I?

Oh, my God. The contest.

I rip the envelope and pull out a single sheet of paper. Scan it, then read it again more slowly.

We are delighted to announce that Archibald's Aria *was chosen from over five hundred submissions as the winning entry in our Picture Book division. You are invited to attend the reception and awards ceremony at Summerwind Cove on March 9, where you will be presented with a certificate and a check for three hundred dollars. Please let us know . . .*

Forty-five

I want to capture this moment and keep it in a bottle like a firefly on a hot summer night, press it like a wildflower and display it in a shadow box on the wall.

I can't remember the last time I felt so special, so rewarded for my efforts. Stuff like this happens to other people, not to me. I usually come in last, like the time Sophie and I ran the three-legged race at Parents' Day. We fell so many times, the headmistress gave us a consolation prize for being good sports. A book of French poetry. Great for squashing the spiders that lurked in the school's basement locker room. I turn toward Tom, eager to share my joy, but I can't because if I open my mouth, my heart will leap out and clap its hands.

Tom squeezes my knee. 'Congratulations.'

Congratulations?

'Hey, wait a minute,' I say. He looks as thrilled as if he'd won the prize himself. 'How did you know?'

He winks and gives me a thumbs-up, and my pleasure evaporates. He must've been one of the judges, maybe the *only* judge. I choke down my disappointment. For a second or two, I thought *Archibald's Aria* had won fair and square. Now I feel, somehow, as if I cheated.

Tom says, 'My agent's partner judged the picture book division, and before you go off half-cocked and accuse me of nepotism, I'll admit I knew about that, but I had nothing to do with picking the winner. In fact, I didn't know you'd taken first place till I saw your illustrations on Judith's desk last week.' He grins at me. 'She wants to represent you.'

My mind struggles to keep up. 'Who does?'

'Judith Tate, your future agent. She loves opera and parrots, and she's absolutely mad about Archibald.'

Tom rambles on about royalties and copyrights and how Judith's already talked it up to an editor, and she expects them to offer around ten thousand for Archibald and maybe I should think about developing him into a series. Tom's words ricochet around my head like popcorn. Probably all that whisky I drank.

Ten thousand dollars.

Reality check here. Ten thousand, minus agent's commission and taxes, won't put much of a dent in my debt. But I don't give a shit because it's doing wonders for my ego. So is the win. I read the letter again.

Oh, my God. First place.

Tom hugs me and I don't want him to let go.

Sophie cracks a bottle of champagne and we toast my success. I pinch myself because I still can't believe it. Is Tom stretching the truth? Can I be sure he had nothing to do with all this? He's flying home tomorrow night, says he looks forward to having me back on the beach, and how about we drive to the city and meet Judith?

'We'll take her to lunch and you can sign the contract,' he says.

Jeez, I'm going to *do lunch* with a New York agent?

What on earth will I wear?

On Monday, Hugh rents a van and drives to Cornwall with Sophie to fetch Claudia's cat, her clothes, and a few pieces of furniture. I remind Sophie to bring Alexandra as well. I stay behind and finish painting the downstairs bathroom. Better that way. I'm not quite ready to face Claudia's cottage.

After lunch, I take the underground to Guy's. Claudia sits by the window in the patients' recreation room, bending over a card table. Two spindly brushes stick up from behind one ear like a TV antenna. A jar of muddy water sits at her elbow and tubes of watercolor lie in twisted shapes beside her sketch pad. Paint rags spill from her pocket. She looks up and grins, her face a smorgasbord of color, and my heart does a victory roll.

She's going to be okay, she really, really is.

I tell her about Archibald and she whoops with joy, then shows me her latest creations, caricatures of the nursing staff, her doctors, and the woman who trundles in with her meals every day. She will give them as parting gifts when we bail her out of the hospital on Wednesday.

She takes my hand. 'Thanks to you, I can afford to keep my cottage. If you hadn't helped get my squirrels off the ground, it'd be on the market by now.' She leans toward me. 'I want you to promise me something.'

'What?'

'That one day, you'll go back there with someone special.'

'Fat chance of that,' I say.

'I wouldn't be too sure, if I were you,' she says, and her lips curve into a saucer of a smile.

Does she know something I don't?

Sophie's downsized her business so that she can spend more time at home, taking care of her mother. Claudia, of course, insists she doesn't need taking care of, so they squabble about this all the way home in the car, along with Claudia's decision to volunteer at the animal rescue center.

'Just what you need,' Sophie says. 'More bloody stress.'

'Rubbish,' Claudia retorts. 'I can't sit around all day twiddling my fingers, doing nothing.'

Like I said, she's going to be okay.

Proudly, we escort Claudia into her new room. Narcissus and early daffodils bloom in pottery bowls. The smell of lemon polish wafts up from the floor and the sprigged curtains I hung this morning frame a view of Sophie's back garden where winter jasmine tumbles over a brick wall. Alexandra's portrait hangs above a bleached pine dresser. Claudia's quilt and soft linen sheets cover her brass bed. On the armchair, Max dozes amid a nest of pillows. I bend and stroke his silvery fur, tickle his ears. He opens one blue eye, yawns hugely, and goes back to sleep. Does he remember me?

I look at Alexandra and wonder the same thing.

Forty-six

Sands Point
February 2009

My train pulls into Sands Point at six o'clock. I gather up my luggage and climb down the metal stairs, feet crunching on crusty snow as I cross the tracks and step onto the platform. Lights twinkle above the lone ticket window. A brisk wind tugs at red balloons tied to the guardrails.

Leftovers from Christmas?

Paper hearts cut from pink doilies adorn the timetable board, and two plastic cherubs dangle from a push pin. A wizened carnation droops from the stationmaster's buttonhole.

Valentine's Day.

I'd forgotten all about it, probably because the greeting card companies haven't brainwashed people in England quite as thoroughly as they have here. I drag my suitcase into the waiting room. A basket of candy sits on the table beside a pile of Amtrak schedules, and I'm about to scoop up a lollipop for Anna when someone taps my shoulder.

'Jill?'

I turn and come face to face with Gary Kesselbaum. I haven't set eyes on him since he spurned my proposal for last year's festival. He carries a brown leather briefcase; an umbrella is tucked beneath his arm. Was he on my train?

'I've been trying to reach you,' he says.

No sense telling him I haven't been home. 'Why?'

'Do you still have those designs?'

I have no intention of making this easy. 'The ones you turned down?'

His face reddens. He sets down his briefcase and removes his glasses, wipes his forehead with a handkerchief the size of a tea towel. 'Stop by my office next week.'

Not till you ask me nicely.

Avoiding his eyes, I take my time choosing two lollipops and a Snickers bar. May as well make him sweat a bit more. Even though I'm desperate for work, I'm damned if I'll lick his boots. And he'd better bloody apologize, too.

Behind me, Gary clears his throat. 'Jill, your presentation was excellent, really first-rate, and I'm sorry about last year, really sorry, but it was out of my—'

Sorry?

Yes!

I turn and flash him my warmest smile. 'Gary, I'd be delighted. How about next Tuesday at ten?'

Harriet's car waits at the curb, engine running, puffs of exhaust scorching a hole in the snow. She pops the trunk and I heft my suitcase inside. I blow on my hands to warm them, and kick the snow off my boots before climbing into the passenger seat.

'Welcome home,' Harriet says. 'We missed you.' She leans over and kisses my cheek. 'How's Claudia?'

'Doing great.' I glance in the back. 'Where's Anna?'

'Saying a fond farewell to your cat,' Harriet says. 'I left her with Bea at your house. We turned up the heat and I bought you some eggs, milk, and bread.'

'Thanks, you're a lifesaver.'

'Want to stop at the market for anything else?'

I shake my head. Scrambled eggs on toast and a cup of tea are all I need right now. Harriet guns the engine. We slide across the parking lot and fishtail onto the road, only to get stuck behind a snowplow.

'Damn.' Harriet thumps the steering wheel.

'In a hurry?' I ask.

She grins at me. 'Not really.'

We follow the plow down Bay Street. Familiar landmarks drift by. The Contented Figleaf, Denison's Hardware, Tuttle's Market. Former clients. Will they come back now the chamber of commerce has bestowed its blessing on me? If they do, I might have a chance of jumpstarting my business. In the center of town, Harriet stops to let pedestrians cross the road and I spot a green and white sign in front of the vacant building next to the post office.

Coming Soon. Village Realty.

Must be that new real estate company owned by a woman who used to work for Elaine. She bailed out just after my meltdown. I remember liking her because she didn't fit the pattern of Elaine's clones. Wore glitter socks with Tevas and drove a pink Jeep. Maybe I'll list my house with her, after I have a go at selling it myself.

One well-placed ad in *The New York Times*, Lizzie always said, and I'd have a herd of buyers out here, waving money at me.

In February?

I'd get a better price in April or May. Can I hang on until then? I make a mental list of stuff that needs to get done.

Bulldoze the attic, ransack my closets, plunder the garden shed. Toss out those *National Geographic*s I've been hoarding since 1982. Haul crap to the dump, donate books to the library and clothes to the Goodwill. Do I really need two sets of dishes, and what about that bentwood rocker I keep meaning to mend, but don't? And then there's that exercise bike I bought and used once, the basketball hoop we never got around to putting up, skateboards and ski boots long outgrown but still in good condition. Jordan's old guitar. Alistair's football pads and helmet, size large.

I'll need to organize a tag sale.

Find another house, another job.

Another life.

Harriet swings onto my dirt road. No lights at Tom's house, just a low-wattage floodlamp aimed at the front door. Looks kind of nice, welcoming. Maybe I should get one of those. Hold on a minute. What's the point? You're selling the cottage. Remember? Suddenly, I can't wait to be inside. Alone. I hope Harriet and Bea won't be pissed off if I shoo them out right away.

Beatrice flings open my front door, laughing as if she's just heard a good joke. She reaches for my hand and squeezes it hard, then Anna rushes up and latches onto my legs like a clip-on toy. I wrap her in a hug and she puts her feet on top of mine and we shuffle together over the threshold. Why is it so dark in here? I'm about to reach for the switch, when out of the gloom Zachary saunters by to see what all the fuss is about. He rubs against my ankles, gives me a look that says, '*Okay, so you're back, big deal,*' then slinks into the shadows. Harriet hauls my suitcase up the porch steps.

Somebody giggles.

'Shh!'

I glance at Beatrice. 'Who's that?'

'*Surprise!*'

Forty-seven

Sands Point
February 2009

Bea hits the light switch and suddenly I'm surrounded by people. Lizzie and Fergus spill into my narrow hall; Carrie and Tom with Molly astride his shoulders stand behind them. Paige emerges from my kitchen; Joel and the kids bring up the rear.

Everyone yells hello, welcome home.

Lizzie pushes Beatrice aside and gathers me into a hug. 'Congratulations. I knew Archibald would win.'

For once, I'm speechless. I sneak a look at Tom and he just grins and shrugs, like it wasn't his fault he couldn't stop himself from spreading the good news. Hands pull me into the living room where red and white roses bloom on my coffee table and helium-filled balloons dance across my ceiling. A parrot piñata with green wings and a red beak hangs in the stairwell. Beneath it, a plastic baseball bat leans against the wall. My God, they've thought of everything. Someone shoves a drink in my hand. Pink, with white blobs floating on top.

'Marshmallow punch,' Fergus booms. 'My secret recipe.'

Lizzie nudges me. 'Battery acid.'

Cripes.

Casseroles and cold cuts, baskets of warm rolls, and bowls of salad appear out of nowhere. Plates and silverware, napkins and glasses materialize like magic. My friends. *My friends*. I can't believe they did all this. Tom takes my hand, whispers in my ear. Agent Judith is looking forward to meeting me. How about next Thursday?

Yes, yes. Of course, yes.

Someone pops a bottle of champagne.

Alistair rings from Boston, excited about Archibald. Lizzie admits to e-mailing my sons. Jordan calls five minutes later even more excited than his brother because, hey, Mom. Guess what? Bridget and I are getting married.

Oh, my God. A wedding.

'When?'

'September.'

Fabulous.

My heart soars. 'I'll call you tomorrow,' I yell down the phone. 'It's a mad house in here.'

'I can tell,' Jordan yells back.

'Congratulations, and I love you.'

'Love you, too.'

I close my eyes, open them again. I'm still not believing this. A welcome home party *plus* my son's getting married?

Wow. Double wow.

Lizzie gives me a glass of champagne. 'Dutch sends love and best wishes.'

'Jeez, Lizzie, who *didn't* you tell?'

She grins. 'Elaine Burke.'

Joel slots in a CD and 'Moon River' wafts from the speakers. He scoops up his daughter and swings her in circles. Beatrice and Harriet join hands and sway in time to the music. The kids squeal and jump up and down. Fergus and Lizzie glide into a well-practiced waltz.

Tom bows and offers me his arm. 'May I have this dance?'

335

I nod and pretend I'm the mother of the groom and we're taking the floor at Jordan's wedding. I'll be wearing a floaty dress and matching high heels. Maybe a wisp of a hat. I wonder where they'll hold it. Some place in Pennsylvania, I suppose. Where will I be living then?

Don't even go there. Not tonight.

Holding me tight, Tom whirls me around and around, faster and faster. Faces zoom past, my feet barely touch the ground. Finally, when I'm way beyond dizzy, we slow down and my partner leans me over in a backward dip and I feel myself curve into a shape I wasn't meant to be.

Will I be able to stand up in the morning?

Big round of applause. Lizzie yells for an encore and I realize we're the only ones left dancing. Last time we did this, Tom wore a hideous mask. Tonight, he wears an idiotic grin.

My face aches from smiling.

What the hell did Fergus put in that punch?

We crack another bottle of champagne and the children gather around Beatrice as she reads *Archibald's Aria*. Not all the illustrations are complete, but the kids don't seem to care. Some are just pencil, others pen and ink. Unfinished sketches.

I think about my mother.

Is she sharing this moment with me? Does she have any idea how much I love her? Tears well up, trickle down my cheek.

I need a few moments alone.

When nobody's looking, I slip upstairs and change out of my rumpled travel clothes, splash water on my face. Then I sit on the bathtub and run my hands over the terracotta tiles I glued down and grouted, the walls I colorwashed three times before I got it right. I contemplate the towel rails I chose with such care and the pedestal sink I found at a yard sale, brand new and still in its box. What will the new owners think of my house? Will they love it or tear it down and begin all over again?

Someone taps on the door.

'Jill, are you in there?' Harriet says.

I run a brush through my hair. 'Be right out.'

Sipping a glass of champagne, Harriet leans against my dresser. She points to a manila envelope on my bed. The flap is unsealed, my name's printed on the front.

'What's this?'

'Happy birthday, Jill.'

'It's not for another three weeks.'

'So shoot me, I'm early for once.'

I pull out a sheet of paper and begin to read, but the legal-sounding words blur and run together. Baffled, I shrug and look up.

'It's a letter of intent,' Harriet says. 'The insurance company decided to settle out of court.' She grins and raises her glass. 'I knew they would. They can't afford the negative publicity.'

'You mean—' I sit down hard on my bed.

She nods. 'Forty-five thousand.'

Oh, my God.

'We'll have their check the beginning of next month.'

Good thing I'm already sitting, because now I have a strong need to lie down.

'I had a feeling that punch was dangerous,' Harriet says. I open my eyes. She's fanning me with a magazine. 'Are you all right?'

'No, I'm gobsmacked.'

'And jet-lagged,' Harriet adds. She hands me a glass of water. 'Here, drink this.'

I ask her to repeat, in words of one syllable, what she told me before I zoned out. I need to make sure I wasn't imagining things. Her hands fly about as she describes how easy it was. Mine wasn't the only complaint, and my former supervisor no longer has a job.

Forty-five thousand dollars?

Enough to pay off all my debts?

I'll do the math tomorrow. Right now, my head's full of cotton candy and my stomach's doing cartwheels. I couldn't add two and two and come up with four if I tried.

With a final whack, the piñata explodes and candy falls into the hands of eager children. Fergus snatches up a Tootsie Roll, hands it to Lizzie with a bow and a flourish. Their daughter comes in with a cake, and oh, what a cake. Tiny green parrots – God knows where they found those – perch on a nest of chocolate twigs. Hearts and roses cascade over the sides. No candles, thank goodness.

Lizzie hands me a knife. 'Make a wish,' she says.

But I don't need to. I've got it all. My house, my friends, my business, even good old Archibald. But best of all, I've got myself, back where I want to be. What more could I possibly want?

I slice and serve and we dive into the cake and wash it down with more champagne, and I'm wobbly on my feet by the time I bid my last guest goodnight. Now it's just Tom and me. And my cat. I gather him up and flop on the couch, head spinning, exhausted and too wound up to sleep. My eyes twitch with fatigue. According to my watch, it's 3 a.m. in London. Way past my bedtime. Zachary yawns, curls up, and goes to sleep on my lap. His whiskers are covered with frosting.

Tom bustles about, collecting plates and glasses, picking up trash. I hear the fridge door open and close. Dishes clink as he loads the dishwasher. It wooshes into action and he brings me a mug of tea, then hunkers down by the hearth.

'Feel like a fire?' he says.

I cradle the mug with my hands. 'Now?'

'Sure, why not?' He picks up a log. 'Got any kindling?'

'I doubt it.'

'Newspaper?'

'Nope.' I shove Zachary to one side and struggle to my feet. 'But there's bound to be something in my office we can use.'

A stray balloon hovers above my desk. Its string dangles in front of that photo of Colin and me. Just what I need. I rip the picture off the wall, take a final look at his face, and tear it in half. Then I place both pieces together and tear them again . . . and again.

Should've done it sooner than this.

I toss the bits in my overflowing waste basket and carry the whole lot out to Tom. He crumples paper and stacks logs, then strikes a match, and as I watch the flames curl around Colin's pink shirt, I feel a final pang of sadness for the boy I once knew.

Tom nods toward the fire. 'Letting go of the past?'

'Something like that, yes.'

'It was time.'

'I know.'

There's an awkward silence. We've never been short on words before. Why now, why tonight after we've danced one another's feet to ribbons? I lean against the mantel, move a candlestick two inches to the left, move it back again. Now what do we do?

'Shall we sit?' Tom says.

I tell him that will be fine.

So we sit. Another silence. Tom drapes his arm across the back of the couch. Crosses his knees, taps his foot. Hums a bit. I think he's nervous. I certainly am. He just watched me

339

toss my past into the fire, so he knows I've worked my way through it. Just like he said I would. Is he going to kiss me?

Oh hell, I don't know what to do.

What if he does? Will I like the feel of his beard? What if it tickles and I laugh, or scratches my face enough to make me flinch? Tom moves closer, takes my hand off my lap and raises it to his lips. Oh my, I didn't expect this. His beard is much softer than it looks, and I'm wondering what it'd feel like on my mouth, when I find out for sure.

Let me tell you, kissing a guy with a beard is pretty special.

We kiss a bit more and hold hands, and that's all I want. I'm not ready for anything more. Not yet, anyway. I don't want to rush. I did that before and I won't be making that mistake again. We're not on a cruise ship. We have all the time in the world, except for right now. I push him, gently, off the couch and out my front door. Tell him I'll commit a mischief if I don't get some sleep.

I'm living on borrowed time here, can't wait to fall into bed.

But when I do, I can't fall asleep, dammit. My eyes refuse to stay shut. Sighing, I get up, slip into my robe and go downstairs. I wander from room to room, weak with relief and gratitude. I came so close to losing all this, and it gives me the collywobbles to think that only a few hours ago I was readying myself to let it go.

My best memories lie within the fabric of these walls. That stain on the ceiling where Jordan chucked a lump of pastry dough to see if it would stick. The grooves in the floor from my bentwood rocker. Those dents in the utility box outside that Alistair used as a backstop when playing baseball. I got an irate call from the power company about that one. They thought someone was tampering with the meter.

The doorframe where Zachary sharpens his claws.

Climbing the stairs, I run my hands along the banister, down the spindles, feeling drips of paint I neglected to sand off. I adjust a couple of pictures that never seem to hang straight and find myself looking at two little boys as they build a castle on the beach. From this angle, I can't tell which one is which. They used to look so much alike.

Am I ready to fall asleep yet?

Almost.

I wrap myself in a quilt, shove my feet into loafers, and step onto the balcony. Winter taps its frosty fingers on my face. I shiver and pull the quilt tighter. A breeze ripples through the willows. Their ice-covered branches glisten and tinkle like wind chimes. Curls of snow tumble off the roof and spiral down to the patio. In the distance, waves roar and rumble up the beach.

My beach.

My home. I take a deep, cleansing breath. Fill my lungs with hope and fresh air. I look up at a black velvet sky dotted with stars and see Claudia's smile in the curve of a fingernail moon. It hangs, suspended on invisible strings, directly over Tom's house. What's she trying to tell me now?

Promise you'll go back to Cornwall with somebody special.

You bet I will.

But first, I have to stitch my life back together again.